NEEDING
NAPOLEON

Needing Napoleon

Published by The Conrad Press Ltd. in the United Kingdom 2021

Tel: +44(0)1227 472 874
www.theconradpress.com
info@theconradpress.com

ISBN 978-1-914913-21-1

Printed and bound in Great Britain by Clays Ltd, Elcograf S.p.A

Typesetting and Cover Design by The Book Typesetters
www.thebooktypesetters.com

The Conrad Press logo was designed by Maria Priestley.

NEEDING NAPOLEON

GARETH WILLIAMS

OF
1979 - 1983

To my parents Bunty and Rhys

Chapter One

'Please let this work!' he hears himself saying and opens his eyes.

'What was that? You're babbling, man! What are you doing here? Open your eyes, damn you!'

Richard's vision is blurry but there is no mistaking the polished voice and tone of command. As his eyes focus, he confronts a stern face beneath a black shako topped with a white and red plume.

Richard looks the man up and down from the gold emblem on his hat to his red jacket with its rows of silver buttons and epaulettes at the shoulder. A white sash crosses from right shoulder to left hip where his sword is suspended. His waist is encircled by a burgundy sash. His upright collar, cuffs and lapels are dark blue with silver detail. His grey trousers reach his ankles. His black footwear is glossed to perfection.

He looks magnificent in what Richard recognises as a light infantry lieutenant's uniform.

'You are lost, sir. Your place is back on the ridge with the rest of the gawpers from Brussels,' snaps the lieutenant. 'Sergeant!'

Immediately an NCO appears. 'Yes, sir! Lieutenant Tarleton, sir!' His coarse voice matches his grizzled features.

'Find a reliable man to escort this gentleman to the viewing compound,' orders Tarleton. 'He seems to have lost his way. A little too much wine with your lunch, sir?'

Richard tries to protest, tripping over his words, as if his mouth has forgotten how to shape the simplest phrases.

The sergeant salutes, turns and trots off bellowing, 'Private Goodbody, to me, now!'

Richard stands swaying under the hawk-like scrutiny of Lieutenant Tarleton. He sees the man examining his clothes critically.

'Forgive my intrusion, Lieutenant. My name is Davey. I am a man of letters. I am in Belgium as a correspondent for *The Times* newspaper. I hope to report on our success here.'

The lieutenant nods brusquely as if such considerations are beneath him. A gangly private runs up and salutes, standing to attention, eyes flicking between his officer and the unexpected civilian.

'Private, kindly escort this gentleman back from whence he came. To the viewing area over yonder. Do not let him wander off or you will suffer the consequences.'

A smart salute and Richard is ushered away. The private holds his musket across his chest at an angle. He is reticent about touching him, Richard senses, but needs a way to persuade this gentleman along. The sight of his weapon is quite enough for Richard who walks in wonder towards the sights and sounds beyond. He smells the soldier's musk of sweat and unwashed wool, tobacco and stale spirits.

They take a dusty lane that soon joins the major north-south road linking Charleroi and Brussels. Turning north, they follow the paved thoroughfare up the gradual slope towards the red tiles and whitewashed walls Richard recognises as the farmhouse of Mont St Jean.

The farm's gates are topped by a squat tower, bright against the grey sky. Richard can hear the pigeons cooing inside, content despite the feverish activity all around.

He is astonished at the cacophony as Wellington deploys his troops. Horses pound in all directions. Groups of soldiers march to shouts of command. Carts and carriages trundle on complaining axles. Whips crack, trumpets blare and artillery drills echo.

Yet still the birds sing. A light breeze sways the barley, wheat and rye filling the fields below. With the farm behind them, they head for the rear slope of the escarpment.

A modest group of buildings huddled around a crossroads come into view. Tiles and slates, pale stone and whitewash, perhaps half a dozen substantial buildings, a few lean-tos and a couple of clapboard barns.

As they draw close, Richard studies an area cordoned off to the left, filled with elegant pale muslin, bright frockcoats, tall hats, gay bonnets and liveried servants with trays.

Richard comes to a stop before the astonishing assembly. Brussels society has decamped to the countryside for a mass picnic on the eve of battle. The young private collides with him and curses under his breath.

'I'm so sorry,' Richard offers weakly as he moves towards the roped enclosure.

The private lifts the rope so that Richard can duck under. He complies, holding his hat in place, before turning to thank the pasty-faced youth. But he is already making his way back to his unit.

Richard stands at the periphery of the merriment feeling awkward in his dated clothes, uncertain what to do.

'Good afternoon, sir. You seem lost. Have you become separated from your party? Might I help?' Her voice is warm. 'My name is Miss Arabella Fortescue. Pleased to meet you.' She gives a little curtsy.

Richard looks at her round face framed with dark ringlets, long lashes shielding hazel eyes. Her pale skin and the elegant curve of her neck rise above a muslin dress of pale yellow. She is shorter than his five feet nine inches but not by much. Her yellow bonnet sports embroidered flowers in pink and blue.

A new expression reshapes her features. She is puzzled.

'Forgive me, Miss Fortescue. Richard Davey, man of letters, at your service,' he tumbles the words out, blushing as he fumbles a bow.

Her face returns to resting cheerfulness. 'Pleased to meet you, Mr Davey. Have you come to see Wellington thrash Boney? My father says there is nothing to fear. He is over there.' She points with the tip of her parasol.

Richard sees an earnest party of uniforms and civilians in close conversation towards the far side of the roped area.

'He does something incomprehensible at our legation in Brussels,' Arabella explains. 'What do you think will happen?' she adds eagerly.

'I think it is going to rain,' replies Richard as the breeze freshens and the sky continues to darken. 'and sections of this battlefield will turn to mud. That will play its part.' Should he have said that?

'What an interesting perspective. I had not even considered the weather. When I awoke this morning, it was hazy but cleared before we set out. By the time we arrived I needed my parasol, the sun was so strong.' She shakes her

10

head. 'My father would love to discuss your opinions. If you are on your own, you must join us!'

Richard watches a servant serve drinks to a party. Glasses of champagne clink and laughter swells. Arabella places a small hand in the crook of his right arm and begins to navigate her way through the throng to her father's circle.

The senior officer next to her father spots her and makes room. Her father is speaking. He is a tall man with an erect bearing. His hair is grey to match his eyes and wrinkles radiate from his proud nose. He is resplendent in the court dress of a diplomat. His dark blue jacket is swamped by silver oak leaf embroidery. It covers his high collar, his chest, cuffs and his long tails. His white breeches are immaculate. His height is exaggerated by a bicorn hat, like an upturned ship, pointing fore and aft, edged with ostrich plumes.

Listening hard, Richard catches something about Blücher's defeat by Napoleon at Ligny the day before. Noticing his daughter, Arabella's father concludes.

'Mr Davey, may I introduce my father, Sir Reginald Fortescue? Father, may I introduce Mr Richard Davey? He is a writer!' She delivers this last piece of information with a flourish, clearly proud to have ferreted out someone new to add to their society.

'I am pleased to meet you, Mr Davey. How is it that you come to know my daughter, I do not recall encountering you at any of the tedious gatherings I am compelled to attend in Brussels?'

Richard looks at Arabella with a worried expression.

'Oh Papa. I have just met Mr Davey. I found him looking lost and took him under my wing.'

Ramrod straight, Sir Reginald smiles indulgently. 'So typical of Arabella. Since her dear mother died, she has had to play hostess for me. It has made her very forward, I fear.'

Polite smiles and suppressed chuckles from the elite group.

'Well, Mr Davey. What do you make of Boney's chances?' asks Sir Reginald.

Richard inclines his head and takes a breath. He is on firm ground here, safe from small talk. 'He certainly can move troops with remarkable speed. Gave the Prussians a lesson yesterday, by all accounts. But he's not having it all his own way, the Black Watch, the 95th Rifles, the North Gloucestershire's all did well defying Ney the crossroads at Quatre Bras.'

'You are remarkably well informed, sir.'

'I intend to write an account of the campaign for *The Times*, Your Excellency.'

'All subject to His Majesty's censor, I trust?' Sir Reginald quips, the smile on his face defusing his words, 'And what do you think of Wellington as a commander?'

Richard hesitates; he needs to tread carefully. 'In truth, sir, I think tomorrow's battle will be a close-run thing but I'm not fleeing for Antwerp! Wellington has taken up a strong defensive position. I think he wants Bonaparte to make the first move.'

The civilians in the group exchange looks.

'Well said, well said!' chorus the two men in military uniform. One wears a red coat faced with dark blue, punctuated by gold buttons and lace. From the two pairs of downward pointing chevrons on his sleeve, Richard discerns he is a major-general. The other officer wears a similar uniform with silver buttons. Richard is not sure but thinks it signifies a member of the adjutant general's staff. Their bicorn hats are devoid of white feather trim. They do not look like they mind.

Sir Reginald nods noncommittally and smiles warmly at his daughter. 'It was nice to meet you, Mr Davey.' With that Richard is dismissed.

He moves away, without realizing Arabella is still with him. 'You didn't get your chance to say that clever thing about the weather!' she complains. 'Father can be so brusque. That's why he needs me.' She has cheered up already. 'Oh look, those soldiers look like they are going to fire that cannon.' She points to an artillery battery just below the village.

They will have a perfect view from the south-east corner of the roped area. Richard lets Arabella weave their way to the prime spot, greeting people as she leaves them in her wake. Everyone smiles and knows her name.

Wedged into the corner of the rope cordon, Richard watches as the gun crews are put through their paces. He should be thrilled to see it done for real. But Arabella has pressed herself against him in a surprisingly forward manner. Her body is warm and firm with tantalising curves he feels all too clearly through the thin layers of her summer dress.

He forces his attention back to the drill but does nothing to discourage the contact. Could this really be happening? He is on the field of Waterloo, on the eve of battle, watching a British gunnery team work, in the company of a very pretty girl who seems to like him. A rumble of distant thunder goes almost unnoticed by the assembled society.

Five men man each gun. Richard thinks they are six pounders from their size, mounted on simple wooden carriages bound with iron. A sergeant oversees the drill for all four field-pieces in the battery. The weapon closest to them is near enough to watch the details of the procedure.

The ordnance is aimed by the gun-captain, sighting along the barrel and allowing for the fall of shot. The second member of the crew is the sponge-man, now swabbing the barrel with a rammer headed by wet fleece. At the same time a third man, the vents-man, puts his thumb over the vent at the sealed end of the barrel to ensure nothing smouldering blows back on the sponge-man.

The loader inserts the cartridge and mimes loading the round shot. The sponge-man reverses his rammer and pushes the charge down the barrel. The vents-man inserts a pricker to pierce the cartridge and fills the vent with a paper tube of powder. The team steps away and the fifth member of the crew uses a slow match in a holder to ignite the charge.

Arabella jumps and grabs at him as the gunpowder explodes. All four guns discharge within a whisker of each other.

'Not too bad, lads!' bellows the sergeant as the din dies away, 'Now do it again!'

Richard pats Arabella's hand and looks at her coloured cheeks. Guiltily, he realizes she is no older than the girls in his year thirteen class. Not his class anymore!

She is chewing her lip. 'Where did the cannonball go? I didn't see it at all. Just a big cloud of smoke and all that noise.'

'It was just a drill. They are saving the projectiles for tomorrow. Besides, there's an awful lot of troop movements

14

across the ridge and in the valley. They don't want to hit their own men.'

'You sound just like my old tutor,' she chides.

Once a teacher always a teacher it seems. Somehow it doesn't matter anymore.

The sky is very dark now and thunder rolls around the horizon, edging closer. A persistent wind tugs at them. The local dogs begin to bark and the first flash of lightning rips through the lowering clouds.

Arabella tenses as the first fat raindrops fall. She cowers under her flimsy parasol. 'I must re-join my father. You will come with us, Richard? Share our carriage. Then you can call on us. Brussels is so dull, the same people, over and over.'

He smiles. It is a tempting offer. Her company is soothing. 'I don't doubt the shortcomings of your social circle if adding me to it is something to aim at!'

The drops are closer together as they draw alongside Sir Reginald. The officers have already disappeared and clusters of revellers hurry towards a park of carriages, trailing overburdened servants in their wake.

'There you are, Arabella. Good, now we must go before the roads are churned up too much.' Sir Reginald takes his daughter's arm and begins moving with the tail of the crowd, forcing her to release her grip on Richard.

She looks over her shoulder with wide eyes. 'Promise me we will see you in Brussels? We can celebrate Boney's defeat together!'

He just hears her as the wind tries to snatch her words away. The rain is insistent now.

'After the battle,' he shouts, cupping a hand to his mouth. It is a lie but the truth seems unnecessarily cruel. She is like a puppy. She will imprint on someone else tomorrow and forget all about him. The thought makes him sad.

He doubles up to get under the far rope and heads towards the last few carriages. He crosses behind them to a wooden barn set apart from the main hamlet. Its swaybacked, shingle roof looks intact although the clapboard walls are heavily weathered. No one pays him any attention.

Reaching the tall barn door, Richard pries it open against the resistance of trampled earth. Countless hooves and feet have compacted the soil to a hard crust that catches the splintered bottom of the door, scoring the earth as he heaves.

When he has it ajar, he slips inside the gloomy space and pushes the door within a hand span of shut. He leans against the barn wall, waiting for his breathing to settle. Rain patters syncopated drumming across the roof.

Over the off-beat rhythm, he hears the last carriages chasing away to the Brussels road. Thunder rumbles again not far away. Sheltered from the rising wind, he is secure for the moment.

As his eyes adjust to the dim interior, he makes out a rickety cart, one axle propped up on an overturned barrel where the wheel is missing. At the back of the barn lies a jumble of timber, as if a hayloft has collapsed.

Peering around the edge of the door, he watches soldiers and camp followers moving around the hamlet.

He checks his watch, unsure whether he can trust it. The dial is bright in the low light. It reads just after three in the afternoon. He has not seen the sun but Arabella referred to the afternoon.

It will not get dark until nine o'clock. There is no prospect of moving unnoticed for long without the cover of darkness.

He shuffles around the interior perimeter, one hand on the wall. The dominant smell is horse manure. No different from outside. There is also a hint of tar used to treat the wooden structure. The air is stale and motes of dust float in a slender shaft of weak light creeping in from the hand span gap by the door.

Clambering awkwardly through the broken structure at the rear, he hears a scuttling and notices spilled grain. He hopes it is mice but fears rats are more likely.

As the rain grows heavier and more regular, leaks reveal themselves in the roof. Most of them are in the rear section of the barn, away from the abandoned cart. Raised above the ground, it promises separation from the unseen rodents he still hears.

Richard removes his knapsack and clambers up onto the cart with it. He unbuckles the top flap and withdraws his carefully folded overcoat. The wooden bed of the cart is caked in mud and smells of turnips. He spreads the coat out and lies on it, shuffling the bag to the end facing the door as a pillow.

He is not cold and he is not wet. He has food in his pack but decides to save it. His bed is far from comfortable but he is surprised at how tired he feels. He closes his eyes but does not really expect to sleep.

The next thing he knows is jerking into a sitting position with a fuzzy head. His pulse races and rain still hammers the barn. What woke him? He cannot hear anything over the noise of the storm. Thunder rumbles. He smells fresh dampness. A flash of lightning flares between the boards that enclose him.

Richard hops off the carriage and crosses to the door. Squinting through the downpour, he spies on the hamlet. Visibility is poor and not just because of the rain. The light is fading. He sees a yellow glow at windows, the occasional form rushing between buildings, plumes of smoke from chimneys and cook fires for the troops. They must have some shelter to preserve the flames. There is nothing he can see that could have woken him.

More thunder booms and lightning flashes soon after. The storm is almost centred on Mont St Jean. It must have been the thunder, he tells himself. Otherwise, he would have to consider rats and that is not something he wants to entertain.

While he has the opportunity, he reaches into his frockcoat and pulls out his pocket watch. It is almost eight in the evening. He winds the watch gingerly to avoid over-taxing the spring and restores it to his inside pocket.

He returns to the carriage and rummages in his bag. He extracts his penknife and the dried sausage wrapped in his handkerchief. Standing at the open end of the cart, he spreads the square of linen as a tablecloth and carefully cuts several slices.

He throws the small hunk of meat attached to the string to the back of the barn. At least he will know where the rodents are for a while. The sausage's pink flesh is mottled with white fat and shreds of garlic. The skin is covered in fine white mould with the texture of paper. He teases it free and adds it to his offering among the fallen timbers.

He chews each slice slowly, savouring the taste as the rich meat replenishes his energy. When finished, he takes a gulp from his round, wooden water canister. British army issue is pale blue but his is plain inside a hessian jacket. It would not help his cause to fall into French hands in possession of British army kit. He replaces the cork stopper and repacks his haversack.

He flinches as thunder explodes overhead and sheet lightning pierces the barn in a hundred places, destroying his vision. He waits at the end of the cart for his sight to return. The flaring abates quickly, leaving after-flashes tinged with red. Gradually, the predominant colours settle back into shades of black and grey.

While he waits, he shrugs into his overcoat and, once he can see, fastens the buttons. The temperature has dropped. He rubs his hands together and takes a turn around the interior, steering clear of the rear of the barn, where scuttling and scuffles still sound.

His eyesight restored, he shoulders his bag and returns to the main door. The rain now falls at an angle across his narrow line of vision. He hears the snap of canvas in the wind. No doubt from the rows of tents beyond the hamlet.

Whinnies of complaint reach him from the horse lines nearby. He can only see the buildings clustered around the crossroads as a less intense darkness than their surroundings. The fires are out now.

It is time. There is no point checking his watch again. His heart hammers against his ribs. He is impatient to be off before his nerve fails.

Putting his shoulder to the door, he opens it far enough to slip out, sodden ground reducing the friction. He closes it and circles to the western side of the barn, with the building shielding him from the hamlet of Mont St Jean.

He sinks his chin into the fur collar of his coat and hunches into the wind gusting across the plateau like waves crashing ashore. He edges to the south-western corner and looks across the flat top of the ridge towards the farm and the edge of the escarpment beyond.

A flash of lightning allows him to get his bearings. There is a lot of open space with nowhere to hide before the shoulder of the rise hides him from the sight of anyone in the hamlet or among the tents beyond.

He trots across the compacted ground, keeping as low as he can, the soles of his boots slipping on the slick surface. Twice he flails his arms to keep upright as a foot skates away.

He manages to pull level with the farm without encountering a sentry, although he hears them calling to each other in the murk. He even picks out an exchange in Dutch, its cadences so like English, as grooms calm the horse lines of the Netherlands cavalry division.

Beyond them are the Household Cavalry under the command of Henry Somerset, who will be commemorated by a stone tower near his home in Gloucestershire.

Richard is heading downhill now. Keeping west of the road he was escorted along this afternoon, he maintains a southerly bearing to draw level with the farmhouse of La Haye Sainte, halfway down the gentle slope.

Trying to spot the mass of the buildings enclosing the courtyard, he trips on a root and sprawls into a thorny bush.

He lies, partly suspended by snagging branches, the wind knocked out of him.

'Halt, who goes there?' The shouted challenge comes from not far off and he stops struggling immediately.

'It's only me, isn't it, Knotty, and some fox making off with a hen from the farm.'

Richard relaxes as the sentries dissolve into laughter. One throws out another comment that is stolen by the wind and whipped away.

He begins unhooking his clothing from the snaring claws of the bush. As he frees himself, his knees drop to the sodden earth which soaks his breeches. His coat has ridden up, bunching around his waist. His hat has been dislodged, and he endures stabs and scrapes searching the shrub before he recovers it.

His hair is dripping wet and his fingers are growing numb. The rain is heavy again and the sharp wind accentuates the cold.

Still on all fours, he conjures up Aunt Patricia. What would she say? Get up, you foolish boy! Get out of the rain and dry yourself before it's too late. His shivering is uncontrollable and his vision blurs with the deluge. He forces himself up and brushes at his clothes. If Aunt Patricia is talking to him, then he is in trouble.

He continues towards the foot of the slope as quickly as he can manage, feet squelching in flooded boots. He reckons the pickets guard the crossroads north of the farm. The Wavre road should be just ahead, running west to east. Somewhere nearby is Wellington's elm, the tree beneath which he regularly surveys progress throughout the eighteenth of June.

Richard creeps forward, trying to control his shivering, aware of how many sentries are likely to be posted along the main front line. He sees a brief flare of light to his left and the sound of a pipe being sucked. He freezes, heart pounding.

The bowl glows, casting a furrowed face in demonic shadow, eyes crossed with effort. An unintelligible curse slips from the side of the soldier's mouth but his thin lips remain clamped on the clay pipe. He shields the bowl with a hand and sucks deeply.

Richard starts forward as the sentry sighs contentedly, keeping one hand over his precious bulb of tobacco, while the other hand holds his musket carelessly at half-mast.

Richard feels dampness on his shoulders where incessant rain is defeating the protection of his overcoat. The cold is inside him now, dulling his thoughts. He clings to his aunt's advice. He needs to dry out and get some warmth into his body.

Another fork of lightning slices the dark, revealing the road ahead. He is astonished to find it thronged with troops marching in either direction, smartly holding formation despite the horrendous weather and sucking mud. Carts of provisions are whipped along, some driven by soldiers, others by civilians.

He sees women and children walking hand in hand as if on the local high street, shawls over their heads. Camp followers call to passing soldiers; messengers ride by in a hurry; furtive figures slip along at the edge of the route, darting forward whenever anything falls from a cart.

With the next flash, Richard spots he is within thirty feet of a gun emplacement on the southern side of the road, four wet barrels jutting defiantly across the valley towards the French lines.

There is no cover. He sucks in a breath and strolls to the road, merging with the traffic heading west before angling to the far verge. None of the pedestrians spare him a look; the nearest carter is so hunched over that the horses appear in charge. A passing cavalryman curses as he navigates the slow-moving traffic, including Richard in his contempt.

He steps off the sticky road surface, across a shallow ditch, into a field of rye as tall as his chest. Wading into the field he feels more secure. He trails his hands in the crop as he moves, feeling the heavy seed heads and their horsehair fronds. He lets the repeating chevrons of the wet ears run through his fingers as he walks further into the field.

He wonders what damage the storm will do to the crops and has to suppress a laugh as he imagines the fields after the battle. The ground is almost flat now, but little imperfections cause him to stumble and snag a foot.

He cuts diagonally across the fields to avoid the main north to south road with its nest of 95th Rifles opposite La Haye Sainte, the farmhouse on his side of the thoroughfare. He wants to steer clear of their position and come at the farm from the west. He needs to find shelter.

He crosses from one field to another, differentiated by a drainage channel. The crop feels the same, although he knows the valley supports rye, barley and wheat.

The wind stills for a moment and voices sound from what he believes is the road arrowing south towards the inn of La Belle Alliance. Beyond lies Napoleon's headquarters at the farm of Le Caillou. He thinks they are speaking English in a variety of accents, suggesting the riflemen, stationed in what was nicknamed the sandpit, on the far side of the road.

He crouches and strains forward until the crop thins to nothing. Straight ahead looms the outline of the farm of La Haye Sainte. He runs to the hedge surrounding the north end. He burrows stubbornly through the dense foliage, trying to protect his hat as he forces his way into the vegetable garden.

He can make out features now, as light spills from the main farmhouse facing the garden. Row upon row of greenery stands on parade as if awaiting the battle to come.

The farmhouse abuts the road with a wall dividing the courtyard beyond from the thoroughfare. Directly ahead of Richard, the same wall continues beyond the house to define the roadside edge of the garden.

Against that wall is a substantial outhouse, a glorified garden shed with a red roof and whitewashed walls.

Where the curtain wall ends, the hedge takes over at a right angle, defining the southern and eastern sides of the kitchen garden before reaching a long stable block. This slate-roofed structure runs the length of the courtyard to a taller barn furnishing the southern wing. It stops short of the road, where the wall springs up again, to complete the corner and run along the roadside to the farmhouse.

The wall grows taller to accommodate a gateway that could admit a large cart and again where a lean-to provides additional storage against the inner flank of the wall.

Most of these details are hidden in darkness beyond pale pools of light leaking from the four ground floor windows in the main house but Richard has studied every element of the battlefield.

Richard hears voices and watches a figure pass behind one of the outward facing windows. He knows the soldiers inside are the lucky ones. They fought the previous day and survived. They are dry and warm. There is a party mood as German jokes are tossed back and forth by the Hanoverian light infantry of the King's German Legion, loyal to the German monarch of Great Britain and Ireland.

He imagines many of them are settling to sleep, having gorged on meat cooked over open fires, provided by their major who has ordered the farm livestock slaughtered for the purpose.

Richard hugs the inside of the hedge, following it around the planted area to the start of the sheltering wall. He is just behind the small garden building. A blank wall stretches above him to the roof ridge. There is a modicum of shelter but his teeth chatter as he inches around the building. The door into the glorified shed is opposite one of the two farmhouse doors.

He hears a curse in German and a door slam. He is just at the margin of the illuminated area. He needs to get inside the building. The tips of his fingers are insensible as he removes his hat and takes a first exposed step.

He edges around the outbuilding until his back rests against its wooden door. He fumbles with clumsy hands. The latch lifts easily and the door swings inwards.

Richard turns into the dark interior, closing the door quickly. His nerves do nothing to still his shivering.

He explores the interior with his hands as much as his eyes. There is a rack of garden implements against one wall, a drying rack and a pile of sacks against the other. The far end is occupied by a small hearth with a modest shelf above. Richard's fingers discover a fire laid in the grate, just waiting to be lit.

He fumbles along the mantle and discovers a round, metallic object with a rudimentary loop handle. He lifts it down and sits on the wooden plank floor, back wedged in the north-east corner.

If he can just light the fire. There is little danger smoke from the chimney will be spotted on such a night. The building is well made. The roof does not leak and there are no windows. He doubts a modest blaze will be visible from outside. His biggest risk is a sentry.

He tries to prise the lid from the circular container but his wet, numb fingers struggle for purchase. Clenching his teeth, Richard puts all his strength into another attempt and the lid flies open, scattering the contents in his wet lap and onto the floorboards.

He scrabbles desperately, trying to rescue the precious tinder. If it becomes sodden, he is lost. He manages to gather a palm full and tips it back into the tin receptacle. Shavings of wood and frayed shreds of cloth form a damp mass while the finest particles, little more than dust, have to be brushed from his hands, already waterlogged.

He quarters the floor around him until his right hand finds the steel, shaped like a knuckle duster. He grips it firmly and continues to feel the floor, on his hands and knees. Surely there must be a flint?

At last, he feels something against his left thumb and his hand closes awkwardly on a piece of sharp stone.

He removes his sodden coat and spreads it on the drying

rack. He places the tinderbox in front of the hearth and strikes steel against flint over the opening, trying to keep his wet body clear.

His strike is clumsy and nothing happens. He is struggling to hold the two tools. His third strike produces a spark but it misses the contents. He alters his angle of attack and tries again; this time the spark flares above the kindling.

Again, and again, he produces a brief orange shower of tiny daggers, stabbing the dark before they die. At last, he finds the perfect approach and sparks fall on the miserable clump of shavings.

His hands shake. He puts down the tools carefully and rubs palms and fingers together until they are dry and painful feeling returns to his fingertips.

What if a sentry hears his repeated strikes? He has seen no one since that banging door. He remembers reading an account of the Hanoverian occupation of the farm. There was a sentry in the garden! He abandoned his post in search of straw to sit on and met his brother at one of the gun batteries. What were their names? Something about a carriage? Landau! Searching for straw, they found wine and the sentry did not return until midnight when he promptly fell asleep!

Richard picks up the steel and flint to try again. He produces sparks every time and they shower the little heap of combustible material. But not one spark catches.

With his forefinger, he stirs the material, producing a shallower layer. There is enough dampness for some lint to adhere to his finger. He shakes his head, fearing the worst, but returns to his task.

A tiny meteor shower plunges into the bowl. There is no

flame but Richard smells a tiny tendril of sweet smoke. He strikes again and again. A brief glow peters out before he can fan it. One more try, another glow, he blows too gently and it expires. He is ready for the next one and coaxes the little red ring into an unsteady flame. He edges more of the kindling inwards and it takes.

Tapers, where are the tapers? He forgot to look for them when retrieving the spilled tinder. He slides his hands across the floor urgently, oblivious to splinters from rough boards.

He snares a length of wooden taper and hurries it over the guttering flame just before the meagre fuel is consumed. It catches and he uses its flickering light to locate a substantial pile of kindling, set in the heart of the hearth.

His vulnerable flame leaps into the dry kindling and flares upwards, lapping at dry sticks and setting them aglow. He sees the base of a log catch, glowing red as bark chars away and true wood begins to burn.

As the hearth fills with flame and light, Richard crowds as close as he dare. The chimney is drawing well. The heat is on his skin and his clothes steam.

Wind howls over the eaves and thunder rumbles periodically. He has stopped shivering and his teeth are still. His jaw aches fiercely. Warm fingers reach beneath his waistcoat and down his legs. He removes his boots and wrings out his socks beneath the tool rack. He puts the socks back on and angles his boot openings to the fire.

He has to scuttle backwards when a log pops, ejecting a red-hot ember onto his right foot. But he edges back as soon as he has extinguished it.

He snags his backpack and pulls it towards him. He undoes

the straps and lifts the lid. The interior is decidedly damp. He extracts his cloth wrapped sausage and rummages until he finds his penknife. He exposes one end of the salami and carves off several chunks.

He sits munching the rich, hard meat, sucking energy from the fatty snack. He watches the flames and chews. He watches the flames and sips from his canteen. He watches the flames and rubs his feet. They are barely damp now.

He takes his coat from the wall rack and holds the lining as close to the fire as he dares. Coat and boots will take some time to dry.

He closes his eyes, barely able to think about where he is or when. It is easier to think back, or should that be forwards, to 2018?

Chapter Two

He shut the door on the screeching but roaring blood pounded in his ears. He looked along the corridor and gulped gratefully. It was empty. He hitched his satchel on a tense shoulder, trying to ignore the sweat slick and humid beneath his tweed jacket.

Although each footstep distanced him from Room Fourteen, the sickness in his stomach persisted.

Autumn sun slipped through gothic windows. At the start of term, it struck the polished floor tiles by the lunch bell but now only reached the wall to his right, illuminating the paintings of saints.

Laughter confronted him from the staff room a corner away and he hesitated. He didn't belong in there. It was full of purposeful people whose jobs fitted their lives.

An exchange of giggles made him realize he had stopped. He clenched his shoulders and thrust his left foot forward, making it around the corner before a pair of year thirteen girls sauntered past, leaning on each other in a chaos of limbs, files and hair.

'Tosser!'

'Totally. Couldn't keep order in a kindergarten,' agreed a faint American accent.

He paused again, trying to hear what came next. 'Yeah, even Boozy copes with us better than him, which is mad because she's the worst teacher in the school!'

He could hear a larger pack heading for the dining hall so

forced himself along the staff corridor.

'Richard! Might I have the briefest of words?' The deputy head's impassive features confronted him from her office, leering over half-moon spectacles.

'Of course, Mrs Streight.'

She stepped back from the threshold and he followed her in, dreading another awkward exchange where she tried to mask her exasperation and he grasped at excuses. She sat behind her large, tidy desk rather than in the armchair. Never a good sign in his twelve years' experience.

He looked over the deputy head's square, linen clad shoulder. He saw his reflection in the window framed with roses still thrusting pink blooms into clear October air.

He raised a hand to his short, receding, light brown hair, trying to flatten an insistent tuft at his crown. His hazel eyes looked tired and his shirt bulged around a pot belly. He sat up straight at the sight of his stooped shoulders.

The deputy head seemed reluctant to begin and that was unusual. He began to list possible reasons for his summons. It would be a complaint; that went without saying. It must be from an exam class or it would have been his head of department speaking to him.

He reviewed the week so far, two and a half days old and already several scenes suggested themselves. He had raised his voice to Mary Hunter. He had given Maeve Tillison an E grade for her essay on the Coup of Brumaire. He had made his year eleven class re-sit their test on the Munich Agreement. He had put Ellie Griff in detention and reported Trixie Rushmore to her head of house for swearing.

It was little consolation that all but the first were justified.

Parents rarely saw things from his point of view.

'Richard, thank you for giving up your lunch hour.'

His stomach roiled and his throat tightened. He stifled a cough with a strangled gulp. So much for the briefest of words.

He nodded to cover his discomfort and attempted a smile. At the best of times, he could coax a facsimile of a grin, although he never let his lips part to reveal uneven, yellowed teeth. This was not the best of times and all he managed was a grimace.

Mrs Streight gave a restrained nod. 'Would you say you were happy with us, Richard?' Her tone left no doubt how he should interpret the question.

He thrust down all the fantasy responses that clamoured around the truth.

'Very much so, thank you, Mrs Streight.' He was pleased with the warmth he managed to project.

She actually smiled. On another face it might have been pleasant. Her teeth were white and even between shapely lips brushed a delicate pink. Her skin was elastic and washed in a restrained tan. Her bone structure was good and her proud nose suited her. It was just her eyes that spoiled the effect.

There was a knock behind him and he turned to see the Chaplain looking concerned.

'Not now, Rupert. Could you see Peter? I'm rather in the middle of something. Just shut the door.'

The bald Chaplain retreated. Richard slumped in his chair.

'I'm sorry about that, Richard.' Mrs Streight pressed a red button on her desk. 'Now we won't be disturbed. You were saying?'

Half-term was only a week and a half away. 'I was agreeing with you that I am happy at St Anne's.' He decided against going for another smile. His mouth tasted of ashes.

'Well, that's very good to hear, although I simply asked for your opinion. In truth, if I was asked the question, I would have been far from sure.'

A robin landed on the head of a rose and stared at him through the office window, head cocked as it ruffled its feathers.

'I had always assumed you loved your job, Mrs Streight? It's hard to imagine St Anne's without you.'

Something shifted in the room. Had she leant forward or was it just a tightening of her features? He made himself look into her eyes and immediately regretted it. Somehow, he had said precisely the wrong thing. He dropped his gaze, noticing a scuff on his left shoe which he immediately moved behind his right leg.

'Richard, really. We aren't here to talk about me.'

He flushed, heat suffusing his body, new pricks of sweat along his receding hairline and at the back of his neck. He dry-swallowed and opened his mouth to speak. How had things gone so wrong before the deputy head even mentioned why he was there? 'Forgive me, Mrs Streight. I... I misunderstood. Is there something specific?' He couldn't bring himself to go any further. Let her do it.

'Specific? Well, I do have several matters on my desk.'

Richard scanned the unencumbered sweep of faux wood. Telephone, monitor, keyboard and a desk calendar from the school's photographers. Nothing else. No file, no print out, no message.

He bit his lip and imagined stepping off the Eurostar at the Gare du Nord with a complete week beckoning. 'I will happily discuss any concerns, Mrs Streight.' Thoughts of a busy café by the Seine and a glass of ropey, overpriced red wine unable to deaden the well-judged *plat du jour* emboldened him.

Steel grey eyes held him. 'Thank you, Richard. That will not be necessary.'

He shifted in the too soft chair, awkwardly trapping the tails of his jacket.

'You have been with us a long time. I just thought it a good idea to sound you out before the majority of jobs appear in the TES. I like to have a sense of all the staff's intentions well in advance. For planning purposes, you understand?' She sounded so reasonable.

Richard wasn't sure she was allowed to ask about his intentions but thoughts of Paris melted away. Was he going to stay? He always did. He was in his thirty-seventh term. There was a litany of examination groups with results that could be directly traced to his teaching.

He remembered the queasiness with which he studied his pupils' results on that first, unusually damp August day. As a set they were not perfect but contained few surprises. More importantly, they looked just as good as those of his head of department and two of his classes were undeniably weaker.

He knew his material. He loved his subject. He had been qualified for fifteen years. He understood the exam specifications and he designed lessons that delivered what was needed. Richard cringed; it was all so much less than he had hoped for on that first day.

For some reason an image of his parents, the only one he knew was not the afterglow of a photograph, slipped into his head. He thought of them seldom but here they stood, smiling in Kodachrome beside a bronze-coloured car with a black vinyl roof. His father had one hand on the bonnet and the other around his mother's bare shoulders. They looked so happy and proud. Their first car and their last. Ironically, it looked more like a photograph than anything else.

'I, I very much hope to continue here.' A decade ago, a list of plans and goals would have hurried after those words. Richard let his reply hang in the lightly perfumed air, glad he could not smell himself.

Mrs Streight gave no sign his response was a disappointment. For an uncomfortably long time she did nothing but then, as if resolved, she leant forward an inch and placed her neatly manicured hands on the desk. 'Well, that is good, very good.' It didn't sound like it. 'We pride ourselves on developing talent, whenever we find it.'

Richard knew enough to play the game. 'Of course. I know what an opportunity I have here at St Anne's and even after my many years of teaching I know I still have a lot to learn.' He was a coward. He knew it every time he saw his parents' smiling faces, fixed in that moment from 1984.

'Quite right. This is a continual learning environment, for staff as well as pupils. Anyone who thinks they are the finished article has no place with us.' A shadow of a smile toyed with her lips.

Richard could not imagine a moment of self-doubt in Mrs Streight, let alone the humility to reshape her practice.

Most teachers were at lunch by the time he escaped to the relative safety of the staff room. He checked his pigeon hole for messages. There was nothing but a key stage three circular and a mailshot from an excessively expensive speaker on exam technique. He put them in the recycling bin and turned to the slew of papers and magazines littering the table.

The workroom-cum-lounge served as a central hub for those without departmental spaces. He pushed aside *The Daily Telegraph* and *The Times*, hovered over *The Independent* but moved on until he surprised himself by picking up one of several copies of the *Times Educational Supplement*.

He started at the back and leafed through the jobs section. It would grow to fill three supplements later in the year but for the moment consisted of less than sixty pages. He counted the history posts. There were eleven. In the heads of department section there were three.

A few colleagues came and went, some greeting him, others not. By the time he had finished reading he barely had time to eat before his next class.

Stuck in traffic that evening he tried to lose himself in the meandering guitar and surreal lyrics of The Bevis Frond, his favourite band of the moment. He smugly wondered if anyone else in Britain was listening to the same thing? Such transcendent music with so little recognition. It was the ultimate irony of his listening pleasure. The more obscure, the more he loved it; the more unfair the music industry seemed.

As he crawled bumper to bumper, car length by car length, away from school towards his comfortable flat, he lost the groove and gave up. He was going to have to confront the events of the day at some point. He hadn't been sacked. There was no immediate crisis to weather. Half-term was near. Paris. Les Invalides. Napoleon's tomb.

He inched forward in his ageing GTI, staring straight ahead, sick of Y378 UCF, black on yellow, with a stain across the final three letters and rusty screws exposed where the matching yellow caps had fallen off.

Did he still want to teach? Did he want to be at St Anne's? The answers should be simple but he started sweating and had to turn up the faltering air conditioning.

Should he have stayed at university all those years ago? He had fitted in. Not with people but with a purpose. He enjoyed study. He loved the subject. He could lose himself in the past. He achieved a good degree. Research beckoned. So why had he barely considered it?

His parents were dead. He didn't owe them anything. He was six when they crashed. Aunt Patricia had taken him in. Never reluctant, never resentful, never unkind. What did he owe her? A respectable career as reward for her pains?

History as a subject had been his salvation. Bereft of parents, living in a creaking Victorian pile so different from fading memories of a sun-filled Sixties home. Thrust into a new school mid-year with little to cling to but Mr Armour's round face whose warm eyes lit up when it was time for history.

Mr Armour was his guide but he was soon off on his own. Exploring the past, jumping around, delving, drifting back from the present, beyond the black tear of loss into another world. He owed history. History had been his refuge. It had saved him.

The number-plate drew away, a horn sounded behind, coarse and insistent. He eased off the clutch and kept pace as the traffic flowed around the roundabout. He would be home in ten minutes.

Home? Was his half-floor of a 1930s brick block that? As he closed the front door he glanced at the familiarity. Nondescript furniture in muted tones and walls of history books. It was all he had.

He would show those girls.

His year twelve class tumbled through his classroom door, filling the high-ceilinged room with piercing voices. They slid into their seats, eyes on each other as they dropped their bags and rummaged for textbooks and files.

'Settle down, settle down, ladies. Today we are going to consider the following question.' He cued the projector and waited a few seconds before reciting, 'Was Napoleon the first great European?' He looked around at the twelve occupied seats. Every face was visible. Several appeared to be actively considering the matter. 'Any initial thoughts?' he asked, cueing the second page of his presentation.

A series of images jumbled into a collage on the whiteboard behind him. Napoleon signing legislation, Napoleon leading troops, Napoleon being crowned emperor, buildings he commissioned, a map of his conquests, all interspersed with the improbable names of states he created. Richard's favourite was the Cisalpine Republic.

'Well, he wasn't the first European, was he? I mean, there were loads of people in Europe before he was born!' Sniggers. 'Is this going to be in the exam?'

Here was the moment. Seize the lesson, coax them to consider the very concept of Europe. Elevate their thoughts. Challenge them, reveal something of the splendour of analysis. 'Settle down. Why don't we start by deconstructing the question? We've done this a lot so take a moment to consider.'

He scanned the room and was relieved to see files opened and pens uncapped. For a glorious minute there was thoughtful silence.

The first hand in the air was Tilly's, it was always Tilly's. In the six weeks of the year twelve course, she had never failed to be first. In all that time her questions remained the same. He smiled encouragingly.

'Mr Davey, please sir, do we have to analyse every word? I mean, what about *was* and *the*?'

He sighed inwardly. 'Key words, Tilly, remember? Just the key words.'

Her arm shot up again but he dipped his head to study his lesson plan. He knew she would be waving by now, eyes beginning to bulge, colour rising. Any second and she would just blurt it out. 'Yes, Tilly?'

'How can you tell if a word is a key word? I mean, they are all needed to make the question!'

Groans, whispers and unkind laughter.

'Someone want to help Tilly out? Libby?' Richard turned to his most studious pupil. He needed an ally before the lesson slipped away.

'European is the key word. We know we are studying Napoleon, assessing his impact on the early nineteenth century. We have to define concepts. To understand what we mean by European we must define Europe. We will also need to consider how to evaluate great and then decide whether or not Napoleon was really the first to meet our criteria.' Libby ran a forefinger up her long nose as if repositioning the spectacles she had worn until the end of year eleven.

Shuffling from the back but most of the girls were writing. They knew whatever Libby said was right and more often in language they could understand than anything he might add.

'Well done, Libby. Succinct and accurate. Let's leave the secondary issues to one side and concentrate on this key concept of Europe. What do we mean by Europe today? Does the question mean the same thing we do?'

'My mum says Europe's a conspiracy of bureaucrats to frustrate business.' Mother a CEO.

'Churchill's biggest mistake.' Father a Eurosceptic MP.

'The only way to get the Ryder Cup off the Americans!' School's best sportswoman, resident in Washington.

'Wogs start at Calais.' Suspended for smoking within three weeks of joining for the Sixth Form.

Richard raised his hands to quell the onslaught. 'Anyone have anything to offer that they haven't heard said by someone else?' A cloud blocked out the sun. Richard switched on the lights.

Eyes dropped or drifted. A nudge, a yawn, no one spoke. He had lost them. He took a deep, sad breath and ploughed on. 'Have the many countries of the continent always acknowledged they were part of something bigger? When did anyone first refer to the idea of Europe?'

They sat in pairs at tables. He walked slowly down the central aisle looking at each girl in turn. Some looked away, others stared defiantly. He left Libby alone. Returning to the front he began to lecture. They dutifully wrote in their files.

From time to time, he keyed another slide. They barely looked up. When the bell was two minutes away, they began putting their files, pens and assorted items into their bags. He was still talking. He ignored it, made a note of where he had got to and asked them to make an essay plan for homework.

They were already filing from the room. The bell rang as he was tidying their abandoned chairs.

That evening he called his aunt. It was something his conscience required at least once a month. 'Good evening, Aunt. How are you?' This was a question she never answered. 'I just thought I should say hello. I'm going to Paris for half-term so if you need me, I'll be on my mobile.' He heard a noise which might have signified acknowledgement. 'I had a meeting with the deputy head yesterday. She was asking about my plans. I told her I was very happy teaching at St Anne's.'

Richard went on and on uninterrupted, inferring reactions or responses from static on the line and the absence of contradiction or cross-examination.

The first clear word Aunt Patricia emitted was, 'Goodbye.' It was only after these one-sided conversations with his aunt that Richard imagined what Patricia really thought. He rarely liked his conclusions.

He went to the pub on the High Street and drank too much in the corner, a bubble of misery amid raucous pleasures.

He arrived back at his flat drenched by a sudden downpour

that stopped as he reached the door.

He stared at the ceiling, frustration keeping him from sleep. He was forty years old and he did not expect much from life. He just wanted a sense of purpose; a satisfying job; not perfect nor easy but satisfying. He had no close friends and no real sense of family.

The one thing he did love was currently in jeopardy. That one, pure thing was being tarnished. Every day, in so many little ways, he was losing that love amongst the poor test results, slapdash essays, snide responses, low level disruption and barely disguised contempt of his pupils.

He curled up facing the wall and thought about Paris. In his mind it was warm, late spring, flowers everywhere. He would arrive on the twenty-fifth of October. It would still be Paris. Eight days to himself.

'Passport, tickets, money,' he recited as he checked his pockets. His single case was designed to fit in an overhead airline locker. It contained enough clothes and toiletries for the week plus a couple more books than he needed. It was quite heavy but rolled easily on its wheels.

The taxi dropped him at his local railway station and for once the train was on time. As the suburbs grew denser, he felt himself coalesce. When the Circle Line spat him out at King's Cross, he was no longer a fractured shadow haunting the corridors of St Anne's.

The Friday crowd's inconsiderate rush could not impede him as he threaded his way to St Pancras International. Richard smiled. The station's Victorian magnificence had been restored with sympathy and style. He nodded to the statue of John Betjeman gazing at the sweep of railway cathedral roof he helped preserve.

Summoned by Bells, such an apt description of school life. A rigid routine he could defy for the next week.

It was late when he arrived, even later by local time. He took a taxi to his hotel and waited impatiently for his key which he fumbled in the lock. He really wanted to get some sleep. He slipped into bed, face tingling from the cold tap and mouth alive with spearmint. He never slept well in a new bed and never when he was excited.

His next thought was to register a sparkling Saturday morning. His Marais hotel room was tucked into the mansard roof, plain but spotless and only a short stroll from the cafés and boutiques scattered carelessly around the rigid symmetry and secrets of the Place des Vosges, the oldest planned square in Paris.

He took his time over coffee and croissant with yesterday's copy of *Le Figaro*. He was too early. His French was a bit rusty but he pieced together the lead stories well enough.

At half past eight, local time, he paid his bill and set off for a five-kilometre walk across the city. He reckoned it would take a little over an hour, meaning he would be there for opening time.

He passed Sainte Chapelle and for the first time was reminded of his school, a Catholic institution with a fine chapel of its own, decorated with plunder from the Low Countries.

He distracted himself with the immensity of the Louvre,

recalling his first attempt to see the Mona Lisa through both security glass and a horde of tourists.

Crossing the Seine, heading for the Musée d'Orsay where he had spent one of the most perfect days wandering from room to room awash with wonder. A day when strike action meant the whole extravaganza was free.

He resisted heading south, staying with the flow of the river, metallic in the cool sun, arcing westward with the Eiffel Tower growing taller ahead.

The National Assembly fell behind him to the left and then he was at the junction of the Pont Alexandre III, all beaux arts swags, with Avenue du Maréchal Gallieni driving south through broad lawns to the imposing sweep of Les Invalides' gilded dome.

And then he was beside the vast buildings, dwarfed by the vision that had conjured them. He was a speck. There were so many ways the sight of Les Invalides defeated him. He had tried so many times to capture it with a camera, in words, even with watercolours. He had tried explaining it to his aunt and to his classes. He had turned to poetry without success.

Nothing captured the essence of it: majestic, audacious, generous, arrogant, stylish, compassionate. The Sun King's legacy; guilt for his fallen troops acknowledged. Gift, duty, patronage, vision. It would dwarf many modern hospitals, having once contained five thousand casualties from Napoleon's campaigns.

Richard walked through the main entrance into the vast, cobbled courtyard defined by its two-tiered arcades. The rhythmic arches were topped with steep slate punctuated by ornamental attic windows awash with military symbolism. Each flank was centred with a pediment while above it all rose the massive, part-gilded dome of the chapel.

His eyes were drawn in and came to rest on the central arch of the second tier beneath the pediment.

A figure filled the space, resplendent in the uniform of a colonel in the Imperial Guard cavalry, partly obscured by that familiar frock coat. A stocky, lifelike figure topped by the ubiquitous bicorn hat, one hand slipped between the buttons of his waistcoat, his gaze fixed on an impossible distance. Cannonballs piled behind his booted feet.

He looked through Richard with bronze eyes, frowning at his frozen fate. The statue was actually four metres tall to appear proportionate among its grand surroundings.

Richard waited patiently until he could buy his ticket and then crossed the courtyard away from the military museum occupying the north facing courtyards. He was enjoying the relative quiet.

Walking beneath the statue, he at last escaped Napoleon's gaze and made his way into the cathedral. Inside were displayed many of France's military honours from the bottom of the barrel vault. The altar was festooned with tricolours.

He headed into the former royal chapel, the domed church that housed Napoleon's tomb. A tour guide waited discreetly as he entered. She smiled at him, the first visitor of the day. She wore a smart navy twin set edged in red, redolent of French uniforms. Her lipstick was the same bold shade and her lustrous raven hair was cut in a fashionable, offset bob. Her skin was pale but her large brown eyes were warm.

Richard smiled back, forgetting to hide his teeth. She

walked towards him, assured on her heels, shapely legs sheathed in stockings so fine he had thought she was bare-legged.

'*Bonjour,* Monsieur. Is this your first time seeing the emperor's tomb?' Her accent was impeccable. He had long given up trying to fathom how the French could divine *les étrangers* from a distance. Nevertheless, he replied in French that he had been here many times. She nodded and her eyes sparkled.

He held her gaze and reciprocated before dropping his eyes to her name badge. 'Amélie Durand. Beautiful.' She raised an eyebrow but a smile teased her lips apart. He blushed and cursed his clumsy command of the language. 'Yes, yes you are… but I was referring to your name. Durand means steadfast, to endure, I believe?' He explained in English. It was her turn to colour. A group arrived, trailing their guide. 'While Amélie means industrious, hard working. A lot to live up to!'

She laughed aloud, a throaty sound that echoed around the sombre space. The group's guide had started his introduction. His audience turned towards the source of unexpected mirth. Amélie blushed more deeply and gestured that Richard should follow her.

She moved confidently to the other side of the vulgar plum porphyry sarcophagus on its green granite base. The circular space was bounded by pillars bearing classical figures that supported the main floor of the church. The whole central area of the crypt was open so that those above could peer over a balustrade, while the tomb sat directly beneath the baroque dome's allegorical paintings.

'They excavated this space to house the emperor.' She had reverted to English seamlessly. 'It took twenty years to do it without bringing the whole thing tumbling down.'

Richard had never really thought about the conversion of a seventeenth century royal chapel into a nineteenth century mausoleum. He asked Amélie about the paintings on the dome.

She told him all about Charles de La Fosse and his admiration for Le Brun.

He asked about the twelve figures surrounding the tomb and she explained they represented military victories and then pointed out the reliefs. She showed him how they chronicled different phases of Napoleon's career, celebrating his achievements from engineering to legislation.

They walked a full circle as the stone story unfolded with Amélie's charming commentary.

'I teach about Napoleon, you know?' Richard offered as they completed the tour.

She stepped close, 'Really? In England?' He told her about St Anne's and the A Level syllabus. How much he loved this period of French history. She asked questions; he knew the answers. He could see she was pleased before she said, 'I did not think the English would want to study their great foe. I suppose it is wise to know your enemy though?'

Richard had a lot to say on this subject. Napoleon was not a natural hero for a British citizen but he had devised an explanation that deflected even the most insistent inquiry. 'What better way to celebrate our ultimate victory over the French Empire than to lionise your emperor? The greater the man we defeated, the more impressive the achievement.'

She peered at him, brows slightly furrowed, a delightful crinkle appearing at the top of her nose. 'That is what you choose to tell people, yes?'

He looked away from her stunning face to the now busy crypt. Selfie sticks abounded. 'He was remarkable.' It was a relief to tell the truth. 'I wish I had lived in his time.'

She put her hand gently on his shoulder with a look of understanding. 'The past can seem so much more meaningful, yes?'

He nodded, mistrusting his words.

She grinned, 'But you would be on the wrong side, I think?'

Richard shrugged. 'It would be no bad thing to be born French.'

'You do not speak for all your people, I think?'

He did not want to talk about Brexit. 'No. But I am on holiday from them. I have a week to spend. You seem to know a lot about Napoleon. I notice you always refer to him as the emperor? What would you do to get closer to the man?' Amélie frowned. Richard blushed, 'I'm sorry, have I overstepped the mark? I'm monopolising your time. I should go.' The words tumbled out to stave off his awkwardness.

She extended a hand to detain him, her fingers were long and beautifully manicured with clear varnish. 'Please. I was only thinking. I know a place, a shop that might interest you. I used to spend a lot of time there as a child. It is full of wonder. You will like it. I will write the address.'

Richard took the notepaper from her outstretched hand and studied it. Her handwriting was florid and leaned jauntily to the left. The paper was what he thought of as graph paper, so typical of French notebooks. Amélie had written the name of the shop, the address and a few brief comments.

Her script was not easy to decipher and he couldn't help reading the first line aloud just to check, 'Madame Odillet's Pieces of the Past. It can't really be called that, here in Paris? You've translated for me?'

Amélie shook her head without disturbing a single hair. 'She was at Woodstock. Don't let her put you off.'

Richard headed for a bistro he remembered that catered for artistic types frequenting the museums nearby. It was lunchtime but he secured a table by agreeing to share with a lively, bohemian trio immersed in a conversation he could barely follow.

He ordered a half-litre of house red and the *plat du jour* without opening the menu.

It had been a perfect morning and yet meeting Amélie had left him melancholy. He pulled her note from his pocket and studied the address. He loved walking the streets of Paris.

Deciphering her ebullient script, he realized the shop was right back where he had started his day, in the Marais district, housed in his favourite square, the Place des Vosges. Its early seventeenth century majesty hummed with the same red brick and warm sandstone tones the Victorians celebrated in at St Pancras. He would save his visit until tomorrow.

A waiter brought his wine and poured half a glass from the earthenware *pichet*. Richard sipped it and tried to tune into his tablemates' conversation. They were comparing artists but none of the names meant anything to him.

Realizing his glass was almost empty, he reached for the glazed jug and smiled as the lightly watered liquid filled his glass. It was not bitter or sour, in fact it was very drinkable.

His meal arrived, *entrecôte frites* with a simple salad, ideally suited to both his mood and his drink. He chewed his medium rare steak, mopping blood with his fries, and sank another glass of wine.

His mood lightened, the simple oil-based salad dressing was perfect, the tenor of his table was infectious, the service was relaxed but friendly and he could hear nothing but French. Inspired by the artistic atmosphere, he determined to spend the afternoon in the company of Maillol. It had been years since he had visited the nearby museum.

Surrounded by Maillol's statuesque bronze nudes, Richard was glad of the wine he had drunk. It made him bold enough to look properly despite the other visitors. He knew the model, Dina Vierny, had only died in 2009 just shy of her ninetieth birthday. She was everywhere in the museum.

Metallic curves radiated heat, the effect she had had on the ageing sculptor was palpable. Love, lust or a dispassionate appreciation of form? Richard knew the answer, seeing it in every deft detail. Stalled by one particularly charming image, he imagined Amélie's face and knew it was time to leave.

He decided against walking back to his hotel, taking the *Métro* instead. As he rattled beneath the city, braced against the sway of the carriage, his melancholy returned. Such a good day but no one to share it.

The hotel bar was open and Richard ordered a bottle of Châteauneuf-du-Pape. The barman recommended the 2016.

It was pricey but he agreed. He sat in a corner as he always did. It was only six-thirty and the bar was almost empty. Just a couple with their heads together, holding hands. He drank the first glass too quickly to appreciate it.

In an effort to pace himself, Richard tried to imagine Madame Odillet from the few hints Amélie had offered. She was an Anglophile, an antiques dealer and a child of the sixties. He pictured long grey hair, a little flyaway, framing a lined face. Thin and just a little hunched, her bangles rattled as she moved, draped in a tie-dyed cotton shift, on scuffed boots.

Richard shakes his head, dispelling his past now more than two hundred years in the future. How long has he been sheltering? He spreads the coat in front of him and pulls out his watch. It is far from dry but still ticking. It reads a little after eleven. He has no idea how relevant that might be in 1815 where there is no nationally standardised time.

He cannot risk being discovered by the sentry. He needs to get moving.

Chapter Three

He wrestles into his damp overcoat, settles his pack and clamps his hat on his head. He eases up the latch and peers out. He can see lights in the farmhouse but he cannot hear any voices from inside.

Nothing stirs in the garden except the wind through the hedge and rain angling from the sky, pattering against thick cabbage leaves.

Richard closes the door and scuttles beyond the lights to the rear of the shed. He works back around the hedged perimeter until his hands find the hole he forced earlier. He removes his hat and begins to wriggle.

A shout from across the vegetable patch in German. He heaves himself through to the other side. He hears a metallic strike and a hissing puff, like a miniature steam engine. Curses ride off on the wind as he runs along the hedge to the outer corner of the farm courtyard.

Richard lopes along the outer wall of the stables to its south-easterly extremity. He is breathing hard, more from fear than tiredness. Ahead is a slight dip onto the valley floor. He supposes the soldier's musket misfired in the rain. A few hundred paces through fields should bring him close to the next building on the road, the inn of La Belle Alliance. Tomorrow it will be Napoleon's base of operations.

He stumbles into the grain, hunches over and keeps going, tending right until he finds the field boundary and a shallow ditch. Instinctively, he follows the dyke due south, parallel with the road.

It is about half a mile to the inn along the highway. The wind tugs the anonymous corn heads from side to side like an agitated sea. Rain fills the air with chaotic waves, thrown about at the mercy of the gusting wind. Richard makes good time along the field's edge, only slipping once where saturated earth gives way beneath his feet.

He crosses a berm into a second field where the crop is taller, and angles across the expanse towards a pinprick of light ahead to his left. As he draws closer, he sees a pair of sentries and a small group sheltering beneath the overhanging roof of the inn.

Richard lowers himself against the bank between field and road, crushing stems beneath him. He cannot hear what is being said but they are clearly an advance guard, securing the inn for the emperor's use as his field headquarters.

His destination is only one thousand five hundred yards south, the farm of Le Caillou where Napoleon will try to sleep tonight.

Slipping back into the field, he presses on, large seed heads at shoulder height weighty as they bounce away from him. He winces at the noise he is making but the storm masks everything.

He has cut through the Allied lines from their rear depot to their most forward outpost without being detained. Now he is beyond the advance post of the French dispositions. He marvels at how narrow the space is between the two armies, like no man's land at places on the Western Front in World War One where the opposing armies lobbed grenades at each other.

He strides on with growing confidence. All he needs is to fall into the right hands, steady hands not panicky conscripts, and he will have survived the most remarkable battlefield walk in history!

He is beginning to believe he will succeed so he rehearses what to say when he confronts French soldiers, inside their lines. If he doesn't make this convincing, one nervous finger could end his adventure less than twelve hours after it began. He grimaces and starts polishing his words.

Before he is finished, he hears the jingle of harnesses and the sound of shod horses passing on the road. Challenges are shouted and replies offered. The riders trot on into the spill of light that surrounds Napoleon's headquarters.

Braziers burn at each corner of the main house and to each side of the front door. The interior is bright, brighter than Richard expected. How many candles and lamps to push back the night like that?

He can make out every detail of Le Caillou. An imposing two storey façade, fresh whitewash contrasting with the red-tile roof. Windows flanked by wooden shutters and four stone steps rising to a recessed front door.

Two sentries patrol between the braziers. They pause at the end of each shuttle to warm their hands before resuming their deliberate pace.

Richard steps onto the road, arms raised, his wet, white handkerchief clutched in his left hand. 'Do not shoot! I am unarmed. I bring intelligence for the emperor.'

Both sentries turn at his voice and advance, muskets trained on him. Ten yards from him they converge, shoulder to shoulder, presenting a wall of blue and white trimmed with red. Their shakos flare from brow to top, more stylish than those of their counterparts on the other side of the valley. Richard can see the imperial eagle on each hat.

'Who are you? Where do you come from?' demands the older of the pair, his drooping moustaches grey at the tips.

'He sounds funny,' chimes in the younger guard, his face a moonscape of pockmarks, 'but not like the locals.'

The older man wears an extra chevron on his sleeve denoting his seniority.

'Corporal, please take me to someone in authority.' Richard keeps his voice level, amazed how calm he feels despite two sixteen-inch steel bayonets pointed at his belly. The pair advance within lunging distance. 'I have information vital to the campaign, to the outcome of tomorrow's battle!' Richard pleads.

The corporal's steely eyes scan him from muddy boots to sodden hat. 'Show me your papers!'

Richard tries to reach the tails of his frock coat but cannot navigate beneath the sodden weight of his close-fitting overcoat. He lets his hand drop, ambivalent about the efficacy of his outdated pass. Tension locks the muscles in his shoulders and the sinews of his neck bulge with tension. 'I will happily produce my credentials to an officer.' He keeps his gaze steady and his face calm.

The acne scarred youth jabs his bayonet forward petulantly, mouth twisted in a sneer. 'I think he's a spy! Gathering information for his bloody English paymasters.'

The older man is scrutinising Richard closely. 'Maybe so,' he admits, 'but he revealed himself to us. Why do that?' His gravel voice is low and measured, the sound of a man who has witnessed a lot and learned to calculate.

'More fool him! Let me run him through. We can tell the duty officer we killed an enemy informer. We might get double rations, brandy too!' Tiny eyes glitter and wrists twitch, jerking the young private's long blade menacingly.

'Stand down, Henri!' bellows the corporal. 'Go fetch Lieutenant Béraud, he's the officer on duty.'

Richard feels the knots in his muscles release. He has survived his first encounter with the enemy. Enemy? He is here to help Napoleon win the battle of Waterloo!

He is about to strike up a conversation with the corporal when a figure appears, framed in the farmhouse doorway. The bright light of the interior casts the newcomer in perfect silhouette as he fits his headgear.

He emerges onto the steps adjusting his chin strap and takes them in a single bound, trotting forward with the young private trailing. Private Henri joins the corporal and whispers in his ear.

Richard looks at the officer he has heard named Lieutenant Béraud. He has presence. His face is not old but his green eyes are wells of experience. His long side whiskers and moustaches are neatly trimmed. He has a proud nose and full eyebrows beneath his squat fur busby.

In contrast to the blue and white of his subordinates in the infantry, his uniform is bottle green with red facings. Double rows of decorative gold lace fill the front of his jacket. There are gold buttons everywhere. Across his shoulders drapes a pelisse in red and gold, trimmed with white fur. This is a cavalryman of the Imperial Guard.

'I think he has something under his coat, sir!' blurts out Henri in an ingratiating whine.

The magnificently dressed lieutenant ignores him. 'Corporal Hubertin, your report?' A fine baritone.

'He just appeared, sir. Surrendered willingly. I asked for his papers but, well, I decided to send for you, sir. He's certainly not French even if he does sort of speak our language. Not a local either. He doesn't assault the ears with that Flemish guttural!'

Richard tries to look confident. This is the man he has to convince. 'A pleasure to meet you, Lieutenant Béraud. I see you belong to the Imperial Guard cavalry. I would very much like to talk with you. I have intelligence vital to the emperor.'

Lieutenant Béraud raises a well-trained eyebrow and strokes his bare chin. A brisk nod suggests he has made his decision. A decisive man. 'Follow me! You two, return to your posts. When your duty is complete you may report to the quartermaster for an extra tot of brandy.'

The sentries hurry off smiling to each other.

At the front door, Lieutenant Béraud takes hold of Richard's arm, guides him inside and then immediately through a door to the left. Richard finds himself on the threshold of a small office.

Béraud indicates a plain wooden chair and Richard sits. The lieutenant removes his sword and hat before circling his simple, uncluttered desk. Richard struggles to unbutton his coat.

The lieutenant picks up a poker and agitates the embers in the hearth, adding a split log and watching the flames catch. 'May I take your coat?'

Richard's hands freeze, the bottom button still fastened. He nods as he returns to his task. He stands and shrugs awkwardly out of the garment.

Lieutenant Béraud waits expectantly, one hand outstretched. Richard yields his overcoat and tries to reclaim the initiative. 'My papers are in the tail pocket.'

The lieutenant feels around for a moment and then withdraws his hand, clutching an oilskin wallet. He hangs the coat on the back of the door and closes it. He then places the oilskin package on his desk and takes his seat. 'Perhaps you would like to introduce yourself fully?' suggests Béraud, his green eyes sparking. A lamp on the desk throws a sickly light across its scarred surface but as the fire grows more vigorous it is replaced by a healthy orange.

'Thank you, Lieutenant. My name is Richard Davey. As you will see,' Richard indicates the damp package on the desk, 'I am an American agent working against the interests of the British. Britain has bankrolled opposition to France for decades. This is what, the seventh coalition? From across the Atlantic, we wish to weaken British dominance. The enemy of my enemy is my friend.'

Béraud laughs, a rolling, weighty sound. 'You have a fine turn of phrase, sir.' Richard colours but the uneven light masks it. 'Pray continue,' requests the lieutenant.

'I have been among the Allied positions this very day. Once it was dark, I made my way to your lines. I wish to pass on what I know to Bonaparte. I believe he can win tomorrow but not if he remains ignorant of certain matters.'

The lieutenant sits quite still, a single finger tapping the arm of his chair.

'His Imperial Highness is yet to return, although he is expected. You appreciate the gravity of what you ask? Should your intelligence prove weak, I will pay the price alongside you. Convince me and I will consider what should be done.'

Richard sighs and slumps in his chair. Although the warmth of the fire is welcome, he is bone tired now. 'I can tell you are a reasonable man, Lieutenant Béraud. A thoughtful one, too, I suspect?' Béraud inclines his head. Richard adds, 'In truth, there is one further motive behind my appearance.'

The lieutenant's finger stills and he leans forward a fraction. Richard presses on before he can be misunderstood. 'I have admired the emperor since he came to prominence under the Directory. He is the outstanding man of his age. It has been my ambition to meet him for many years. I engineered my assignment. Fortunately, Washington have reason to value my services. President Madison is a man of like mind. He fought the British in 1812. The effect of their naval blockade has convinced him we must continue our opposition by other means. I carry a letter of recommendation for the emperor's eyes from the president himself.'

Richard sees he has made an impression on the lieutenant, who leans back, hands steepled in front of him, elbows on the arms of his chair. He waits hopefully.

Lieutenant Béraud claps his hands and stands up. He leans across the desk and picks up the oilskin wallet. He has almost finished unwrapping the package when there is a knock at his door.

He apologises and relinquishes the parcel, slipping into the corridor where Richard hears him in conversation.

The lieutenant does not return immediately so Richard

stands and inspects his documents. A little water has wormed through the packet's defences.

His forgery is untouched but his expensive warrant from Davout has run in several places, most particularly at top right where the date was marked. What remains is a general pass for the bearer signed by Marshal Davout. It is even more creased than when he bought it but that can be explained by its recent treatment. The discolouration is barely noticeable in the flame light. Richard slips the documents back into the cover as he hears footsteps in the hall.

The lieutenant returns with a serious look on his handsome face. 'The emperor has arrived.'

Richard's eyes widen. 'He is here, now?'

Béraud nods. 'Upstairs with his staff, finalising orders for tomorrow. He looks tired. He is much changed since the Battle of the Three Emperors.'

Richard smiles at the alternative name for the great French victory at Austerlitz.

The lieutenant continues, 'He is grown stout and his head hangs between his shoulders. His belly is a bulging pot. His complexion is pasty, almost waxy and he is heavy on his feet.' Béraud pauses and pinches the bridge of his nose. 'But his eyes still blaze with ambition. He is still my emperor. Now, let us return to the matter in hand.'

Richard puzzles at the officer's accent. Years of service have glossed and abbreviated his natural dialect but he still has a tendency to pronounce every syllable and end words with exaggeration.

Béraud resumes his seat and removes the two documents from their protective wallet. He puts them carefully on the desk and opens a drawer from which he extracts a bottle and two stemmed glasses.

'You are *Provençal?*' enquires Richard.

'*Camarguais*. My father was one of the *gardians*, horsemen of the wetlands, caring for the bulls. That is where I learned to ride.' His face lights up as he talks of home. He pours two full measures of brandy and pushes one glass across the desk.

The glass is a greenish, thick and almost opaque. The rim is chipped.

'To the emperor and victory!' toasts the lieutenant.

Richard leans forward and grasps the glass, raising it. 'To the emperor and allowing him the best chance of victory!'

Béraud shakes his head and picks up the pass. He scans it and returns it to the table without comment. He then takes his time reading the fake letter from Madison. When he has finished, he reads it again. 'Your credentials are impressive. Now we must judge whether your information is of similar quality.'

He has passed scrutiny. The lieutenant believes his cover story. Now he has his chance. He begins describing Wellington's dispositions in detail, adding convincing details from what he has seen that afternoon.

The lieutenant produces pen and paper from another drawer. He writes rapidly what must be close to a verbatim account.

Richard speaks to the crackle of the fire and the scrape of the nib, pausing occasionally to sip brandy. When his glass is empty, Béraud holds up his hand, refills Richard's glass, sinks his own drink in one gulp and replenishes it. Once his pen is

61

back in his hand, he nods and Richard continues.

It is done soon enough. He has one last card to play. 'Bonaparte must not underestimate the Prussians. Yes, he beat them on Thursday but they are far from a spent force. Blücher is a wily old fox. Grouchy will not contain his forces. He will find a way to play his part. If I could just discuss the emperor's thinking on the matter, I could ensure his success.'

Lieutenant Béraud rests his pen on a sheaf of scribbled notes and massages his right hand with his left. He smiles as he drains his glass and pours again for both of them. 'I would like you to call me Emile. May I do likewise, Richard?'

He nods. 'Thank you, Emile. I have been fortunate, I think, to find myself in your hands.' It is flattery. He still hopes to persuade the lieutenant to put him in front of Napoleon but it is also what he thinks.

'Perhaps. It is true others might have acted first and asked questions too late. I am persuaded by what you have told me. It is clear you have seen the enemy emplacements in detail. I will ensure the emperor has access to everything. But how can you claim to know the importance of the Prussians to tomorrow's battle? Let alone dismiss Marshal Grouchy so roundly? How do you even know of his command? You speak as if you have already witnessed the day!'

Richard feels things unravelling. Has he overplayed his hand? 'Please, Emile. Put aside concerns for yourself. I promise you, all I have described is accurate. The emperor will be defeated unless you give me an opportunity to explain!' His voice is uneven and slightly slurred.

Emile tosses back his drink, slaps his hands on the table and stands. 'I shall convey all you have said to those closest to the emperor's ear. More than that is not within my power. You think I spend my time at his side? In a way that is true. I have served him for more than a decade in a regiment he loves so much he wears our uniform on campaign. I have often, as now, commanded the duty squadron from our regiment. And yet I have been in a room with him no more than a dozen times and exchanged words with him less often than that. Your dream, I fear, is simply beyond my gift to give. I am sorry, Richard.' With that, Emile calls through the door.

A sentry, not in cavalry green but the blue, white and red of the line infantry, appears with alacrity.

'Escort our guest to my quarters and arrange for a second bed to be installed.'

The soldier salutes and waits in the doorway until Richard reluctantly rises, accepting his coat and hat from Emile.

He has come so far. He is so close. He exits the office to an exchange of pleasantries and follows the infantryman along the corridor and out of a side door into the main courtyard of Le Caillou farm.

The rain still falls, although the wind has dropped. They head beyond the well towards a two-storey barn with a carriage door to the right and a smaller door dead ahead. As they reach this door, he glances behind him across the sweep of the wide courtyard, up to the first floor of the farmhouse, where a pair of bright windows is visible. He sees figures bent over a table. One of them is the man he has come so very far to meet.

Inside the barn it is murky but he sees most of the ground floor to the left is filled with carts and farm implements.

Fresh straw is scattered on the dirt floor. To the right is a run of stabling from which emerges the sounds and smells of horses.

The soldier indicates a rudimentary ladder propped against the mezzanine floor. Richard climbs cautiously, closely followed by the guard who points left and then escorts him past a series of shoulder height cubicles fashioned of raw planks. They halt at the end of the row, facing an enclosure slightly wider than the rest. There is a blanket hung at the opening.

Pushing through, Richard finds a camp bed, a washstand, a chair and a travelling chest. On pegs protruding from the far wall hang spare items of uniform and equipment.

'You are to remain here. I will arrange for a second bed.' With that, the soldier retreats, muttering.

Richard eases back the hanging to look through the end window. He watches the guard emerge and traverse the courtyard to a smaller barn. He is only inside for a minute before he and a companion appear at either end of a cot. As they reach the door to the barn he occupies, Richard ducks back into Lieutenant Béraud's billet and sits on the single, armless chair.

He hears the two privates manhandling the pallet as they mount the ladder. One curses and then the other. Their breathing labours as they throw back the blanket and put the bed down parallel to the one already in place. The second soldier produces what looks and smells like a horse blanket and then they are gone.

Richard lies back on the bed and closes his eyes. He has no hope of sleeping but it feels good, even if he imagines Aunt

Patricia's disapproving face projected onto the inside of his eyelids. At least he has found shelter, he reminds her.

The next thing he knows is the sound of someone moving around the space. A nub of candle gives a pale light from a holder on the small trunk. Richard rolls onto his side. Emile has removed his black fur hat, bright jacket and polished boots.

'I am sorry I woke you, Richard. It is a little after midnight. Get some rest. We have received our orders for tomorrow. My men are to escort the emperor. We must be ready at four-thirty. The army marches at first light. One of my men will wake us in time for breakfast.'

Richard is surprised he has dozed. He checks his watch and adjusts it so that the longer minute hand is just visible beyond the vertical hour hand. 'It has been raining for hours now. Most of the roads and lanes are not paved. There will be much mud. I think things will be delayed.' Richard knows.

'The emperor is a master moving an army at speed. If he says we march at dawn, then that is what will happen.'

Richard keeps quiet. He knows. He closes his eyes to wait.

Richard opens his eyes to find Emile looking down at him, a hand on his shoulder. 'Breakfast,' he says gently.

Richard smells coffee and sits up, swinging his legs onto the floor. He accepts a cup and a cold bread roll. His head clears as he drinks the weak blend and munches on his roll.

His muscles have relaxed as he slept, the canvas sling of a bed proving more comfortable than many he has tossed and turned in. He checks his pocket watch. It is just after four and no light creeps under the blanket.

The candle gutters but Emile ignores it, dressing efficiently in his finery, brushing every element carefully first.

'How is the weather?' Richard asks.

'Drizzle but mild.' A knock on the exterior of the cubicle interrupts. 'Enter!'

An infantryman appears and salutes. 'New orders, sir!' He holds out a sealed message.

The lieutenant takes it and dismisses the man. He breaks the seal and reads. 'It seems you were right, Richard. Our departure is delayed. We assemble at eight o'clock. The army is to be in position to engage by nine.'

Richard smiles. Napoleon has been told how scattered his troops are and that many minor ways remain impassable. He will be back in bed now.

Dressing, Richard is delighted to find everything more or less dry, even his overcoat. His hat looks scuffed and is the one thing still obviously damp. He borrows one of the lieutenant's brushes and does his best to restore it. It is cold when he tries it on and he gives an involuntary shiver.

'I do not think your hat is quite the thing for today. You must remain by my side at all times.'

Richard looks quizzically at the hat. 'Is it too scruffy to be seen in the company of the emperor?' he jokes.

Emile grins. 'Perhaps. More to the point, is your balance so fine you can ride without it being dislodged?'

Richard freezes. Dare he admit he cannot ride? Might that leave him confined to this farm? So close and yet so far from the action. He bites his lip and sits his hat on the camp bed.

They talk of small things in a desultory way even though the lieutenant brims with energy, itching to be off. Richard tries to remain calm but thinking of the day enervates him. They drink more coffee and Emile makes his rounds, visiting his troopers and checking the arrangements to secure the farm.

Richard watches the courtyard, peering across to the windows of the farmhouse, hoping for a glimpse of Napoleon as he shaves, cuts his nails and dresses. He does not know which window to choose. Napoleon checks the weather regularly this morning, he knows, but he sees no one.

It stops raining around seven-thirty and the wind gets up. Richard imagines Bonaparte's excitement. He will while away some time eating breakfast with his inner circle, including his brother and Marshal Ney, along with Reille, whose force is still an hour and a half away. Satiated, Bonaparte will start pacing, one eye on the weather as he dictates to his aide.

Time passes slowly for Richard and Emile. Both men avoid looking at their watches. Eight o'clock comes and Lieutenant Béraud is summoned from below. When he returns, he is scowling. 'Another delay!'

They lie down and doze. Richard lets his mind wander back to the first time he stood outside Madame Odillet's extraordinary shop.

Chapter Four

Richard studied the double-fronted window displays flanking an ornately framed glass door. To the left were miniatures, inlaid boxes, shoe buckles, travelling cases for writing and medicines, clocks, Sèvres porcelain and fragments of tapestry.

He doubted there was a single thing he could afford. He felt queasy from too much wine the night before. To the right were larger pieces, mostly furniture, more eclectic but unified by the quality of craftmanship: a pair of gilt-edged chairs, a black and gold secretaire on lion paws, an ornate velvet footstool and a pair of ormolu and amethyst lamps.

Most of it dated from the late seventeenth and early eighteenth centuries. Napoleon himself could have sat on or written at or rested his feet on these very pieces, they really were that fine.

Richard took an unsteady step back. This wasn't a shop for him. It looked like you needed an appointment. He didn't feel sufficiently well dressed in his open collar, herringbone jacket and navy corduroys, even if his brown brogues had a good shine lost in the shade of the cloistered gallery.

The place would be shut anyway, after all, it was Sunday. He looked at the shop one last time only to see a figure beckoning from behind the decorated glass door. It was so unexpected he looked around, convinced the gesture was aimed at someone else. The whole gallery was deserted.

Reluctantly, he moved forwards and gripped the polished

handle. A delicate bell sounded. Soft lighting subtly emphasised key objects but discretion reigned. His swimming head was grateful. He penetrated the ornate cave until he was at the centre of an authentic Aubusson rug.

'Come in, all the way in! I have been expecting you.' Once more his nationality determined before he spoke.

Richard hesitated again. 'I don't understand. How can you have been expecting me?' He was still trying to discern the features of a woman's face. 'Madame Odillet?'

'But of course. I am she.' She moved a little and light washed her face. She looked much as he had imagined her the evening before. 'My dear friend Amélie told me all about you. Look around, take your time. I shall be just over here.' A slender armful of bracelets indicated a wingback chair, its gold leaf frame perfect against the pale blue silk upholstery. It sat beneath a floor lamp with a pleated ivory shade. A glossy magazine spread, face down, on the plump seat.

Richard looked around. There was no diminution in quality in sight nor any hint of a price tag. The shop was large but so full it reminded him of a Victorian salon, fussy to modernist taste. Richard liked it even if he was there on false pretences. He was on holiday, so he started browsing. It didn't matter where he walked or looked, there was something to enchant. He moved deliberately between pieces, relieved that the shopkeeper was not hovering. Indeed, she seemed entirely oblivious, engrossed in a fashion magazine for someone under forty.

There was no sense of time in the emporium despite the ticking and chiming that punctuated his exploration. He discovered display spaces beyond those he had first seen. It was the most eclectic collection he had encountered in a shop.

One room was a jumble of art deco and art nouveau, bold angles and repetition contrasting with floral, organic forms reminiscent of the *Métro* sign he had seen the day before.

In the very next space was a display of posters from the late sixties, filling every inch of wall space with psychedelia and the names of dead musical greats like Jim Morrison, Janis Joplin, Jimi Hendrix and Mama Cass.

Richard looked at his watch and was astonished to find two hours had passed. Had Madame Odillet forgotten he was here? He couldn't remember hearing the shop bell ring in all the time he had been browsing.

He really should make his excuses. She might already expect him to buy something. Perhaps one of the more obscure posters would be within his budget?

On his way towards the front of the shop he became disorientated and stumbled into a small, tidy kitchen. He began backing out but collided with a wiry form coming the other way. 'I am so sorry, Madame. I should not be in here. I took a wrong turn.'

Two veined, freckled hands gripped his forearms and steered him back towards the row of units above a sink and white-tile worktop. A tinkle of laughter and a rattle of jewellery. She really did fit Amélie's description to a tee.

'Not at all, not at all. You are just where you should be. Share a *tisane* with me.' Her voice was throaty but kind. There was no doubt he was expected to stay.

'I cannot impose. I have already stayed too long and I fear your wonderful collection is beyond my means.' He tried a self-deprecating gesture with his arms, an awkward Briton caught up in the moment, trying for some Gallic nonchalance.

The venerable shopkeeper tutted, busying herself with herbs and hot water. By the time she turned back she held two steaming, pale yellow drinks, in glasses set in filigreed silver.

The scene could not have been more French and Richard determined to see it through. Why should he cut and run when this lonely old lady wanted someone to break the monotony of her customer free day?

She gestured with the drinks that he should retrace his steps to the front of the shop where she sidled past him, back to her chair beneath the lamp. He had not noticed the exquisite inlaid side table nor the second chair. She set the drinks on a pair of coasters, shunted her magazine to one side and sat elegantly.

Richard edged past her booted feet to sit in the vacant seat. Madame Odillet took a sharp sip of her beverage and let a beatific grin stretch the lines from her face. 'So, tell me, what brings you to Paris?'

Richard took a sip of his drink as he decided what to say. The herbal concoction was bitter but softened on his palate with a hint of coconut. He found himself smiling. His stomach felt more settled and he relaxed into the firm upholstery. 'Napoleon Bonaparte. He is the main cause. I have visited your wonderful city many times and he is always at the heart of it. I studied history at university, I am a teacher now…' His explanation sounded so trite, fell so short of what he wanted to say.

Madame Odillet swallowed another mouthful and closed her eyes. Her wide cheekbones were feline in the warm glow of the lamp. 'I sense you wish you had been alive to meet him, perhaps?'

Richard spilled a little of his drink but his host was oblivious. He gulped a mouthful and his thoughts became unnervingly clear. 'My life is underwhelming. He did so much, so young. I admire that. So many victories, so many other achievements. By the time he was my age he stood astride Europe. Wagram.'

The antique dealer sighed. 'But that was the year he divorced Josephine. His principles ebbing away. A marriage of convenience to come.'

Richard realized he had almost finished his drink. The ornate surroundings were crystal clear and yet his vision pulsed gently. 'For a son. He needed a son.'

'Like Henry VIII?' Her tone was disapproving. 'To abandon love for expediency. It is not very French.'

'Well, he was only French by accident, really. Born just one year earlier and he would have been, what?' It was clear this woman knew her history, he expected her to speak of the Republic of Genoa, but her reply wrongfooted him.

'Corsican. It is true. A different thing, a particular thing, a thing that shaped him, I think.'

Richard thought about Bonaparte's early life, an outsider at military school, teased, cold shouldered, taking refuge in his brilliance. Transferred from Brienne to Paris, a step up and then everything became possible. 'But then the revolution. *Les Jacobins*. Such tumultuous politics he is almost undone yet, within the blink of an eye, he goes from obscure artillery officer at Toulon to command in Italy.' Richard smiled, "He begins to redraw the map of Europe.'

Madame Odillet set her glass down on the table. It was empty. 'I know the story. Republican or not, we French love *le petit caporal*. But if you could see one thing from his life, what would it be?'

Richard gnawed at his lower lip with an uneven incisor. 'Austerlitz?'

'What if that were really possible? If you wanted it enough.'

He laughed, swept along by the heady idea. 'To witness his greatness. That would be something.'

'Something? That is not sufficient. You must want it more than anything, anything binding you to the present. You must be prepared to go back and never return.'

Richard shook his head. The herbal drink was affecting him. This kindly, lonely antiques dealer couldn't have said that. 'I must have misheard? It sounded like you believe…' He swallowed the rest of his sentence. It would sound too ludicrous if he voiced it.

A gravel chuckle and Madame Odillet's twinkling eyes were upon him. He tried to hold her gaze but could not manage it for long. 'I'm sorry, I really must be going.'

Before he could lever himself out of the plump chair, Madame Odillet was up and in front of him. She leant down with surprising ease, placing a hand on either wing of the chair, drawing her face close.

Richard could smell her breath, rich with the concoction that made it so hard for him to just laugh and leave.

'Why do you think Amélie sent you to me? Because you are

a fan of the emperor? Because you love history? Because you might spend some of your British pounds in a poor old woman's modest emporium?' She leaned in even further, forcing Richard to press his head against the chair back, raising his hands but hesitating from touching her.

'Please, I have no wish to offend…' He cringed at the plaintive note in his voice.

'But this is part of your problem. You exist and yet you avoid. You were sent to me because you have nothing. That is the necessary precondition. To travel back, there can be no ties. You are alone, yes?' Her words echoed in his head, his vision swam and he thought he might vomit.

Gulping for air, he pressed his forehead against a wing of the chair, cool silk soothing his feverish brow. Was he really in the shop or just sweating out last night's excesses in an unnerving dream, trapped in the sweaty sheets of his hotel bed?

Strong fingers seized him by the chin, turning his head. 'Listen to me! This is your chance to live. I know how it may be done,' She paused theatrically, 'but only you can make it happen. Do you want to spend the rest of your life avoiding offence, trying to please people who do not matter and conform to a society with which you are not sympathetic?'

Richard froze. It was as if she knew his deepest, most shameful secrets.

'You are right. My life is such a disappointment. I am drifting towards death. There truly is nothing for me to lose. I sorely wish what you say could be true.' He tried to sound apologetic, eager to avoid offence.

'But it is true. Will you let me tell you a story, a true story?

74

One story and then you may leave. If you still want to.' She straightened and stepped away. Moving to the front of the shop, she turned the sign to display *fermé*. Richard wondered if she ever had any customers.

She smiled as she returned. 'Another drink?'

He declined, still feeling the effects of her concoction.

She nodded but looked disappointed as she sat. 'So, I will tell you the story of my Louis. The man I married many years ago. It was a different world then. We are all time travellers, you see. It is but a matter of direction and speed. We wanted children but first, we thought, one great adventure. Woodstock!' She looked at Richard as if unsure he would know what she meant.

'Max Yasgur's farm,' he said.

She shook her bangles theatrically, as if dancing to unheard music. 'Yes. It was not perfect. But we were in love. The counterculture was going to change the world for the better. Great days.' Richard could feel melancholy fill the room. 'We came home,' she continued. 'It was not the same. The harder we tried to recapture it, the further away it felt. Louis began to use drugs. He tried to persuade me it was a portal to how things had felt in America.'

Richard squirmed in his chair. 'Please don't tell me you think drugs can induce time travel?'

Madame Odillet held up a hand. 'My story. Just listen. Afterwards, I will answer anything you wish.'

This was certainly not the holiday he had expected. A thought of tormenting pupils insinuated itself and he felt nauseous again. 'Please, go on.'

'Louis slipped away from me into addiction. He started

75

selling our few possessions to fund his habit. I discovered I was pregnant and had to get away. He barely noticed me leave.'

Richard saw tears welling in her kind eyes, a loss that never healed. 'Somehow, he managed to get enough money to go back to America. It was so pointless. By 1971, nothing was the same. Nixon was president! Louis took his only possession, a drumstick he caught in the crowd watching Santana play 'Soul Sacrifice'. He went back to the farm. I often wondered what the cows thought. He so wanted to recapture his memory of that festival. He never returned.'

'How can you know this if you never saw him again?' Richard asked as neutrally as he could manage.

The old woman wiped her face and sighed. She got up and disappeared at the back of the shop.

He could hear her moving things around and then what he thought was the shuffling of paper.

When she returned, she had regained her composure. She did not sit but handed him what looked like a number of air mail letters in a clear plastic folder sealed with a zip. Richard took the transparent wallet and opened it.

He extracted four flimsy letters in their original envelopes edged in red, white and blue. In the right-hand corner of each was the printed fee of thirteen cents and the profile of JFK imposed on the shaded image of an aircraft. At the bottom of the envelope, just above the border, in neat red printed capitals it read *Aérogramme. Par Avion.*

All four were addressed to Marianne Odillet at the same Left Bank address. The handwriting was spidery. One address was smudged, another looked as if it wanted to slip off the right side of the page. In the top left corner where three blue lines tamed the writing, was the sender's name and address.

It was hard to make out the franking but Richard shuffled them into what he thought was chronological order. They were sent in 1968 and 1969, then 1972 and 1975.

As he tentatively extracted a single thin sheet from the first envelope, Marianne Odillet sat back down and put a hand on his arm, stalling his action.

'These are all I have,' she said, surrounded by treasures from across the centuries.

Richard handled the first letter like a valuable part of an archive, guilty his bare skin touched the translucent blue paper and its meandering text.

'Why was he writing this letter? You were with him at Woodstock in 1968.'

Marianne said nothing but gestured towards the letter. He read slowly, piecing together the words into a semblance of meaning. He shook his head and tried again. 'My French must be rustier than I thought.'

'I suspect there is nothing very wrong with your French, Richard.' It was the first time she had used his name. He didn't remember her asking and was sure he had not given it. Amélie, he supposed. 'Why don't you read the opening aloud, just to be sure?'

He hesitated, as if giving shape and sound to the words would make a difference. She continued to look at him invitingly.

'I arrived a week ago from New York. Hitchhiking was easier with you. I slept in a barn that first night. The following morning was warm but hazy. I got up early and walked to the place. You would not know anything had happened there. Just black and white cows and a dog that barked until I gave it the last of my food. I sat down and cried. Everything hurt, cramps and sweats and ants biting under my skin. I sat for a long time remembering what it was like with four hundred thousand people. I wanted to be back there so much. I gripped the Santana drum stick so hard. My body was shaking. I passed out. When I came to, I could hear 'Soul Sacrifice'! There were people everywhere lost in the music. I don't know how you could believe me. But I want you to know I am sorry.'

Richard stopped and looked at Marianne. Tears streamed down her face. 'It was a one-way trip,' she mumbled. He must have looked confused because she went on, 'If you read the rest, it becomes clear. He had wished himself into the past but there was no coming back. He was trapped, living his life from 1968 on, unable to catch up to the present... when Woodstock was over, the counterculture faltered... His last letter was from 1975. It's obvious he has given up. He's using heavily, rambling, talking of a final escape.'

Richard slipped the first letter back in its envelope and handed all four back to Marianne. He didn't know what to say. He wasn't an addict; he wasn't trying to recapture the feeling of a single moment that cast the rest of his life in shadow. 'I'm so sorry,' he managed, surprised he no longer doubted her. 'How many people have you told?'

A chaos of grey hair fell across her face as she shook her head. 'Who could I tell? I have no wish to be committed. My daughter needed me. I have a kind of life with my antiques. My life with Louis was over before this happened. Yes, he

78

talks of us being together again but it was impossible. He was lost. So, I kept my secret, year after year.'

'Did you never try to go back, I mean, to wish yourself into the past to be with him again?' The words were awkward on his tongue.

'You have to want it with your whole being, to be there forever.' She fished a delicate handkerchief from a hip pocket and wiped her eyes. 'I suppose I was too conflicted for it to work. I had my daughter. To give up my present to reconnect with the man who broke my heart? It's hard to want that without reservation, don't you agree?'

Richard watched a couple peering into the shop, puzzled to see them sat there as if they too were for sale. 'I fear I'm scaring off your customers,' he said rather than answering her question. His head was spinning. Was it last night's excess, the old woman's narcotic tea or the idea that he could live in the past?

Marianne stood up. Her face was drawn and the bags beneath her bright eyes had darkened. Her eye liner was smudged and she looked frail. 'Come back tomorrow.'

Richard stood but she was not going to let him just slip away. 'Promise me? I will have something that will really interest you.'

He glanced at his watch and realized he had spent half the day in the shop. 'What have you got to lose?' she insisted.

He was halfway to the door but halted. He looked over his right shoulder and nodded. 'I promise. I'll see you tomorrow.'

He sucked in a deep breath of urban afternoon and had to catch himself against the brickwork. Gradually, the repetitive symmetry of brick and sandstone, slate and glass enclosing the formal gravel, grass and trees soothed him.

At the centre stood the mounted statue of Louis XIV looking imperious. presiding over the square he had caused to be built three hundred and fifty years ago. It was a kind of time travel. Possible for the Sun King, an absolute monarch with limitless resources.

He thought of the performers at Woodstock. Fifty years later, some were mere footnotes in the history of popular music but others, often those dead too soon, cast long shadows, their music echoing ever after them: Hendrix, Joplin and Keith Moon just three taken too soon after performing at the festival.

Back in his hotel, Richard resisted the bar and climbed the stairs to his room. He tried to read but couldn't find anything that held his attention. A siren sounded nearby. Laughter in the corridor receded.

He put the book aside and stared at the ceiling. Was he really going back to Place des Vosges, to the antique shop and its eccentric owner? Surrounded by the pleasantly mundane, it was hard to credit how seriously he had taken her story.

He could only imagine a snort of derision from Aunt Patricia should he be foolish enough to tell her.

He didn't doubt Madame Odillet believed but surely there was a more likely explanation? Louis, the stoned ex-husband, had played a cruel and sustained joke on her. He forged those air mail letters and had them delivered to Marianne, probably from somewhere in this very city. Best he kept his theory to himself.

He could just avoid the shop. It would be kinder. It would avoid having to pretend.

He turned in early but sleep defied him for a long time and when it did come it inflicted troubled dreams of separation and loss, a terrible jumble of his childhood and Marianne's delusion.

The next morning, he put some distance between himself and the seductive idea of escaping St Anne's and all his disappointments.

He took a double-decker train to Versailles, sitting on the upper level, watching the sprawl of Paris that had swallowed the town of Versailles. He was reminded of his journey into London and all the frustration he had felt drain away as a week of freedom opened up in front of him. Now he was avoiding the one person who suggested there was an alternative to that existence.

He fished his guidebook from his jacket pocket and started to read about the court of the Sun King. It did nothing to distance thoughts of that shop in Place des Vosges.

By the time he disembarked, he no longer had the appetite for a long day revisiting the great palace and its grounds, its stunning stables and historic tennis court, subsidiary palaces, fountains and faux village.

Madame Odillet had told him a story too incredible to believe. A story suggesting he could live in his own dreams. It could not be true but the thought of it cast a shadow.

He had an *espresso* and a *pâtisserie* in a café and returned to the station. He caught the next train back to the centre, not even bothering to sit above the noisy mob of students turning

81

the carriage into their mobile common room.

By the time he reached Madame Odillet's Pieces of the Past emporium it was lunchtime and she was not open for business. He peered inside but no one occupied her chair. There was not even an abandoned magazine in evidence.

He would just have to lunch nearby and return later when she would, surely, be back in her seat, ready to confront any customers bold enough to enter her domain.

As he searched for a restaurant not awash with tourists in the surrounding side streets, he wondered how many customers had passed through Marianne's shop, unaware of the secret she clutched to her? If she was to be believed, and he did believe her, then he was the first person she had told. What were the odds of that? Why him? Even though he felt eminently suitable. How could she have known? What had moved Amélie to point him in Marianne's direction? Fate?

He stayed away as long as he could but when he returned at almost half past three, the shop was still sleeping. Perhaps Marianne didn't open on Mondays?

It was a wet Tuesday but Richard ignored the rain as he crossed the square once again, oblivious to its magnificence. He dodged the pigeons flapping at his feet impatiently.

Reaching the shelter of the arcade he made himself slow down. He tried to peer through the gloom into the shop. It looked deserted. There was no hint of light inside. He reached the door.

The closed sign was displayed. He tried anyway. It was locked. He actually stamped his foot, startling an old lady walking her small terrier in the shelter of the repeating arches.

He mumbled an apology to her retreating back, the dog yapping over its shoulder.

The restaurants on either side of the shop were not the sort that opened for breakfast but one more door down a florist was setting out her displays for the day.

Richard wondered where the dazzling roses came from at this time of year. 'Excuse me, I was hoping to visit Madame Odillet's shop today. You know, the one with the odd name in English? Do you know what time she is likely to open?'

The florist straightened and rubbed her reddened hands on the front of her green apron. She had a simple face. No more lines or angles than necessary. A perfect face to surround with an array of blooms shouting for attention. 'Marianne does whatever she feels like. She has been here forever. She actually owns that place. Do you know what the rent is like here?' He didn't but he could imagine. 'I think she just works for the fun of it,' the florist continued. 'So, when it doesn't feel fun, she stays home.'

Richard dug his nails into his palms before he realized he had balled his fists. He was making such a mess of things. She had asked him to come on Monday. He promised he would but had gone to Versailles instead. Then he changed his mind but got back too late. This was what he deserved. Always hesitating, procrastinating and avoiding things. Look where it had got him.

'Do you think it likely she will be back this week?' He sounded desperate and the florist noticed.

'I'm sorry. I cannot say. Sometimes she is here every day and then closed for a week.' She shrugged sympathetically.

He thanked her and retraced his steps to stand in front of

the glass door. He stared at it for a long time before he focused on the letter slot, set in the metal frame between the two panes.

He hurried back to the florist who was now putting buckets of pink and white peonies into metal stands. 'I am so sorry to bother you again.'

A neutral face looked up. 'Would you like to buy some flowers, sir?' Her voice was just a little sharper than the last time.

'Yes, of course. What do you suggest?'

She gestured all around her at roses in every colour he could imagine, tight buds yearning to open. 'Yes, roses, lovely. I'll take a dozen, not red.' He blushed as she selected a bunch of yellow blooms edged with pink.

He followed her into the shop where a tropical green backdrop set off a floral rainbow. He recognised blue irises and hyacinths, hydrangeas in pink, blue and white and gladioli in red, yellow and orange.

There was much more but his attention had come to rest on the counter where he saw what he really wanted. He fumbled with his wallet and parted with more euros than he expected to spend on lunch. Accepting the roses, wrapped neatly in a waxy, patterned paper, he asked, 'Might I have a sheet from your notepad and the loan of a pen?'

The florist ripped a leaf from the wire bound pad and held it out with a biro. Richard accepted them awkwardly with his right hand and looked around. Pale arms extended to relieve him of his flowers, placing them at one end of the counter. He smiled gratefully and bent to his task.

He wrote a short, apologetic message, providing his mobile number and asking Marianne to call him. As an afterthought he added he was leaving on Saturday. He folded the note in half and wrote Marianne's name. Richard then very deliberately returned the pen, swept up his flowers and retreated, spouting appreciation.

He pushed the single piece of paper through the letter plate and checked it was visible on the mat. It looked insubstantial, like one of Louis' missives from the past. Well, they had reached Marianne.

Reluctantly, he stood up and walked towards the nearest exit from the square. There was one more thing he could do.

Ignoring the drizzle, he went in search of a taxi. Despite the rain, there were several waiting at the first rank he reached.

'Les Invalides, please,' he said as he settled into the back and fastened his seat belt. He put his nose to the flowers he had bought. They had no scent at all. He put them on the seat beside him and sighed. He caught the driver looking at him with a sympathetic expression. He shrugged at him and the man returned his attention to the road.

The traffic was tolerable considering the weather. He was trying to stay positive. They arrived and the fare consumed another chunk of his currency. Perhaps he should start paying with a card when abroad? Somehow that seemed like a loss of control. Exchange rates varied. He knew he was living an outmoded life. He just didn't have the energy to invest in his current existence. He wanted to be elsewhere.

Standing in the queue with his roses he noticed the skies had lightened. He watched the people ahead of him, couples and families on a day out, mostly tourists from their clothes. Once the father ahead of him wrangled his three boys out of the way, Richard approached the ticket window.

'Nine euros fifty please,' asked the moustachioed face behind the glass.

'I'm sorry, I don't want to buy a ticket.'

'Information is over there.' A long forefinger indicated a curved desk covered in leaflets staffed by a middle-aged woman. Above her was a large banner bearing a stylised information symbol.

'I'm sorry, I was hoping to speak with one of your guides.'

'You will need to join a group. Here are the times.' A leaflet was pushed under the glass towards him.

He did not pick it up. 'I must apologise again. If I may just explain?' he kept going, 'I spoke with her on Sunday. Her name was Amélie Durand. Is she working today?'

Dark eyes blinked rapidly above the moustache. 'I am afraid she is not working today.'

'What about tomorrow?' Richard asked hopefully.

'No, sir. She is on holiday. A wedding, I believe.' The official's eyes caught sight of the flowers in his hand and his expression changed. 'I see you knew about the happy event. I am sorry you missed her. She will not be back for a week. You can find another use for your flowers, I hope?'

People were swapping out of the queue to get their tickets at the window for groups. This started an argument when they were told they needed individual tickets and should go back to the line they had just vacated. When they tried, another disagreement broke out as those who had stayed put would not let them resume their places.

Richard winced and shuffled away, holding the flowers behind his back. There was not much else he could do for now. Amélie was a dead end. He had left his note.

He did have the telephone number for the shop. He rang it but there was no answer. He left a message.

He decided to walk back to the hotel but even the splendour of Baron Haussmann's avenues had lost their sparkle. He walked in a daze and inevitably his thoughts turned to next week. He would be back at work. A clammy sweat prickled his skin. The topics he would be teaching began to crowd in. His dread compounded his frustration. Lost in a sea of self-pity he was almost mowed down by a delivery lorry when he stumbled off the pavement.

Horns sounded as the rusty vehicle's brakes hissed. There was a squeal of tyres further back along the road. The driver gesticulated in his mirror to those in his wake as he got moving again.

Heart pounding and feeling thoroughly sorry for himself, Richard stopped at a café. He drank too much *espresso* as he tried to block out thoughts of school and convince himself everything would work out.

By the time he had eaten a plate of sliced fruit for breakfast he felt better. It was another day: Wednesday. His head was clear. The previous night he had avoided the lure of alcohol by visiting a cinema. He had not intended to watch a film. He was just out strolling in search of equilibrium, persuading himself to fall back in love with Paris. None of this was the city's fault.

It was the poster that had done it. That impish expression staring down at him, pale face and red lips beneath a quirky bob of black hair. *Amélie!* It was the perfect film for him, quite apart from any coincidence. The actress did look like

Amélie Durand, currently on her honeymoon, he imagined.

He suppressed a pang of loneliness. He was adept at distracting himself. The film was a loving homage to the city of Paris, the city he did still love but had snubbed that very day in his funk. It was about a young woman subtly influencing the lives of all around her to create a world of her own manufacture. And it was funny. For two hours it took him out of himself, despite touching close to home, and he returned to his bed hopeful.

He would not mope around Place des Vosges today. He would not ring Marianne's shop every fifteen minutes. No, he would do the things he had originally come to Paris to enjoy.

He would spend the morning at the city museum, the Carnavalet and then walk to the Musée d'Orsay for an afternoon with the French impressionist and post-impressionist masters. He should try living in the present even if that meant enjoying the masterpieces of the past.

As he stepped out of the museum, he checked his watch. It was already lunchtime. Marianne had not called. He knew he would be teaching on Monday. That was always going to be the case. If she did not call before he had to leave, so be it. That was what telephones were for. He would talk to her soon. He had survived many winter terms. He would be back in December.

He bought a ham and cheese baguette from a street vendor and ate it on a bench, enjoying the improved weather. Small white clouds scattered across the pale blue sky like a flock of sheep grazing contentedly. There was no dog to harry them and no fence to pen them. They wandered slowly wherever the blue grass looked tender.

Sandwich finished; Richard set off for the Seine. Turning along the *quai*, he saw the twin towers of Notre-Dame on the island to his left. He lamented the fire, wishing the restorers the very best as they toiled.

He passed the length of Île de la Cité, moored in the river, tethered by its many bridges. Past the most westerly, the Pont Neuf, and on to the imposing riverside facade of the Louvre in its Renaissance splendour. He felt like a cartoon character passing the same scenery over and over until the building yielded to the open space of the Tuileries gardens. Before he reached the far side of the charming park, he took the bridge to the other bank and his destination.

About to mount the steps to the converted railway station, his mobile rang. He fumbled it out of his pocket. 'Hello, Richard Davey speaking.' His heart was racing and his hand shook.

'This is Marianne. I am so sorry to have stood you up. There was an emergency. An old friend. She is in hospital. Still alive.' She sounded distant.

'Forgive me chasing you. I completely understand. I will be in Paris again. Perhaps we can meet then?' His throat was constricted but he forced the words out.

'Certainly not! You must come. On Friday. I will be at the shop from ten.' Her voice was firmer now. He knew he should dissemble but he bit his lip and kept quiet. 'Are you there, Richard? I said you must come. I have things to show you. We have much to discuss.' She sounded genuinely enthusiastic.

'If you're sure, I'll be there shortly after ten. Thank you for sparing the time.' He could not hide the relief in his croaky voice.

Chapter Five

The sound of marching feet and shod hooves drifts across the courtyard from the road beyond. It is nine o'clock. From the upper storey, Richard can see the slow-moving columns pass. Muddy boots keep time but look laboured. Horses step more easily but the artillery carriages stop regularly with men clustered around them, straining for all they are worth.

'General Reille's men, at last! They were expected at five!' comments Béraud, pinning back the curtain.

Richard nods. Inside the farmhouse, Napoleon talks with his most trusted artillery officer, General Drouot who informs his emperor that the roads will not be dry enough to manoeuvre guns for several hours. Richard can only imagine Napoleon's frustration. But the emperor trusts Drouot and knows how critical his superiority in cannon is to success.

At half-past nine, urgent shouts ricochet around the courtyard, underpinned by running feet. Richard and Emile look down from their eyrie to see the distinctive bicorn hat and grey overcoat step from the farmhouse. Men run to the stables and towards their position.

Lieutenant Béraud does not wait to be summoned. He grabs his sword and busby and ushers Richard into the narrow corridor. They shin down the ladder and out into the breezy air of a June morning. It is warm and Richard can see the sun.

Béraud barks orders at scrambling Chasseurs and infantry

from beside the well, watching the emperor approach his horse, which has been standing patiently in the courtyard since seven.

The equerry on duty is nowhere to be found. Lulled by repeated delays, he has slipped off for a quick breakfast. Napoleon's overexcited page, César, stands in, offering his interlinked hands to the imperial boot. Once Bonaparte's foot is in place, César boosts him up, almost propelling him over the saddle.

Catching himself with a curse, Napoleon flicks his reins and gallops off, complaining. He is accompanied by most of his senior officers and a local Flemish innkeeper as guide. César wrestles his own horse, clumsy with embarrassment, but eventually sets off in pursuit.

One of Béraud's men appears leading two horses, while others check the girths and bridles of their own mounts. The lieutenant takes the tall, bay mare's reins and strokes her long nose affectionately, whispering to her.

The soldier holds out the other reins to Richard who accepts them nervously. His horse is a placid grey mare with a solid look. He glances at Emile, who has already swung into the saddle. 'I haven't ridden for years,' Richard admits.

'Help our guest up, Corporal!' The soldier bends his back and offers his hands as a stirrup. Wary of what almost happened to Bonaparte, Richard hesitates. 'Hurry man, we must catch the emperor!' snaps Emile.

He steps into the offered hands and allows himself to be boosted into the saddle. He finds his seat without trouble, grasping the pommel with one hand for reassurance.

Béraud turns his horse and the imperial escort of twenty-six cavalrymen fall in behind him, a sergeant, two corporals, a trumpeter and twenty-two troopers. Richard saws on his reins and manages to align his horse.

'Forward!' orders the lieutenant, gesturing with his right arm. The beautifully uniformed figures set off as one with Richard's grey plodding in their wake.

By the time his mount turns onto the road, the undulating wall of green backs are fifty yards away and turning onto the north road. Sucking in a breath, Richard squeezes his knees into his mount's sides, flicks his reins and shouts encouragement. The mare ups her tempo but he is still falling behind.

In desperation, he yells and slaps her rear, almost losing his precarious balance. They shoot off in pursuit and soon draw level with the rearmost troopers. By this time, his mount has his measure and settles into a matching pace.

From his elevated position, Richard looks across the fields he traversed the night before. The valley spreads out ahead, tall, ripening crops divided by ditches and hedges. Before he can worry about his mount, they are pulling up just short of the inn of La Belle Alliance. His mare halts as the last pair of cavalrymen bring their mounts to a neat stop.

Richard tries knees and heels, whispering encouragement and shouting orders but nothing persuades the mare to move. Looking around, a veteran grins, wheels his horse out of formation and pulls alongside.

Without warning, he slaps the grey on her broad flank and she lunges forward, around the seated pairs, to the shoulder of Emile's taller horse. Here she decides to stop. Richard is sure he had no say in the matter.

In front of them, Napoleon's party have dismounted and are surveying the vista to the south.

Lieutenant Béraud nods to his men and they dismount, leading their horses from the road to a grassy area behind the inn. Emile vaults from his horse and offers Richard his hand. Safely on the ground, Richard follows the officer to the lee of the main building.

Napoleon Bonaparte is discussing the Allied lines with his closest confidantes, just yards away. Richard stays as close to the corner of the building as possible, straining his ears. The wind is gusty and makes it impossible to catch anything being said.

On the far ridge, where Richard met Arabella just the previous afternoon, Wellington is ready. Most of his troops are hidden by the lay of the land, marshalled on the rearward slope of the escarpment. Richard made this clear when briefing Emile, the previous night.

Bonaparte is determined to be the aggressor by repeatedly attacking the Allied line. Had the Prussians been more effectively bottled up by Grouchy, his forces might manage it. But Grouchy will not sweep the dogged Prussians from their positions around Wavre and they incrementally reinforce Wellington on his left.

As the afternoon wears on, the Prussians create so much pressure that Napoleon is forced onto the defensive on his right. He then bludgeons his army to death on the implacable defensive positions of the Allies, eventually sacrificing the Imperial Guard in a final, desperate gamble. The survivors fall, acting as a rearguard.

Richard digs his nails into his palms. There is another way.

One of the cavalrymen calls something to his lieutenant's attention and Richard seizes his opportunity. He is around the corner and away, along the front of the inn towards the far gable where the emperor stands among his generals.

Richard hears a voice call out behind him and breaks into a trot. He rounds the southerly end of the inn and collides with Napoleon's page, César, who is standing discreetly to one side. César is knocked off his feet by the impact but Richard keeps moving.

'Stop! Now!' There is a panicky insistence in Emile's voice as he slews around the corner and trips over the still sprawled page.

Bonaparte's aide, Gourgaud, moves to intercept Richard. The general, who saved Napoleon's life the previous year, is drawing his sword but hesitates with the tip still in its scabbard when Lieutenant Béraud appears in distinctive green, so obviously part of the imperial escort.

Springing up, Emile lunges at Richard, tapping the back of his left heel against his right, throwing him off balance. Richard sprawls on the ground just ahead of prone lieutenant and winded page.

Gourgaud stares incredulously at the mayhem as he clears his sword to point it at Richard's upturned face.

'I implore you, General, stay your hand!' Emile's voice is still agitated.

Richard keeps still while the lieutenant regains his feet and steps between the immaculate steel and Richard's wide eyes. He looks up between the lieutenant's legs, at a half-circle of astonished faces. His eyes stop as one man, no shorter than the others, steps forward to peer around Gourgaud. His eyes are small but so dark their colour is lost. What they have seen!

'Your Imperial Highness,' he tries a semblance of a bow although he is lying on his side, 'forgive my unorthodox appearance but I bring intelligence that can win the battle!' Why is he so calm? His voice is assured and he holds the emperor's gaze.

Marshal Ney scoffs and Gourgaud thrusts closer with his blade, causing Emile to flinch.

Napoleon waves his aide away and speaks. 'Lieutenant Béraud, you have been with me for a long time. We wear the same uniform. Yet you have allowed this madman into my presence on the eve of my greatest victory? How has this come to pass?'

Emile steps back and looks down at Richard. 'Forgive me, sire. This man is Richard Davey, an American agent. He arrived last night with details of the Allied army. He carries a letter to you from President Madison. I passed the information to General Gourgaud last night. He assured me you would see it.' Emile's voice wavers as he realizes the situation.

Gourgaud snorts dismissively. 'Why would I trouble the emperor with the ravings of an embittered colonist? Look at him!'

Emile drops to one knee, head bowed. 'Sire, I intended offence but the detail of the report, the insights offered were, in my judgement, of great value.' There is resignation in his voice.

'How dare you! I shall see you court-martialled for your insolence,' sputters Gourgaud, eyes like daggers. 'No one questions my loyalty!'

Richard winces as spittle flies from the enraged officer's twitching lips. He is famously over-sensitive.

'Gaspard, calm yourself. The lieutenant meant no offence. Tell me, have I seen this report?'

Hatless, high forehead exposed, face framed by heavy sideburns, the general shakes his head. 'Sire, I did not credit it. I simply threw it in the fire. You had so much to deal with.' He is apologetic but Richard hears suppressed anger as he stares at Emile.

Napoleon removes his bicorn hat and rubs the top of his head. 'I will retire inside. Lieutenant, bring this fellow you have vouched for. You will guarantee my safety. Gourgaud, ensure my orders reach Grouchy. General Haxo, you are my chief engineer. Take an escort and ride close to the enemy line. Check for any defensive entrenchments!' With that, the emperor walks around the roadside edge of the building and into the inn.

Richard gets to his feet, still eyeing Gourgaud warily. Emile takes him by the arm and leads him after Bonaparte. 'So, you have met your hero and almost destroyed my career into the bargain!' Emile hisses. His fingers are tight on Richard's upper arm. Richard barely notices as they cross into the cosy interior.

Napoleon unbuttons his coat and sets his hat on a long bench. He sits at the end of the common-room table in a carver chair.

Emile escorts Richard to within six feet and halts. They remain standing as if immobilised by the seated man's scrutiny. Emile produces the letter addressed to the emperor and places it on the table without releasing his charge.

Napoleon draws it towards him with his right forefinger and reads it without lifting it from the sand-scoured surface. 'I may be Emperor of the French but I was a republican once like your president. There are not many heads of state whose word I trust. But this man,' he gestures at the letter, 'is one of your founding fathers, some even call him the father of the constitution, do they not?'

Richard nods, surprised at the depth of Napoleon's knowledge. Bonaparte flashes a grin, 'I had dealings with him when I sold Louisiana, single-handedly doubling the size of your new nation! I rejoiced when he declared war on the British!'

Richard marvels at Bonaparte's ability to reframe the past. He sold France's holdings in America, in desperation, to fund his wars. The emperor gestures with his right hand. 'Now sit, gentlemen. I would hear what was so important you risked death to convey it?'

Richard steps over the backless bench, breaking Emile's grip, and sits. The lieutenant follows suit, stiffly, swinging his sword clear of the furniture.

Richard has never felt so alive. The sun glances through the small windows of the tavern to the flagstone floor. He takes in the wooden roof beams and a stack of barrels against the far wall, each labelled and fitted with a spigot. Every detail is crisp and wonderful. He feels euphoric.

'Bring wine!' barks Bonaparte.

A rotund figure with a shock of white hair and thick moustaches appears in a clean apron. He immediately fills an earthenware jug from one of the barrels and brings it to the long table with three beakers.

Napoleon nods and waves him away. 'So, Mr Davey, my time is short but I would know how you come to be here?'

Richard wonders what would happen if he tried to tell the truth? He suppresses the urge, realizing his euphoria borders on hysteria. Instead, he recites his story and a summary of Wellington's dispositions.

'Yes, yes, this is as I suspected,' Bonaparte insists. 'Although I believe there are rather more soldiers in Wellington's combined force than you suggest. I am sure General Haxo's observations will tally with what you say. I may not have superiority of numbers but I have more guns. I have routed the Prussians. I am master of my own destiny and that of the French people!'

Richard shuffles on the bench and places his hands palms down on the table. 'Forgive me, sire. I have nothing but admiration for your achievements. You are undoubtedly the greatest commander of your age. But I fear you underestimate the Prussians. They are far from a spent force.'

Bonaparte takes a sip of his wine and winces. He gets up and moves along the far side of the table to stare out at the road beyond. 'You sound just like Marshal Soult at breakfast this morning. He chastised me for dismissing the quality of Wellington's army. I told him he gave Wellington too much credit because he defeated him in Spain! This time, Wellington has me to deal with, something he has not faced before! Soult did not like that, you can be sure. I defeated the Prussians at Ligny on Thursday and I have sent Grouchy to keep them at arm's length.'

'Recall him. Attack now. If you wait for dry ground, it will be too late. The Prussians will get past Grouchy and reinforce

Wellington. With thirty-five thousand more men and almost one hundred guns, you will win the day!' Richard is breathless as he finishes.

Somehow, everything has worked out. He has leapt across centuries and navigated the field of battle. He has found someone to believe him and spoken directly to Emperor Napoleon Bonaparte. He has said his piece. There is nothing else to do but bear witness to the day.

'You speak with such certainty,' Napoleon observes, returning to his chair. 'You know the strength of my forces in surprising detail. But this mud, Drouot and I are in agreement, if we wait for it to dry, our guns can manoeuvre.'

Richard sees an opening. 'But the Prussians are advancing. They will appear in front of the forest of Soignes.'

Bonaparte's hand freezes half way towards his beaker. Is he remembering the bitterness of the wine? 'My brother, Jérôme, heard similar gossip from a waiter yesterday. He was quite insistent at the breakfast table this morning. I wonder?' His hand grasps the cup and he takes another sip. Deep in thought, his face does not change.

Richard fixes his eyes on his own untouched drink while Emile tosses half his measure back in a single gulp. His eyes are fiery and his back rigid. 'No, it is not possible now. The moment has passed and my troops are still assembling.'

Richard's shoulders slump. He pulls his watch from his pocket. It is after ten o'clock. Perhaps Napoleon is right? The moment has passed. He sighs aloud. 'My emperor,' Bonaparte glances at him quizzically, 'I implore you. If you must wait, consider a subtle approach. Just as Wellington has not faced you, neither have you faced him. Do not bludgeon the Allied line. It will hold!'

There is nothing tired or ill about the emperor's demeanour now. His eyes are still dark but glitter like oceanic obsidian. His eyebrows are mobile and colour suffuses his previously pallid cheeks. His lips set and a single curl defies his receding hairline. 'You presume to lecture me on tactics? Austerlitz, Jena, Friedland! Do you doubt my ability? Moments ago, you called me the greatest commander of my age!'

Lieutenant Béraud edges away from Richard along the bench, as if distancing himself from such temerity.

'Sire, you have been the master. You move troops quicker than any other general. You lure enemies into traps. You deploy guns more effectively than any before you. So why do you propose such a direct approach today?' Bonaparte raises an eyebrow.

'You seem to know a lot about my intentions. I thought you were spying on the British? I have better men and more guns. Why shouldn't I attack?'

'Because Wellington has chosen the ground. You have divided your forces. The Prussians will appear. Yesterday, your strategy would have succeeded. Today, I fear it will not.'

Outside, a mounted detachment rides past at speed. Napoleon stares at Richard, his lips quivering. 'You make me very angry, Mr Davey, because you rehearse everything that has run through my mind. I have convinced myself the Prussians are not a factor, that I have eliminated their threat but I have no reliable reports. I wanted to attack early but the weather, my advisors, everything conspired against that. I dare not let Wellington withdraw because he will then combine with the Prussians for certain. British reinforcements will arrive from America and my enemies in the east, those lesser emperors of Austria and Russia, will find the courage to march.'

'Wellington is convinced you will attack. His strategy is to wait. Exploit that! Leave a token force posing as the whole army and reinforce Grouchy. Really destroy the Prussians. Then Wellington is vulnerable.'

Sweat appears on Bonaparte's forehead. His eyes fix on the middle distance, as if the walls of the inn are not there. Is he wavering?

'I thank you for your perspective, sir. You would be an asset on my staff. I invite you to stay with me for the day. We will see who is proved right. Lieutenant Béraud, you and your men will remain with my party. I trust you have let through the only infiltrator I will have to confront today?'

Emile stands and bows deeply, if awkwardly, constrained by table and bench. Napoleon rises, retrieves his hat and sets it on his head. He buttons his coat as he heads for the door. There is a mad scramble to mount up and catch the disappearing emperor and his entourage.

Richard, Emile and his company trail Napoleon Bonaparte as he rides his stallion, Marengo, along the low rise from La Belle Alliance westwards. He brought the horse back from Egypt in 1799. Although small at fourteen hands, the Arab stallion is a magnificent grey.

The troops are aligned in formation and shout '*Vive l'empereur!*' as Napoleon passes. Helmets and hats thrust upwards on the points of bayonets and swords. As Richard struggles to keep pace with the party reviewing French positions, he is struck by the subdued colours. Coated in plain blue or grey against the earlier rain and spattered with mud, they are, nevertheless, impressive.

Artillery batteries front the massed ranks of infantry. The line regiments display their colours with pride. They pass a first, a second and then a third great block of infantry.

Towards the end of the line, set back, Richard studies a fourth formation, comprising more line regiments and a mix of mounted troops. Hussars and Chasseurs sport upright plumes on their shakos while lancers wear brass helmets with black combs. Sabres and lances, pennants and carbines acclaim their emperor.

Richard wonders what Wellington makes of it all from the elm tree at the cobbled crossroads? The Duke certainly lacked faith in a significant portion of his own soldiery.

Returning to the Brussels road, Napoleon leads his party south, plunging through marching columns of infantry on one side and cavalry on the other. With the columns behind him, Bonaparte dismounts to toil up a modest hill near Rossomme farm.

Gourgaud sends three of his staff into the farmhouse. They emerge after a short delay carrying a table and chair for the emperor. Map cases are unbuckled from saddles and their contents spread out. His party gathers around, surveying the battlefield once again, from the prominence. Emile keeps his men apart but close by and Richard remains with them.

Napoleon sits immobile beside the improvised map table for a long time. He slips a hand beneath his tunic to clutch his belly. It is as if the battle doesn't have his full attention.

This is how Richard has read about Napoleon's behaviour.

Leaving almost everything to Ney whose written orders are vague, although the two spoke at length leading up to the battle. Could it be the advance of stomach cancer impairing the emperor? Richard has read a convincing paper supporting that theory.

'Emile, he's just letting it happen!' His friend does not reply and Richard wonders whether he remains angry about the embarrassment he caused.

Checking his watch, Richard sees it approaches eleven-thirty. He braces himself. Moments later the ground shakes, the air explodes, the sky screams, smoke billowing up from below. The artillery bombardment so favoured by the French to open an engagement has begun.

'The Grand Battery,' shouts Emile with a grin. Like most of the army, they have been taught to love their gunners and what they can do. After all, wasn't the emperor an artillery officer who made his reputation with skilled gun placement at the siege of Toulon?

The aerial onslaught starts with the gun emplacements to their left and runs along the line as battery after battery joins in, rolling thunder summoning the gods of war.

As smoke swallows the ridge, Richard slips from Emile's side and makes for the emperor who murmurs, 'My beautiful daughters. Do your deadly work.' His voice is level, even affectionate, but Richard thinks there is an air of resignation about Napoleon.

'Sire, most of Wellington's men shelter beyond the crest. Your bombardment is falling short.' Bonaparte appears not to register. Richard tries something else, yelling to ensure he is heard, 'Sire, you march infantry against Hougoumont?'

Eyes like coals look up at Richard from beneath the brim of his hat, rimmed red as if a fire has just ignited. 'My youngest brother's last chance to prove himself. He has been a great disappointment. But I am loyal to my blood. There must be strength in him if he shares my lineage. We do not intend to capture the wretched place. But forcing Wellington to reinforce the position will weaken his line. Then we pound his centre with guns, cavalry and foot until he breaks.'

Richard kneels beside the emperor to make sure he catches every word. Where is the guile? Where is the judgement? Napoleon has often chastised Jérôme Bonaparte as base, stupid and cowardly. Why then does he entrust so crucial an element of his plan to the man?

'You think I am a fool for risking everything on Jérôme? He has learned his lesson. The 6th Infantry Division will do their duty.' Bonaparte trusts his soldiers, his systems and their years of experience. 'They will have occupied the woods to the south by now.'

Richard looks to the north-west. Through acrid smoke he imagines the chateau and its surrounding walls beyond the woods and orchard. Closer to Richard's viewpoint lies open parkland.

Above the woods, the farmhouse faces south. It is largely of red brick topped with slate. Its friendly windows look out over a walled garden. On the far side of a courtyard, a sweet chapel abuts the chateau.

The house's mass separates the entrance courtyard from the main farm buildings. All is enclosed by a brick wall. A western entrance leads out beside a hedged apple orchard.

All entrances are heavily barricaded. He has studied floor

plans, paintings and computer renderings. He even built a scale model of the place, colouring it lovingly with a fine brush dipped in tiny tins of paint.

Time passes. The artillery quietens. Eventually, his aching eyes see French infantry pour from the oak woods near the chateau. Richard knows they have already faced strong resistance from German skirmishers among the trees. Jérôme overcame that first obstacle by flooding the woods with more and more men. Fighting uphill through trees is one thing but as the survivors move into the open, the defenders have the advantage of height.

Clear lines of sight turn the immediate vicinity into a killing ground. Minute by minute, men fall and others replace them. Inch by bloody inch the troops move closer to the fortified mass. Richard winces as the advancing French line takes savage punishment.

It begins to waver and buckle and then retreat. He can hear the cheers of the defenders as the French are driven back down the slope.

His attention is stolen by the arrival of General Bertrand, who leaps from his saddle and hurries to the emperor.

'Prussians! I am fighting Wellington and always I am distracted by the damned Prussians,' spits Napoleon. 'Well, they will have to wait their turn.'

Richard opens his mouth to remonstrate but Bonaparte stands and walks away, staring to the east.

'Speed will save us!' the emperor announces as he returns. He draws out his watch, staring at the face for a long time. 'Speed? It has been elusive today. We should have started at six. It is already well after noon!' He calls an aide over and scribbles a note, 'Take this to Ney!' Another aide is summoned. 'For the artillery commander! It is time we pounded them again.'

Eighty heavy pieces spit and belch, boom and smoke, thrust and recoil to the right of Napoleon's viewpoint. Richard estimates the range at eight hundred yards.

The French twelve-pounders are monsters and take twice the men to operate compared with the six-pounders Richard watched drill with Arabella. Most of the men are needed to manhandle the two-ton behemoths back into position after the recoil.

The bombardment concentrates on the left half of Wellington's line but the trajectory makes it difficult for the big guns to reach the Allied troops sheltering in the lee of the ridge. The stubby howitzers are proving more effective as they lob their shells beyond the lip of the escarpment.

'Now we come to the crux of the matter. Count d'Erlon has sixteen thousand men. Let us see if the British will stand!' There is fire in the emperor's eyes and his voice is thick with passion as he times his comment between discharges.

The smoke from the cannon envelops them again and the Belgian fields transform into the terrain of an alien planet. For half an hour the barrage numbs the air. Fields of rye close to the muzzles are blasted flat like sectors of a crop circle.

The Allied guns are fewer but they bark defiance, taking a gory tally from the close order battalions on the downward face of the low ridge. They fire shells and round shot but most terrible of all is case-shot, canisters that explode, showering troops in musket balls. Case-shot was designed, Richard recalls, by an artillery officer named Shrapnel.

Peering across the valley, he thinks he sees an explosion among the British guns. He wonders if it was firing case-shot? Occasionally the friction between small balls and powder inside the case caused explosions in the barrels. Whole gun crews could be decimated.

He looks away to see that Drouot, the Count d'Erlon, has his corps divided into four divisions, ready to attack. They begin to move, marching to the drums. They reach the artillery and the Grand Battery falls silent.

Once through the gun lines, the sergeants shout, the ranks dress, officers checking the files. Still men fall to Allied fire, cases splitting apart with a flare of orange, raining sharp death. The ranks hold and the drums start up again, beating out that familiar rhythm that has instilled fear across Europe.

Richard watches it all through a ragged pall of dissipating smoke, his eyes watering. He hears it all with ringing ears, the hair on his neck electrified. He smells discharged powder and sneezes at the heavy snuff of war. His mouth is dry as he tastes the fear of thousands of men marching into a hailstorm of jagged metal.

His skin itches and prickles, mired in sweat, heightened emotion and frustration. It is happening exactly as it should. If nothing changes, Napoleon will lose. He has to do something!

He looks back at Hougoumont to the left of the hillock where they stand. All the imperial staff are watching d'Erlon's advance but around the fortified farm, men continue to die, too many men, good men, to no avail.

'Sire, allow me to carry a message to your brother. See,' Richard points away from the magnificent spectacle of sixteen thousand soldiers traversing the fields of no-man's-land, many waist-deep in golden crops, 'he is destroying the 6th Infantry Division. You will need them before the day is out!'

Napoleon waves Richard away impatiently. Before he can remonstrate, another messenger arrives. Richard edges as close as he dares as Napoleon reads the document with his staff officers. 'Captured from a Prussian hussar. A despatch from Blücher to Wellington. They will be here in three hours, maybe less!'

Bonaparte removes his hat and rubs his high forehead, then strides to the map table. He scans the top chart and discards it onto the dirt, again with a second. The third, after a few moments' study, he jabs with his forefinger. 'Lieutenant Béraud!'

Emile runs forward, shouldering past Richard to bow to his emperor. 'I want you to carry a message to the King of Westphalia!' Napoleon's voice drips with scorn, using his youngest brother's defunct title, lost in 1813.

'Of course, sire,' replies Emile.

'I will not commit the order to paper. We see what happens then!' Bonaparte waves the intercepted communication meant for Wellington. 'Tell him to commit just enough men to convince the garrison at Hougoumont that nothing has changed. Then he must march the remainder of his men back. Impress on him how much I have need of them!'

Standing, Napoleon pulls his signet ring from the little finger of his left hand, caresses the eagle emblem and thrusts it at the astonished lieutenant. 'Give him this so he knows you speak with my authority. Tell him, if he fails, the family is finished!'

Emile takes the ring as if it is a holy relic, bows and retreats. He is about to slip the signet into a waistcoat pocket when Richard seizes it, grasps his left hand and pushes it firmly onto Emile's smallest digit. The immaculate lieutenant stares at the ring so intently, he trips over his own feet and only Richard's steadying hand keeps him from falling.

A grin spreads across his handsome face as he tears his eyes away from the eagle emblem and claps Richard on the back. 'Finally, a chance to taste battle! For too long I have polished and preened. I began as a cavalryman not a decorative bodyguard. It is time I remember why I wear this uniform!'

Richard grins back, caught up in Emile's excitement. 'I must come with you. It is our agreement. I must stay by your side.' Adrenalin surges through Richard. 'We ride for Hougoumont!'

Emile looks doubtful. 'Richard, my friend,' he uses the phrase sincerely and Richard feels a rush of affection for this man he has known less than twelve hours, 'you can barely sit a horse. You are no soldier. Can you wield a sword or fire a carbine?' Richard looks sheepish but defiant. 'I thought not. Well, we had better equip you with both, for whatever good they may do!'

Richard's smile returns as he follows Emile to his horse.

Richard holds his knees tight against the mare's sides. A carbine is holstered at forty-five degrees, wooden butt brushing his lower thigh as his mare labours to keep pace with Emile's mount. A sabre, snug in its steel sheath, hangs from his waist on the opposing flank. The gun is loaded. It is wonderful to ride bareheaded with the breeze in his hair.

They ride north on the main road to Mont St Jean until a lane comes into view on their left, just before the inn of La Belle Alliance. The lieutenant wheels his mount and they leave the partially cobbled thoroughfare for a muddy way. They ignore a track that appears almost immediately on the right, angling straight for Hougoumont, and continue across the rear of the Second Corps commanded by General Reille, until they reach the far end of the line.

This is the sector commanded by Prince Jérôme. His reserve troops stand behind the guns straddling the larger road running towards Mont St Jean from the south-west. The men look nervous and there is no doubt why.

In front of them the woods slope up towards the chateau-farm. At the southern fringe of the trees lie dozens of infantrymen tended by medical orderlies. Their moans and screams are audible despite the gunfire that now echoes across the battlefield.

Emile locates a young lieutenant with green eyes and an unsuccessful attempt at a moustache. 'Where is Prince Jérôme? I have orders from the emperor.'

The young man actually squeaks as he tries to reply. His wavering forefinger indicates a group of officers close by.

A heavy man with an excessively ornate uniform but no hat is gesturing with both hands at a group of more junior officers. His forehead glistens with sweat, pasting the curls, crafted to disguise his hair loss, to his head. 'Send in more troops! It has taken far too long to seize the wood. We must press on. I will wrest this place from the enemy. It will be my gift to my brother!'

Emile dismounts and gives his reins to a groom tending the

officers' mounts. Richard copies him with considerably less grace, as he forgets the short musket on one side and sword on the other.

As the pair reach the fringe of the assembled officers, Richard can read the faces of Jérôme's subordinates. Mistrust borders on contempt. Yet none demur. Instead, they turn away, calling their men to assemble.

Emile seizes his opportunity, circling in front of the youngest Bonaparte brother. Bowing low, he introduces himself.

'Well, what is it? I am not usually troubled by mere lieutenants!' Tiny bubbles of spit accumulate at the sides of Jérôme's mouth.

'Forgive me, your Imperial Highness, but I bring a message from the emperor.'

Jérôme scowls. 'What is it my brother wants now? I am essaying every effort to take this Belgian pigsty for him. Does he not trust me to complete the job?' His voice grows higher, dripping with hatred. 'He stole my wife and failed to save my kingdom! Yet still I serve him!' Spittle flies from his lips but

Lieutenant Béraud does not flinch, even when Jérôme thrusts his prominent nose close.

'The emperor asks that you withdraw the majority of your men, investing just enough in the siege to convince the enemy. You are to march your remaining troops to La Belle Alliance. They are needed to reinforce d'Erlon's assault on the centre,' Emile insists in an even voice.

Jérôme Bonaparte's eyes bulge, his eyebrows shoot up and stick there. His hands become fists which he waves in Emile's face. 'Preposterous! I shall do no such thing! Where are these orders? Napoleon has a huge reserve. He is just trying to deny me my victory!'

The lieutenant produces the eagle signet and holds it out. 'The emperor told me to present this as proof I speak his will. He has intercepted despatches meant for Wellington and fears his orders might suffer a similar fate.'

Jérôme extends his plump hand and snatches the ring away from Emile. He stares at it in horror before flinging it clumsily across the road into the wheat. Richard's mouth hangs open.

Here then is Napoleon's greatest weakness. His family. Emile makes as if he intends to retrieve the ring.

'Lieutenant, do not move! I have new orders for you and you will obey them!' There is a manic quiver in the high-pitched command and a febrile glaze in Jérôme's eyes. 'You are to make your way through that wretched wood.' He points with a quivering finger. 'You are to join the men I have just ordered forward and you are not to return until that bloody farm is in French hands! Do I make myself clear?'

Richard feels sick. It is a death sentence. Before he realizes what he is doing, he has rounded on Jérôme. 'You cannot do that! I was there when Lieutenant Béraud received his instructions from your brother. You are wilfully refusing an order of the emperor. I shall ride to his command post immediately to report what I have witnessed.'

Jérôme's face is wracked with twitches and his cheeks darken to an alarming purple. He grabs Richard's lapels and throws him to the ground. Leering down, he fumbles with his sword, trying to clear his scabbard unsuccessfully.

He shrieks for his attendants, who had moved judiciously

away when he began to remonstrate with his officers. They are pacing the edge of the minor road running north-west but turn at the summons and trot reluctantly towards their commander. 'Detain this man whose French reveals him an agent of the enemy! I want a firing squad assembled!'

Emile's face is a picture of misery, Richard sees, but he shakes himself and steps forward. 'My Prince, I will happily join the assault. But I have given my parole for this man. He is an agent but one who works for us. Let me take him with me. It is likely neither of us will trouble you again.' Somehow, Emile maintains a reasonable tone and it seems to have a placating effect.

'Wait!' Jérôme's aides freeze. 'Find two reliable soldiers to escort this pair to their duty on the far side of the wood!'

Five minutes later, Richard and Emile are stepping around the dead and dying who have crawled clear of the trees. They have two grizzled infantrymen for company.

'There's still skirmishers in these woods, bloody Hanoverian riflemen. So, keep your heads down and your eyes open!' Rough words in a gruff but kindly voice. 'Don't know what you did to piss off old Peacocks but I hope it was worth it.'

The other private laughs bitterly. 'Don't reckon he's going to be happy until we're all dead. How he can have the same blood as the Little Corporal beats me!' His voice is utterly resigned. Soldiers are pawns on the chessboard, sacrificed while their commanders watch from the rear.

Musket fire crackles from the far side of the wood, growing louder as they slip forward from tree to tree. They move slowly uphill but Richard sweats profusely. It is a warm afternoon and his frock coat is too heavy.

As they approach the centre of the wood a louder discharge cracks close to Richard. He drops to the leaf litter.

'Richard, are you well?' asks Emile.

'Yes, but that sounded close by!'

'Indeed. We must keep low.'

The two infantrymen are already lying prone, muskets at the ready, scanning in the direction of the shot. They begin to slither forward using their elbows and knees, clumsy like seals on a beach.

Richard and Emile emulate their approach. It is difficult to generate forward motion, keep hold of his weapon and ensure his clothes and sword do not snag. The floor of the wood is covered in damp leaf mould and smells like a mushroom cellar.

Another shot snarls from a different direction. Richard sees a trunk splinter close to the two foot-soldiers. The snipers must be able to see their quarry because the impact is only a foot above the cowering privates.

It is gloomy between the trees but far from dark. The men of the King's German Legion have been embedded in the woods for long enough to acclimatise their eyesight.

Richard can already make out details, the texture of bark, the shades of brown in dead leaves, the finer branches close to the ground, devoid of greenery.

Ducking under one of these projecting obstacles, he feels a thrum in the air and a sound like an axe striking wood behind him. He does not look around but buries his face in the mulch.

His stomach lurches at the thought of a musket ball hitting him. It is not the initial damage that disturbs him as much as the thought of sepsis setting in. Shreds of cloth driven into a wound were a common cause of infection. He has read enough about medical knowledge in the early nineteenth century to understand the high death rate among casualties.

He lifts his chin to scan ahead and is about to move when there is another discharge from his right. This time he sees smoke as the powder ignites. They are sitting ducks.

'Richard, they have us pinned in a crossfire. We have to act! After the next shot, run as fast as you can in that direction.'

It sounds crazy but Richard understands. Although his every instinct screams at him to turn and flee, he would only make himself a target.

It takes fifteen seconds to load, aim and fire. Effective range is perhaps one hundred yards. Unless they are equipped with rifles. If that is the case, their accurate range doubles!

The two soldiers whisper to each other. They seem to have forgotten their charges. A moment later the pair leap up and dart first left then right, from tree to tree, back towards the southern treeline. Their boots slither as they run, the slope aiding their speed.

Two shots sound in very quick succession. Richard sees the flash from one. The private closer to the brighter light of safety spins around without a sound to lie immobile on his back. His companion throws himself beyond the body and hauls it onto one side against a tree trunk, as a makeshift shield.

Incongruously, the surviving soldier whistles tunelessly. The dead man's black shako is dislodged, revealing the back of his head. It is a shattered mess of blood and skull fragments. Richard vomits.

A musket ball thuds into the corpse with a thwack, causing the other soldier to yelp. Without pausing to wipe his mouth, Richard stumbles to his feet and throws himself uphill, towards the sound and smoke of the sniper.

Another shot sounds from his left but he keeps running. He hears Emile close by; they are converging.

Richard counts as he runs, spitting the numbers aloud from his sour mouth, 'Four… five…'

Emile is ahead by ten yards and pulling away, his carbine, a shortened musket, held ahead of him.

Richard has been running with his carbine in his left hand, gripped in front of the firing mechanism. He now takes hold of the truncated barrel in his right hand and feels for the trigger with his left forefinger. 'Eight… nine…'

He hears a metallic snap. Is that the ramrod at work or the hammer being drawn back?

His ankle turns and he narrowly twists away from a fall. His sword swings awkwardly on his hip and strikes a tree. 'Eleven… twelve…'

Out of the corner of his right eye, in dappled light, he sees movement and pans his head for a better look. He locks onto the long barrel sweeping in a horizontal arc, keeping pace with him.

The distance from muzzle to Richard is no more than fifty yards. He hears the hammer strike flint against the frizzen and imagines its hinge forced back to reveal priming pan and powder. The flash flares bright in the woods.

He tenses for the inevitable impact as he continues to run.

Nothing strikes him but he hears a curse in German. Miss-fires are about one in six, often because the touch-hole becomes clogged with burned powder. 'Fourteen…'

Just ahead, he watches Emile fire his carbine from the hip, drop it and throw himself headlong at a uniform of the King's German Legion, just as the sharpshooter lifts his weapon to his shoulder.

Emile tackles the man around his chest, pinning the gun between them as they crash to the ground. Emile's neck whips back as his forehead collides with that of the Hanoverian.

He rolls off to lie motionless on his back. Richard watches the German retrieve his musket from among the leaves. He thumps the stock into the ground to ensure the charge is still in place and begins raising the weapon. He angles the barrel down forty-five degrees to point at Emile, unconscious at his feet.

'No!' cries Richard, aiming his carbine at the man's chest, the easiest target, with shaking hands. He prays the charge, loaded back at Rossomme, is sound and no damp has penetrated the mechanism as he crawled through wet leaves.

He pulls the trigger. The weapon fires, wreathing Richard's head in smoke as the recoil catches him by surprise. The short musket is torn from his trembling fingers. Behind him he hears twigs break as boots pound down the slope.

He manages to clear his sword from its scabbard only to confront a musket point-blank in his face. He raises both hands to find his left still grips the sabre. He drops it awkwardly to his side. His head spins.

He has shot a man, at least he thinks he has, and now he is about to find out what that feels like. He watches the sniper cock the weapon, shivering at the metallic click. Oddly, the discharge sounds as if it has been triggered from behind him.

None of the expected smoke enshrouds them and the German gapes in disbelief. Richard expected the impact to throw him back, as it did the French infantryman, but he is still standing. It amazes him how a flood of adrenalin masks pain, even if it cannot last. He feels a tightening of his shoulder and braces for the avalanche of agony.

'Richard, are you wounded?'

The rifleman confronting him collapses to his knees, eyes rolled back in his head as he falls flat on his lifeless face. Richard turns from the awful sight to see Emile, cavalry issue pistol still raised, looking at him with concern.

'Apparently not, but you are!' He points to Lieutenant Béraud's bleeding forehead. Emile runs two fingers across the gash and brings them away slick with blood.

'So I am.' With that he staggers in a tight circle, flails for a grip on the nearest trunk and slides down it to the ground.

Richard springs to his side and helps him into a sitting position, back against the tree. The lieutenant is unconscious. Richard looks around in the gloom. There could be more skirmishers hidden in the woods.

He tries to slap Emile's cheek but his wrist clenches and his contact is weak. Steeling himself, he aims again and manages a firmer strike. The lieutenant's head lolls to the side, hat still in place. As he tilts Emile's head perpendicular to his body, Richard can see the colouration from the impact. He slaps the other cheek awkwardly with his right hand. He catches Emile's cheekbone hard and has to grab the lieutenant by his shoulders to prevent him slipping.

'What happened?' asks Emile weakly through clenched teeth.

'You saved my life!' Richard replies. He is beginning to shake now and has to sit beside the reviving lieutenant.

'Not before you saved mine!'

They sit shoulder to shoulder, sharing the rough trunk's support. The sounds of intense struggle from around Hougoumont penetrate the wood. Richard looks at the dead bodies of the riflemen. He can see the shock on their faces even though their eyes are blank.

For a moment Aunt Patricia is there, standing over him, a look of incredulity on her face and absolutely nothing to say.

'The emperor's brother very nearly got his wish.' Richard has never heard Emile sound critical of his superiors. Even now, he seems incapable of voicing such a sentiment but his tone is unmistakable.

'We followed his orders. We engaged the enemy. I think we have done all duty demands. Let's return to the emperor and report,' Richard suggests and holds his breath.

He is half expecting Lieutenant Béraud to insist on continuing. 'If we do not return to the 6th Division, we breach no order. The Prince merely instructed us not to return until the buildings were in French hands. Now, we are required elsewhere. I trust the farm shall fall to us before I am in his presence again!'

Richard grins in relief but realizes he is still shaking. He has killed a man. 'So, we need to find another way out of these trees?' Emile nods. 'What about the horses?' Richard asks.

The lieutenant scowls. 'I have ridden that horse for more

than five years. I'm damned if I'm going to lose her now. I will send a trooper to collect both mares discreetly.'

Having scanned between the trees for signs of more embedded riflemen, they begin to crawl east. It is easy to choose the direction.

They will keep clear of the fighting beyond the wood. They will avoid the raging commander behind the trees. They will make for the edge of the trees facing La Belle Alliance. The inn lies about a mile away.

Richard is relieved when they reach the last of the oaks without encountering another soul, living or dead. Peering beyond the fringe of trees, he sees they are to the north of the French advance line. Behind them, more troops stumble through the wood towards the chateau.

They step into the open. Emile's uniform is so distinctive, any French soldier will recognise it immediately. There is the bearskin adorned with a jet and scarlet plume matching his red jacket with black fur trim. Intricate facings fit over a similarly ornate tunic; while below the waist, deerskin breeches denote Emile as a personal escort of the emperor. Unmistakable even on a battlefield blooming with colour.

Nevertheless, they move tentatively, with arms raised towards the ranks of troops ahead.

Behind them a new sound intrudes. The thump of howitzers followed by explosions. The rending of splintered trees almost as chilling as the screams of shattered Frenchmen.

Ahead of them, a challenge is shouted over the cacophony and Emile replies, 'Lieutenant Béraud, Chasseur of the

Imperial Guard, on an assignment for the emperor!'

A gap opens in the line as they draw near and they slip through. Emile reports to the duty officer on that stretch of the line. A loan of horses is accepted with thanks.

Richard eyes the leggy animal warily as he is handed the reins. Her huge eyes remain fixed on him while rolling in her head. She snorts. Wiping his wet hand on her muzzle, he feels the heat of her. If he stumbles, she will sense his weakness and cause trouble.

He asks for a bunk up and Emile obliges. He swings into the saddle with some conviction and pats the mare firmly on her roan neck.

Emile wheels his borrowed chestnut gelding and salutes. 'I will send a trooper back with the horses.' He promises to the watching duty officer. 'He can ride on to collect our animals. I will ensure he has a written order from Bonaparte himself!'

Richard encourages his gangling mare alongside Emile and nods, eager for the moment when he is back in the saddle of the patient grey. Fortunately for Richard, this mount is conditioned to ride in company, so she holds herself on the shoulder of Emile's mount.

They soon reach the main road and pass the inn of La Belle Alliance, heading south to Rossomme, where the emperor is stationed with his staff.

Dismounting at the foot of the little hill, Richard checks his pocket watch. How long were they pinned down in the woods? Time seemed to stand still. D'Erlon's sixteen thousand were advancing as they left with the message for Jérôme. His watch now reads just after three in the afternoon.

The battlefield seems oddly quiet. D'Erlon's huge assault has been driven back, with heavy losses. The Prussians are arriving from the east in ever greater numbers, shoring up weak points on Wellington's left. Within the hour the weight of Prussians will become decisive.

Napoleon orders men from the regrouping Second Corps to replace artillerymen killed manning the Grand Battery. Emile waits discreetly until he has finished. 'Sire, I conveyed your message to your brother. He declines.'

Richard is impressed with the lieutenant's brevity.

Bonaparte spins on his heel to stare in disbelief at the commander of his personal escort. 'You gave him the ring?'

Emile bows again as he replies, unwilling to meet his emperor's eyes. 'He was angry, sire. He threw your signet into a wheat field. I fear the whole 6th Infantry Division will be lost.' Emile manages to sound calm but contemptuous.

Bonaparte thumps the table. 'Damn that peacock! He has deprived me of the men I need. I must send my reserve to face the Prussians. Jérôme's tittle-tattle was as accurate as his tactics are flawed. It seems you were right, my American friend!'

'But sire, I beg you. Without Grouchy's men, you cannot win today. Look how things stand! Pull back to a defensive position and reunite your forces.' Richard speaks with passion, the sight of that dead marksman urging him to prevent more futile killing.

'You have a good eye for combat, sir. But I have built my success on overcoming adversity not yielding to it. There is still a chance. If I can break Wellington's centre before the full weight of the Prussians is brought to bear, then they will have nothing to reinforce!'

Richard gropes for another argument, anything to turn Napoleon from this course, the course of history, the stubborn refusal to let his army live to fight another day. Soon, Bonaparte will allow Ney to squander his cavalry in an unsupported attack that rips the guts from his remaining forces.

General Gourgaud steps in front of him. 'You have no place here. I cannot understand what spell you have cast over the emperor but it ends now. His Imperial Highness has important work this day and he will complete it with the help of loyal Frenchmen. Make yourself scarce before I have you arrested.'

Richard's knees tremble and the dull sickness souring his stomach flares to an acidic burn that threatens to overcome him. Emile appears on his shoulder and leads him away.

He lets himself be supported from the map table, the stoop-shouldered emperor and his over-confident staff. Emile finds a bench in the farmhouse and sits Richard down. He disappears for a few minutes and Richard closes his eyes.

When he feels a hand on his shoulder, he opens his eyes to see Emile placing an earthenware flagon and two cups on a rickety table. 'It is some kind of fruit brandy.' The lieutenant pours two generous measures. Richard does not move, so Emile places a cup into his slack hand. His fingers tighten automatically but he does not lift it. Emile grasps his hand and steers the drink towards his lips.

He still feels nauseous but the aroma of strong spirits triggers a reflex and he takes a sip. Outside, the massed guns of Napoleon's Grand Battery start up again. Richard gulps then sputters as the harsh liquor burns his throat.

Emile pounds his back. Richard's eyes water; he thinks it is the alcohol. It might be sadness. He grasps the flagon and tops his cup to the rim, even though he has not finished the measure. He wipes his eyes. He swallows down another slug, gasping.

When he can speak without wheezing, he begins recounting the events that are about to unfold. 'Listen, Emile! What a bombardment, have you ever heard the like?'

The walls of the farmhouse vibrate so much plaster falls from the ceiling. Emile shakes his head.

'Wellington will pull his men back from the ridge.' Richard continues, 'Marshal Ney will think they are retreating and order the cavalry to charge. The cuirassiers, eight regiments of them, will be at the heart of that advance. Fine heavy cavalry on their blacks and bays, with their armour breastplates and straight swords. They will have many from your own Chasseurs with them, dragoons and mounted grenadiers too.'

Richard drinks some more, feeling the effects heat his body, calm his stomach and muddy his thoughts. He does not want to think about what will happen when the cavalry, without significant infantry support, reach the Allied lines. 'Five thousand men and their horses against twenty squares of British infantry flanked by artillery.'

Emile frowns but taps one foot on the boarded floor. 'You speak as if you know. Surely the emperor would never order such a thing? Ney's experience would prevent him from such an action without the necessary foot soldiers. It is madness!'

Richard reaches for the flagon but cannot meet the outraged officer's eyes. 'Everything I came to prevent. It is happening anyway.' He lets his chin slump onto his chest.

Richard hears a door bang and his head snaps up. The room, dusty from dislodged plaster, is empty. Richard struggles to his feet feeling light-headed, spilling the remains of his brandy. He lurches towards the door but is only half-way there when everything goes blank. His left shoulder bears the brunt of his fall but his temple strikes the wooden floor.

He is conscious as his head comes to rest. 'Emile, don't do it!' His lips are numb rubber. He can barely hear himself. Rolling over, he hauls himself onto his hands and knees and crawls to the door. Once there, he clambers up the rough wood and lifts the latch.

The door swings open in time to frame Lieutenant Béraud on horseback at the head of the duty escort, galloping away.

'Lieutenant, you are abandoning your post!' shouts one of the staff officers from the side of the building where Bonaparte watches events spiral out of control.

Richard squints into the brightness, his watering eyes following the diminishing green phalanx as it hurtles diagonally down the slope to intercept Ney's trajectory. Dust rises and obscures the magnificent green uniforms and their fine mounts. The mud of the morning has dried but it has done its work.

Hours lost that cannot be reclaimed, hours that allowed the Prussians to manoeuvre around Grouchy and reach the battlefield in time.

'Emile, why choose to believe me now? Why did I even say it?'

Richard does not dare return to the emperor's party. Gourgaud would doubtless keep his word. Instead, he looks for a good vantage point. The main brunt of the cavalry charge will funnel between the chateau of Hougoumont to his left and La Haye Sainte farm dead ahead.

He begins to walk along the cobbled road that runs north to Mont St Jean, nestled behind the Allied front lines. At first, the road drops towards the floor of the valley, which means he cannot see what is happening on top of the ridge.

He cannot see but he knows just the same. Precise squares prickling with bayonets, manned by phlegmatic troopers who have never seen a square broken by horse. Redcoats who can load and fire to order over and over again, front rank kneeling, rear rank standing, alternating volleys of deadly musket balls. They can hardly miss the cavalry bearing down on them in such numbers.

He hears the Allied guns firing, canister wreaking havoc among horses and men, armoured or not. As the charge grows closer, the gun crews will take shelter in the squares. He begins to run, frock coat flapping, oblivious to the incongruity of his appearance at the heart of the battle, a dated Regency gent flinging himself towards the mêlée.

Sweat runs into his eyes as he draws level with Decoster's house, home of Napoleon's unwilling local guide. Soon Napoleon will move up from Rossomme to a hill beside this modest dwelling to get a better view of the action.

By the time Richard reaches what remains of the 2nd Corps lines, he is panting for breath. Past the inn of La Belle Alliance and on beyond the initial French line of battle, now largely depleted by d'Erlon's assault and Ney's charge. Here is the flat bottom of the valley and he heads to his left, away from the road into the trampled rye.

Lifting his head, he realizes he can see the whole downslope ahead, scored and pitted, littered with abandoned guns, corpses of men and horses, craters from howitzer bombs and plugged round shot.

He watches the massed charge pouring over the lip of the escarpment, leaving shattered horses and men in their wake, mostly their own.

Richard comes to a stop in the middle of the field, a flattened swathe beaten down by twenty thousand hooves, wary of advancing any further and putting himself in a possible crossfire from Hougoumont and La Haye Sainte. Ney has kept his charge narrow, to slip between the two Allied outposts without exposing his cavalry unduly.

As the last of the cavalry top the rise, Richard thinks he sees a flash of green. Could that be Lieutenant Béraud and his escort party? He hopes not.

Atop the plateau, beyond that lip, stand some twenty squares of infantry. Again, and again the horsemen will charge the squares but their horses baulk and they are reduced to circling the human fortresses, firing into them with pistols and carbines. Some have such trouble controlling their terrified horses, faced with banks of bristling bayonets, that they dismount, leading their horses as they fire at the walls of uniformed men.

Coordinated volley fire takes a terrible toll on the attackers but rather than retreat, Ney reinforces his assault until he has deployed some nine thousand mounted troops.

There is no way Richard can see any of the action beyond the ridge, he would be afforded a better view if he copied the emperor and headed for Decoster's house behind him.

Just as he reluctantly turns, he feels a stinging slap to the side of his head. His mouth drops open as his legs collapse beneath him. There is no pain but as he lies among the broken crop, he can taste the iron tang of blood.

He tries to move a hand to his temple but finds his arm insensible. He rolls onto his back, freeing his other arm which is still under his control. Trembling fingers explore his head and come away slick and red. His stomach heaves and he has to blink away blood.

The sky is a patchy blue. The sun appears, framed in one of the rips in the cloud cover, the warmth feeling good on his face. He closes his eyes for a moment. Again, his mind wanders, taking him back to Paris, Place des Vosges and Madame Odillet.

Chapter Six

Richard seemed to have spent his week crossing this formal square. He was beginning to feel he had a right to be here. He wasn't just an intrepid tourist wanting more than the Eiffel Tower and the Champs-Elysées.

The lights were on, illuminating prize items, but the closed sign was still displayed. He was about to knock when Madame Odillet appeared on the other side of the glass and opened the door. She was resplendent in a dark blue velvet combination awash with gold embroidery.

As she led him into the shop, he studied the dragon motif on the back of her hip length jacket. Her baggy trousers were gathered at the ankle. She wore leather flip flops which slapped the soles of her feet as she walked. 'Come in, Richard. Something to drink?'

'A long, weak, white coffee please, Madame Odillet.' He wanted to keep his head.

'Call me, Marianne,' she chuckled.

He followed her into the kitchenette. As she prepared his coffee and her *tisane*, she explained a little more about her friend in hospital. A stroke, she was stable now, she would need some help when she came home. Marianne lived in the same building. Things would work out.

When the drinks were prepared, Richard moved towards the pair of chairs at the front of the shop.

'No, no, this way,' Marianne called as she disappeared deeper into the building. She halted at a door to the room directly behind the kitchen. She inclined her head and Richard obliged, holding the door as she entered before following her in.

He gasped aloud.

'This is my private collection.' The lower half of the walls were lined with panelling painted a muted blue. The upper portion was whitewashed. The ceiling was dominated by a glorious chandelier set in an ornate plaster rose. It hung above a circular table covered in green velvet embroidered with golden bees, a favoured Napoleonic symbol.

Sat on the cloth was an intriguing assortment of objects but on the wall to Marianne's left was a portrait that immediately caught Richard's eye. 'Isn't that a copy of Robert Lefèvre's painting? I saw the original at the Carnavalet museum this morning.'

Marianne smiled. 'Someone has the copy but it isn't me.' Richard assumed she was joking and smiled back. 'I think the board of the city museum should look long and hard at their acquisitions team,' she added.

'You're serious?'

She nodded, joining him in front of the painting. 'I have an unbroken provenance from the artist's studio in 1809.'

Richard closed his mouth and stared at the image. Napoleon stood in front of a chair so grand it was almost a throne, its circular back decorated with a crowned letter N. The emperor's right hand rested lightly on a table draped in maps. The top map was of Africa.

Looking closely, Richard could also see Bonaparte held a pair of compasses. On his left hip was a sword. He wore white breeches and black boots. Over a white waistcoat and a red sash was a cutaway tunic in blue with gold epaulettes. Collar and cuffs matched the sash. It was the uniform for a colonel of the Foot Grenadiers.

He was a living tricolour. He was bare headed and looking into the middle distance, envisioning his next battle.

Richard stood next to the aged collector, sipping his coffee and staring. Marianne placed her empty glass on a marble-topped side table supported by black sphinxes with golden wings. She relieved Richard of his half-drunk coffee and gestured towards the table. 'See what you make of these.'

Richard tore himself away from the portrait. On the velvet shrouded table lay six items, apparently scattered at random. There was a pair of gloves, a bicorn hat, a small clock, the baton of a Marshal of France, a snuff box and a sword. Richard's left hand edged to the rim of the table and hesitated. He looked to Marianne.

'Handle anything you wish. What is the point of them otherwise?'

He was a little shocked but found himself lifting the marshal's baton free of its case. Unlike the one he had seen in the Queen's Gallery at Buckingham Palace, this example looked new. The velvet had not faded to mottled brown but sang in blue.

Imperial eagles decorated its length in silver and gold thread. The eagles clutched thunderbolts in their talons. Each end was finished with a gold cap. The box was red Morocco leather embossed with more gold eagles.

Richard held the baton. The wooden core made it lighter than he expected. It was engraved with a Latin inscription. 'Terror in war, ornament in peace,' he translated aloud. 'Do you know who it belonged to?'

Marianne fingered the case. 'It is allegedly one of the batons of Jean Lannes but the provenance is, unfortunately, weak.'

Richard felt a shiver, imagining Napoleon handing the emblem to his friend, one of the first to receive the honour from his hand.

'He was close to Napoleon and he missed him after his death,' she said.

'A blunt man, I recall? Rude even. Rose from nothing. A true revolutionary success story.'

Marianne nodded, her hoop earrings twisting wildly against her unruly mop of hair. 'He was the only one of Bonaparte's generals allowed to address him as *tu*. That tells you everything.'

Richard replaced the baton, still thrilling at the contact and what it conjured up even two hundred years later.

Next, he examined the clock. It was a Breguet. Napoleon had bought a number of timepieces from that firm. The company was still in existence.

Marianne tapped the carrying handle. 'He bought that in April 1798. I have a copy of the bill of sale from the watchmaker's archive. A month later he sailed on his Egyptian campaign.'

The clock was less than five inches tall and about three inches wide. A silver dial with black Roman numerals was pierced by a display of the phases of the moon. The carriage clock case was framed by Doric pilasters in gold. Engraved scrollwork danced at top and bottom of the timepiece. Three small windows near the base displayed the date, month and day of the week.

The antiquarian leaned towards Richard, 'It is said to be of particular importance as the first example of a modern carriage clock.'

Richard's left forefinger traced the columns, revelling in the contact. All four sides sat safe behind glass panels. He imagined Napoleon winding it, checking the time, waking to its strike. The piece was silent and the hands sat impassively at six o'clock. 'Does it still run?'

Marianne started to search in the two voluminous pockets of her jacket.

Richard held up his hands to forestall her. 'Please don't wind it on my account.'

'But I have the key here somewhere,' she replied, delving into her trouser pockets.

'That's really not necessary, it's just lovely to know it is in working order.' He moved on quickly.

The bicorn hat was a particularly good example. There were notoriously many of the hats in existence whose owners claimed they belonged to Bonaparte. In reality, the hats were worn widely across Europe and in the American forces from the 1790s onwards. 'I think I read that one sold for 400,000 dollars quite recently?' he said.

Marianne tutted and rubbed her hands together, bracelets tunelessly accompanying the movement. 'The hat he supposedly lost at Waterloo. A bargain at that price. Some South Korean businessman paid two million dollars for one in 2014. Admittedly in much better condition.'

Richard was barely listening. He was a boy again and all he could think of was putting it on his head and picking up the ornamental sword lying beside it. He heard those bangles again and felt a hand on his shoulder. 'Go on. Put it on. It's so obvious you want to.'

Reaching across the table, he picked it up carefully and turned it over. The lining was yellowed and stained. The felt exterior was more grey than black and so shiny near the rim it looked green. If the hat had belonged to anyone else, he would have hesitated putting something that dirty on. But this had once enclosed the emperor's head.

He settled it gently.

'A pretty good fit!' Marianne observed, patting him on the back. 'There are only nineteen still in existence.'

'How many would he have owned in his lifetime?' Richard was really just musing out loud but the old shopkeeper knew the answer.

'About one hundred and twenty!'

Seeing the direction of his gaze, she picked up the sword that was already unsheathed. The scabbard was relatively plain, tapering from a golden neck along its black length to a gilt point.

The sword itself was another story. The handle and guard glittered under the light of the chandelier, chased with foliage and a profile of Napoleon. The top of the brilliant blue steel blade was fire gilded with foliage from hilt to tip.

'There is no way this was meant for fighting,' Richard observed, as he let Marianne place the hilt in his hand. It was heavier than it looked but still impossibly delicate.

'It was forged for him just before he became emperor by Martin-Guillaume Biennais, a top Paris goldsmith. It is a symbol of command like the baton. For a long time, it was thought there was only one in existence. The one he wore at Austerlitz and always referred to as his sword.'

'That makes sense. I remember seeing a sword very like this in the Army Museum at Les Invalides.'

'You are right. That is the sword or so everyone assumed. After all, no other has ever appeared.' She had an impish tilt to her head as she watched his reaction.

'Are you saying there may be some doubt? I thought the sword stayed in his family until they placed it in the museum?'

'All I know is that there are two swords. Who is to say the emperor did not have more than one? Calling it his sword might refer to the design, don't you think?'

Richard wasn't sure he found that convincing. 'The other one has a pretty strong provenance. Are you sure this isn't a brilliant replica?'

Marianne scowled and shook her head. She paced to the far side of the table and then leant forward, resting fists on the velvet. 'Do not impugn my profession! It has been tested. The blade was decorated using powdered gold and mercury. The heat of the kiln burned off the mercury to leave the gold design behind. The fumes from the process killed workers before they reached forty! That's a pretty dangerous forgery!'

Richard carefully returned the sword to the table and placed the hat next to it. 'Forgive me, this is all rather overwhelming. I had no idea private collections like this existed.' Even as he said it, he knew it sounded unconvincing.

'Come now! You mean you never expected a collection like this to be owned by someone like me! Don't worry, you are not the first to underestimate me.'

Richard wondered if he was outstaying his welcome. 'You've been so generous with your time. I really appreciate it but perhaps it is time for me to leave?'

He could not imagine Marianne was going to give him an artefact from her collection. After all, if she was right, she would never see it again. Not that he believed her tale of time travel, however tempting the idea. How could he dare? Believing it was to admit there was no hope for his actual life and he reserved such maudlin sentiments for the end of drunken evenings.

'What about the gloves?'

Richard had forgotten about the dirty cream leather gloves. They looked like a quality calfskin and were made for small hands. 'No doubt they belonged to Napoleon?'

'Indeed. They were left in his carriage when he had to abandon it during the flight from Waterloo. I acquired them from an impeccable source, just recently. I believe the seller needed to fund some major renovations to his palace.'

Richard was shaking his head but his expression left no doubt he was convinced. 'Truly extraordinary.'

Marianne leant over the table and retrieved the gloves. They were indeed quite small. Richard wondered if he would be able to squeeze his average hands into them. He did not try. He accepted them from Marianne. They were surprisingly supple and still smelled like new despite the discolouration.

He put them back on the table and sighed.

'What makes you sad? The thought of returning home? Melancholy for the First Empire? Your lack of faith?' Her voice was kind but the words cut him.

Chewing his lip, he backed towards the door. 'I do want it to be true. I really want it but how can it be? History would crumble! The present would become chaos as old certainties disappeared without warning. Even if I did believe, if your collection demonstrates anything, it is how sought after such artefacts have become and how many forgeries are in circulation.'

Marianne joined him at the door and opened it. She ushered him into the narrow hallway and then popped back into the room. He waited uncomfortably in the gloomy space, fingers idly stroking the flock wallpaper. Marianne reappeared with a modest wooden box pinned between her hip and the crook of her right arm. 'I have one last thing to show you. After that you are free to go with my blessing.'

As they reached the front of the shop, he was able to make out the rich mahogany of the box. The corners were capped with brass and the lid was a profusion of inlaid flowers in blond and dark woods.

They sat in the twin chairs beneath the pool of light cast by the standard lamp. Marianne placed the box on the occasional table and began fishing in her pockets again. At the third attempt she produced a small bunch of keys.

Selecting one, she unlocked the box and lifted the lid. It blocked Richard's view of the contents. She rummaged for a few moments. 'Aha, there it is! Perfect.' She closed the lid with her left hand and relocked the box. The bunch of keys disappeared into a deep pocket. She kept her right hand hidden inside her velvet sleeve. 'So, you need something of the emperor's to make the trip. Austerlitz, you mentioned? It is in the Czech Republic, I believe?' There was promise in her eyes.

'That's right, Austerlitz was the Austrian name of the town nearest the battle. It's called Slavkov u Brna today.' Excitement drew Richard in despite his scepticism.

'Not a catchy name for a great victory?' joked the eccentric shopkeeper. 'Better use its other title.'

'The Battle of the Three Emperors, yes. Napoleon, Alexander and Francis. France, Russia and Austria,' Richard agreed.

They sat in silence for a few moments. Richard watched the shoppers and tourists who glanced in at the wonderful displays but moved on, startled when they saw the pair of them, like mannequins abandoned during a refit.

'You will be needing this, then.' A heavily veined hand extended over the delicate table. There was a slight waver at the wrist but then she calmly turned her hand over and opened her fingers.

Sitting in her surprisingly pink palm was a single shoe buckle. The gold plate had worn off in places but it was unmistakably from the right period. He always thought buckles looked odd bereft of shoes. Lozenge shaped with a central pivot and sharp teeth for fixing to the leather. They were utilitarian. Certainly not high art.

Marianne took Richard's left hand and placed the buckle in it. 'Before you ask, yes, this belonged to Bonaparte. It was one of a pair in the inventory of his possessions drawn up after he died on St Helena.'

Richard decided against interrogating the provenance. He had learned his lesson in her inner sanctum.

Such a mundane item. Of little intrinsic value without its companion. But what a thrill! He was actually holding something the emperor had taken for granted, using it on a daily basis. At that saddest time in his life, when all his dreams had been hauled down and he was banished to one of the remotest spots on the planet.

His heart sank. 'Say I did believe you, doesn't that mean I could only travel back after Waterloo, when he is exiled in the South Atlantic?' he tried hard to keep disappointment out of his voice.

'You are a sharp one, aren't you?' Marianne stood gingerly, wincing as she straightened her back. It was a rare show of age. 'Stay where you are. I will show you what really convinced Louis to make that trip.'

She was not gone long but when she returned from the back of the shop, she was carrying a big, black leather-bound book. It looked very old. Like a family bible.

He leant forward inquisitively as she sat back down and opened the tome on her lap.

'You must promise me one thing,' she said sternly, looking at him with her steeliest look.

Richard nodded.

'Promise me!' she insisted. 'Promise me you will not tell another soul?'

'I promise to keep this secret, whatever it is.' He meant it.

Marianne Odillet sat in silence for a long time. A tear navigated the delta of fine lines around her left eye and escaped onto the surprisingly smooth hill of her cheek.

'There was a time when Louis and I shared everything. We loved nothing more than spending a day at a flea market seeking treasure. Second-hand book stalls were a particular favourite. One day he brought this home to our draughty little flat. He had found it long forgotten at the bottom of an uncatalogued box of old books a dealer had acquired from a house clearance and forgotten. He got it for a pittance. I think the seller was glad to be rid of the clutter.'

She turned over a few pages so that Richard could see the archaic penmanship and garish illustrations. 'We spent hours poring over it. Puzzling at it. We wondered if it was a clever fake. But then life took over. Woodstock. My daughter. Louis lost himself. It was the only thing he took with him when he left.' She shook her head. 'When I threw him out.'

Richard said nothing; there was nothing he could say. Madame Odillet continued, 'Perhaps something in his drugged state drew him to the book. It is a most peculiar mix of recipes and incantations, mythology and superstition. It is part almanac and part handbook.'

'Handbook for what?'

'I think it is meant as a primer for apprentices.'

'But what kind of apprentice would need the kind of things it contains? It sounds like a book for trainee witches!' Richard looked at Madame Odillet. Her unruly grey hair and bohemian clothes, her unconventional feel. He had taken her for an ageing hippy. For a moment he saw her as something else and Amélie beside her, an assiduous acolyte!

'You are not very good at hiding your thoughts, dear boy! Owning a book for witches doesn't make me one, whatever you think I look like!'

He reddened and squirmed in his chair. 'Forgive me, our meeting has not turned out as I expected. I'm finding it hard to keep my wits.'

She nodded as if that was the most understandable thing in the world. 'The truth is rather less exciting. Once Louis left with the book, I forgot about it. It was only after he took his fateful trip back to the States, I got a call from his landlord. Landlord! Some tough who extorted a few *sous* from each hopeless case dossing there. Supposedly to provide security. Anyway, he said he had a box of things Louis left behind. My contact details were among them. I could collect the box if I got there by the end of the week. Otherwise, he was going to burn the lot.'

She paused and clasped her hands together on the thick pages of the book. 'I thought about leaving them but something made me go. The horrid reprobate made me pay him for storing the box, only a few francs but I was poor back then. I paid up, took the box and headed home. I didn't even look inside until the next day. It was raining, I remember. I had no money for the electricity meter thanks to that nasty man. I ripped off the Sellotape to find a bundle of threadbare shirts, a broken belt, a pair of shoes with one sole adrift, a few posters for local bands and at the very bottom, this book.'

She looked old now, beneath the warm light, with the curious book open on her lap. Sitting quite still for once, staring into the middle distance, just like Napoleon in Lefèvre's painting.

Was she back in 1968 with all its promise or 1971 when disappointments crowded around her? 'I was eight months pregnant and broke. I had time on my hands until I could get a proper job. Meanwhile I was making a few francs buying and selling *bric-à-brac*, more often scavenging cast offs and selling them! Anyway, I spent my evenings trawling through this book. When Louis' first letter arrived in its pretty little air mail envelope, it all made sense.'

Dropping her head, she turned to the back and peered at the page. She leafed forward from one page to another before nodding. Her hands smoothed the rough paper surface and then stilled, obscuring most of the page she had found. 'The French is rather archaic but I think you will get the sense of it. Take your time but remember your promise.'

She handed him the book. He took it gingerly, careful to keep it open at the right page. It was not as heavy as he had expected but he rested it in his lap. In the pool of yellow light, he saw a broad decorative margin of acanthus leaves entwining conch shells, comets and mythical creatures. The greens and blues were still bright, while the creatures leapt off the page in red, black and gold. Inside the bestiary of a border was inscribed a handwritten text of some twenty short lines.

Richard began to read, stumbling over the unfamiliar constructions and delayed by the odd unfamiliar word. Despite the obstacles, the subject matter quickly became clear.

'So, Louis didn't just tumble back to 1968 by accident? He had a plan inspired by this strange guide.' He was no longer denying her story. He believed Louis had travelled back to Woodstock. It didn't mean he could do something similar.

The majority of the text was preamble but the key passage was unmistakable. Richard read the rudimentary rhyme aloud,

'Grasp the property of one you would see,
stand on the ground where you would be,

imagine the day, wish yourself away,
with unreserved intent, renounce the present.'

He looked at the antiquarian sitting beside him in her velvet verve and noticed the tears. She had tried to follow those instructions but failed. She had Louis' clothes. She knew where he had gone and when. She had just been unable to forsake her daughter for the arms of a man who had hurt her deeply. No wonder. 'You actually tried? You went to the farm?'

Marianne didn't answer immediately. Instead, she lifted a locket on a chain around her neck and opened it. She showed it to Richard who leaned in closely to make out the tiny picture inside. 'Liselotte. She's nearly fifty. Married with three children. She lives in London.'

Richard studied the happy face framed by unruly hair. 'She was a lovely child.'

Marianne wiped her face with a handkerchief conjured from another pocket. 'I took her with me to America. I had to borrow money from friends. Liselotte was a toddler but she was so good on the flight. She didn't like New York City but when we took the bus upstate, she became content. For a few hours I thought it was all meant to be. A wonderful reunion. We would fix our mistakes by living a new life in the past.'

It looked dark outside. Lamps were on around the square. How could he have spent all day in this old woman's shop? Marianne had stopped crying but her eyes looked sunken in her head, as if hollowed out by the memory. 'She loved the cows and horses. We even saw some deer. We stood in that field and I tried, I really tried but nothing happened. I could feel Liselotte's warm little hand in mine. She had no idea what I was trying to do. What if I had succeeded? She would have been left all alone in that field and I would have been right there but unable to reach her. How could I wish that with my whole being? How could I have failed to think about it before I begged my friends for money and dragged my daughter across the Atlantic based on the memory of a man who no longer existed?'

Richard looked at the shoe buckle, still awkwardly clasped in his left hand, and then back to the ornately decorated page. 'You were a single mother with a little girl and no obvious way forward. Who wouldn't be tempted by a time when everything was wonderful? When anything seemed possible.'

She reached out her left hand and rested it on his arm. 'You are too kind. I was not thinking straight. I can't even remember what I wished for. Was I trying to get to 1968 or to Louis? Did I think I could have both?'

Richard shrugged while trying to communicate sympathy. 'Thank you for sharing that with me. I know it wasn't easy. You didn't have to tell me. The book was all I needed to see really. I understand the point. That an object must simply have touched the person in question, the person you seek.'

'Exactly. That was what I needed you to accept. The rest was for me. Not even Liselotte knows the truth. I have never found the courage to confess. It was time I found someone to share it with. So, it is I who should thank you. Now keep the buckle and take that adventure you are so sure you need!'

Outside, a gloomy dusk was held at bay by pools of light beneath the arches. A gentle mist was descending and the air grew heavy with suspended moisture. Richard rubbed his face as he crossed Place des Vosges one more time. His hand came away wet.

It was time to pack. Tomorrow evening the train would take him back to England and his modest flat, to a looming Sunday, his least favourite day, when all he could think about was the week ahead.

Fending off images of classrooms and jaded pupils, he began to list the things he would need to get done in the next seven weeks. He was sure of one thing, there was no Liselotte binding him to the present. Perhaps he really could do it?

Waiting to board the Eurostar, he wrestled with the thought of just turning around and finding the best way to the Czech Republic. Why go through another half term of angst? Why not grab this improbable chance and see where it might take him?

And then he thought about Marianne and her ill-considered journey back to upstate New York. So often frustrated by his own caution, this time he embraced it. He meant to try this, so he was going to do it right.

He picked up the phone and rang the familiar number. 'Hello, Aunt Patricia. I hope you are well?' He thought he heard a murmur. 'I've decided to spend Christmas abroad. The Czech Republic. I hope you won't be too disappointed?' He always made a duty call to her Victorian pile just before Christmas. A pilgrimage to the house where he grew up in the same rooms his aunt occupied. He never thought of them as living together but adjacently. Christmas compelled her to speak to him and he was forced to be appreciative. It did them both good, he had always thought, although neither of them enjoyed it. 'I'll post your present. Don't worry about me. I'll call you when I'm back.' Was that agreement?

He rang off guiltily. With any luck he wouldn't be coming back. It was the twelfth of December. Term would end in just a few days. He hugged his secret to him as he turned up the heating. He had given notice on his lease. But that was just the tip of what was keeping him warm. He sat in his one armchair and picked up the letter. He read it through, nodded and folded it carefully in three before slipping it into the good quality envelope.

He uncapped his pen and wrote Headmistress, then picked up the glass of whisky he had poured to fortify himself for his telephone call to his aunt. He tossed back the remainder and swallowed the fire in his throat, enjoying himself.

He had not told Aunt Patricia what he was about to do, just that he was going on holiday again. Nor had he told her what would happen next. How could he? Why would he? He knew what she would think. He poured another glass. He had waded through six more weeks of mediocrity in the classroom, almost as much from him as his pupils.

On Friday term would end and so would his career at St Anne's. A twinge of doubt nagged at him. He drowned it.

It was cold as Richard gazed across the flat farmland that separated him from the Pratzen Heights. Dawn had defeated the night but the sun remained shrouded behind heavy skies.

Napoleon had given up the Heights, despite their dominant position, as part of a ploy. He enticed his enemies to engage, believing the French army weakened and exposed.

Richard looked around his immediate surroundings. There was an early morning dog walker far to his left. He stood in front of a cobbled area flanked by trees. In the centre was a platform topped by what looked like an altar. A rectangular block of grey stone marking the spot where Napoleon placed his headquarters on the day of the battle. On top of the stone box was a bronze map of the battlefield.

Richard hugged his overcoat, trying to move naturally in his Georgian clothes. His legs were cold in close fitting cream breeches that finished below the knee, tucked into the brown tops of black leather riding boots. His white shirt with a matching cravat was mostly hidden by a patterned burgundy waistcoat and his dark blue, cutaway tailcoat. He was holding his squat, black Regency top hat. The fur collar of his overcoat tickled his cheek but the coat's brown wool offered welcome warmth.

He carried a leather satchel slung over his shoulder. Although a little incongruous, it was the sort of thing many soldiers used on campaign. It contained some food provisions, a pen knife, a telescope, a spare shirt and a travelling kit for brushing clothes and polishing boots.

In a hidden pocket of his tailcoat, he carried two documents that he hoped might prove useful. One was a pass from Marshal Davout granting the bearer safe passage. It was dated the twenty-ninth of November 1805 and it was genuine. It had taken all of Richard's modest savings to secure it at auction. The pass was far from pristine but there were plenty of things that could have led to the discolouration and creasing apart from age.

The other document was a forgery in every way. A letter of

recommendation to Emperor Bonaparte from President Madison. It named Richard as in the employ of the American government and commended his efforts to frustrate British ambitions. The paper was linen based and would pass muster. The rest was Richard's invention. He was rather pleased with it. He had wrapped the precious pieces of paper in an oilskin packet.

Richard walked a little way along the top of the hill, away from the bronze map. He decided to drop down the hill rather than appear without explanation in the very middle of Napoleon's inner circle. Some irony to successfully travel across two centuries, only to be shot on the moment of arrival.

There was no way of telling where any ground cover might have been in 1805 but he determined to settle himself in the lee of the hill. He would make his attempt and be ready with his pass in hand. While he unwrapped his packet and extracted the document, he rehearsed his reasons for escaping the present and why 1805 was the perfect destination.

He checked all around. He was alone. He pulled the shoe buckle from his overcoat pocket and grasped it firmly in his left hand. He gripped the warrant from Davout carefully in his right hand.

He sucked in a deep breath and closed his eyes. He screwed them as tightly shut as he could and recited his litany of disappointments, overlaying them with the glories of Napoleon at his zenith. Austerlitz was the midwife of that.

That was where and when he wanted to be. On the very morning of battle. The fighting had started early, around seven o'clock. He wanted to be there for that. He was shaking with the effort.

'Please let this work. Get me to the second of December 1805. That's where I want to be more than anything. Please, don't leave me in this field in fancy dress. Let me live when I was meant to be!'

He repeated every word and held his breath. Red and yellow fireworks exploded on the underside of his eyelids. His head was spinning and his knees gave out. As the explosion of colours faded into darkness he dropped to the wet ground.

He came to on his side. There was something wrong with his face. A strange tugging at his left cheek. It felt wet. He could hear a peculiar snuffling noise. Was he having a stroke? His breathing sounded too rapid and there was a damp, musty smell filling his nostrils.

He heard voices but they sounded like children. He couldn't make out the language. He managed to roll onto his back and opened his eyes. As his vision cleared, he found himself surrounded by inquisitive expressions. Knitted hats and gloves, misty breath and everyone talking at once. Three children, all the same height with matching ruddy faces and blue eyes. Girls or boys, he couldn't tell.

He noticed one of the children was restraining a dog. A second was taking a picture of him with a mobile phone. Now a man and woman knelt beside him and helped him sit up. The third child picked up his hat and brushed it gently. Phone back in a pocket, the second child was about to retrieve Davout's permit.

Richard snaked out a hand to reach it first. He folded it clumsily and slipped it into his overcoat. 'Forgive me for startling you. I seem to have fainted. Thank you for your help. Most kind.' He was acutely aware of his unconventional appearance.

'Ah, are you an American?' the woman said in lightly accented English. Her face was kind but concerned.

'That's right. I seem to have lost my party. We belong to a historical society.' He stopped talking.

The two adults were nodding and speaking quickly in Czech to their children, no doubt explaining about crazy Americans. A flask was produced and a steaming cup offered. Richard accepted. He was beginning to shiver.

He had failed. He had quit his job and blown his savings. For what? To be sitting on the wet ground in a cold field some 750 miles from home, drinking hot chocolate. He swallowed the hot sweet liquid and felt his muscles relax a little.

He nodded his thanks and returned the cup. 'You have been so kind. Thank you very much but I must go now, to catch up with my group. They will be wondering where I am.'

The man took his hand and helped him onto his feet. Richard swayed for a moment but caught his balance and tried to smile. He managed to turn the hand holding into a handshake, bowed awkwardly to mother and children, patted the retriever on its head and started to climb back up the Zuran Hill.

His legs felt weak but he was glad of the need to concentrate on his body. Soon enough he was going to have to confront what he had done to his life.

He stood in the airport in a daze beside the suitcase he had thought he would never need again. Inside were his period clothes. He was dressed like everyone else. People rushed back and forth, struggling to steer overloaded trollies. They jostled about in queues to check in, buy coffee and pay for parking.

He had arrived full of hope with a one-way ticket. Now he needed a way to get home. Where was that? There was space on a late flight to Stansted but there was nothing for him in England. He had quit his job, given up his flat and spent his savings. To return to England was to return to his aunt. He could imagine her reaction.

He slumped onto a bench seat beside a young mother and her grizzling daughter. He fished his mobile from his pocket. 'Madame Odillet, is that you?' He had no one else to call.

'Richard, it didn't work? I am so sorry. You must come back to the shop.'

He patted the zippered compartment at the front of his bag. The buckle was safely stowed in there. 'Of course. I will bring back the shoe buckle as soon as I can work out the best way to reach Paris.' At least that was something he needed to do. After that, his life stretched in front of him like a barren field, sterile beneath a dull sky.

He heard Marianne sigh. 'You misunderstand me, Richard. We must discuss what happened or rather, didn't happen. I know you want this unconditionally. We must work out why you failed.'

Part of him wanted to shout in frustration. It didn't work because the book is a fraud, there's no such thing as time travel, your ex-husband has played a cruel joke on you! But that was a sure route to an empty field of nothingness stretching to an invisible horizon. He quashed the impulse.

'Thank you. I will call when I know my travel

arrangements.' Gratitude and self-pity fought each other as he rang off.

He scanned the departures board. There were no direct flights that day or the next to Paris. He found an information desk and asked about his options. The young man behind the desk was dressed in a dark tie, white shirt and light blue sleeveless pullover. He listened carefully and then tapped away on his keyboard.

'The best route is to take the train to Prague or Vienna and then fly direct from there. Buses leave every thirty minutes for Praha hlavani nadrazi, that's the main train station. It doesn't take long, maybe twenty minutes.' He spoke good English and sounded apologetic.

Richard was just happy to have a plan, even if his credit card would soon feel the strain. He had not intended to be around to pay the bill.

He had arranged to go to Madame Odillet's Pieces of the Past emporium as soon as he reached Paris. She had been adamant she would be there, no matter how late it was.

He was glad the *Métro* ran all night because his flight was delayed by fog. He had left the airport at eleven and reached Prague at just after half past two. By then he had booked a flight online but had to take an underground train and then a bus to get to Terminal One at Prague airport.

His flight was due to leave at six but only taxied onto the runway at seven. The plane touched down at Charles de Gaulle at nine in the evening. By the time he cleared customs and passport control it was almost half past ten. He had to change terminals to pick up the train into the Gard du Nord and then take the *Métro* to the Bréquet Sabin stop.

As he emerged onto the pavement it was snowing lightly. The short walk to Place des Vosges was welcome after a complicated day of travel. The air was fresh, snowflakes stuck to his upturned face and melted.

The city was still awake. Decorative lights hung everywhere. Restaurants with steamy windows emitted a warm glow, casting into silhouette the waiters and diners. Couples passed by, leaning against each other, their visible breath intertwined. Laughter spilled into the street. A group in party hats. It was just what he needed.

Place des Vosges was even more beautiful with its windows and arches spilling light, suffused through snow into a heavenly glow. There were times when the present looked pretty good. Maybe he just needed to get a grip?

And then he was there. Madame Odillet was opening the door and ushering him in. 'Come in out of the snow. You made it! Not a straightforward journey, I take it?' she asked as she locked up. He was about to apologise but she forestalled him. 'A glass of wine?'

He accepted gratefully. Soon they were sitting in the two familiar chairs. The shop was pleasantly warm and smelled faintly of festive incense. No, that was Marianne's bouquet. The shop was redolent of vintage leather and that faint mustiness so reassuringly familiar to lovers of old things.

Outside, the snow grew heavier and started settling across the square.

'Thank you,' Richard said, feeling better than he had since coming round on the battlefield.

'It is nothing. Now tell me what happened.'

He described everything. By the time he had finished, Marianne had refilled his glass. It was a very good Côtes du Rhône and it coaxed more out of him than he intended. He spoke of his embarrassment and frustration and how bleak things seemed now.

'Enough!' exclaimed Marianne, not unkindly. He turned to her and saw such compassion in her face, he felt tears well up. 'That is done with. We must look forward!' She was wearing a loose-fitting dress that stretched from neck to ankles. It was a wash of orange and blue tie-dye. Beneath its strappy top, the shopkeeper wore a translucent black top finished with frilly cuffs. Her feet were hidden in heavy work boots of scuffed tan leather.

'But I did everything right! Why should I think another attempt would have a different outcome?' He winced internally at the whining tone.

'I do not think you wanted Austerlitz with all your heart.'

He opened his mouth to reply but she held up a hand and he gave way.

'I believe you want to go back. I believe it is Napoleon or nothing for you. I know how much you admire him, how great a victory he achieved on that day. But search your heart, what is it you truly love about him? After all, for many he was a dictator, a ruthless warmonger, an upstart, a betrayer of the revolution.'

Richard sat silently. Clocks ticked all around, one struck the hour quite out of step with modern time. Marianne topped up his glass.

'He was an outsider who defied the odds to dominate his

age. He was a flawed man, full of contradictions. But he was so full of life, of ambition, irrepressible. To come back from Elba! Like a retired boxer craving one more big day in the ring.' He sipped at the wine, knowing he was tipsy. 'The Hundred Days! Perhaps it was folly but there was nothing inevitable about Waterloo.'

Marianne patted his hand, bracelets chiming against each other. They seemed tuneful now. 'So, you wish to witness the denouement?'

Richard shook his head. A gulp finished his glass. 'The chance to help him. To nudge him towards different tactics. To ensure his decisions were based on good intelligence. Yes, that would be the greatest thing I could imagine. To help Napoleon defeat Wellington on that day and then remain with him, wherever that might lead.' He knew his voice had grown louder, excitement and alcohol pushing up the volume.

'It sounds like you need to book a ticket to Brussels. But first there is another bottle. You must sleep here. Tomorrow will be a very different day.'

Richard woke to the sound of a mechanical street cleaner working around the periphery of the square. Its brushes scouring in gutters and against kerbs, consuming litter and spraying slush.

He rolled over and dislodged one of the cushions Marianne had used to fashion him a bed on the floor of the shop. He was a little groggy but the quality of the wine meant he was mercifully free of a hangover. He struggled from beneath a heavy velvet drape serving as a blanket.

He stood and looked out onto the square. The snow of last night was in retreat, fraying and greying at the edges, only pristine on Louis XIV's statue, comically accentuating his hat.

'I see you are up. Come, have some breakfast.'

Richard smelled warm croissants and joined his host in her tiny kitchen. She had brewed him a coffee without asking and he accepted it gratefully. She was already halfway through her *tisane*. They stood in the small space, chewing contentedly at the buttery flakiness.

It was a companionable silence, but in the end, Richard broke it. 'Do you really believe it can work?'

She looked at him with a disappointed expression. 'You know I do.'

He rubbed his scalp, set down his finished coffee and reached out his hands to touch her gently at her elbows. 'Come with me, then!'

She did not pull away but looked very deeply into his eyes. He blinked repeatedly. 'Why would you want an old woman tagging along? This is something you have to do alone. If anyone knows that, it is me! Had I not had Liselotte, had I not been tied to her, what might have happened?'

He knew she was right but that didn't stop him feeling disappointed. 'I'm afraid. If this doesn't work. What am I going to do?'

'It will work, if you believe completely. At the moment, you are riddled with doubt. Having me with you is just perpetuating your uncertainty. Besides, I have commitments here. When I came back from the States with my daughter, I embraced my life. I had a precious gift, a reason to move forward. I had to build a life, earn a living, raise a child. Even now, I have commitments. My friend…'

Richard let her go and smiled. 'Of course. I understand. You are right. I have to find a way.'

Richard opens his eyes to the sound of music. Loud martial music. Patriotic French songs played on massed drums, fifes, oboes, French horns, clarinets and bassoons.

He sits up. His skin is tight against the right side of his skull but his head is clear. The music swells above the desultory sounds of fighting from further off. Have the French somehow defied history and won the day?

He turns his head and sees some hundred and fifty bandsmen playing with gusto as the Imperial Guard marches on, acknowledging their emperor who raises his hat in salute as they pass him, seated on Marengo.

'The Guard is advancing!' echoes between the columns as one veers from the road.

'Long live the emperor!' Scattered infantrymen and cavalry troopers emerge from behind hedges and folds in the land to swell the ranks of bearskins with shakos, peaked and plumed helmets in brass, steel and copper, topped with feathers or horsehair in tails, crests or combs.

Despite the chaos at the fringes, the main phalanxes of the Guard keep their shape like the disciplined troops they are. The remnants of other regiments coalesce into a ragged skirmish line.

Richard watches the Guard march towards him, massive under their bearskins adorned with the red plumes of their dress uniform, ready for the celebratory ball scheduled for that evening in Brussels. They are kitted out in their blue greatcoats with red epaulettes. It is a magnificent sight, one he has imagined many times, aching at the pathos of the scene.

But this time it is different. He is actually present. Up close, the marching boots are muddy but keep perfect time. Allied guns bark defiance, hurling shot at the columns.

Belatedly, Richard hauls himself to his feet and scuttles to one side as the vanguard follow the route beaten by the cavalry. He edges back towards the massed band and the stocky figure of Bonaparte as he takes his final gamble.

Clear of the advancing troops, ignored by everyone, an utter irrelevance as the day reaches its final crescendo, Richard can only imagine the slaughter to come.

For a moment he flashes back to the wood below Hougoumont and the two dead Hanoverians in their King's German Legion uniforms, blank eyes staring accusingly. He shivers as he hears the shot he thought would kill him, only to find it was Emile's pistol saving him.

Reaching Napoleon, he keeps his distance, unwilling to put Gourgaud's threat to the test.

He is alone, dislocated by more than two centuries from his own time, watching the climax of the most famous battle in European history. He can see the tight set of the emperor's lips as he replaces his bicorn hat on his balding head. His eyes are full of pain.

Richard has fooled himself into believing he had some part to play but he is just a bystander, a witness perhaps? Either way, he is on the side lines in 1815 just as he had felt two hundred years later.

Chapter Seven

Richard looks at his watch groggily, it reads half past seven. From where the emperor stands, whenever the smoke parts, he can see across the six hundred yards to the enemy.

Seventy men abreast, the two columns march away, one thrusting past La Haye Sainte, the other further to the west, closer to Hougoumont. As they climb the slope towards the ridge, the French artillery falls silent. The drummers change their rhythm, muskets lift from shoulders to face forward, bayonets menacing.

The Allied guns continue to fire, tearing through the ranks with ball shot, grape shot and case shot. Every time a gap appears, men form up to fill it and keep marching, keeping time.

Richard edges around to see Napoleon's face. His look is stern but tears leak from his eyes. A curtain of smoke descends, hiding the French advance from the Allied defenders, who peer across the valley, tight with tension.

Cannon fire ceases. Muffled orders drift to them from ahead. A resounding volley. Screams from the wounded. The sound of the charge. Steel against steel.

For a moment the mist of war parts to show the Imperial Guard held at bay but standing firm. A battery of guns targets them. More men swarm the ridge, reinforcing the red wall of Foot Guards, commanded by Major-General Maitland.

Richard had studied the Frenchmen's faces as they marched

off. How many are already dead? It is not clear who has the advantage. Across to Richard's left, unseen, he thinks he hears the other attacking column or is it the British defenders? Volley fire echoes again and again.

Richard sees the emperor wince as the waves of firing continue. And then the first bearskins appear, blue coated with white waistcoats and red trim, hurtling towards them out of the smoke, all semblance of discipline dissipated in headlong flight. At first, single soldiers and pairs, then small groups, coalescing as they reach the valley floor but not stopping.

Like a contagion, the panic spreads to the column facing Maitland and they too break and run. The first men to clatter past Richard turn away, unwilling to see the look in their emperor's eyes.

As the Guard breaks, the news spreads like a virus. From regiment to regiment, infantry to cavalry to gunners, men hear the news they never expected to hear. The Guard is defeated. All is lost.

Artillerymen cut horses free of gun carriages and ride them away, abandoning their weapons as the Allied forces pour down the slope. All is pandemonium.

Richard wonders how much he is seeing and what his brain fills in from his detailed reading? It doesn't really matter. He is here and if he doesn't move soon, he is going to be run down.

Napoleon wheels Marengo, who favours a rear leg from a wound to his hip. With his entourage, Bonaparte trots dejectedly down the road up which he so recently led his beloved Guard. All optimism burst. At the inn, a remnant of order among the free for all, the three reserve battalions of the Old Guard.

'Save yourselves!' men cry as the Allied cavalry barrel down the road. The reserve Guard ignore the mayhem. They form squares and retreat, repulsing British skirmishers and enduring sporadic artillery fire.

Richard runs alongside them, still invisible as men strive to extract themselves from the inferno.

At Rossomme, where everything started so hopefully, the squares halt, occupying ground on either side of the road, supported by a battery of huge twelve pounders.

Richard marvels as the drummers beat their rallying tempo and men emerge from all directions to swell their ranks. There are cavalry uniforms without horses, line infantry, gunners, engineers and even marines in dark blue jackets and orange braid. He thinks he sees a few green jackets. Could Emile have survived?

He has to get inside one of the squares or die. Men are falling all around. Even the orderly squares are taking substantial punishment as enemy cavalry, infantry and artillery are brought to bear on their stubborn resistance.

One of the squares buckles inwards and falls apart, men scattering in all directions. At that moment, the emperor dismounts, barely slithering from his saddle.

A shell falls nearby and even sanguine Marengo baulks, reins slipping through Napoleon's gloved hands. The stallion shies away and is lost in the smoke. Briefly, Napoleon stares after him before shaking his head and indicating his wish to enter the square of the 1st Grenadiers.

At the order, a tidy gap opens for the imperial party and Richard runs forward, slipping through on Marshal Soult's coattails. He receives a couple of frowns but nobody speaks to him. There are several clumps of men inside the square. Men without muskets or bayonets, wounded, medical orderlies, buglers and drummers. Assorted remnants of other regiments, whose presence in the lines would only hinder the drilled precision of the veteran Guard.

Richard looks around, trying to appear inconspicuous, keeping clear of the outward facing troops and endeavouring to seem, at least loosely, attached to the imperial party. It works. He is close enough to hear Soult pleading with Bonaparte. 'Sire, you cannot remain here.'

'Where else should I be?' Bonaparte's voice is defiant.

'Safe, sire,' Soult's baritone cracks. He enlisted as a private when his father died. One day, he will be Prime Minister! Richard wonders how any of them are going to survive?

'Where safer than among the bravest of the brave, my Old Guard?' A touch of petulance from the emperor.

'They will die for you, sire. Do not make that sacrifice pointless!' the Marshal chides gently, his words thick with emotion.

'I have lost my horse, my dear Marengo. If I must march, let it be among my men!'

'There are other horses, sire. Take mine. He is sound.'

Richard watches as a series of emotions play across the emperor's face. He sees annoyance, despair, sympathy and finally resolution. 'Very well, Soult. Let us be gone from this miserable patch of Belgium. The battle of Mont St Jean must not be what I am remembered for.'

A hand comes to rest on Richard's shoulder from behind. He tenses, expecting a rebuke.

'Richard, is that you?'

He spins around. 'Emile, you're alive!'

His friend grimaces, for he is a friend, even if they met only a day ago.

'Why, I do not know. It was slaughter!' He says no more.

Marshal Soult gives the order and the disciplined lines of veterans step in and to the side, opening a channel for the emperor's exit, like a tiny honour guard.

'Hold firm, my glorious Guard. Remember, we are France!' As Napoleon speaks, Emile propels Richard along in his emperor's wake.

Soult salutes with his drawn sword but remains inside the human fortress as the wall reforms.

There is still a good supply of fresh horses in the stables of the Rossomme farm. Emile finds a mount very similar in frame and colour to his lost beast. He also identifies a horse he thinks suitable for Richard.

As the party mounts, Richard sees Napoleon's eyes settle on Emile. He inclines his head before urging his horse away. Bonaparte rides through the smoke of battle like a ghost, grey coat atop his borrowed horse, Soult's bay stallion.

Everywhere the air billows with the discharge of musket and cannon, the noise buffeting against Richard's chest. Emile reaches out a hand to steady him before pulling alongside his emperor and exchanging words. Grasping the bay's reins, he heels his own horse urgently and they shoot away from the crossroads. La Belle Alliance, where all had still been possible this morning, falls behind them.

A few guns still bark defiance from the nearby artillery. A motley assortment of cavalry troopers holds steady along with the reserve battalions of the Old Guard. They know the battle is lost. Defeat is bitter like cordite in their dry mouths but they stand firm when all around them, the roads are flooded with fleeing troops. All order is lost in a breakneck race to slip from the battlefield before the advancing Prussians roll them up and cut them down.

The Guard's sacrifice is magnificent and it buys the time Bonaparte needs. Beyond the inn, on the road south, sits the emperor's carriage, blue bordered in gold with the imperial arms decorating its doors.

His driver paces nervously amidst a detachment of the Guard forcing refugees from the battlefield to by-pass them. Emile saws on his horse's reins and pulls Napoleon's mount to a halt with his other hand.

Bonaparte's head slumps between his shoulders, hiding his eyes from the sights around him. Somehow, his bicorn hat is still on his head. His hands are entwined in his replacement horse's mane and his toes sit tenuously in the stirrups.

The driver steps forward and offers his exhausted commander a hand. Napoleon stirs and reaches out but his weight slews to his left and he slides from the saddle, taking the liveried driver by surprise. He tries to brace himself against the weight of Bonaparte's slack body but he loses his footing and collapses with the fallen emperor on top of him.

Emile shouts in horror. Richard throws himself from his steady mare, hitting the ground with force. He rolls on impact and is straight back to his feet. Five strides and he kneels beside Napoleon. Emile joins him, having retrieved the ubiquitous black felt hat.

'Help me get him into the coach! I will travel with him,' Richard says.

'Be quick, for God's sake, we are almost overrun!' exclaims Emile. 'Driver! Get us moving as soon as the emperor is on board.'

Richard and Emile lift Napoleon under his arms and the driver opens the door before springing onto the box seat for the off. Richard enters first and hauls Bonaparte forward, with Emile pushing from behind. They manage to get Napoleon upright.

Emile steps away, shouting, 'Ride man, stop for nothing!'

Richard hears the coachman's whip and the carriage jerks forward. A few mounted guardsmen accompany Emile and the other outriders, while the grenadiers stay behind as a final rearguard.

Turning to Bonaparte, Richard is struck by his sallow, slack features smeared with the dirt of battle. His eyelids droop and his chin is on his chest but he mutters under his breath. It is dim inside the carriage, the interior lamps unlit, and it grows darker as dusk descends. The sounds of panic outside are muffled by sumptuous, quilted velvet.

Searching the interior, he finds a mahogany travelling case containing a pair of decanters and silver cups. Richard sniffs both and pours a generous measure of what he thinks is rum. He holds the cup to Napoleon's slack lips, tilting and supporting his head with one hand. The fumes cause a flutter of eyelids and he coaxes some spirit down his patient's throat. Slowly, more rum leaves the cup and Napoleon opens his eyes fully.

Richard cannot help staring. He holds his hero in his arms but he is looking into the face of utter desolation. 'Sire, it is good to see you recovering.'

'I recognise you. The American? It seems you had the right of it this morning.' The emperor's voice is hollow. 'I needed more men. Joseph was wasteful and Ney unimaginative. Why did I not take closer control? Why did I not heed your warning and send after Grouchy to return?'

Richard shakes his head sympathetically. 'Questions for another day, sire. We must keep you from the clutches of your enemies so you may fight on.' He pours more rum and Napoleon does not resist, guzzling it greedily, as if eager to numb his synapses from firing more painful questions. They sit in silence for some time as the coach bumps over the cobbles.

'Will they even remember me?' It is a slurred mumble, probably part of an internal monologue, but Richard cannot help replying. 'You cannot doubt it. You remain my hero, sire. You raised France up to glory! Your name will be familiar to everyone even two hundred years from now.'

Bonaparte looks at Richard sharply but then a hint of a smile trembles at the edge of his mouth. 'I fear you picked a poor day to meet your hero, sir!'

The coach slows dramatically and shouts echo all around. Emile leans down from his saddle and taps on the window. Richard reaches across the emperor and releases the spring-loaded blind.

'The traffic is impossible,' complains Emile. 'The bridge at Genappe is constricting everything. We must abandon the coach. Can the emperor ride?'

Richard supports Napoleon as Emile opens the door and helps him stand, head ducking as he exits. Richard retrieves the bicorn hat. His own headgear is long lost, left at Le Caillou early this morning.

He glances around the plush burgundy and green interior for a final time and spots a pair of calfskin gloves. He reaches for them.

'Hurry Richard, we must go!'

He withdraws his hand. 'Enjoy them, Madame Odillet!'

Outside, Emile and a tall guardsman help Napoleon remount. As the emperor sits in the saddle, the stallion whiffles and paws the cobbles, eager to be off. His nostrils flare and he looks willing to run until his heart bursts.

Richard manages to mount his mare without help, despite his aching body. They ride along the verge beside the road pursued by four imperial guards who have cut the carriage horses free from their traces and are riding them bareback, hands knotted in immaculate manes.

As they close on the bridge, out of the deepening dark, a jam of baggage wagons appears, spilling onto the soft ground either side of the road, along with discarded artillery pieces. Men are abandoning carts to join the fleeing soldiers crawling underneath their vehicles, dodging horses' hooves to reach the bridge.

Emile leads the mounted party cross country, over an already trampled field of rye to the river bank. The river Dyle is not wide but the current menaces after the recent rain. Lieutenant Béraud signals for the grenadiers to escort their emperor into the moonlit water.

Richard has his hands full staying on his placid mare's back as she high-steps down the bank into the flow. Her head comes up but she wades forward, following the bareback riders, the lieutenant and the emperor until water touches Richard's boots.

He clings to the reins, sitting stiffly until the water recedes. His mare reaches the far side and with a heave of her powerful haunches, springs up the bank to join the others.

No sooner are all clear of the river than they are away, hooves clattering on cobbles as they trot through the chaos of the village. Men jostle each other and swear while others slump against the church wall or forage for food or drink.

The atmosphere is febrile. Torches flare and desultory gunfire suggests the killing is not finished. Richard shivers and edges his mount closer to Emile and Bonaparte.

They press on to the south, further from the sounds of pursuit, into clearer air where the moon illuminates the scene like an old Dutch master painting. As they reach the crossroads at Quatre Bras, Emile shouts to Richard, 'Such a nondescript name but Wellington did well to hold it on Thursday!'

Richard nods, surveying the loose array of buildings, pock-marked in places, shattered in others. Suddenly, the emperor sits bolt upright, reclaims his reins with his left hand and raises his right.

'Halt!' Bonaparte's voice is unnaturally high as he gazes at the surrounding fields. Glistening in the moonlight are thousands of naked corpses. Among the bodies prowl black cloaked carrion crows, buzzards and furtive furred creatures with sharp eyes; foxes, rats and stoats.

'Stripped and picked clean!' exclaims one of the grenadiers

with a shudder, doubtless imagining how easily this could be his fate.

'Dead because of me,' Napoleon confides to Emile, who shakes his head.

'They died for France. There is no greater honour than to fall in service to the emperor!'

Napoleon stretches out a wavering arm, as if trying to bat away the lieutenant's words. He slumps in his saddle again and Emile catches up the slack reins. He coaxes Marengo's replacement forward and they ease back to a trot, ever southwards.

Through Charleroi and on to Philippeville. Sunday becomes Monday. Joined by Marshal Soult, Count Bertrand and Drouot. Numb with exhaustion they approach the French border. It is morning; another day. The eighteenth of June 1815 is history. Again!

'French soil,' says Marshal Soult. Napoleon ignores him. Emile tries to smile.

'I must write to my brother Joseph,' insists Bonaparte, trying to bring his horse to a stop. It is the third mount he has ridden since losing Marengo in the chaos. This gelding does not like him, black flanks always twitching, head too high, eyes wide, froth around the bit and sweat staining ebony muscles with salt.

They stop in a quiet village. The houses are shuttered, the street empty. A dog barks. They hear chickens disagreeing. A child cries and is hushed. There is a coaching inn. The gates to the courtyard open. They ride in and guardsmen hold their horses.

Richard slides from the saddle aching everywhere. By the time he straightens his back, Napoleon has been helped down and is disappearing into the inn. Several guards begin watering the horses from the trough while others look for feed in the stable block.

Inside the inn it is gloomy. Count Bertrand disappears in search of the innkeeper. Drouot produces pen and paper for the emperor and sees him settled by the window, where the light is a little better. Motes of dust float in pale shafts that pierce the distorted panes of the window. Bertrand returns accompanied by a sour man with a warty face and a staring eye.

'Breakfast!' commands Soult. Reluctantly, the proprietor bows and exits to the far side of the common room. He shouts coarsely and receives shrill replies.

Richard sits at the far end of the table where the emperor is poised, pen in hand, a frown on his face.

Bertrand approaches. 'May I, sire?' He gestures at the blank page. Napoleon cedes the pen. Bertrand sits beside him and slides the paper along the table. His face is composed, his eyes kind and his hand steady.

Drouot, whose artillery was so frustrated by the mud but bellowed fiercely for most of the previous day, sits motionless, staring at his dirty boots.

Bonaparte begins, 'My dear eldest brother, all is not lost. I estimate that collecting all my forces, I shall have 150,000 men left.' A plate is dropped deep in the building; a curse and a slap. Gentle sobbing.

Soult stands up glowering but Bonaparte waves him back to his seat. 'Leave it! These are the sounds of the living. I relish them today.'

Tears spring into Richard's eyes, surprising him. He wipes them away surreptitiously but the emperor sees.

'Thank you, my American friend. I must continue, time is short.' He pats Bertrand's wrist, causing a drop of ink to fall. 'The National Guard and other battalions will give another 150,000. I can drag my artillery with carriage horses.' Drouot sighs but does not move or speak. 'I can raise 100,000 conscripts.'

A phlegmy cough interrupts, the landlord appears with a full tray of cold meats and cheese along with a pitcher and some rough glasses. He sets them down close to Richard, keeping as far from Napoleon as possible.

Richard cannot bear to listen any more. He walks across the common room and finds himself standing beside the patron, who wipes a table with a filthy rag. 'Where's your uniform? Got rid of it already? Don't blame you!' His voice is unhealthy, words bubbling through wet lips.

'I am not a soldier.' Somehow the truth sounds forlorn.

'Me neither, but I had a son who was. Jean. Conscripted into the bloody Marie-Louises. Rags was all they had to wear. A new blue cap with a red number. A grey coat with holes in it. That and a musket!'

Richard tries to look sympathetic as the landlord spits loudly onto the tiled floor. 'He was only fourteen. Wanted to be a blacksmith. Two weeks' training was all they got. He was only in the army two months when he died.'

Richard knows how short of men Napoleon became after the debacle in Russia. Assaulted on all sides, he resorted to desperate measures. He tries to imagine the boy's terror facing his first engagement but all he sees is the blank face of a dead

German rifleman.

What would Aunt Patricia's reaction have been, had she seen him marched off to war at fourteen? Uncharitable thoughts crowd in and he chases them away angrily.

He watches Napoleon dictating and wonders if the man has a conscience? From two hundred years away, it was easy to excuse the losses. He was a man of his time. War was just diplomacy by other means. The coalitions raised against France gave him no choice. Big answers to big questions but they miss something fundamental.

Richard glances at the dissolute landlord. In every crease of his face, underneath every dirty nail, ingrained in his worn clothes and swimming in his watery eyes, is loss. Not the loss of a generation or the loss of an empire, neither the loss of reputation or a gamble but the loss of hope in the loss of a single boy plucked away before he could become a man.

'You blame him?' Richard askes sotto voce.

The innkeeper shoots him a furtive look and then another towards the grey-coated figure. He wipes his face with the same rag he was using on the tables. 'I do. What did my boy die for? This,' he waves his rag at the other side of the room, disturbing the dust motes, 'is Jean's epitaph? To die in service to him? He could have wrought a lifetime of metalwork that would do service for generations. That would have been a life. To fall in love, settle down, have children perhaps? That man stole it all and more. He stole my legacy. Jean was that.' He is teary now and wipes his face again, rubbing the dirt deeper into the crevices and creases, wrinkles and lines. Richard looks away. 'He should have stayed where they put him.' There is no doubt who the innkeeper means.

'A gilded cage?' Elba. The words are out before he can stop them.

Colour spreads across the grieving father's face, broken veins lurid against coarse skin. 'Better than a pine box under six feet of soil.'

There is nothing to be said to that. He nods and leaves the distraught man in search of Emile.

They are in a carriage, donated by General Dupuy, commander of the Philippeville garrison. Richard is still with Napoleon. He cannot believe it. He feels dirty and he aches everywhere. The hours of creaking springs blur. He falls asleep and dreams.

He stood at the foot of the Lion's Mound. A vast earthwork, looming over one hundred and forty feet high and one thousand seven hundred feet in circumference. He peered up the steep grassy slope to the statue at the apex. Richard knew the bronze lion weighed thirty-one tons and was over fourteen feet in length.

He had climbed to the top more than once but today he turned his back to gaze along the ridge of Mont St Jean, the site Wellington chose to anchor his dispositions. There was a hamlet on the reverse slope, while the farm of the same name stood closer to the escarpment facing the French positions. Richard had decided on the day before the battle, to give him the best chance of making his way to Napoleon.

He was acutely aware of the flaws in his preparation. His clothes would look dated to a discerning eye. His warrant from Marshal Davout was ten years old. He had forged a second letter with an appropriate date commending him to the emperor.

Unsure of his paperwork, he had decided to fall back on the one fact that might play to his advantage. He was English, as was a fair part of the Duke's army. He was most likely to be convincing in his own language, certainly in the first seconds after his arrival.

He walked across the ridge top towards the farm that was at the rear of the Allied lines on the eighteenth of June 1815. To appear unexpectedly in no-man's-land was to be shot. To surprise the French inside their lines was equally risky. He hoped stumbling around among English troops, he could forestall a musket ball, with a few well-chosen words.

As he walked, he audited what he was carrying. Apart from two documents wrapped in oilskin, he had a wooden handled pen-knife and a good Belgian dried sausage folded in a clean handkerchief. He carried a decent pocket-watch that kept reasonable time. His knapsack contained a change of clothing and a canteen of water.

Although the sun was shining and the sky unbroken blue, he had arrived wearing his overcoat. It was now in the bag, folded carefully to avoid excessive creasing.

He did not have the battlefield to himself. He needed to find a discreet spot. He had no way of knowing how time of day might translate across the centuries. He was hoping it would be instantaneous, apart from the small matter of some two hundred years.

It was late morning. Many tourists had enjoyed their tours and headed for a meal or other distractions. He heard them milling around the farm buildings housing a museum, microbrewery, distillery and shop.

Beyond the farm, he veered left to keep clear of the crowds and sought an empty spot at the foot of the slope, where a country lane meandered towards the route to Wavre.

This was where Major-General Ponsonby's cavalry was stationed for the start of the battle, immediately behind the 5th Division under Lieutenant-General Picton. The troops were a mix of English, Scottish and Irish, hence their name, the Union Brigade. Here he was certain his language would be an advantage. Elsewhere, Wellington's army spoke Dutch and German.

Richard looked across the valley floor to the south, marvelling at how compact the battlefield appeared. Just a thousand yards away, was the slope where the French marshalled their forces for the battle.

Napoleon would base himself at the inn of La Belle Alliance while Wellington kept returning to an elm tree at a crossroads on the ridge his forces commanded. The distance between those two spots was three-quarters of a mile.

Richard wondered if they could see each other as the events of the day ebbed and flowed? Surely with a spyglass?

A small tour party approached him, led by a guide holding a flag on a short pole. Phones appeared as he became the centre of attention in his Regency finery.

'Don't you just love it when they wear period costume?' asked a southern drawl.

'I do indeed, so authentic!' replied her much larger friend as she videoed the scene.

Richard managed a grimace they took for a smile. He had

always loathed re-enactments and avoided sites where staff pretended to be characters from the past, particularly when they insisted on staying in that character no matter what.

Fortunately, the group was on a tight schedule and they were soon hurried away by their guide. Their chatter dwindled and Richard took another look around.

There was no one close by. This was his moment. He pulled the shoe buckle from his pocket and held it firmly in his left hand. He screwed his eyes shut and conjured all his dissatisfactions into a dense cloud.

He spared nothing. His personal shortcomings. His stuttering career. The lack of love. Each element added to the dark density of the cloud. He pressed in on it, condensing it, keeping it low in his stomach, an oily, sickening maelstrom.

Satisfied, he summoned everything that attracted him to 1815. The drama, the significance, the scale, the two combatants.

He let the colour of it explode inside him, swelling with his own emotions, never so bright, so safe, so excited, so happy as when immersed.

The immensity threatened to burst his chest, filling his throat and dazzling him. He grew rigid as he forced the crescendo of colour and wonder down into the black whirlpool of angst.

As the kaleidoscope reached the seething morass, glittering tendrils snaked out, like an octopus enclosing its prey. At first, the prismatic brightness stalled, slipping along the surface tension of his darkest thoughts and feelings. But gradually they penetrated the inky perimeter, diffusing colours deep into the well of blackness.

The nature of the darkness began to change, no longer an absolute absence of light. Richard was weakening. He talked to himself, coaxing his hopes onwards, no longer downwards but inwards, to penetrate and dilute.

Shadows of grey flickered near the core. The concentrated vitriol disintegrated around the edges while the centre grew pale.

'Please let this work! Let this be 1815! There is nothing else. I only want this!' He cannot hear his words because blood pounds so loudly in his ears. Shaking violently, his vision ignites. He staggers but keeps his feet. It is over.

There is an empty feeling in his chest and his stomach churns. Jolted roughly, Richard opens his eyes, there are no British lines readying for battle, just the shadowy interior of a coach juddering at high speed.

Paris in 1815. No Eiffel Tower. The Arc de Triomphe is still being built! No wide avenues flanked by elegant buildings. No sprawling suburbs but a scatter of separate towns, moons circling their planet. Narrow streets, leering buildings, the smell of too many people and too little sanitation.

The cobbles are hard beneath iron bound wheels. It is early as they approach the centre. The streets are empty, as if the city does not have the heart to wake this morning. Every shop is closed and every house shuttered.

'The city looks dead. Rats are most active at such times.' There is steel in Napoleon's eyes but he looks and smells defeated.

The magnificence of the Elysée Palace appears. Richard

looks up and recognises its mansard roof. Below, two floors of tall windows flank the entrance beneath its classical portico. The wings of the building extend comforting arms around the party. The pale stone washed in early sunshine makes Richard think of lemons.

As the carriage halts, a figure appears on the steps. Napoleon winces.

'Caulaincourt. He has not loved me for a long time. But when I left him, all things were possible. Now? He will no doubt tell me!'

Richard sits in the coach as Bonaparte steps tiredly out, helped down by a liveried servant who appeared as if by magic. 'Follow on, my American friend. You have come this far, are you not intrigued as to what will happen next?'

Richard grins and hurries from the cocoon of the coach into the stark daylight. Emile still sits on his horse.

'Stay close, Lieutenant.' Bonaparte pauses and frowns. 'You have seen the best and worst of me. Stay if you wish or depart with my blessing.'

Emile dismounts in a fluid motion despite his tiredness. He bows deeply.

'To the end, sire!'

Napoleon sniffs. 'That may not be long in coming. I must seize my fate back from the hands of others.' With that, he strides up the steps and enters the palace with Caulaincourt immediately behind him.

Richard follows, still expecting to be chased away at any moment. Looking back on the threshold, he sees Emile lead his horse away, no doubt in search of water, feed and a brush like any good cavalryman.

They pass through a succession of lavish rooms overwhelmed by gold. Richard wants to stroll through the splendour but Bonaparte is in a hurry. All he can do is glimpse the magnificent tapestries, portraits, ornate furniture and rich carpets from the corner of his eye. Everything looks improbably new.

Napoleon smiles as he reaches his study. 'A bath at last!' he announces.

Richard looks down at himself and blushes. He is scruffy in the extreme. What was once white is grey, what was blue is grey with dried mud and ingrained dust. He has sponged the blood from his head leaving his shirt pink at the neck. His breeches are torn and his boots scuffed.

As Napoleon's valet begins removing his master's clothes, another servant appears to usher Richard to an adjoining room. A copper bath is man-handled into the elegant withdrawing room. Richard hears no orders given. Perhaps his need is so obvious nothing needs to be said.

He submits to the attentions of a slender, precise manservant with elegant movements and a discreet habit of looking away at the right times. Other liveried servants appear carrying steaming gilt ewers to fill the bath.

Once he is sunk beneath the surface of the hot water, Richard closes his eyes. There is a lot to think about.

He has witnessed Waterloo. He has tried to help Bonaparte avoid his fate. He has failed. It seems some things are just meant to be, simply too large to be nudged in a different direction.

He squirms as more hot water is added. He doesn't want to think too hard about his predicament. Better enjoy the bath, scrub himself clean and emerge ready for anything.

He does not see Napoleon again that day. He hears people come and go next door where the emperor struggles with his new reality.

Once washed, he eats greedily from trays that appear, laden with enough food for four, wrapped in a robe lined with a fur he cannot identify. It is so soft he only reluctantly takes it off to try on a selection of clothes brought for his consideration.

He passes the whole morning making his choices. More food appears and he gorges again.

He dozes the afternoon away on a day bed, reading fitfully from recent editions of *Le Moniteur*. From the newspapers, he would not know Bonaparte had suffered a catastrophic defeat!

At first, the Battle of Mont St Jean is a resounding victory and the emperor celebrates in Brussels. '*Veni, Vidi, Vici*,' is the message Napoleon sent to Paris at three in the afternoon from the battlefield.

The next two editions continue to talk of victory, supplying spurious details like forty captured cannon and thousands of prisoners.

The official announcement of defeat is only in the latest copy and glossed heavily as a glorious achievement. It is Wednesday. Tomorrow, Napoleon Bonaparte will abdicate in favour of his son, a gesture that means nothing.

Richard cannot read the full account of the battle. He lets the paper slip to the floor and closes his eyes again. He is clean and comfortable and full of food. He sleeps but his dreams are not happy.

He is back in the sloping woods below Hougoumont. It is darker between the trees than he remembers and the noise of the desperate struggle around the chateau is louder. Their two escorts melt away as soon as he thinks of them, leaving Richard and Emile alone.

In his mind, the wood is crawling with snipers so skilful they merge with the trees, red uniforms invisible as if, asleep, he is colour blind. Creeping forward, every leaf and twig shifts beneath their boots emitting improbably loud noises. Even their breathing is like the panting of a mastiff.

He watches helplessly as Emile spots a skirmisher and charges him, sword drawn. Where is his carbine? Richard tries to follow but his feet become impossibly tangled in the roots of a tree.

He topples over and hits his head against the trunk. Red and green fireworks explode in his head, he spits out leaf mould again and again, fighting for breath.

Emile is struggling too, feet mired in molasses. He is moving too slowly. The rifleman is calmly reloading.

Richard raises his hands to loose a shot only to find they are empty. No, his left hand holds a marshal's baton!

He throws it in frustration and watches it hurtle like a projectile straight for the soldier. It strikes end on, piercing the man's forehead with such force it bores through his brain and pins the poor wretch to the tree behind him. There he dangles, astonishment on his face as life drains from his eyes.

Richard hears the thump of a howitzer launching its deadly cargo skywards. A whistle announces the bomb's descent. It lands at Emile's feet, fuse uppermost and sizzling dramatically.

The lieutenant stares in puzzlement. It explodes with a devastating blast, filling the spaces between the trees with smoke. Richard fights the snagging roots to hobble forward.

The smoke clears from around the shattered stumps of trees to reveal a crater where Emile had been.

Richard opens his mouth to lament the loss of his companion but words die on his lips as another Hanoverian marksman steps from his hiding place and pulls his trigger. The ball punches into Richard's chest, hurling him backwards.

He comes to rest in a sitting position, back to a tree, legs in front of him. Skin ruptured and burnt, muscle torn through, blood vessels severed, deep tissue penetrated, bones cracked. He feels each element of the damage as his blood leaks away, no longer channelled by arteries. Fragments of powder and cloth drive deep into his chest cavity.

The start of sepsis, a building pressure of yellow pus filling his wound and spilling through his shattered system.

He shuts his eyes tight but he is still inside himself. His dispassionate assessment of the damage gives way to pain. He screams but the trees muffle the sound. They dampen the sound but not the sensation. He moans and rolls onto his side. His shrieking gives way to raving as fever wracks his body. He is slipping. His shoulders shake, cold sweat prickling hot skin.

He opens his eyes. Looming over him is the manservant who has looked after him with such discretion. His aesthetic face is a picture of concern. He grips Richard by his shoulders, preventing him from rolling off the day bed. The shaking was his attempt to wake Richard before his nightmare disturbed the emperor next door.

'Forgive me,' he whispers feebly. His lips are cracked and his mouth as dry as a desert. Before he can ask, the servant produces a glass of water. 'Thank you. What is your name?' He does not know the protocol. He is not sure he cares.

The man raises an eyebrow. 'I am Pierre, sir.' He helps Richard sit up and plumps a cushion for his back.

'Thank you for your care, Pierre. My name is Richard Davey. I am an American supporter of the emperor.'

A flicker behind Pierre's grey eyes.

'Does that surprise you, Pierre? We are a republic and Bonaparte was born of the revolution.'

Pierre looks away, as if he does not want to see the lie in Richard's eyes. 'What is it, Pierre?'

'It is not my place, Monsieur Davey.' His speech is as exact as his actions.

'Please, speak freely. I have no standing here. We are equals, you and I.' Pierre allows a sceptical look to cloud his slim face. 'I have known some Americans, Monsieur. You do not sound like them.' There is a hint of apology in Pierre's observation but the set of his mouth is resolved.

Richard has never really thought clearly about his future in the past. He fixated on that Sunday in June 1815. Now it is in the middle of the next week and his implausible web of deceit is unravelling.

'And where were these men from? Just as there is much difference between the Languedoc, Alsace, Brittany and Paris, so there is great variation in my country. We trace our roots to England and Ireland, Scotland and many other parts of Europe too. Some preserve the accents of their forefathers while others do not.' He cannot read Pierre's face. 'In truth, I have spent much time as an agent in England where it has paid me to be taken as a local. One slip might betray my life, so necessity becomes habit.'

Pierre looks distinctly uncomfortable at having compelled a guest of the emperor to justify himself. 'My deepest apologies, Monsieur Davey. I have heard it said a little knowledge is a dangerous thing.' He smiles, revealing remarkably well-preserved teeth.

Richard smiles back and hopes his relief is not too obvious.

Chapter Eight

Richard turns in after supper. He expects to lie awake, imagining the contradictory thoughts assailing his host. Preferable to dreams of death. But sleep he does, as if he has not rested all day.

No dead men's eyes accuse him and he wakes to the smells of breakfast. Another feast! He eats all the fruit and pastries he can, washed down with several small cups of aromatic coffee.

'Pierre, I would like to explore the palace. Would that be permitted?'

The valet bows. 'You are the emperor's guest, Monsieur.'

Richard smiles awkwardly. Within hours Napoleon Bonaparte will cede his title, his authority, his empire.

He lets Pierre hold the towering white and gold doors aside for him and goes exploring. He wanders back and forth.

Finding the library, he feels at home despite the grandeur of the bookcases and the ancient languages he cannot read.

There is a room where blue wall coverings match the opulent pattern of its gold framed furniture.

In another, the walls are painted with geographical scenes. Map cases are arrayed in fine cabinets, each leather tube labelled in copperplate script.

Yet another room is entirely hung with tapestries celebrating great events from French history.

He even finds one inspired by French discoveries during the invasion of Egypt.

Finally, he reaches the *Salon d'Argent* in the East Wing, decorated by Napoleon's sister Caroline. She is married to Murat, that dashing, charismatic cavalryman, the dandy king of Naples. She certainly knew what she liked and she liked silver!

He sits in an ornate chair looking at a white desk on tapered legs, picked out with silver detail. This is where Bonaparte will finally accept his fate and sign his abdication.

Richard has always believed there was nothing inevitable about the emperor's demise, even after Waterloo. He had choices as his brother Lucien has pointed out.

What if he engineers another meeting with Napoleon, might he sway him to stand firm? He imagines himself by Bonaparte's side as he fights to rescue his regime!

He jumps from the plush seat and walks briskly from room to room, heading for the imperial study.

He finds Marchand, the valet, guarding the door. 'I am afraid you cannot be admitted, the emperor is in conference.'

The valet is a handsome, well-spoken young man with fashionable chestnut side whiskers and matching eyes. His manner is studious and impeccably polite but he gives the impression he will die before he opens the door.

'May I ask when the emperor might be free to speak with his guest? I have an important perspective to share with his Imperial Highness.'

Marchand inclines his head respectfully. 'He will be busy until lunch. Perhaps in the later afternoon?'

This sounds like a brush off. 'But that will be too late! He will have already abdicated!' Richard's voice is frantic and echoes in the vast corridor, 'Abdicated... abdicated!' He winces.

Marchand looks horrified, his hands and face pleading with Richard to keep silent. 'Please, Monsieur! Do not say such things! His Imperial Majesty, long may he reign, must not be disturbed.'

Richard raises his hands in frustration but turns away, a sense of inevitability settling on him.

He retraces his steps to find the grand entrance where the carriage deposited them the previous day.

He detains a servant in the entrance hall. 'Can you tell me where I might find Lieutenant Emile Béraud of the Chasseurs of the Imperial Guard?'

The plump, powdered lackey looks blank.

'The lieutenant who accompanied the emperor upon his return?'

A glimmer of recognition. 'Try the stables, Monsieur.' The liveried servant indicates the left wing curving around the courtyard.

He finds the serried stalls without trouble. Carriage horses munch contentedly from nets of hay. He is almost at the end of the cubicles when he hears a voice talking in soft, affectionate tones. A whickering is the only reply.

'Emile, is that you?'

The lieutenant's head appears over the half door to a stall. 'Richard! Tell me, what is it like to share accommodations with the emperor?' he teases but his smile is kind.

'I have not seen him since we arrived but the palace is very fine. I feel entirely out of place.'

Emile nods. 'I am happier among the smell of dung.' Emile opens the door to the stall and steps out, latching it behind him. He wears a pair of green overalls and has removed his jacket and waistcoat. He replaces a pair of brushes on a nearby shelf and sighs. He pats the horse's nose and rubs beneath his long chin. 'I do not even know where this beast came from but he is in my care.'

Richard understands taking refuge in the familiar but he doesn't have that option. 'Emile, I don't know what to do. Bonaparte is going to abdicate today. I know he is with his advisers but they cannot be relied upon to give him impartial advice. Half of them served Louis XVIII when he was exiled to Elba. They will be positioning themselves to do so again. Most of the rest are either too loyal, too dislocated from reality or too greedy.'

He expects the lieutenant to object to his assassination of the emperor's inner circle but Emile places a hand on his shoulder. 'I doubted you once. But at Mont St Jean everything occurred as you said it would. This time I do not doubt. What do you need?' There is steel in his voice and his eyes spark.

'I need to speak with Bonaparte alone and I need to do it now.'

Emile pulls his waistcoat from a peg and slips it on.

Five minutes later, Richard is hurrying in Emile's wake as he strides purposefully over the polished floors of the palace. One more corner brings them onto a long corridor with the emperor's study at the end.

As Richard expects, Marchand stands by the door eyeing them with suspicion. '*Messieurs*, I have already told this one,' he indicates Richard, 'the emperor is not available.'

Emile does not bother speaking; he simply grasps the valet

by his lapels and sets him to one side. He then seizes the ornate handle and hauls the door open, gesturing Richard inside.

A group of dignitaries surround Napoleon. They are all talking at once. As Richard and Emile enter, they fall silent, staring in disbelief. Fouché moves forwards frowning, cheeks flushed, eyes like daggers.

The family are there. Napoleon's mother sits primly beside Hortense, a living memorial to Josephine, her mother. They do not look at each other. Lucien looks fiery, Joseph beaten down and Jérôme unperturbably arrogant.

General Solignac, representing the Chamber of Deputies, scowls impatiently. Carnot, the reformer and mathematician, engineer, politician and soldier looks up with interest, a late addition to the inner circle but yet to disappoint the emperor.

Fouché reaches out to detain Emile but Napoleon intervenes. 'Desist! I have been remiss with my guests. They have languished while I think only of myself.'

'No sire, you are thinking of France!' Lucien is not finished; to Richard he looks as if he would see every citizen's blood spilt before the end.

Napoleon shakes his head. 'Leave us!' Richard starts to turn. 'My dear family, we will lunch together soon. But until then,' he waves at the still open door, filled with the apologetic figure of Marchand. 'Fouché, I have seen enough of you for a lifetime. General, the Chamber shall have my answer this very afternoon. Count Carnot, it has been a pleasure, we are more alike than you might imagine.'

The force of Napoleon's personality has recharged in these grand surroundings. Nobody demurs as they file out, not

189

even Fouché, chief of police, spymaster and consummate survivor. Marchand closes the door as the last of the party departs, no doubt positioning himself to inform all comers that the emperor is in conference and cannot be disturbed.

Emile bows low, holding the obeisance for a long time. 'Forgive me, my emperor! There was no other way. Monsieur Davey felt it essential he speak with you this morning and there were obstructions.'

'Marchand is loyal. It is a good quality for the most part, would you not agree?' He sounds tired but uncowed.

'Indeed, sire. I presume to claim the same attribute.'

Napoleon nods, apparently satisfied. 'You have done as you saw fit. Now it is for me to judge whether your action was justified.'

He turns his face to Richard. 'So, my American friend. Here you are again. Let us see whether your presence can turn the tide of history this time!'

Richard inclines his head briefly but he is studying Bonaparte. He looks worn. 'I believe you still have options, sire.'

Emile stands beside the door, looking guiltily at his green overalls, a clear breach of protocol. The imperial escort always wears buff deerskin breeches on duty.

Richard sees his discomfort and smiles. Bonaparte seats Richard opposite him in a chair backed in blue silk embroidered with an N beneath a crown of golden bees. The well stuffed upholstery makes Richard sit up straight, as if he is in the deputy head's study.

Napoleon does not have the demeanour of a teacher. He is dressed as colonel of the Imperial Guard Grenadiers, as he

190

usually is at home. Resplendent in royal blue and white, with red at his cuffs and gold epaulettes on his shoulders, he sits in front of Richard. A single lick of hair curls across his deep forehead, accentuating his receding hairline. There is a blue tinge to his chin although he appears to have shaved.

His eyes astonish Richard. They have always looked so deep and dark their colour was obscured. But here he is, looking intently at Richard with piercing eyes, all redness banished. They are blue! The blue of the ocean through a light sea fret, the horizon lost against the pale echo of the sky.

The emperor's white waistcoat is only buttoned at the bottom, allowing him to slip his right hand inside. It looks awkward as he sits back but Richard knows it is regarded as a gesture of power, often favoured in portraits. Perhaps Bonaparte is grasping at anything that suggests he is still in control?

'Tell me.'

Richard takes a deep breath. 'Dissolve the Chamber of Deputies and the Senate. Dismiss Fouché and Talleyrand. Arrest your enemies in the city. Declare emergency powers. Rally the city defences. Send someone trustworthy to negotiate with the Coalition. Accept the old borders. Appeal to the ordinary people of France, promise them the revolution is not dead. Topple all the cronies and schemers, place-men and royalists. Sweep the city clean. Coordinate with Grouchy in case you have to fight for time.'

It comes out in a rush and a jumble. Everything he thought studying Napoleon's demise from two hundred years away.

A crease forms on the emperor's pale forehead. 'You have been inside my mind, my American ally. Not one of these ideas but I have entertained it! Yet the Allies would denounce me as a dictator and vow to depose me.'

Richard clenches his teeth and presses on. 'They denounced you as the instrument of the revolution and again as a tyrant, an illegitimate ruler and a warmonger, what insults do they have left that can touch you? You are Napoleon Bonaparte, Emperor of the French!'

'My brother Lucien is of your mind. He reminds me of times when I did not hesitate. I had such certainty. Now the fates conspire against me! Those devilish English moneylenders have financed my enemies again and again. They have denied France peace! They forced me to fight when I would not. Enough! Time to end the sacrifices of the French people by sacrificing myself.'

'But sire, you would surrender your empire to pygmies! These wretched cowards in the Chamber, these men who kow-towed to fat Louis are preparing to do it again. Can you surrender France to him?'

Bonaparte stands and walks to the window. He draws aside the net curtain. He opens the window and the sounds of the city drift in.

There is a crowd in the surrounding streets despite Fouché's best efforts to have his police disperse them.

'Long live the empire! Long live the emperor!' There are shouts of agreement but cat calls too, merging with the sound of hawkers selling their wares and complaints from carriage drivers and their masters at the obstruction.

'The mob! It is a thing to be feared. We learned that in the revolution. Those people down there are vagrants and troublemakers. They thrill at moments like these. It makes them feel alive, as if they matter! But they are here because they have no jobs, no responsibilities.'

Richard joins the emperor at the window. 'Then give them jobs and responsibilities. Arm them, train them, harness them to your purpose.'

'My days as a radical are over. It is for your young country to realize such dreams. Perhaps we should travel there together?'

Richard senses the spark. There is still an appetite for life beneath the sallow, sagging exterior. But his own lie will unravel quickly if he agrees.

Emile has not said a word, standing stiff as a statue against the wall. Richard glances at him, imploring him to intervene.

'Sire, if I may speak?'

A weight lifts from Richard. Napoleon nods without turning from his view of the sky and the sounds of the crowd.

'I am nobody, but here I stand. You raised me up! There are many thousands like me across your empire. What are we to do if you leave us?'

At that, Bonaparte does turn, a look of profound sadness on his face. 'You are my children. I have helped you grow but you are infants no more. You must live for yourselves and your families, for the future of France.' There are tears in his eyes.

'Sire, what future will France have without you? The fat king returned, a lackey of your enemies. The Allies will occupy France and strip her bare. They will crush our spirit and persecute those who have given most in your service.' Emile speaks from the heart, his hands reaching out expressively, as if addressing a brother. Richard is moved.

'You ask what will happen if I go and paint a sorry picture. Better to ask what will happen if I stay?' Napoleon sounds dejected.

So, it is done. Napoleon Bonaparte is no longer Emperor of the French. He has abdicated in favour of his infant son. Napoleon the Second will never rule.

Richard has been in France a week; he has been in 1815 for a week. What has he seen? The defining battle of the age and the end of an era. The end of Napoleon as a political figure. Vanquished by the antipathy of the ruling houses of Europe, determined to crush the idea that a man could simply make himself a monarch. No wonder they are resolved to prevent a second Napoleon on the throne of France. Richard smiles. There will be another within forty years!

Richard and Emile leave Bonaparte's study knowing they have failed. They flee the glamour of the palace for Emile's utilitarian quarters to drink cheap wine until it doesn't hurt so much.

'What will you do now?' asks Emile, lounging on his bed in breeches and a creased shirt.

Richard has existed in the moment but now the prospect of living the rest of his life in the nineteenth century mocks him. Did he give up everything for this?

Suddenly he is awash with affection for the little things of his modern life. Music, beer, football highlights and yes, even Aunt Patricia! 'What is there for me here?' He sounds hollow to his own ears.

Emile refills his glass from a flagon sitting on the boarded floor. Richard does the same. He is drunk and will pay for it tomorrow but he has no intention of stopping. Aunt Patricia would disapprove, letting him know without a word. He drinks deeply.

'I think the emperor was serious when he talked of America. You could be his companion? It is your country after all.'

Richard scowls as if objecting to the sour wine. How much to tell? He is silent for a long time. He wonders whether Emile has fallen asleep?

He looks across the small room to find his new friend's eyes on him.

'I could come too. I should have died in that charge but I didn't. I have lived to see the end of everything I believed in. I will not live in a humiliated country ruled by a collaborator and occupied by enemies. America is a new land, perhaps I could make a life there?'

'What about your family, won't they miss you?'

This time Emile is quiet as Richard continues to drink steadily. Finally, he says, 'I fear I have seen little of them since I joined the army. My parents are dead. My sister is married. There are others to care for the *mandane*, the farm and the bulls.' He sounds as if he is trying to convince himself.

Richard opens one eye and rolls over. He feels bilious and his head is gripped in a tightening vice. He moans. Emile is nowhere to be seen. Slowly, he forces himself into a sitting position. There is a washbasin and a jug half full of water. He tips the water into the bowl and immerses his face, splashing water over his head and neck. A rough towel hangs on a hook and he gropes for it.

If only he had some paracetamol. He needs to drink water, a lot of it. He briefly contemplates the hazards of the Paris water supply in 1815. Footsteps sound in the corridor, hurrying.

Emile bursts in. 'They are evicting him!' He begins to dress in his escort uniform. Richard reaches for his coat hanging beside his makeshift bed on the floor. 'I will join my fellow Chasseurs in accompanying him. Let the world see who we still serve.'

'I'm coming too.'

They hurry into the courtyard. The imperial coach waits at the foot of the steps below the portico. The sun is shining. Napoleon appears. He holds his head up and enters his carriage without a backward glance. A groom hands Emile his horse and is sent scuttling off to saddle one for Richard.

The carriage and escort leave the palace grounds before Richard is mounted. Emile sets a rapid pace and they soon catch the colourful procession as it forces its way through the streets of the city.

Napoleon's coach is emblazoned with a large letter N surrounded by laurels and topped with a crown. His escort of Chasseurs are resplendent in green, gold and red.

People stop and stare. Some wave and a few cheer but many look away awkwardly. News of the abdication has spread through the city like wildfire.

Richard thinks of Elvis near the end, reclusive and addicted, overweight and paranoid, the Elvis his fans never saw even when they were looking right at him.

They head west, cutting across two great meanders of the Seine on fine bridges. Skirting the southern fringe of the Bois de Boulogne then to the north of Saint-Cloud's formal forest pathways. Marie Antoinette's rose garden was there. Richard thinks of all those executions at the height of the revolution, clearing the way for men like Napoleon. Now it is he who is being swept from the stage.

The approach to the chateau is from the north-east, a fine gravel drive flanked by trees, a lawn guarded by topiary pyramids. The house is honeyed stone. The entrance is designed to resemble a military pavilion; a confection in teal, glass and gold. Its faux drapery is flanked by obelisks plundered from Egypt.

The carriage stops smartly, aligning the carriage door with the entrance. Napoleon steps out briskly but does not immediately enter the house. Instead, he strolls along the façade, pausing to caress one of the obelisks with a faraway look on his face. Richard wonders if he is back in Egypt, when he believed the whole world was his for the taking?

Following Emile's lead, Richard dismounts and stands respectfully to one side of the entrance. The main body of the escort remains mounted, horses still as statues, arrayed in pairs along the drive. The former emperor's personal staff make their way into the house to ready it for their master.

Napoleon reaches the far end of the building Josephine lavished so much money on. He turns, his stride measured, hands clasped behind his back. 'Lieutenant Béraud, it is good to see you here. Will you form my personal escort while I remain at Malmaison?'

Emile salutes in acceptance, a grin splitting his handsome features. He turns to the escort party and cuts out the men he wants for their final duty as Chasseurs of the Imperial Guard.

Emile confers with the captain at the head of the column before issuing orders to his chosen sergeant, two corporals, twenty-two troopers and trumpeter. The main body of Chasseurs wheel away at an order from their captain and trot immaculately down the drive.

Emile's men fix bayonets to their musketoons and form a loose perimeter around Bonaparte. They are rigid and alert. Emile, as officer commanding the imperial picket, moves to Bonaparte's side as protocol requires.

'Thank you, Lieutenant. See to your men. Ensure they are billeted comfortably. I would spend a little time with the American, Monsieur Davey. If I need anything, I will send a valet to you.'

Emile salutes, turns and informs his sergeant of their orders.

Napoleon strides over to Richard. 'Will you walk with me? I have need of company but my guardsmen remind me too much of what has passed, and this house,' he gestures fondly, almost indulgently as the shutters are opened, 'Malmaison is another character from my past. I spent happy times here. But in truth, I look at these gardens, overgrown as they are, and I see Josephine as I choose to remember her. Spectacular, extravagant, capricious but most of all, mine. I did not always give her the attention she craved nor did she always show me the respect I was due. Still, that is as it has always been between a man and a woman, am I not correct?'

Richard keeps silent. Napoleon leads them onto the lawn which is in need of mowing. 'Did you know there used to be a whole menagerie wandering through the grounds?' Richard looks suitably surprised. 'It is true, Josephine had all manner of creatures brought here from the furthest places in the world. There were kangaroos and emus, zebras, ostriches, black swans and llamas. I forget what else. Ah yes, she even had a seal!'

Bonaparte smiles, that indulgent look on his face again. 'I should like to see the places from which these exotics came. Pineapples too, she grew hundreds of them, over there.' He points a pudgy finger towards a large orangery. 'Roses were her passion, two hundred and fifty varieties and plants of all kinds sent from Martinique, where she was born.'

Richard hopes companionable silence is what Napoleon wants. They walk in a wide loop, penetrating the fringe of the woods. The shade is pleasant but Richard feels claustrophobic. The smell is too familiar, the slanting shafts of sunlight like the trajectory of projectiles. His mind furnishes a martial soundtrack and he heaves a sigh when they return to the open lawn.

'Enough! I must face my demons. Let us go inside.' Napoleon sounds resolved.

Richard has never visited Malmaison. Now, Napoleon Bonaparte is his guide!

That evening Richard is invited to dine with Napoleon. Marchand shows Richard into a room lit by a beautiful chandelier, shedding golden light onto a white-draped table. The floor is like a chessboard. The walls are salmon pink, decorated with nymphs and classical ruins. Arched glass doors reach from floor to ceiling, their shape echoed in the mirror.

All of this Richard takes in greedily as he is seated at the end of the table opposite Napoleon. Four chairs flank the table on each side. None of them is occupied. No other places are set.

'I hope you do not mind the lack of company? I shall endeavour to be a decent host. I must pay attention to the niceties of existence now they are all I have!'

'It is a great honour,' gushes Richard incredulously.

Who did Bonaparte eat with on this evening, his first back at Malmaison? Perhaps he dined alone?

'I am determined to think of the future. I cannot pretend the events of the last week have not been a staggering blow, but I would prefer to face what comes next with dignity. If I can still make choices about my retirement, then that is what I shall do.' He pauses and looks through the windows where servants are weeding the flower beds in the fading light. 'Let us talk of America. I have ordered some books on the subject but I am impatient. I prefer to hear about it from a son of the Founding Fathers.'

Richard squirms in his chair. His glass is already filled with a red wine. Without thinking, he reaches out and drains half of it.

Napoleon raises an eyebrow but says nothing. The wine is very good. It is a Burgundy. Chambertin, Richard thinks.

Napoleon reaches for a water pitcher and dilutes his own glass which has been left half full to facilitate his habit.

'Sire, I have spent much of my life in service to my government out of the country. I fear I will prove a poor source of accurate information.'

Napoleon takes a fastidious sip and sets his glass down. 'Come, come, Monsieur Davey. You have the advantage of me. I know very little of America. I will enjoy whatever you tell me. Although, I do now regret a certain piece of business I contracted with President Jefferson. I believe your current president was secretary of state at the time. He played a major role in convincing your Congress to pay up.'

'The Louisiana purchase?'

'Yes, you could call it that. Had I managed to retain that territory my options might be rather different today.' Bonaparte seems to have forgotten talking of the very same thing on the day of the battle.

What Richard knows about early nineteenth century America is the result of one undergraduate course taken twenty years ago augmented by some casual reading. He does his best. Napoleon seems satisfied. They sit at table until late.

Richard starts watering his wine before the dessert.

He sleeps well in a grandiose bed with a mahogany frame, inset with gold sphinxes and lotus blossom.

He wakes early and goes exploring. There are few staff and no one questions his right to wander.

Many of the rooms are painted in pastels reminiscent of Roman villas or with friezes of classical figures and garlands of flowers.

More than one room is draped to echo the tent effect of the entrance hall. Josephine's bedroom is swathed in a rich claret backing a riot of gold. An eagle-topped canopy floats above a swan flanked bed draped with patterned silk. It looks like a fairground carousel. He does not linger.

Soon after, he finds the small library and sits for a while, leafing through a copy of the *Life of Alexander* by Plutarch, translated on alternate pages into French.

When his eyes grow tired, he moves on, stumbling across the billiard room where he finds Emile. The walls are acid green. They hit some balls but neither of them is sufficiently skilled to make the game interesting.

They share a modest lunch in the grounds.

'It is to be America, then?' asks the lieutenant.

Richard nods slowly. He does not want to mislead his friend. 'That is Napoleon's intention. He plans to travel to Rochefort before occupying forces make it impossible.'

'Then that is where I shall go. I hope he will allow me to accompany him?'

Richard smiles. 'He has asked me to be his guide. It would be good to make the journey together, wherever it may lead. I fear the Prussians and British have other ideas, another island, more remote perhaps?' He is trying to temper Emile's enthusiasm.

As they sit sharing their simple picnic on the lawn, shouts emanate from the house.

'It is the emperor!' cries Emile. 'Whatever can be the cause of his distress?'

They run towards the front entrance and hurry inside, following Bonaparte's agitated voice.

'The ungrateful pygmies! First an unending queue of debtors and now this indignity! Perhaps I should marshal those still loyal and march on the Provisional Government? I could compel them to recognise my boy as Napoleon the Second!' His voice is shrill and his eyes lance the air like daggers.

As Richard and Emile enter, Marchand is beseeching his master to remain calm, offering him a brandy.

Incensed, Napoleon seizes the delicate glass and flings it to the floor where it shatters into fine shards, glistening in the spilled amber liquid. The noise brings Bonaparte up short.

He slumps into a nearby chair, head on his chest, wringing the fingers of first one hand and then the other. He is pale and his breathing sounds laboured. The valet kneels beside his master with a bottle of smelling salts, scowling at both of them. Emile pulls Richard away.

Napoleon spends the following day reading the books that have just arrived. He is sequestered in his study and sees no one.

The day after that he receives everyone who comes, be they bankers or relatives, old friends or members of the interim government. Richard sees them coming and going, a parade of carriages along the drive, chaos as they jostle for position.

It is summer. The sky is blue and Richard can smell cut grass. A knock at his door and Marchand appears, hiding any antipathy he might feel. 'The emperor asks that you join him for dinner this evening.'

One of the suits of clothes he was gifted at the Tuileries is a replica of that which Napoleon wore as First Consul for a painting by Ingres. Richard has never dared wear it; worried what Bonaparte would think. But this evening, the last to be spent at Malmaison, if history remains on track, is different. He will try to make it a celebration rather than a wake.

The coat is a red brushed velvet with gold embroidery and buttons. The collar is a high, exaggerated lapel. The tails are long but it is cut severely at the waist, revealing matching crimson breeches, white stockings and black patent slippers.

It is dated and rather tight but Richard does not care.

This evening he does not have Bonaparte to himself.

'Good, this is good. We are all here. Allow me to make introductions.'

General Gourgaud looks at Richard with contempt as he enters but Napoleon claps his hands in delight.

General Bertrand is smiling beside his tall, attractive wife, Fanny.

The Comte Charles de Montholon is Napoleon's aide-de-camp. His comely wife, for whom he is a third husband, is called Albine.

Her hair is in long ringlets. Her eyebrows arch neatly over small but proportionate features. There is nothing remarkable about any part of her face but the sum is enchanting.

Emmanuel Las Cases, the former chamberlain, inclines his scholarly head in an enigmatic gesture.

Richard is glad to see Bonaparte in his Chasseurs uniform. He looks around the room, trying to learn the faces. This will be the inner circle from now on. Everyone here will sail for St Helena. He clenches his hands together, schooling himself to be careful. Everyone here expects to travel to America.

Bonaparte is determined for everyone to get on. He is an attentive host, particularly to the wives but he fosters a comradely banter with the men, making sure to include Richard, who is acutely aware what a latecomer he is to such company.

Conversation tip-toes around any reference to the past. By the time the remains of a dessert of cream filled waffles are cleared away, topics are running dry. No one wants to be the first to leave. It is as if they know this is the last time that they can even pretend everything is alright.

In the end, Napoleon rescues them. 'My loyal friends. I fear we must end our evening. You have all been so kind, offering to remain with me wherever I may go. I believe America will be good for us. Now go and pack, for tomorrow we journey to the coast!'

They are standing on the harbour wall looking out at the grey swell of the Atlantic. Gulls wheel overhead, their cries mocking the frustration on Bonaparte's face.

On the horizon loom the hulls of Royal Navy ships. The port is blockaded. Richard looks towards the inner harbour. Two French frigates, the *Saale* and *Medusa*, sit powerless at their moorings. The deposed emperor's party had hoped to step from French soil onto French decks, trusting in French sailors to see them to their destination.

A large gull with a strong yellow beak banks low, releasing a stream of fishy white excrement that spatters the despondent party. Napoleon removes his bicorn hat and examines it. His nose wrinkles and Marchand whisks it away. He says nothing. His gaze is fixed on that horizon.

Soldiers and sailors, politicians and local dignitaries all come calling. Day after day they offer advice. Some make pledges but others are transparent in their manoeuvring. They want him gone, they want him in British hands, and they want him wiped from memory. He is not fooled. Even his brother's plan to act the decoy while he slips away from Bordeaux is rejected.

'I will not risk being hunted down like a common

criminal,' he tells Joseph in Richard's hearing. 'To sully my reputation like that would be insufferable.'

Richard wonders if Napoleon has any idea what people think of him? Small crowds of fishermen and troops implore him to stay, to fight on, to defy the tide of history. Every time it happens, Richard sees a spark kindled in his blue eyes but as soon as they are gone, it gutters and dies. There is not enough oxygen to support such defiance.

'The British are steadfast. I will request asylum. General Gourgaud, I have a mission for you. Prepare to sail for England!'

A fine drizzle blows in off the sea. Richard licks his lips and tastes salt. Everything is playing out as expected. Richard has not tried to convince Napoleon to run the blockade. He does not see America as his destiny. He has a life to live. Does he want to bind himself to this defeated man?

Sitting with Emile in a sailor's bar on the seafront, Richard drinks steadily. Emile is talking of England and America, asking Richard to teach him the language. 'I will be a fine pupil. I must find a way of supporting myself. Perhaps I will be able to serve the emperor in some capacity?'

Richard hears the words but he is thinking of himself. England in 1815. An interesting prospect. Might he convince the authorities to grant Bonaparte's request for a country house near London? How? What standing does he have? He is a fraud no matter what nationality he claims. He is certainly not an American agent. He is English but to all appearances a traitor and in reality, a man entirely out of time.

Where he has been accepted is in France, first by Lieutenant Béraud and then by Bonaparte himself! That is what makes sense of his existence now. Wherever they go; he will go. Otherwise, he will be lost and alone.

The days in port are sultry. They are on the very fringe of France. In Paris, the survivors are getting to work. Louis XVIII is restored, again.

Napoleon talks of Fouché. 'Once a necessary evil but now he will not stop until I am gone. I cannot wait any longer for confirmation from London.' He pauses. 'I need Marchand.' His valet appears as if by magic at his side. 'Good, pack my things. Wake me at midnight. Enough of this limbo. I wish to be moving again. I must trust this Captain Maitland. At least his ship is deserving of my presence. HMS *Bellerephon*, she fought at Trafalgar, you know?'

Everyone present nods.

'Billy Ruffian, that's what her crew call her,' offers Richard, hoping to lighten the mood. The joke is lost in translation. By the time he has explained, the moment is also lost.

Chapter Nine

Richard cannot sleep. He lies on his bed for an hour listening to the waves break on the sea wall then gets up. He lights a candle and shaves slowly. Anything to pass the time. Emile is sleeping soundly on the other side of the room. He hears a scuttling along the wainscoting. Rats! He shivers but holds the blade clear of his throat until it passes. He wants to look his best.

He must try to help Bonaparte. He does not want to be stranded on St Helena waiting for his hero's death. He looks at the bags beneath his bed. They are packed. He has selected a sober set of clothes. His jacket is a blue of which the navy would approve. His feet are sheathed in high gloss black. He sits on the bed, trying to avoid creases in his buff trousers.

'Is it time?' Emile's sleepy voice barely crosses the room.

'Not yet. Another hour at least. I'm sorry I woke you.'

Emile sits up and rubs his jaw. 'A blessing. My dreams were not happy. I am afraid of the sea.'

Richard smiles sympathetically. He is not the only one embarking on unfamiliar territory. 'The Royal Navy is the best in the world. If Bonaparte had persevered with his invasion plans, it would have been a disaster.'

The lieutenant gets up and crosses to the small attic window. 'I do not doubt their expertise but my own. I cannot swim.'

Downstairs, lamps are lit. Their shadows loom menacingly on the stairs as they descend but the smell of coffee and freshly baked bread disperses any sense of threat.

'It is Saturday? The fifteenth of July. The day I leave my homeland.' There is a melancholy in Emile's manner that Richard understands, even envies.

'Almost.' Richard greedily consumes a warm bun, washing it down with black coffee. He thrills as the caffeine jolts his system.

Emile picks at his food as if seasickness has already claimed him. Richard is far from a good sailor but he would rather start with something in his stomach.

A door opens, Bonaparte appears. He is dressed in the green of his General of the Chasseurs uniform. Emile jumps to his feet and salutes, grinning. He too is in uniform.

'I am glad you are with me, Lieutenant. We are still the glory of France!'

Marchand serves Napoleon but he eats little. His blue eyes watch as the rest of his party assemble around the table. The women are elsewhere, caring for their children.

'Gentlemen, you have come far enough. I cannot ask you to abandon France with me. You have families and futures. I can promise you nothing. I have asked the Prince Regent for favour, for leave to travel to America or become a private citizen in England. These would be bearable to you, perhaps, but what if my requests are refused? There is talk of exile. Elba was a farce. This time it will surely be worse. We should say our farewells.'

There is uproar. Everyone is speaking at once, professing their desire to remain. Napoleon holds up a pudgy hand, it is trembling. 'Think of your wives and children.'

General Bertrand looks uncomfortable.

'Yes, General, Fanny loves you. She will go where you go. England seems an adventure to her but she has endured Elba and must know the risk: it will be forever this time.' There is a deep pain in Bonaparte's voice.

Bertrand begins to cry.

'Montholon, Las Cases, you too have children, will you sentence them to my fate?' asks the deposed emperor.

They clamour that they will. The rest of the meal is eaten in an awkward silence. When Bonaparte stands, everyone rises. Marchand helps him into his grey overcoat and buttons it. They leave and the party breaks up.

Servants are called, orders given. Richard and Emile carry their own bags out into the darkness.

Braziers are lit. A cart appears for the luggage. Soon they are all at the dock. The brig, *L'Epervier*, is flying a white flag that hangs forlornly for a moment and then stirs against the dark.

They board carefully, the women and children handed across the gangplank by sailors. Richard's shoes slide on the damp cobbles but the cleats in the boards provide grip. Emile follows him reluctantly. The whole entourage file across to huddle on the deck of the twin-masted vessel.

The women and children are escorted below, along with the servants. The rest of Napoleon's companions remain with him on deck. The sea and sky are indistinguishable except fore and aft where lamps cast a localised brightness, illuminating spume as the craft gets underway.

'It is done,' mumbles Montholon.

'So, it begins!' replies Bonaparte, a general lying to his troops. The captain approaches and requests a word in private. They move off together towards the stern.

When Napoleon returns, he is frowning. He turns to Bertrand. 'The captain has offered to run the blockade. He is convinced the British will betray me.'

'There is that possibility, sire,' replies the voice of a man walking a tightrope.

'I shall surrender myself to Captain Maitland. I trust he is an honourable man.'

Richard says nothing.

Maitland sends his ship's barge to collect Napoleon's party. The crew of the brig cheer Bonaparte throughout the transfer. As the sailors draw close to HMS *Bellerephon*, they raise their oars to the perpendicular. The wooden walls of the ship tower above them in the gloom.

The barge pitches about and Emile, sitting beside Richard, begins to look pale. A ladder is lowered from the main deck to the shallow barge.

General Bertrand climbs first. Napoleon mounts with care followed by his entourage. When it comes to Emile's turn, he clings to the railing but hurries upwards. 'Surely a bigger ship means a less aggravating motion?' he whispers to Richard who is absorbed by the first encounter between Maitland and Bonaparte.

There is a guard on the poop deck but they do not present arms as is customary when a person of high rank boards. Once on the quarterdeck, Bonaparte removes his hat. 'I am come to throw myself on the protection of your Prince Regent and your laws.'

'Welcome to HMS *Bellerephon*. Allow me to show you my

cabin. I have put it at your disposal for the duration of the voyage.'

Napoleon looks puzzled. Richard steps forward. 'If I may, Captain? The emperor does not speak English as yet. I would be happy to act as interpreter. My name is Richard Davey.'

'That would be most welcome, sir, as my French is very much of the school room and that was long ago!'

They move towards the hatch together, Richard on Maitland's left and Napoleon to his right. Other officers escort the remainder of the party below.

'How does an Englishman come to be in the company of Boney?' asks Maitland affably.

'I am from America, Captain. Our countries were at war but a year ago.' The captain nods but wears a slight frown as he shows them into the great cabin at the stern of the ship. It is bright and orderly.

'This is a fine cabin,' remarks Napoleon.

'The captain has put it at your disposal for the duration of our journey,' replies Richard.

'Please convey my thanks. He is a generous host and I look forward to getting to know him.'

Richard translates the sentiments.

'There is an inevitable awkwardness about our situation but I am determined to play my role with respect. Although the former emperor's status is yet to be determined by my government, I shall regard him as I would any senior commander of a belligerent nation. I cannot call him by his former title. I shall address him as General. I trust that will be acceptable?'

Napoleon is looking on with interest.

'The captain wishes to address you as General Bonaparte,' Richard explains.

Napoleon unbuttons his grey coat and draws it back with a flourish to reveal his immaculate green and white uniform. 'As you see, I am indeed a general and proud to be called such by my beloved Chasseurs of the Imperial Guard.'

Captain Maitland smiles. No translation is necessary. 'I shall leave the general to get settled. I hope he will dine with my senior officers this evening? Perhaps you would be so good as to be in attendance?'

Richard checks with Napoleon. All is agreed.

The wardroom is a plain space and the ceiling formed by the deck above is low enough to compel a tall man to stoop. There is a single table in the centre of the cabin covered by fine linen and set with a smart dinner service and crystal.

Hats are removed and seats taken after introductions are exchanged. Present are First Lieutenant Bowerbank, blond mop atop a pink face with small eyes and a permanent scowl. The captain of Royal Marines is distinguished by his uniform, his jet-black hair and boxer's chin. The surgeon is an Irishman, Barry O'Meara, another dark-haired fellow but young and alert with an open face. Two other lieutenants look like peas in a pod, their features are so similar. Finally, there is the chaplain, ruddy-faced with copious white whiskers and watery eyes.

The remainder of the officers must be dining elsewhere, Richard supposes. He is seated opposite Captain Maitland, who has Napoleon to his right and his ranking lieutenant to his left. Richard is flanked by two more lieutenants, while the doctor and chaplain are opposite each other closest to the door. The captain of Marines perches awkwardly on a stool at the foot of the table.

At first conversation is inconsequential. They talk of the weather expected, the accommodation for the remainder of Bonaparte's party and the quality of the vintage. As usual Napoleon waters his wine.

He watches everything but says very little. The party breaks up early, leaving with what appears to be relief.

The captain asks Napoleon and Richard to remain. 'Please forgive my officers, it is not an easy thing to sit at table with an enemy of the general's stature. They will grow used to it and the quality of discourse will improve. Will the general take a glass of port?'

Napoleon asks Richard what has been said, listens to the reply and then gives an entirely Gallic shrug. 'It is only natural they should be wary in my presence. It is not every day you sit at table with an emperor, even one who has lost his throne!' He accepts the glass of port but does not raise it to his lips. 'Tell the captain it is fitting I should be on board a warship such as his. He will understand.'

Richard complies, although he only translates the second half of what Bonaparte has said.

'The general is knowledgeable about our ships, I see. It is true, the *Bellerephon* has seen much action against the French. She was first bloodied on the Glorious First of June and again most severely at the Battle of the Nile. She lost her captain at Trafalgar. Billy Ruffian the men call her. A tough ship to be sure and one I am proud to command.'

Bonaparte listens calmly as Richard translates. There is a

hint of defiance in Maitland's manner but his guest smiles before pounding the table with his fists.

'It has always been your fine navy that frustrated my ambitions!' There is admiration in these words but regret too. 'If it was not for English money and English ships I would have conquered and held the Levant. I should have crossed the channel with my barges of men and fought you among your fields and villages. How different would that have seemed for your people! My infantry in their streets rather than their taxes funding the crowned heads of Europe to make war on me!'

Captain Maitland's mouth naturally curves upward but now it sets in a thin line. His large eyes study his guest and his strong chin juts forward as he finally replies. 'Had you made that crossing, you would have been surprised at the resistance you would have been offered.'

Napoleon inclines his head. 'The Norman bastard and Julius Caesar both succeeded. The Vikings in the north also imposed themselves.' The two men are playing chess with historic events as the pieces.

Richard translates for both, doing everything he can to soften what is suggested.

'Indeed, they all did what you could not.' Richard holds his breath as he conveys the captain's retort.

Napoleon stands and offers his hand across the table. 'I have always found the Royal Navy a worthy opponent.'

The days settle into a kind of routine. Richard keeps close to Bonaparte, although he rarely needs him during the day as the officers and men of the ship do not speak to him unless he speaks first, which he rarely does.

Emile is not enjoying the motion of the larger vessel any more than he had the brig. He keeps to his cabin, which he shares with several others.

Napoleon walks on deck for an hour before supper each evening. On the day the last vestige of French coastline is visible at Ushant he stands for a long time, staring at the outstretched finger of France. Was it an accusing finger or a beckoning one? Most of the party join Bonaparte but he speaks to no one.

He does not appear for the evening meal, sending his apologies, claiming an upset stomach. That night Richard sleeps soundly and wakes to shouts from above. He climbs onto the main deck to see the coast of England has replaced that of France.

Richard goes in search of Maitland, hoping to gauge his thoughts. He finds him talking with the purser about the state of the ship's supplies. When they have finished, Maitland greets him. 'I have just received my orders from Admiral Keith. It seems we have outstripped the authorities' discussions. The general is to remain on board until a decision is made as to his future. It will not be passage to America, I am afraid, you can be sure of that.'

Richard tries to play his part. 'I am sure the president would not wish a situation to develop that might threaten the Treaty of Ghent or imperil the improving relations between our two sovereign powers.'

Marchand appears and gestures to Richard. 'The emperor is asking for you.'

General Gourgaud boards the ship through a throng of small boats selling wares, sightseeing, perhaps even spying. He looks grey and glum. He has failed. He has not even been allowed to land. All he brings are recent newspapers. They talk of Bonaparte the tyrant and warmonger and call for him to be imprisoned in the Tower of London or exiled to the furthest fringes of the British Empire.

Bonaparte insists Richard reads him everything. Colour rises from his red collar to his cheeks. 'So, there is to be no honourable settlement with my most implacable foe? They insist on total humiliation.'

Richard knows now he cannot exercise any influence here. The British Empire will revenge itself on its most feared enemy. The course is set. It will be St Helena. He excuses himself and heads up on deck.

There is an offshore breeze. He can smell England. Cut grass, wood smoke and a hint of sheep reach his nostrils. He breathes in deeply, over and over again. The sea is calm. A gauze of mist pulls apart to reveal the coast, separating the sea from the sky.

He knows how it will go. Day after day of waiting; hope diminishing; resentment swelling.

Richard hears shouts from the main deck and sees Fanny Bertrand standing atop the rail, one hand clutching the rigging. Richard crosses the deck as her husband appears, closely pursued by the other women in the party. Soon a crowd has gathered at the rail.

'I could endure the thought of England, although it meant living in the bosom of the enemy, dependent on English whims. At least I have family in Ireland. But they will not let us land!' She is almost purple with rage, her eyes bulging and her neck ropes of tension. Her bonnet comes adrift and her auburn curls blow loosely in the breeze. 'I cannot live on some vile speck in the middle of an ocean!' Spittle gathers at the corners of her mouth and is whipped away by a gust of wind.

Richard feels wetness on his face.

She wears dainty slippers and her balance is precarious as the ship rolls. Her left foot slips and she screams; the sound of an animal caught in a trap.

She is hanging now, left wrist tangled in the rigging, both feet kicking outside the rail.

Her dress accentuates her tall, elegant body. A blue ribbon defines the base of her high bust. Modest layers of chiffon drape to her ankles but billow on the breeze, revealing long, athletic legs.

Henri Bertrand leans over and locks his wife's loose wrist in his firm hand. She goes slack. He pries her other hand loose from the rigging and hauls her back over the rail like a mermaid caught in his net.

He lays her gently on the deck. Barry O'Meara produces a small bottle, unstoppers it and wafts it beneath her delicate nostrils.

Her pale lids shoot up and she moans quietly. Most of the crowd move back, leaving her in the care of her husband and the doctor. Richard backs away but remains in earshot.

'Fanny, my darling. I know you dread St Helena. But if that is where the emperor goes, then that is where we must go.' She struggles in his arms, trying to escape his news. She shakes her head wordlessly, tears pouring down her flushing cheeks. There is something compelling about her despite the histrionics. Bertrand pleads, 'Do not distress yourself, my darling. I promise we will not remain very long.'

Fanny relaxes against her husband's broad chest and manages a weak smile. Richard envies the general.

It is Monday, the last day of July. The weather is damp. Admiral Lord Keith is piped aboard. He introduces Under Secretary of State Bunbury to Captain Maitland. They disappear below.

Richard tries to follow but two marines are stationed above the hatch and his way is barred.

Later, once the visitors have left, he is allowed below and heads straight for the rear cabin. He knocks. There is a pause before a sharp voice calls out. 'The emperor is not receiving.' It is Marchand.

'It's Richard,' he shouts, ignoring the valet.

After a few moments, the cabin door opens and the reluctant face of Marchand glares at him.

Bonaparte is standing at the stern, gazing out of the rear windows that make the space so light. Richard notices a crumpled letter on the table.

'Read it to me, although I know what it says. The admiral would not look at me while that foppish underling Bunbury translated it.'

Richard wonders why Napoleon wants to inflict this on himself. He picks up the fine linen paper and scans the contents. One phrase stands out: prisoner of war; and then exile and St Helena. 'Sire, do not make me read this again.'

Bonaparte looks over his shoulder. He looks utterly defeated as he did in that coach some six weeks ago. 'Perhaps that is best. I shall compose my objections but there can be no doubt, I am to be cast so far adrift they hope the world will forget me.'

Richard sees Bonaparte draw a small red bottle from his pocket. He runs his thumb and forefinger around the gold stopper. 'I could cheat them of their final punishment.' His chubby hand encloses the vial. 'I could force them to explain my death on board their warship? Even their own press would struggle to vilify me then!'

Marchand hurries across the room and gently lays a hand on Bonaparte's arm. With his other hand, he pries open Napoleon's fingers and relieves him of the deadly dose of opium.

Richard sits at the table, the letter forgotten in his left hand as he rubs his face with his right. 'Sire, I know you do not fear death but nor should you fear life. You once said you would drain the glass of life to the very bottom. It takes a certain courage to do that. Perhaps dignity is the one lesson you can still teach your enemies, even as they seek to humiliate you?'

The defeated general, the deposed emperor, the despondent man in a fine green uniform, returns to the table. 'I shall write the story of my life. I shall relive my past glories and ensure the world knows what I achieved! I cannot allow the English to write the history of my life. They would make themselves the heroes!'

Plymouth recedes as HMS *Bellerephon* navigates out to the open sea. It is Thursday the fourth of August and they are heading for a rendezvous out of sight of land. Richard is still on board. He stands with Emile at the rail of the main deck watching England disappear.

'I suppose this is our last chance?'

'For what?' asks Emile.

'To change our minds. To avoid weeks and weeks at sea,'

Emile grimaces. He is pale and has barely eaten anything but crumbs of ship's biscuit for a fortnight.

'To do something else with our lives than go into exile on a rock in the middle of the South Atlantic, hanging onto the tattered coattails of a broken man?' Richard sound plaintive to his own ears.

Emile stiffens. The line of his jaw knots and he turns hurt eyes on Richard. 'I promised to follow him. It was not contingent on the destination.' His voice is thick with emotion.

Richard can hear the sacrifice. 'Forgive me. My bonds are perhaps not as strong. Nevertheless, I am here and I shall board HMS *Northumberland* if I am still welcome. But one day I shall want something more than this.' He pats Emile's shoulder and moves away; aware something has shifted between them and unsure if it is permanent.

HMS *Northumberland* disrupts the horizon, growing larger with infinite slowness. At first, she is a beetle crushed between sky and sea. Then her three masts are discernible. As they draw closer, Richard can make out sails and then her rigging.

To his eye, she looks much like the *Bellerephon*, if a little longer from stem to stern. Up close, her paint is fresher, her wood smoother and her gun metal brighter.

Richard packs everything he has and joins the party waiting to be transferred by jolly boat. He sees the ladder extended from main deck to water level against the hull of the *Northumberland*. He watches it unfold, complete with handrail. There will be no accidental drownings today. The sea is calm.

Bonaparte appears. He looks glum. He bids farewell to those of his party who will travel with him no further. There are tears. Richard sees the envy in Fanny Bertrand's face.

Captain Maitland shakes Napoleon's hand. 'I wish you a safe voyage, General.'

Napoleon nods and doffs his bicorn. 'I do not blame you for this travesty. I believe you acted in good faith. You have been a generous host but your country treats me with a contempt history will condemn.'

They hear the rowers ship their oars and come alongside. It is time. Napoleon sees Richard and his luggage and crosses the deck immediately. 'My American friend, what is this?' He indicates the two bags. 'Surely you have a life to live? Get away from me. Why should you suffer my fate?'

Richard realizes he is trembling. Tears flood his eyes. It is only in this moment he realizes he has made his choice.

Far away, Aunt Patricia scoffs, shrugs and turns away.

'Please, sire, do not send me away. I have nowhere else to go. I wish to remain by your side, if you will allow it?'

Napoleon's blue eyes study him intently, as if divining his motive. He nods. 'Very well, Monsieur Richard Davey, henceforth you shall be my tutor. I command you to teach me the language of my enemy, so that I might contest with them on equal footing.'

Richard bows. When he raises his head, Bonaparte is still there. 'One more thing, the post comes with its own uniform. I believe you have it with you?' Napoleon points at the leather bags at Richard's feet. 'The garb of First Consul is to be repurposed. It suits you and it cheers me, a reminder of happier days. I expect you to wear it when you attend me.'

Rear Admiral Sir George Cockburn is long of limb but narrow shouldered and portly. Nevertheless, he has an air of authority. This is his command. The honour guard salute. Napoleon acknowledges them but they are greeting their captain.

Everything is efficiently done. Richard is to share a cabin with Emile. He is pleased.

'I saw the emperor speak with you before we left HMS *Bellerephon*.' Was Emile jealous?

'It seems I am more attached to him than I realized. He wants me to teach him English.'

'It is not an easy language. I wonder what kind of pupil the emperor will be?'

Is that a warning, wonders Richard as he smooths the red suit on his bunk? He has a small hanging space but it is sufficient. Emile has an identical arrangement across a narrow gap. There is a small desk against the bulkhead. The door opens onto a passageway.

After a week on HMS *Northumberland* the whole household assemble in Napoleon's cabin. He looks surprised and a little put out. 'What is the meaning of this assembly?' he asks crossly, setting aside the Morocco leather-bound volume he had been reading.

They all wish him, '*Joyeux anniversaire*!' There is a cake and other treats. Wine flows. The mood is happy. Napoleon expresses his gratitude. An orderly knocks and is admitted. Napoleon is invited to dinner with the captain.

'I would be pleased,' he replies in English. He does look pleased. 'May I bring a companion?'

The orderly looks confused, Napoleon has reverted to French. Richard translates. The orderly does not know. They are still eating cake when he returns. It is fine. Napoleon turns to Richard. 'I would be grateful for your company this evening. Words are weapons.'

The meal is civil. The naval officers toast Napoleon but Richard senses tension between Bonaparte and Cockburn. The subordinate officers at table talk amongst themselves. When the meal is done, the admiral invites Napoleon into his quarters for a game of cards. The offer is accepted and Richard is asked to remain.

'We don't have a fourth for bridge so what shall we play?' Cockburn looks at his captive; he is to be governor of St Helena once they arrive.

Richard talks with Napoleon. 'He suggests Twenty-One. Do you know it?'

Cockburn smiles. 'A game of chance rather than skill. No matter, it will pass the time.'

He is not unkind, Richard decides, just careful to set no precedent he will suffer by once they reach their destination.

Marchand is summoned and instructed. He leaves and returns quickly with a purse for his master.

'Ask the admiral if he is happy to wager on the cards?'

Cockburn does not really need a translator for this. He

nods and retrieves some coins from a drawer in his desk. Richard takes a seat a little back from the table.

The admiral deals the first hand and Bonaparte wins it with eighteen to seventeen.

Napoleon deals and draws twenty; Cockburn has fifteen and takes another card. It is a seven and he loses.

He deals and turns up a king and ace to Napoleon's nineteen. He claims his winnings and smiles for the first time.

It proves a rare win. The pile of coins in front of Napoleon continues to grow while the admiral is forced to augment his twice. Richard knows Napoleon's confidants ensure he wins their games of chess and billiards. Does he think Cockburn is doing the same? Does he know how long it has been since he played in a straight game?

'The admiral is not lucky nor does he have good instincts. This game might be more interesting with three?'

Richard is embarrassed. 'I would be honoured to play but unfortunately, I have no coin.'

Napoleon pushes half his winnings across the table to a vacant space. He gestures at Richard and raises an eyebrow at Cockburn.

'I have no objection,' the admiral says stiffly. He is not enjoying losing. This man is the enemy and he has been defeated. He is not playing his part.

The first time Richard deals, he wins and apologises.

Napoleon deals and Richard wins again.

Cockburn deals and Richard takes the pot. Bonaparte gives him a long look. For the next two rounds Richard recklessly draws a card and goes bust. Napoleon claims both pots.

Cockburn offers port. Richard declines. Bonaparte accepts

a glass but barely touches it. The admiral empties his glass and pours another. Conversation is inevitably stilted, channelled through an intermediary.

Cockburn is very interested in Bonaparte's military record, although he is keen to discuss the Peninsular and Russia whereas Napoleon wants to recount Austerlitz. Richard thinks of his brief time on that battlefield, some two hundred and fifteen years in the future.

Talk turns to other French victories; Friedland and Jena. Eventually, inevitably, as eight bells sound for midnight, Cockburn mentions Waterloo.

Napoleon gazes at him with a slight frown. 'Tell him I will not discuss that battle unless he calls it by the proper name, Mont St Jean.'

Richard tactfully communicates the gist of the request.

Cockburn sips his port thoughtfully, eyeing Napoleon over the rim. 'I fear that is not possible. History is written by the victors. Waterloo is a British victory even if Wellington admitted it the nearest run thing you ever saw in your life. So, the battle will be remembered as Waterloo and its memory will overshadow all those French victories that went before.'

Richard drops a pair of aces onto the table without noticing. He looks imploringly at the admiral.

Bonaparte's eyes flick between Richard and Cockburn with amused interest.

Richard is about to reluctantly convey a watered-down version when Cockburn raises his hand. 'Very well, let us save discourse on that matter until we are better acquainted. I wish you a happy birthday, General Bonaparte.'

Napoleon methodically stacks the coins in front of him

before tipping them into his purse. Despite Richard's late winning streak, he has taken a substantial amount from the admiral. He weighs it in his palm and nods in satisfaction.

As the cabin door closes behind them, he glances at Richard, 'Now if I had faced the admiral on the battlefield, no matter how skilled and knowledgeable he is, I would have trounced him!' He waves his purse under Richard's nose with a grin.

'He has had a distinguished career,' Richard counters.

'You only say that because he burned Washington!'

Weeks pass. There is a tedium to the voyage that Richard does not mind. So much has happened so quickly since he arrived in 1815. It feels good to have time on his hands.

He is planning lessons for Bonaparte. Sometimes he is allowed to put them into practice but there is no rhythm to these opportunities.

In Napoleon's cabin, his valet has set up the imperial campaign bed shrouded in green curtains. There is a writing box that also came on board with Napoleon's effects and his portable library in six mahogany cases.

Richard does not have any English books nor are there any in Bonaparte's collection of military histories, classical works and contemporary texts on philosophy, politics and morals.

Instead, he spends hours writing texts in English. Simple primers are easy. He recreates the stories of his early childhood. They are timeless and make Napoleon smile as he puzzles at them.

Richard is also writing longer tracts for future use. He tries Shakespeare, the plots are reasonable simplifications and he gets some key passages close from memory but his prose sounds hollow abutting a soliloquy. He spends days at this when the weather is benign.

Emile has decided to take advantage and within a month can construct simple sentences in English. His friend has finally found his sea legs, although he takes refuge in his bunk whenever a storm hits. Richard finds he is better on deck when the ship is battling rough seas but sometimes it is not safe and he has to suffer below decks.

Napoleon stays in his cabin for most of each day reading and dictating to Las Cases.

He walks on deck for an hour at five and dines at six, often talking with Cockburn for hours. They have grown more comfortable with each other, although Napoleon still plays the emperor and the admiral ensures he knows he is a prisoner of war.

The weather changes as they plough south. The sun is directly overhead at noon. Fortunately, south-easterly winds are a near constant and moderate the heat. There are downpours but they are neither frequent nor protracted. It is October now but they have crossed the equator. Richard wonders if that means it is like a northern April?

Emile takes to speaking only English around the ship and has become quite friendly with some of the crew. 'We should make landfall within a fortnight. It will be good to have earth beneath my feet again,' the lieutenant says.

Richard agrees. He has borrowed some spare charts from the Admiral and is studying them.

'Show me this St Helena,' Emile asks, standing behind him as he sits at the small desk, the chart still rolled at either end and held in place with brass weights.

Richard points to a small speck far from any other feature. 'It looks like a mistake.'

They laugh together but stop at the same time as if sharing a single thought. This is going to be their home. It will be the scope of their lives.

'How far is it from somewhere bigger?' asks Emile seriously.

Richard traces the coast of Africa from the equator to the Tropic of Capricorn. Much of the interior is labelled as unknown parts. He also looks at South America. There is more detail but that continent is even further away.

He picks up a pair of compasses, calibrates them from the key and steps out the distance to the nearest point on the African coast. 'One thousand two hundred miles. Two thousand kilometres. It is one of the most remote places in the world.'

Emile sighs. 'And is it as small as it looks?'

Richard pulls a smaller chart from below the one he has been studying. It contains a detailed coastline but almost nothing about the interior. However, it is to scale. He measures again. 'About ten miles by five. That's sixteen kilometres by eight.'

Emile is very quiet. Eventually he asks, 'So, there can be no hope of escape?'

Richard traces the vast empty ocean between St Helena and the coast of Africa with his forefinger, back and forth, as if he can wear away the distance.

Emile returns to his bunk and lies down, facing the bulkhead. Richard glances at him and then returns his attention to the map.

The winds are kind and twelve days later the island is sighted. Richard can sense relief among the crew. It is Saturday the fourteenth of October.

All of Napoleon's party appear on deck to peer through the haze at the island that is to be their home.

'It is not France,' says General Bertrand, patting his wife's arm.

'It must be the most remote place in the world.' Nobody contradicts her, not even Admiral Cockburn who has been appointed its governor.

'The cliffs look almost black. They have an evil look,' Napoleon comments. A shaft of sun pierces the light cloud and a flash of white appears in a cleft.

'Jamestown,' the admiral announces, peering through his telescope.

Chapter Ten

Napoleon is to be accommodated at Longwood House but work has not finished. The admiral sends the ship's carpenters to help. Bonaparte takes up residence at Briars Pavilion, owned by an employee of the East India Company. It is a warren of small spaces. Some of the party have to take rooms at a nearby hotel.

'So, this is my court now!' he scoffs one day to Richard as he struggles with his English lesson.

'Sire, in English?'

'This is my ... kingdom?'

'Court.' Richard explains the difference but Bonaparte isn't listening. It has only been three weeks but St Helena is crushing him, its dark walls of rock closing around his ramshackle court.

They hear through the thin wooden walls an argument between General Gourgaud and Marchand, the valet. Napoleon clenches his fists. This is not for his ears. There is an insistent knocking at the door. Bonaparte looks away, as if he cannot admit what is happening all around him in the humid, heavy air.

Richard goes to the door and opens it a fraction. Gourgaud is red faced and pushes past him. 'Sire, this is insupportable. Your servant exhibited the utmost disrespect. I insist he be punished!'

Napoleon gets up and crosses to the solitary window. The view is of rooftops. There are a few clouds above, moving fast.

The wind is back. 'It should cool down soon,' Bonaparte observes, his voice tight. 'You should do the same, General. Your manners are atrocious. Do not think I will forgive everything because you twice saved my life. Many men can make the same claim. Most of them are dead. Marchand is my man and he is loyal. Are you? You insisted on accompanying me into exile. What was your purpose? To increase my misery with your outbursts?'

'Sire, I protest in the strongest terms! I am the wronged party here.' He is almost purple with suppressed rage, eyes bulging and spittle on his lips.

Marchand enters silently and stands by the door, his eyes full of loathing as they dart between Richard and Gourgaud.

Napoleon turns back to the interior. A sardonic smile flickers on his lips. 'General, I have a task for you.'

'Anything to be of service, my emperor.' He bows with a flourish.

'That is good to hear, Gourgaud. I want you to apologise to Louis.' Silence fills the room.

'Sire, I do not know a Louis.'

Bonaparte steps close to the uniformed officer and takes him by the shoulders. He turns the general so quickly the threads of his epaulettes sway. Bonaparte's right arm extends, forefinger pointing towards Louis Marchand.

'This is Louis. You have known him for years. I want you to apologise to him for your high-handedness.'

The look of astonishment that blossoms on the general's face is so exaggerated Richard has to stifle a giggle. Gourgaud stammers and mumbles but eventually he forces the words out.

Napoleon nods and dismisses him. 'Marchand, send messages to my court. We will dine together tonight, even the children. I need to set the tone before we sink to the level of the savages that infest this awful rock!'

The meal is modest but there is wine and most of the party drink too much. The few candles gutter in the breeze that infiltrates the room through cracks in the walls.

When Gourgaud arrives, there is no place set for him, even though every one of the children is seated. Marchand lays another place with deliberate fingers and a neutral expression.

Napoleon waters his wine and sips abstemiously. He is watching his entourage with sharp eyes. Richard drinks little. Marchand spills soup on General Gourgaud who seethes silently, his face promising retribution at a later date.

Albine Montholon sits beside Napoleon while her husband has been placed at the far end of the table. Napoleon's left hand is in her lap. She wriggles but says nothing. By the end of the meal, she is flushed and Napoleon is whispering in her ear. Her husband pretends not to notice.

Las Cases boasts how the emperor's memoirs will be the best seller of the century. 'But sire, I must protest the time you are wasting with this American.' He gestures clumsily towards Richard, forgetting his glass and spilling red wine across the table. Drops spatter the chest of Fanny Bertrand who wears a cream silk gown with a square neckline and white applique flowers. She dabs delicately with her napkin.

'Forgive me, Madame Bertrand.' Las Cases subsides. His son looks mortified, he is a touchy fifteen-year-old, dressed as a miniature replica of his dark-coated father.

General Bertrand, resplendent in his blue and gold uniform, glowers at the secretary in his plain frock coat. 'Know your place, sir. By rights you should not be sitting at table with the likes of us.'

'I couldn't agree more,' Gourgaud blusters, also in his dress uniform.

Las Cases colours but speaks with control. 'I renounced the title of marquis to return to my homeland. I was conquered by the glory of the empire. The emperor saw fit to make me a count. Bertrand, your family are bourgeois. Gourgaud, your father was a musician. So, I have double the credentials of anyone here!'

There are mutterings from the pair but it is Montholon, immaculate in his military finery, who speaks up. 'A secretary should conduct better research. My family is aristocratic while I too received the title of count from our emperor.' He is controlling his anger, Richard can see. 'But my service was on the battlefield while you pedalled your atlas around Europe!' Montholon sneers.

'Enough!' bellows Napoleon, rising from his chair and banging his fist on the table so hard the plates chatter. 'This is precisely why I summoned you together this evening. You are my dignity on this putrid pimple of British territory. Yet you behave like bickering children! I will not have it. Anyone who cannot learn to get along will leave my presence permanently.'

Eyes are downcast around the table. The Bertrand children are only three, five and seven but have sat at dinner with impeccable manners. Henri and Hortense begin to cry and are ushered away by their mother while the older boy, also named Napoleon, bites his lip but remains. Albine Montholon seizes the opportunity and escorts her sleepy three-year-old Tristan from the room.

'See what you have done!' rails Napoleon, thrusting his hand into his white waistcoat. 'You have shorn my table of its embellishments. The children who are a balm to my aching father's heart, denied my own son's presence, are removed, along with the beauty of their mothers which is some comfort to me, exiled as I am from the arms of the empress.'

Richard remains silent. He is an interloper. This dysfunctional group is all that remains of the French Empire. He is a fraud and a liar. Perhaps he belongs in such company? He sits in his red and gold suit of impossible richness and ponders.

He pushes Aunt Patricia's voice away before he can hear what she thinks. He preferred it when she judged him in silence.

When the remainder of the party breaks up, Richard goes in search of Emile. He finds him in his room in an annex. The room is small and lacks a window. Emile keeps the door open to moderate the heat.

'I thought everyone was summoned to dine with Bonaparte?' Richard asks.

'General Gourgaud despatched me on an errand. He takes every opportunity to humiliate me. I carried letters to the governor and had to wait for a reply. I waited until the shutters were closed but I was ignored. So, I ate in town, I cannot say what type of bird it was, and then returned to my cupboard!'

Richard is uncomfortable. This man has been loyal to

Napoleon for his whole adult life. Richard arrived a little over four months ago. Yet he is dressed as First Consul and granted intimate access to the former emperor, while Lieutenant Béraud of the Mounted Chasseurs of the Imperial Guard acts as messenger.

'Tell me about the meal. What was the mood?' Emile asks.

'Napoleon is exasperated with all the squabbling. He demanded everyone get along or leave the island!'

Emile nods slowly. He is dressed in just his shirtsleeves, breeches and stockings. His hair is damp with sweat despite the welcome breeze wafting through his open door.

The smells of Jamestown drift into the room. Wood smoke doing its best to mask the smell of too many people living close together in the tropics.

'It is not easy to adjust. I cannot imagine the emperor remaining here until he dies. Surely that cannot be his fate?'

Richard looks at his feet as he leans against the door jamb and says nothing.

'And what of you, the emperor's American friend? Are you content to remain here, watching his decline year after year? He is only forty-six.' Emile takes a pinch of snuff, as if that can protect him from the rotting fish guts and cesspits.

He offers his silver snuff box to Richard who surprises himself by taking it. Tentatively, he snorts a pinch, gasps, sneezes and wipes at his watering eyes with the heels of his hands. When he has recovered, his nose is full of spices and flowers. The stink of the town is quite gone.

He smiles at Emile. 'As you can tell, I am not a user! Forgive my intrusion. I came in search of someone I can really talk to. You are my friend and yet I feel I have mistreated you.' His voice is low, his hands clenching and unclenching. He really wants to tell someone the truth. It is madness, no one will believe he has travelled back in time. He must start with something less incredible.

'I do not understand. You have never done me any discourtesy,' Emile sounds genuinely distressed.

'I have lied to you from the beginning. I am not the man you think I am.' He pauses; he must confess he is English. 'I am just a teacher.' He winces. His own words betraying him with an unintended truth.

Lieutenant Béraud raises an eyebrow but remains on his bed, reclining on his side. 'What does it matter? You spied on Wellington and sided with the French. You act for President Madison. You were vouched for by Marshal Davout. Now look at you!' Emile gestures at Richard's clothes, 'You are a member of the court.'

Richard gnaws at a thumb nail. There is a faint buzzing in his head. It is the nicotine, he supposes. Dare he say more? If he does, he will likely alienate Emile. He could end up regarded as a traitor by both the French and the English. Where would that leave him, stranded on St Helena? 'But I don't deserve any of this,' he looks down at his red velvet splendour, 'I don't belong here.'

'None of us do, Richard. It is the vicissitudes of fate that brought us here.'

'I don't believe in fate,' Richard replies petulantly and grimaces.

'Then we must forge a future for ourselves, although I cannot quite imagine what, at present.'

The chart of the South Atlantic comes into Richard's mind,

with St Helena adrift at its centre. He shrugs and makes his excuses.

He traces his way through narrow corridors to his own room and shuts the door with relief. Emile is right, it is an adjustment for everyone.

Longwood House is finished. Napoleon has taken up residence. His court still bicker but they take care to do it when he is not present. Richard is tolerated by the inner circle but none of the men want him there. Emile is his only friend but spends large parts of each day riding a horse he has managed to acquire. The women of the party are more willing to spend time with him.

Today he is calling on Fanny Bertrand. The Bertrands have not moved into Longwood. The general likes to keep his wife and children to himself and has had a small house built opposite Longwood.

The general is in attendance at Longwood so it is Fanny who opens the door to Richard's knock. She smiles and her pretty porcelain face becomes beautiful. Richard realizes he is grinning as he enters. His heartrate is elevated and his palms sweat.

A maid ushers the three children from the parlour, which Fanny has made homely with the addition of a few throws and ornaments. 'It is pleasant to see you, Monsieur Davey. Will you take tea? There is not enough coffee but the English never run out of tea!'

Richard is seated by the window. He can see Longwood House. It is freshly painted a light buff colour. The roof is grey. It rambles across its site, a central block and two uneven wings. The beginnings of a garden are in evidence. 'Tea would be delightful, Countess,' he replies, sounding too eager.

General Bertrand's wife looks knowingly over the teapot as she pours.

'Call me Fanny. We can speak English if you wish, I am rusty but I learned it from my father before he was killed. It will help us pretend we are somewhere else.'

'Very well, but you must call me Richard.'

They continue for a while but the conversation is stilted and they lapse back into French.

'I could give you lessons if you wish? I am supposedly tutoring the emperor, although he does not spend the time he should on his lessons!' Her laugh is a trill of notes and thrills him. 'I have also taught Lieutenant Béraud. He is a model pupil,' Richard adds.

Fanny smiles. 'The lieutenant is making quite a reputation for himself among the island population.'

Richard is not sure what she means.

'He turns all the women's heads with his good looks, his fine uniform and his dashing about from place to place. He seems capable of making anyone his friend. Even the British like him. I think they would have him in their army if he would ask.'

Richard gapes at the suggestion. 'Emile, join the British army? I cannot imagine such a thing!'

Fanny smiles knowingly. 'As we are all discovering, Monsieur Davey, we must make adjustments, if we are to go on living.'

Richard remembers Emile saying the very same thing soon after they had arrived. Now it is a new year, the seventh of

239

January 1816. 'Even so, that seems a step too far.' He does not know if she is testing him, joking or serious. 'What are your plans?'

This time her laugh is harsh and her eyes flit from side to side. 'My plan is to leave this hateful island at the first opportunity. I want a good education for my children but I want my husband's devotion. The emperor chose him for me but I have grown fond of him. Alas, he is in thrall to his master. He has yet to imagine an existence without him.'

She stops talking, colour rising from her lace neckline. She smooths her hands on her flower-patterned dress and refills their cups. As she leans forward, Richard can see a hint of cleavage and crosses his legs in embarrassment at his reaction.

'What about you, Richard? You are not bound to remain here. Unless you are part of an American Bonapartist plot to spirit the emperor away from captivity?'

Yet again Richard wants to shed his false identity. He fantasises telling Fanny everything and imagines her believing him, pitying him, comforting him.

He shuffles in his seat once again. 'I have been caught up in events, it is true. I have few ties. But now that everything is settled, I do find myself rather alone.' He had not meant to put it quite that way but Fanny's face is kind and compassionate.

'I too miss proper society. I am a social creature. I am still young.' She stands, unfolding her exquisite length, the light material of her dress sliding against her athletic form.

Richard rises but she waves him back to his seat with a graceful gesture. 'I want to dance and shop and travel. I want to dine and attend concerts and flirt.' Her long eyelashes dip and rise. She spins around, her hair breaking free of its styling. Her breathing is accentuated and Richard stares at the rise and fall of her chest.

The maid appears. 'Excuse me, Countess. There is news.' She holds out a handwritten sheet. It is in Las Cases' hand.

Fanny reads, her colour fades. She slumps into a chair, holding out the note to Richard. Murat, King of Naples, has been shot after attempting to regain his throne. Refusing a blindfold, he is reported to have fearlessly faced his demise, saying, 'Soldiers! Do your duty! Straight to the heart but spare the face... Fire!'

In a strange parallel, another of Napoleon's longest serving commanders, Marshal Ney, has also been shot by firing squad, having declined a blindfold and given the order to fire! This is the only news from Europe to have reached them since they arrived.

For the next few weeks Richard tries to stay away from the Bertrands' cottage. He asks to ride out with Emile. He insists on lessons with Napoleon.

Adrift in the Atlantic, isolated by the governor's refusal to allow the court access to newspapers or journals, Richard begins to believe history is no longer unalterable. After all, he has infiltrated the past. None of his interactions with these people was meant to happen.

While he was unable to turn the tide at Waterloo, he is not so sure that applies on St Helena. He imagines the battle's place in history. How many words have been written and spoken about it? How many major consequences flowed from it?

It was the defining event of an age. It has been studied and celebrated for more than two centuries. No wonder he was unable to alter the outcome.

But now Napoleon is being forgotten. Side-lined, nothing he does from now on is significant. He may snipe and complain, he may write his memoirs, reshaping the past to suit his ego, but he is a spent force.

Richard is not sure what becomes of Fanny Bertrand. He remembers she suffers miscarriages on the island but survives to be at Napoleon's bedside at the end. Then, at last, she will have her husband to herself and the family can escape St Helena. The general will be pardoned and have his titles and property restored. There is a happy ending waiting for her.

That is what history tells him. But is that fixed? Is there the possibility of an alternative? Might he not figure in the rest of this vivacious woman's life?

Richard rides hard, prepares more lessons and tries to charm the men of Bonaparte's court without success. He attends functions held by Governor Cockburn. He toys with the idea of diary, begins and then burns it. The days go by but his nights are disturbed.

He dreams too much. He dreams of Fanny. Fanny dressed in gauzy dresses that cling to her body. Translucent dresses that reveal her perfect pale skin. Fanny smiling enticingly at him, gesturing for him to follow her, her throaty laugh teasing him. He dreams of her touch, her elegant fingers removing his shirt and brushing his skin.

He enters her chamber in the dark and awakes bathed in sweat with the face of a dead German soldier leering at him. As the weeks go by the soldier's skin grows pale and pasty and then takes on a greenish tinge. One day maggots crawl from his nostrils and force themselves out between his barred teeth.

On other nights, when Fanny does not appear, he dreams of his parents for the first time in decades. They are always happily planning a trip they will never complete. Joking with each other and imagining what they will see. Then he is reliving the accident, night after night, the accident he never saw. His imagination renders it in 1970s colours. The crumpled car, the twisted limbs, the blood and the smell of petrol.

Aunt Patricia appears; cool but sympathetic. He is grateful to see her face. She says nothing but he feels guilty wallowing in his misfortune.

On the fourteenth of April 1816 the new governor arrives. Two days later Napoleon is invited to an interview with General Sir Hudson Lowe at Plantation House, the governor's official residence.

'It will be good to deal with a soldier again. These navy men are alien to me,' comments Napoleon at the end of a lesson. Richard holds his tongue; he knows how difficult the pair will find each other. 'I believe we may have exchanged a few cannon balls in the past and that is a noble connection!' Bonaparte smiles, albeit briefly.

Richard is pleased to see the former emperor in better spirits. He looks a different man from the one who fled the battlefield slumped on his horse, barely coherent.

His secretary, Las Cases enters and glowers at Richard in his red velvet finery. 'Sire, I believe it is time for your memoirs?'

Napoleon claps his hands together. 'Indeed, today, I think we shall revisit the Siege of Toulon, for that was the moment I became a part of history for the first time!'

Las Cases smiles and settles himself at his desk, one leg extended beneath, hand gripping a pen, nib already charged from an ornate ink well.

Richard makes his excuses but Napoleon has more to say. 'My American friend, I am not yet confident enough in my command of your language. I hear the new governor wishes to converse in Italian. I would prefer to speak French at our first meeting. Therefore, I require your attendance at our interview.'

They are received formally by an impassive, ramrod-backed butler and conducted into a waiting room decorated in unconvincing faux-baroque. Hudson Lowe opens the door to his study himself. 'Good day, General Bonaparte. We will not require your over-dressed lackey; I am conversant with your native language.' Curiously, he utters these words in English and with a smile.

Napoleon looks to Richard, although his expression suggests he understands the new governor perfectly well. Richard translates.

'Tell him I was Emperor of the French. That is my language now, I will speak no other.'

Richard communicates the sentiment as politely as possible. The governor's face folds in on itself in an exaggerated frown. His long chin and prominent nose reach for each other as his forehead furrows and his red brows lower. He reminds Richard of the seaside puppet, Punch. At least he isn't threatening them with a stick!

'As the general is a guest in my home, I will concede but he must know who is in authority here and it is most certainly not him.' There is a pedantic edge to the voice but his face is open again. A small smile appears as he shows Bonaparte and Richard into his inner sanctum. 'Lady Lowe is not impressed with our lodgings. She will be taking them in hand,' offers Hudson Lowe, sweeping an arm around the room, the carved wooden walls awash with curlicues and painted to imitate gold and marble.

They sit either side of a nondescript desk. The small talk is at an end. 'I gather relations with my predecessor were sometimes strained?' Richard translates and Napoleon nods cautiously. 'I trust we can begin on a civil footing. I would be happy to put my library at your disposal, General.'

Richard thinks the governor sounds calculating but offers Napoleon's thanks.

Bonaparte then seizes the initiative. 'Tell the governor I am pleased to be dealing with a soldier once again. We come from the same world. This should make for easy relations.' This comment receives a nod and a smile. 'Also tell him, I know something of his career and his dealings on Corsica. He raised a force of Rangers to serve against France. He reduced those men to mercenaries enslaved to an unjust cause, the destruction of my empire!'

Richard wordily conveys the sense that Napoleon knew of Hudson Lowe and his achievements but refrains from passing on any criticism.

'You may tell the general, I found his island a trifle warm but that its people have fierce hearts.' Hudson-Lowe replies.

Richard is not sure what that last phrase suggests but renders it as brave and passionate. Napoleon looks pleased.

Once they are back outside after the conclusion of the meeting, Richard realizes he is sweating. It was warm in the governor's study but that does not explain it. He is used to the climate now.

He knows there was some dispute about the course of this first meeting between Napoleon and the governor in the records. He senses he has exerted an influence. What is he trying to achieve? More cordial relations? His reflection is interrupted by the appearance of their carriage.

Once they are seated in the interior, Napoleon turns to him with a raised eyebrow. 'That man is horrific! What a face! Still, we should not judge a book by its cover. Although it was strange, the way his expressions did not always reflect his words.'

Richard shoots his eyes sideways to look out of the carriage window at an ochre landscape punctuated with bursts of intense green. The carriage halts at the front entrance to Longwood. Richard notices there are more guards than under the former regime. He glances at Napoleon but he either has not noticed or is studiously ignoring the fact as he strides inside.

Richard follows, unsure whether he has been dismissed. He loiters in the entrance hall as Napoleon removes his hat and gloves. 'You are looking tired, my American friend. Does the heat of the tropics not agree with you?'

Richard shakes his head. 'My sleep is troubled with dreams, sire. Whereas you appear to be thriving here?'

Bonaparte freezes in the act of patting his thin hair into place in front of a mirror. 'On those wretched voyages I was tormented by nightmares but since we made landfall, poor as it is, I have been more at ease. I have decided to defy fate. It would be too easy to end my life. I wish I had fallen on the battlefield but it was not to be. So here I am. I shall defend myself for posterity. I shall not let those scribblers and caricaturists defile my memory!'

Las Cases appears from an inner room and grins at Richard. Bonaparte notices him. 'Give me a moment, Emmanuel. I appreciate your dedication but I do have other responsibilities.' Dismissed, Las Cases shoots Richard a look of pure loathing as he departs.

'Now tell me, what is it that troubles your sleep?' They are still standing in the hall. Napoleon has his hands clasped behind his back, feet as wide as his hips, chin jutting forward. The sun is bright outside but the interior is in shade.

Richard returns Bonaparte's gaze. 'Death.' Before he can go on, he is interrupted.

'It is always there. Every fallen comrade makes me more aware of my own mortality. That is why I must preserve my legacy!' Silence fills the space between them. 'Forgive me, we are talking of you not I. Tell me about these dreams of death.'

Richard describes his recurring nightmare. The soldier in the wood. How the corpse grows more putrid with the passing weeks.

Napoleon crosses the hall and places a hand on Richard's shoulder. It is such a natural, kind gesture, he feels tears well up. 'The first man you killed. A difficult lesson but one to which I have the answer. You cannot dwell on what is done.

That soldier is dead. If that were not so then you would not be here now. Is that not a fact?' Richard nods. 'Then that is your solution. When he appears to you, you must thank him for dying. Let him know his death had purpose. Do that and he will trouble you no more.'

Richard is in no doubt Napoleon speaks from personal experience. He is deeply touched at such intimacy. That his hero should offer him such caring advice is remarkable.

'Emile, it was not until that conversation three weeks ago that I ceased wondering why I came to St Helena.' Richard sits with his friend at the top of a cliff looking out over the vast ocean.

The unfaltering breeze cools the sweat as their horses, tethered nearby, nibble optimistically at the sparse vegetation. It is late afternoon and the sun will soon set.

'Why is that?' asks Emile kindly.

'It is hard to put into words. After the excitement of the battle and the rush of days after that there was so much time.'

'And so many waves,' laughs the lieutenant.

'So much vomit!' parries Richard with a grin. 'But those days crossing to England and waiting in limbo on board were difficult.' He pauses to watch as the lowest point of the sun touches the tangent of the horizon. In his head he hears a hiss. 'I had tried and failed. My task was over. What was to come next was uncertain. I travelled with the emperor because he let me, because I had allied myself to his cause, because I was in awe.'

Hearing a whinny, Emile stands and walks towards the horses. He pats his mount's neck and returns to Richard who continues, 'For so long I had wanted to meet this man. I was like a moon trapped in his orbit. But he was no longer the dominant force of his age. He was defeated, deposed and distraught. In its way that was hard to walk away from. Like the first time you discover your father cannot do something or the inability to look away from a terrible accident.'

Richard is so adrift in his thoughts he is not sure whether he is still talking. The sun is now sliced in half, the upper hemisphere backed by unclouded sky floating above a perfect reflection. The sky steals colour from the sun as it sets. The ubiquitous pale blue, dazzling but hard to look at, washes away and bleeding in comes every shade from yellow through orange to purple. 'I was caught up but uneasy. What was I supposed to do? It was just easier to remain.'

'But nothing binds you here, Richard. You are free to go and yet you remain, month after month.' Emile is clearly puzzled.

'You are right. I was drifting from day to day. But then I became ensnared in other ways. Our friendship,' he holds up a hand to forestall Emile's objection, 'is valuable to me but I have found myself drawn to another, a woman who cannot be mine.'

Emile laughs heartily, laying back on the ground oblivious to the dust besmirching his uniform. Richard stares at his friend in surprise. This is not the reaction he expected.

'Anyone who sees the pair of you must know the truth. You speak of Countess Françoise-Elisabeth Bertrand. You are awkward whenever she appears and she devours you with her eyes. I tell you everyone knows of this.'

The blood drains from Richard's face. He feels sick. He has

tried so hard to hide his feelings, to deny them, to avoid situations where they might show.

'But no one has said anything!' he exclaims, clinging to hope. 'Surely her husband would have called me out?'

Emile has composed himself. He sits up and brushes ineffectually at his dusty clothes. The upper rim of the sun, now blood red, slips beneath the horizon. It is a little after six o'clock and it will get dark quickly now. 'General Bertrand is so jealous of Fanny he imagines everyone has designs on her. Yet, he loves her so much, so gratefully, he trusts she is never more than friendly in return. I promise you he is the only person on the island who does not suspect the pair of you of the deepest intimacy.'

The sun has gone, swallowed by the immensity of the southern Atlantic. Dusk deepens.

'But why has no one told the grand marshal of their suspicions?' Richard realizes he has not bothered to deny Emile's assumption there is more to his relationship with Fanny than mutual attraction.

'I expect they have. Las Cases for one loathes you. Gourgaud too. But as I say, Bertrand trusts his wife. Has she suggested he is suspicious?'

Richard shakes his head. He wants to laugh, mainly at himself, because nothing intimate has happened with Fanny. Mainly because he has tried so hard to avoid it. 'Very well, if everyone believes we are conducting an affair, so be it.' Richard stands and gathers up his horse's reins in the rapidly fading light. He will have to ride carefully on the way back to avoid a fall. 'You ride on to whatever island girl waits for you tonight, Emile. I will take my time.'

He watches his friend urge his horse into a canter and disappear into the night. He will seek the first opportunity to see Fanny and explore just how far she is willing to take their flirtation.

As he approaches Longwood, all is confusion. British soldiers run towards the far side of the residence from which come raised voices. An unseated horse gallops along the road, causing Richard to pull up his mount and calm her with a gentle hand on the neck. When the mare stops circling, he walks her briskly towards the epicentre of the noise.

He hears Albine Montholon pleading with her husband, 'You are aide-de-camp to the emperor. General Gourgaud is grand officer of the crown. You stand above him in rank. You do not have to accept his challenge!' Her voice is shrill.

'Montholon, draw your sword and defend yourself like a man. I will not suffer your impudence any longer!' Gourgaud has shed his jacket and unsheathed his sword.

Montholon is staring with contempt. Richard dismounts and ties his horse to a nearby post. Lights bloom inside Longwood, illuminating the scene more clearly.

Fanny appears at his shoulder and slips her arm through his. 'Two over-sensitive peacocks!' she scoffs. 'They make my husband seem the sanest of the lot.' There is no irony or regret in her tone.

Montholon has shrugged out of his tunic and brandishes his sword, swinging it back and forth with panache.

'Should we not find your husband? He is the grand marshal of the palace.'

Fanny leans into his hip and his breath catches. 'Let the

boys play! My husband is with the governor, trying to smooth over the latest offence given him by the emperor.'

Richard is all too aware how rapidly relations between Napoleon and Hudson Lowe have deteriorated. He was present at two more meetings between the pair before he was banished from proceedings by the infuriated governor. Now Napoleon is forced to converse in Italian which only facilitates opportunities for him to give offence to the pedantic governor.

As he watches with Fanny, the adversaries approach each other and cross blades. The sound of metal on metal raises the hair on the back of Richard's neck.

Fanny presses closer, her bosom crushed against his side. It is a deep dark now and everyone is transfixed by the drama. He slips a hand across her buttocks then grips her tightly around the waist. She moans into his neck. He can smell strawberries on her breath and his head spins. It is an effort to keep his eyes on the duel.

There is a surfeit of shuffling and a flurry of feints. Soon each man is breathing hard. Their sword tips clash once, twice, three times but neither man makes a decisive lunge.

Fanny slips a hand into his hip pocket and sighs as her fingertips make contact with his aroused manhood through the lining. Richard flinches and bites his lip. He leans against Fanny to remain upright.

'Stop immediately!'

Richard freezes and Fanny rapidly withdraws her hand. It is a voice used to command, a rich baritone that can only belong to one man. Napoleon descends the steps and crosses the trampled ground beside the main house. 'What is the meaning of this?'

Fanny pulls at Richard's arm, drawing him away from the back of the small crowd. 'This is perfect. The court will be in turmoil for hours before things settle down. Henri will report to Bonaparte when he returns from Plantation House and become embroiled.'

Richard trips over his own feet. 'My quarters are cheek by jowl with those of servants. You cannot risk being seen in the vicinity. There could be no convincing excuse.' He sounds fraught, almost frightened.

'Calm yourself, Richard, for just a few minutes. Our cottage is nearby. My children are spending the night with their friends, the Balcombes, and my maid is in town. She has an admirer in the garrison and will not return until the early hours. I will be finished with you by then!'

Oddly, Aunt Patricia invades his thoughts and for once she seems pleased.

Chapter Eleven

Marchand looks worried as he opens the door. 'The emperor is unwell. Dr O'Meara is with him.' Napoleon has sequestered himself inside Longwood, refusing to expose himself to spying eyes. The army detachment picketed around the house is strangling him. He declines all invitations. He walks just once a day in his garden, where the paths are cut so deep, he cannot be seen from outside.

Richard turns to leave.

'Do not go! He has been asking for you. He says he must maintain his lessons.' It is the first time Marchand has not sneered at him. Richard follows the valet through the gloomy house to Napoleon's bedroom.

The lighting is low. The polished wood floor is mostly covered by a carpet of black and white floral wreaths set in squares. The walls are a pale-yellow wallpaper patterned with small flowers.

Napoleon lies in his camp bed, the green curtains drawn back. His shoulders are propped up with pillows and he is studying his English exercise book.

Las Cases sits at the desk on the far side of the room. He is transcribing notes and does not look up when Marchand introduces Richard.

Dr O'Meara, formerly of HMS *Bellerephon*, is an Irish surgeon who seized the opportunity of accompanying Bonaparte to St Helena. Richard has never quite worked out why. Perhaps the doctor's motivations are not so different from his own?

'He needs rest. I have told him repeatedly. When he is better, he should exercise more and take better care of himself.' The doctor looks pointedly at Marchand who is deeply offended and storms from the room.

'I can return another day?' Richard offers.

O'Meara nods and returns to his ministrations. He uses a pipette to add drops to a glass of water. He then holds Napoleon by the back of the head and helps him drink the medicine.

When he has finished drinking, Napoleon raises a hand. 'My American friend will stay and help me with my lessons. I am resolved to win my battle of wills with Hudson Lowe. I will not speak with him again until I can do so in his own language!' His voice is weak and his skin sallow. 'When I rid myself of this terrible gripe in my guts, I will take your advice, Dr O'Meara.'

O'Meara packs up his case and makes to leave. Richard catches him before he exits. 'Forgive me, doctor. Is there any possibility the emperor's condition is the result of poison, arsenic perhaps?'

O'Meara's freezes. 'What makes you suggest such a thing?' he asks guardedly.

'It would be convenient for the British, would it not?'

'That Bonaparte be poisoned?' O'Meara sounds puzzled.

'That he dies swiftly, obviating the need for all of this. An end to Bonapartist plots and the bad publicity associated with his treatment.'

The doctor draws Richard into the corridor, glancing up and down before replying. 'His digestive complaints could be the result of arsenic poisoning, although there are other explanations. I have been tending towards a diagnosis of stomach cancer, although I implore you keep this information secret at present.'

Richard nods. 'How might arsenic be administered?'

'Swallowed in food or drink. It has no smell or taste.'

'Can you run any tests?' Richard asks.

'There are tests. Samuel Hahnemann devised one involving hydrogen sulphide and hydrochloric acid. It requires a fluid sample. Tell Napoleon I will return later. I will let you know what I find.'

'Be careful, doctor. If it is poison, the poisoner is likely among us.' Napoleon calls out impatiently and Richard hurries back to his bedside.

Bonaparte has been working much harder at his exercises and is pleased with his progress. The lesson goes well despite his weakness and Richard's distracted state.

When they are finished, he calls for a small glass of wine to celebrate. Marchand returns, his usual composure restored. Richard accepts a glass but notices a tremor on the liquid's surface.

'This is my new favourite. It is astonishingly good. They have grown grapes near the southern tip of Africa for many years, I am told. Old vines are always the secret.' He holds up the small glass of golden liquid to the weak light from the window. 'It is a dessert wine but I drink it whenever I wish, although always in moderation.'

It is the first time Richard has seen Bonaparte drink wine without watering it first. 'It looks delicious,' he says, holding it towards the light of Las Cases's desk lamp.

Las Cases is still at work. Marchand has retreated to his post by the bedroom door. Could either of them be implicated? Richard tries to push away the idea. He must wait to see what Barry O'Meara discovers. He turns his thoughts to his current situation. He no longer feels like an uncertain hanger-on who followed Napoleon into exile.

'The taste of good soil, benevolent sun and great care,' sighs Napoleon. 'I should like to see the place where it is made.'

Richard has a lover. He is an intimate of the emperor. He has never been happier. But an idea comes to him nevertheless. He sees the naval charts he studied on the voyage from Portsmouth. He remembers his fingers caressing the coast of Africa. He looks at the ailing man in the bed. 'I believe that could be arranged, sire.'

Napoleon's blue eyes transfix him. He looks at Las Cases hard at work.

'Emmanuel, my faithful secretary. You have worked so hard today. Go, spend some time with your son. Marchand, show him out and give us some privacy.'

Once the pair depart, Napoleon gestures to a chair. 'Come, sit by me. I fear my hearing is faulty. I thought you suggested a trip beyond the confines of my cage?'

Richard can tell he has piqued Bonaparte's interest because he is whispering. 'Sire, if you remain, I foresee your end. Yes, you will complete your memoirs, reliving the past. But you will grow sicker and weaker. This climate does not suit you. Your feud with the governor has caused you to retreat into this gloomy house. You will continue this spat until your strength is gone and you die in this very bed, too young, too soon,' Richard's voice starts conspiratorially but his sure knowledge of Napoleon's fate overcomes discretion. He has said more than he intended and braces for Napoleon's ire.

'Once again, you have the knack of echoing my thoughts, my American friend. I too feel this prison closing in. It is crushing me, squeezing the life from me. I have entertained thoughts of putting an end to it all.' He produces a small black pouch from beneath his night clothes. It hangs from a leather thong. He opens it to produce a tear-shaped glass vial.

'Opium?' asks Richard.

Bonaparte nods and puts it away. 'I will not give Hudson Lowe the satisfaction but that is a poor excuse for living. I would rather die attempting an escape. Gourgaud has suggested it but he is such a hothead I cannot trust his judgement. His plan involved sliding down a cliff face to a sailing boat hidden inside a blue barrel to mimic the sea! Ridiculous. But you, Richard, you are a man of perception. Do you think it possible? My supporters in America?'

Richard's heart is racing. 'We will need accomplices, certainly. Some we can select but for the others we must trust to fate.'

'Am I to risk my life on those devoid of loyalty to my person?'

Richard smiles. 'May I tell you the story of Bonny Prince Charlie's escape among the western isles of Scotland?'

'His was a tale of defeat was it not?' asks Napoleon critically.

'Yes, sire but he was successful in evading capture.'

As Richard concludes the story, Napoleon shifts in his bed, pulling irritably at the sheets. 'You propose dressing me as a maid?' There is no amusement in the question.

'I merely illustrate the surmountable nature of your famous appearance, sire. Forgive me, if I gave offence.'

A smile stretches Napoleon's wan face. 'It would help too, no doubt, were I to shed this.' The prostrate man indicates his protruding belly. 'In this you are in agreement with the good, Irish doctor?'

'A new body for a new life, sire?'

They laugh together and Richard has to fight to keep from hysteria. 'Albine does not complain but it would be good to have more stamina.'

Richard doesn't know how to react. It is unspoken knowledge throughout the court that the emperor is bedding the Countess de Montholon. She is clearly pregnant, but no one would raise such a matter with the emperor, not even her husband.

'Do not look so shocked, my American friend. You are not above reproach in such matters, I am told?'

Richard flushes and feels his chest tighten. He splutters and has to reach for the remains of his wine, all thoughts of poison forgotten.

Bonaparte smiles. 'This is a good thing. Co-conspirators must be bound together, although neither of us should plan on bringing his paramour on our adventure!'

Richard lies on a rug enjoying the breeze on his bare chest. He can hear Fanny's regular breathing and knows she is asleep. He rolls onto a hip, marvelling at his flat belly.

Fanny is completely naked. He is familiar with every inch of that body now but his eyes catalogue her charms hungrily. He lazily traces the curve of her hip, entwining his fingers in the soft shock of red hair at the base of her belly.

She moans and scissors her legs, trapping his hand between her thighs. Looking to her face Richard realizes she is still asleep. Very gently he extricates his hand from her warm flesh. Her scent fills his nostrils and his head spins.

He has never enjoyed a woman this much nor for this long. In his previous life, he was a confirmed bachelor, suppressing his desires and living out an empty existence.

Here, on St Helena, two hundred years earlier, he tingles with life. Virility courses through him. How is he going to leave Fanny behind? She looks so content. She looks so vulnerable. His chest constricts and he fights for breath.

He needs someone to talk to but there is no one. He lies back and closes his eyes. The sun is warm but the breeze is kind. He begins to doze. Aunt Patricia's face appears, looking peculiar. She is smiling. 'So, you have found what you were looking for?' she asks with genuine warmth.

He sees Napoleon bright on the battlefield. The image fades into a sallow Bonaparte struggling with English grammar. A lively gust scatters his frowning face, only for it to be replaced by Fanny in a floating white gown, pale skin colouring as she laughs, eyes sparkling at him.

'Yes, she is wonderful,' he gushes like a lovestruck teenager.

'Foolish boy,' scolds his aunt, 'you are infatuated. I hoped some healthy sex would be good for you but you lack the emotional maturity. This woman is using you! Do not think you are the only one. She is a particular type just as you are. She will never leave her husband. Think! What does she yearn for most of all?'

Richard does not hesitate. 'She wants a life of high society.

She wants her children healthy and educated. She wants to escape St Helena.' He realizes how naïve he has been. 'I am an amusement to pass the time. She is waiting for Bonaparte to die.'

He shudders and moves a few inches away from Fanny on the rug. Aunt Patricia's expression is one he has only seen once. The day his parents died. She looks compassionate. 'So, what you have found isn't a woman's love, then?'

He shakes his head. 'Bonaparte?'

His aunt shakes her head. 'We are talking about you, dear boy, not that ageing has been.' She is laughing.

Richard bridles but does not wake. He finds himself examining the past year. So colourful, so full, sparking such emotions. 'I've found a life worth living.'

Aunt Patricia claps her hands in ironic applause and disappears. A stronger gust stirs the hair on his chest and he opens his eyes.

Watching Fanny more critically, he is astonished he was so taken in. He still enjoys her company. She is bright and attentive. She is a passionate lover. She has casually kept her husband content while easily ensnaring him. She charms everyone and flirts indiscriminately. Richard is no longer so engrossed that he is deaf to the small court's rumours of her other dalliances.

'There is something unhealthy about this place, Emile,' he confides to his friend over a shared bottle of wine.

They are sitting in the garden at Longwood. Emile is on duty but Napoleon is exercising inside on a newly installed see-saw he designed himself. Birdsong chatters on the sighing breeze disturbing the larger bushes. It is early June but the weather remains fine and the humidity of the past few days is gone.

Emile studies the maturing gardens and turns his handsome face to the sky. 'I rather enjoy the climate,' he says sleepily.

'I don't mean the weather. I was talking about our situation. This so-called court is a cesspit of deceit!'

Emile shrugs. 'I imagine there is always intrigue. It is of no concern to me. I am a simple soldier serving my emperor.'

Richard shakes his head and finishes his glass. They are drinking a watered red as Bonaparte's taste now runs to sweet whites from the Cape. Dr O'Meara has confided to Richard his findings. It is certainly safer to consume a wine no one thinks Napoleon will order. 'To what purpose? Are you a funeral guard in waiting?'

Emile had been leaning back in his chair, balancing on the rear feet but now he flings himself forward to stare into Richard's eyes. 'What is this you are saying?' His tone is stern with warning.

'Are you truly prepared to serve the emperor at the expense of your own life?'

'I assure you my life is quite satisfying!' Emile grins and raises an eyebrow but his forehead is lined and there is a tightness along his jaw.

'Are you prepared to die for Napoleon, even now, when the fighting is done and there could be another life for you?'

The lieutenant stands, smoothing his breeches, resplendent, as always, in his green and gold. 'How can you doubt it? Am I not a man of my word?'

Richard nods and holds up his hands in a placatory manner. 'Emile, I mean no offence.' He pauses and looks around. There is no one in sight. 'I need an accomplice. Bonaparte wishes to depart this place and I aim to help him.'

Emile scans the perimeter of the garden and checks the house, its windows mostly shuttered as they always are. 'What are you saying? I know the emperor has been depressed but we must not let his thoughts turn to suicide,' he whispers as if his throat can barely shape the thought.

'No, no Emile. He may loathe Hudson Lowe and St Helena but he no longer contemplates using the vial hung from his neck. Quite the opposite. But there are those conniving at his early death. Someone is slowly poisoning him, so he means to board a ship in secret and sail away to new possibilities.'

'Poison? Who?' asks Emile incredulously.

Richard holds up a hand. 'We can discuss that later.'

Emile looks deeply troubled but allows himself to be redirected. 'America?' he asks dubiously. 'There is no way off this rock. It is garrisoned for one purpose. Eight hundred men to hold the emperor here. The Royal Navy patrols offshore and no trading vessels are permitted to land. It is a hopeless dream!'

Richard pauses before replying, allowing his friend's scepticism to dissipate. 'Not America but Africa.' Emile looks aghast. 'Let me finish,' Richard insists. 'The island is still supplied by East Indiamen and privateers. They may have to hold off while they unload but there is opportunity there. The lighters that row back and forth could be utilised. If we bribe the right captain…'

'And if you select the wrong man, what happens then?' Emile cannot bring himself to spell it out, Richard notes.

'Let me explain my plan. It has the emperor's approval.'

Richard sits in the modest room he has hired close to the main dock in Jamestown. The dock is close to the cliffs that loom beside the harbour mouth and the main fort.

He has already interviewed five ships' captains from a recent convoy without finding one he felt he could rely on. He is expecting a visit from another.

A month has passed since he took Lieutenant Béraud into his confidence. Every day he spends at least a few hours around the docks.

Meanwhile, Emile has become obsessed with finding the source of the arsenic poison.

Richard has the governor's permission to trade with the ships visiting the island subject to checks by both the army and local administrators. Many East India Company officials remain on the island they so recently administered.

He cultivates their favour. The British Government will tax his profits, they warn, but he does not care. He is not speculating with his own money. He has purchased as much coffee from the island growers as he can. This will be his cargo.

A knock at the door announces his visitor. 'Enter!'

The door opens and a tall, thin man's silhouette fills the frame. As he steps over the threshold, features fill his outline.

'Captain Simpson, I presume?' Richard stands and shakes the man's bony hand. He gestures to the one other chair. 'Please sit. May I offer you some refreshment?'

The captain holds his hat in his left hand. He has a full head of white hair and a wind-scoured complexion. His eyes are a watery green. His nose is proud and straight above a mouth inclined to smile. He wears the East India Company uniform. 'Thank you. I am partial to the coffee grown here, if you have any?'

Richard nods. 'I rely on a local man who provides such essentials to those of us without servants. Please excuse me for a moment.'

Richard leaves the office and calls across the dock front to a small man dressed in oriental pyjamas and a conical hat, squatting over a fishing line. 'Two coffees, if you please, Wang Xiu.'

The little man bobs his head and rushes towards a nearby building. When he returns to the office, Richard finds the captain studying a small, leather-bound book.

'Forgive me, my accounts. I do not come from money and it took every penny I had to purchase my command. Couldn't afford a marine chronometer so the bloody Company threatened to replace me if I didn't sail without one!'

Richard smiles. The hint is plain. 'I do prefer doing business with a man who pays attention to the details.' Richard unlocks the small strongbox sitting on his desk and opens the lid to reveal a mass of gold coins.

He watches Captain Simpson carefully. The gleam of avarice in the older man's eyes is unmistakable. He licks his lips and rubs his hands together. Richard assumes he never plays cards or he would be destitute. 'I was given your name by a clerk who works for your company. I understand you are open to additional investors?'

Simpson tears his eyes away from the box and studies Richard carefully. 'I am a loyal Company man but if there is unused space in my hold and an opportunity presents, I am not averse to a little commerce on the side. I am particularly keen at present; this voyage has been a disaster. We would not usually put in at St Helena on our outward voyage but freak weather drove us from the usual sea lanes. We were then becalmed for an inordinate time, necessitating our visit to resupply.' He smiles knowingly and licks his lips again.

Richard is sure. This is the man he needs.

There is a tentative knock at the door. Richard answers it and returns with a wooden tray bearing two porcelain bowls of steaming liquid. The aroma of coffee fills the room.

'I should like to make use of any spare capacity you have to transport some goods to the coast of Africa. I assume you will round the Cape of Good Hope on your way east?'

Simpson nods. Richard shows him the grant to trade he secured from the governor in exchange for a guarantee Bonaparte would accept an invitation to Plantation House.

Simpson reads it and returns it looking disappointed. 'I do not have much capacity. We sailed fully loaded. However, I always reserve a little space for the highest bidder.'

Richard understands. Clandestine commerce pays better than officially sanctioned trade. 'Do not worry. As this is our first venture together, I intend to make a gesture of good faith. I will pay handsomely for you to transport my,' he pauses to hold up his bowl, 'coffee across the Atlantic. I also require a cabin for three.'

The East India captain's tongue shoots out, as if testing the air. 'May I know the identity of these persons?'

'Certainly. I travel with a good friend and one servant.'

'Then you require both a cabin and space for your servant.'
It is not a question.

'I shall pay to your satisfaction but all three of us will
occupy a single cabin.'

Captain Simpson leers in a surprisingly lurid manner. 'Do
you take turns or wick her together?'

Richard acts his part, feigning embarrassment, stammering
and making a half-hearted denial. 'I shall be paying for your
discretion in all things. I hope I make myself clear?' Richard
insists abruptly.

The captain nods with an expression of complete
understanding. 'Very well, just one thing remains for us to
discuss. The price.'

Bonaparte bursts through the doors of Longwood House in
a fury. He is dressed in his Chasseurs uniform which now
hangs loosely on his frame. Richard has been waiting for him
in the hall.

'Hudson Lowe is a buffoon! Can you imagine what he
wanted to talk about? That I should pay for my own firewood
and contribute to my upkeep. He is a petty clerk not a man
of honour.'

Richard is smiling. 'My American friend, do not test my
patience! I am irate and you would do well to show me
respect.' He strides into his study and chases Las Cases and
Marchand away.

Richard hands Napoleon a glass of his favourite sweet
wine. Barry O'Meara has certified it safe to drink. 'Forgive,

me, sire. I do not smile at your tribulations but rather bring news they may soon be at an end.'

Immediately Bonaparte is calm. 'You have secured passage?'

Richard nods. 'We sail in three days. All we have to do is spirit you from this house, beyond the cordon of troops, across the plain and into Jamestown harbour.'

Napoleon snorts. 'If we pave the way with gold we will succeed. What about the formalities at the port?'

'Captain Simpson is a familiar face in these parts. As a Company man, he resents the army takeover. He is used to conducting business here. He will take care of those matters.'

Richard can see the excitement filling Napoleon's body, engorging muscles that have replaced his former flabbiness.

'What of the men we bribe to carry messages and smuggle newspapers? Will they help breach the stranglehold around the house?'

'It will drain your coffers, sire but Lieutenant Béraud should have it arranged by tomorrow evening. He is on very good terms with several of the young officers.'

What of the governor's spies? Richard has thought long and hard about this. Hudson Lowe insists the duty officer guarding Longwood must make a confirmed sighting of Napoleon every day. Any failure to do this will result in troopers forcing entry to search the house.

'We need to bring one more into our confidence, sire. He needs to dress in your uniform and distinctive hat. He need only appear periodically at a window to ensure no suspicions are raised. Meanwhile, we will have you on your way.'

'Marchand. He will do it. He is unmarried. He can claim

I ordered him to hoodwink the guards. I will arrange it. I will tell him I sail for America.'

Richard would like to object. Marchand could be the poisoner. But Napoleon will hear no criticism of his valet. Emile is certain the arsenic comes from the poison Marchand distributes carelessly around Longwood in a losing battle against a plague of black rats.

Richard and Emile flank Napoleon who rides a leggy grey with a black mane. The officer commanding the cordon around Longwood tips his hat. He has been well paid. He will confirm he sighted Bonaparte today. It is only a ride. His prisoner will return before sunset.

The three men settle into a steady trot north-west, dust pluming behind them as they cross the desolate plain dotted with stunted trees. At the edge of the plateau, they slow their horses, taking a path into the hills above Jamestown. Rising to their left is Bunker's Hill as they thread through Rupert's Valley.

Well hidden from the troops on the flat land behind them, they pull up their horses and dismount. Richard pulls a bundle of clothes from his saddle-bag and passes them apologetically to Napoleon who accepts them with a wry smile. Bonaparte begins removing his Grenadiers uniform.

Richard calms his horse while Emile does the same for the other two. Richard checks his pocket watch.

Marchand, who is proving an enthusiastic accomplice, left Longwood House two hours before his master. He made himself very obvious as he headed out on the main route to Jamestown. Before he was funnelled towards the harbour by steep hills, he cut right, climbing at first and then dropping down into Rupert's Valley.

A clatter of stones makes all three men look up as the faithful valet leads his horse towards them. He is dusty and hot but unscathed by his cross-country exploit.

As Napoleon sheds garments, he passes them to Marchand who replaces his own clothes with the distinctive blue, white and red uniform.

When the exchange of clothes is complete, Richard surveys the party. Marchand is a fraction taller than Napoleon but he will pass all but a close inspection.

On the other hand, Bonaparte looks grotesque in a dress Richard acquired from Fanny's maid. It is a yellow cotton patterned with tiny blue flowers. The length is good as is the fit at the hip. However, the bodice hangs emptily and Napoleon's scowling face looks like he is posing at a seaside attraction.

Emile pulls a wig from his saddle-bag and fits it awkwardly on his emperor's head. It helps. Emile then offers two bundles of cloths which Bonaparte stuffs into pockets sewn strategically into the front of the garment. When he has finished, the dress is a fuller fit.

Marchand steps up to his master and produces a compact with which he powders his face. Rouge is applied to his lips and used to put colour in his cheeks. His eyelids are shaded and his eyelashes thickened with the careful application of lampblack. A bonnet is then fastened over his wig and knotted beneath his chin.

'It will be dark,' Richard says reassuringly.

'It will need to be, I suspect, judging from your faces!' jokes Napoleon.

Marchand looks mortified. 'I have done my best, sire.'

He receives a kind pat on his arm. 'You are a most loyal servant and deserve a reward.' Napoleon produces an envelope from the saddle-bag on his horse. It bears his wax seal. 'You do not need to read this now. Suffice to say, I have elevated you to the status of a count. There is also a wooden box in my study. The one with inlaid ivory stars. The contents are for you. For your future.'

Louis Marchand is in tears. His hand shakes as he accepts the envelope. 'I would forgo it all to remain by your side, sire.' His voice crumbles and he stares at his feet.

Richard glances at Emile. They have been wrong about Marchand. The poisoner is still at large. If they get away, it will not matter.

A gust of wind, funnelled along the valley, threatens to dislodge the frilled bonnet from Napoleon's head and he grasps at it clumsily.

Emile spends some time fussing at the fit of the general's uniform on Marchand. The much younger valet has shaved off his side whiskers to mimic Napoleon's thinner hair. Thanks to Bonaparte's recent exercise regime and stricter diet, there is no need to pad the young man out. The uniform looks a little slack, as it has on its owner in recent weeks.

Richard looks again at Napoleon in drag and suppresses a smile. He has only the slightest of paunches now, which could easily be accepted as middle-aged spread in a woman.

Richard consults his watch once more. 'Time to be on our way, Louis. You have proved yourself loyal and I wish you good fortune.'

Marchand has never liked Richard but this undertaking

has brought a kind of understanding. 'Take good care of the emperor. One day I hope to serve him again.'

Napoleon steps close, kisses him on both cheeks and gives him a sustained hug. 'I salute you, Count Marchand! Now return to Longwood House and play your role. If anyone knows my mannerisms, it is you.'

Richard and Emile mount up with Marchand.

'I shall hide myself behind that stand of brush until it is time,' says Bonaparte. Richard senses how keen he is to take charge. There are so many people they are depending on, some motivated purely by avarice. There are too many ways this could go wrong. Too many to think about, Richard chides himself as he turns his horse and leads the way back towards Longwood House.

As they draw close to the outer pickets, Richard tries to keep his hands light on the reins. He counts his breaths and when the blood pounding in his ears becomes deafening, starts up a stilted conversation with Emile about the quality of their horses.

The first pair of soldiers stand smartly to attention as they pass. Richard nods in acknowledgement and the older man, wearing a corporal's insignia, winks at Emile, rubbing his thumb against his two longest fingers.

They pass a company drilling on the flat ground close to the site of Bertrand and Montholon's aborted duel. Not even one soldier looks in their direction.

Close to the front of the house, the duty officer is in conversation with a sergeant as they approach. 'I trust you enjoyed your ride, General Bonaparte?' The captain's voice is like china dropped on flagstone.

Marchand nods and makes a small gesture of assent with his hand, such a studied motion, a perfect facsimile. Richard and Emile keep their horses between the captain and Marchand, who wears the bicorn hat.

They hand off their horses to a groom and enter Longwood House. Richard claps Emile on the back. 'We board the ship tonight. We sail in the morning. With luck it will be several days before Hudson Lowe realizes something is wrong.'

'He will soon deduce which ship we took, will he not?' Emile sounds like a man who wants to be convinced.

'If no one discovers the precise day of our departure, there will be several possible vessels to chase. I doubt the Royal Navy has sufficient ships on patrol to chase them all.' It is far from a watertight reply.

'So, we trust to luck?' Emile asks.

Richard thinks about all the men who have been paid to make this happen. None of the emperor's court will reveal anything but can they trust men in the king's uniform willing to assist their sworn enemy for money? He would rather trust the captain of the East Indiaman for whom everything is a commercial transaction. 'Luck, yes, that and the strength of our bribes.' He tries to sound jolly.

'I would not worry too much about the garrison. Military justice is swift and merciless. They will not want to admit involvement in such a thing. Imagine being held responsible for their greatest enemy's escape!' Now it is Emile trying to cheer the mood.

The wind tugs at them as they ride towards Jamestown, filling their nostrils with smells both tangy and fetid, salty and fishy.

It is dark as they approach the crossroads with the path to Rupert's valley. Bonaparte is waiting crouched behind a thorny bush. His horse is tied to a ragged stump a little way off.

No one speaks as the frocked form reclaims his horse and mounts. Richard smiles in the dark at how easily the forty-six-year-old springs into the saddle. A far cry from the fiasco in the courtyard on the morning of Waterloo!

They ride patiently down the narrow valley until they reach the first outpost of Jamestown, a modest farm supplying fresh goat's milk to the inhabitants. The pale moonlight illuminates the buildings as silvery outlines. The goats in their pens pay them no attention.

They dismount and walk their horses to the wooden barn. Emile opens the high door to reveal a musty blackness. They lead the animals inside, remove their saddlebags and wait. Each man strokes the muzzle of his horse and whispers reassurance. Gradually, Richard's eyes begin to pick out features. There are no stalls but a cart is parked to one side and the three men tie the reins of their horses to its yoke. It reminds Richard of his hiding place atop the ridge at Mont St Jean.

Emile finds some feed and scatters it on the dusty floor beneath the horses' hooves. They drop their heads and begin to feed methodically.

The door creaks as they leave but no one stirs in the small farmhouse surrounded by a rickety veranda. A few goats bleat half-heartedly as the three men find the road and step out along it.

Richard wonders what the farmer will do when he finds

three decent horses have appeared in his barn. Informing the authorities seems unlikely. With a twinge of guilt, he walks on. Most likely, the three beasts are destined for the pot, fresh meat being in short supply for all but the wealthiest residents of St Helena.

Slowly the road is enclosed by buildings built from volcanic rock and painted white, reflecting the moonlight. A dog barks but no one appears.

The town is little more than a snake of buildings squeezed into the narrow floor of a steep valley threading from the interior down to the coast.

They walk briskly, saddlebags over their shoulders, and soon reach the more densely populated area where houses abut each other. They approach two soldiers manning a guard post. Emile, resplendent in his lieutenant's uniform, is a familiar sight. They are waved on with an exchange of pleasantries.

Here, some of the dwellings rise to two storeys, fronted by balconies. They surprise a couple in an alley who shuffle deeper into the darkness without disentangling.

As they near the port itself, they encounter three-floor constructions with dormer windows. Here there are soldiers and sailors, dockers and clerks. Some are working and others taking the air, smoking, joking, or just chatting to pass the time.

The hotel is well lit and a few revellers spill outside laughing drunkenly. Nearby, the officers' barracks is a fine shuttered building with a portico. The British flag flaps noisily in the insistent breeze and Napoleon clutches at his bonnet.

The church looms next with its fine spire just discernible. The three of them pause in the shelter of its porch to survey what lies ahead. In front of them is the sea. Between them and it, spreads the wharf, warehouses, fort and sea walls. They also see the curious barrel-roofed customs shed with grilled windows either side of its door.

As they forsake the shelter of the narrow street for the open spaces of the quay, Richard shivers. They approach the guards manning the fortified lines with Richard and Emile in front of Napoleon.

The fortifications still look fresh having been built less than ten years previously. All three of them slip their luggage from their shoulders and pile it in a heap. Napoleon looks particularly relieved to unshoulder his burden.

'Good evening, gentlemen.' Richard produces his letter from the governor granting him permission to trade and some papers in Captain Simpson's own hand beneath the East India Company letterhead.

He has deliberately spent time over recent weeks around the docks in the evening. Several times he has been accompanied by Emile. Richard recognises the sergeant who accepts his document, he has a scar on his left cheek and no front teeth. 'I have arranged passage on the East India vessel moored offshore. We are to accompany my shipment to the Cape.'

As he speaks, a plump private with a tick in his left eye props his musket against the dressed stone wall and circles behind their party. Richard resists looking around.

'I think some of the crew are drinking over in The Anchor.' The sergeant indicates a tavern nearby.

Richard is about to enquire after the third mate, a man called Skelton, who is to meet them, when he is pushed in the back. He staggers against Emile but keeps his feet, turning to see what has happened.

The chubby private has looped an arm around Napoleon from behind while attempting to get his other beneath the skirt. 'C'mon darling, let Billy have a feel between your legs. I ain't got two farthings to rub together 'til payday but you see me right and I'll show me gratitude when I'm flush.'

Richard looks back to the sergeant who is watching with amusement. 'Sergeant, aren't you going to control your man?'

'Looks like your maid can take care of herself!' replies the NCO with a chuckle.

Sure enough, Bonaparte has managed to twist in the soldier's grip and is wrestling for all he is worth.

Giving up reaching beneath his skirt, the private gropes for his chest. 'Blimey girl, you've got nothing but stuffin' for tits!'

Bonaparte seizes his moment. The soldier is facing him as he drives his right knee upwards. Air explodes from the private and he doubles over, moaning.

The sergeant is now laughing uproariously. 'Serve you right, Billy!' he manages.

Emile ushers Napoleon away from his attacker.

'Bloody bitch done me good, Sarge. I'm goin' to give her a fair slap for that.'

Richard feels sweat prickle his forehead. This is getting out of hand. 'I want that soldier's name immediately, Sergeant and yours too if you do not comply.'

The scar on the sergeant's cheek pulls tight. 'That's enough Billy. Apologise to the missy and have done with it.' His voice

277

is firm and the injured private nods, trying to straighten up.

He spits, wheezes and collects his musket. 'There you go, gents. No harm done. What do you say to leaving it at that?'

Richard agrees hurriedly. The sergeant steps aside and the three of them duck beneath the barrier.

It is only then Richard realizes he has not asked about Skelton. He scans the seafront as they walk. He sees Wang Xiu fishing from the dock and heads over to the Chinese man.

A quick exchange provides Richard with what he needs. He thanks the coffee seller and gives him a coin that will feed his family for a week.

Standing on the very edge of the naval yard, Richard can see a set of steps that angle from town level down to the sea. At the bottom, a lighter is moored with a single sailor lounging towards the stern.

'Is this lighter from the East Indiaman *Arniston*? I'm looking for Third Mate Skelton.' The man sits up promptly and moves forward to access the steps. He bounds up two at a time and doffs his hat. 'Your servant, sir. Captain Simpson instructed me to offer you all assistance. A party of three he said?'

Richard sees the young sailor eyeing Napoleon dubiously. 'That's right.'

The sailor's fresh face nods and smiles a little uncertainly.

'The captain is well aware of the composition of our party. How long until we can be transferred to the ship?'

The third mate looks towards the town and shrugs. 'The boys are in the tavern but they'll be back when they run out of money. No hurry, we don't sail until the morning tide.'

There is no sense arguing. The last thing they need is to get into a confrontation with the very men who are to row them away from St Helena. 'Very well, Skelton. I have an office by those warehouses. We will wait there. Please send a sailor when you are ready. My sign reads R. Davey, Esq. Merchant Trader. It is easy to find, at the end of the row.' Richard points.

'I'll send Simpkins if he's not too drunk. He can read.'

Chapter Twelve

The knock on the door takes Richard by surprise. He checks his pocket watch. It is a little after nine in the evening local time. All three men spring to their feet. Richard crosses to the door and opens it gingerly. He hears Emile ease his sword in its scabbard behind him.

An unshaven face grins in the doorway. The smell of rum is noticeable but the bow-legged sailor looks steady. 'Third mate's compliments, sir. We're ready to push off as soon as you is all aboard.'

They follow the messenger out of the office and down the steps. His rolling gait prepared for whatever he finds beneath his feet. As they reach the top of the stone steps, Emile takes the crook of Bonaparte's left arm, startling him for a moment before he remembers himself.

'Wait! I say, wait there!' calls a stentorian voice across the quay.

Richard freezes. A small, stooped figure ambles across from the Customs House, dragging his left foot. He wears a dated frock coat and tricorn hat, all in mid-brown. His black shoes bear square brass buckles which accentuate his crab-like progress. He is carrying something under one arm and waving at them with his free hand.

He arrives short of breath and stands for a moment gesturing at the air as if encouraging it into his labouring lungs. He looks over his half-moon spectacles, 'Glad I caught you. My name is Travers, I'm a clerk here. I have a package for Captain Simpson and some letters I'd be obliged you see delivered. I will settle up with the captain on his return.'

Third Mate Skelton tugs his forelock and takes the package and the bundle of letters. Travers nods to Skelton and his three companions. 'Please forgive the delay. Safe journey. You need fortune given the absence of an escort!' With that he drags himself about and disappears with surprisingly speed.

The third mate casts off from a ring in the sea wall and uses a boathook to nose the skiff out. The sailors dip their oars with a mixture of grunts and pull away. They keep in unison without communication.

The onshore breeze makes them work hard and Richard soon sees the most inebriated begin to struggle. He peers ahead through the darkness at a pinprick of light. It looks a long way off.

As they clear the inner harbour the water grows choppier and one sailor catches a crab, almost falling off his bench. A stream of curses rain down on him from the rest of the crew as the tender loses way.

Richard hears a sharp intake of breath from Emile and looks back at his friend seated beside Bonaparte on the stern-most bench just ahead of the third mate at the tiller.

'I can see a light at the stern,' he shouts over his shoulder encouragingly.

Emile nods and grips the side of the rowboat.

There is something depressingly familiar about life on board, Richard thinks to himself as Emile moans in his bunk. The creak of the ship's timbers, the slap of the waves against the hull, the whistles in the rigging and snap of sails filling with wind.

He studies the modest cabin, cramped with the three of them. The timber interior is dark and there is no porthole. The single candle is cheap and smells awful. It is placed close to Napoleon who reads a book he has borrowed from Captain Simpson. His English is improving rapidly.

'May I ask what you are reading, sire?'

Napoleon looks up slowly and blinks as if travelling back from the world in the book. '*Travels in the Interior Districts of Africa* by Mungo Park. This continent we travel to is so vast, so alien, I must read what I can. This Park explored far to the north and west of our destination. Still, I believe I will learn something of use. It distracts me from the intermittent pain in my guts. I must find a purpose. I need a plan.' With that Bonaparte returns his attention to the book, hunched over, seated at a tiny drop-down desk.

The mattress he and Emile take turns using on the floor is rolled and tied with a cord. Stored on the bunk, it prevents Richard from stretching out so he sits with his back to the bulwark, knees bent. He is glad Bonaparte is looking forwards. He must do the same.

They are four days out from St Helena and have already lost sight of the other ships in the convoy. The *Arniston's* route is due east until they sight the African coast close to Benguela in Portuguese territory.

From there, they will hug the coast south to reach Cape Town, newest addition to the British Empire, ceded by the Dutch in 1814. From that staging post at the very tip of Africa, the vessel's route is across the Indian Ocean to Ceylon.

'Sire, we must prevent Captain Simpson putting us ashore at the Cape. There is too great a risk that you will be recognised, particularly if news of your escape reaches the colony,' Richard suggests.

Napoleon sets his book aside. 'I have been considering this matter. The Portuguese are the key, I think. They have a presence further up the east coast, a place called Delgoa Bay.'

Richard nods. That makes a lot of sense. 'How do you come to know of this, sire?'

Napoleon scoffs. 'I was Emperor of the French. I never envisioned the empire's interests in terms of colonial acquisitions, that being England's game. Nevertheless, I needed to safeguard our trading interests and understand the ambitions of my enemies. I could map the dependencies of every European power for you.'

Richard worries every time he hears the call of a sailor on watch. The Royal Navy are not escorting the convoy. Its unexpected arrival at St Helena meant there were no available ships. However, the squadron patrolling the area could still overhaul them if their deception is discovered too soon.

They are on board an East Indiaman, broad in the beam, built to carry heavy cargo, a slow vessel and difficult to manoeuvre. The winds could be fickle, even in these latitudes.

They have bought passage to the Cape but Richard and Bonaparte have agreed they must avoid landing there. He favours a quiet portion of coast, beyond the reach of the fledgling colony. Perhaps Portuguese territory would be best?

Closing his eyes, he tries to assess what has happened in the last few days. The historian in him is abashed at what he has done. Napoleon spent his last years on St Helena. He died there. It is a matter of record.

But that will not happen. Anything is possible. If Napoleon does not die on St Helena, then does he die in 1821? He certainly looks far healthier than he did a scant ten weeks ago. He keeps to a strict regime of sit ups, squat thrusts, push ups and stretches. His muscles grow hard beneath his pallid skin.

He still complains of stomach pains, although there is no threat from arsenic on board. Perhaps it takes time for the symptoms to abate? Richard chews at his bottom lip with his uneven teeth. Stomach cancer is another matter. Like any Napoleonic enthusiast, he has pored over contradictory autopsy evidence and subsequent test results.

Has he sprung Napoleon from his imprisonment only to watch him die painfully in a different foreign field?

What about himself? He travelled through time to Waterloo but his madcap scheme to help the emperor proved sheer hubris. But the universe did not prevent him meeting his hero. More remarkably, he has become his close companion.

He smiles as Bonaparte turn a page of his book and Emile tosses in his discomfort. He is responsible for their presence on this merchant ship, ploughing through the waves towards a new adventure. His smile broadens. Thanks to Richard Davey, Napoleon wears a floral dress and has agreed to confinement in this stuffy cabin for the duration of the passage.

For two thousand miles, the *Arniston* will fight the prevailing south-easterly trade winds, beating her way south to pick up the Westerlies south of the African continent. A perilous journey of some three weeks.

How does he feel about his situation? The battle is done. He is closer to Napoleon than he could ever have hoped. He has engineered their escape from St Helena. He has given only the haziest thought to what may happen next. Get away, reach Africa, evade British influence.

Does he mean to spend his life with Bonaparte? Asked that question back at St Anne's, he would have had no doubt. Reality is different, it must be lived day by day. Something stirred in him on St Helena, holding feisty Fanny in his arms.

He has let her go but taken hold of his life. He has wrestled history and broken the rules. For the first time in his adult life, anything seems possible. He imagines Aunt Patricia would be pleased. What does he want?

Sighing, he struggles out of his bunk and leaves the cabin. He heads up the ladder to the main deck. He stands beside the port rail, amidships, trying to keep out of the way. It is late afternoon and the sun sinks towards the horizon astern.

Richard has never fathomed the technique for sailing into the wind. He studies the sails and attendant cat's cradle of rigging.

'A fine sight.' While Richard gazes aloft, Captain Simpson has joined him. 'She's a good ship. Over twenty years old but plenty of life still left in her.'

Richard nods. 'Do you expect good weather on our passage to the Cape?' he asks hopefully.

'Does no good to speculate. Weather changes in a moment. Seen most things in my time. I fear pirates more than storms. Particularly running without Royal Navy escort.'

The revelation doesn't make Richard feel any better. 'Are pirates a common problem in these waters?'

Captain Simpson gestures along the length of his ship. 'We carry fifty-eight guns on a cargo ship. That should tell you something. 'Still, now we have control of the Cape, perhaps more Royal Navy ships will prove a discouragement?'

Richard's journey from Portsmouth to St Helena was uneventful on board a seventy-four-gun ship of the line. HMS *Northumberland* was such a daunting vessel that Richard never felt in the slightest danger. It seems things are different on board the *Arniston*.

Captain Simpson watches the smooth working of his crew with what Richard reads as satisfaction. They are all dressed in short blue jackets over white smocks tucked into loose, canvas trousers. Most go barefoot.

'Is it usual to sail out of sight of the other ships in a convoy?' asks Richard to make conversation.

'In truth, a Royal Navy escort acts like a sheepdog with a flock. Without them snapping at our heels, each captain chooses his own route into the wind and trusts his boatswain. Each vessel has its own characteristics. We are all slow but some are slower than others or handle better in certain conditions. So, we have scattered.'

Richard marvels at the difference between Captain Simpson the grasping profiteer and Captain Simpson the experienced sailor. He is a different man. His eyes still calculate but not the size of Richard's purse rather the performance of his ship.

'Your crew seems smaller than I expected,' he prompts.

'One hundred and thirty-nine souls,' Simpson replies. 'A Navy ship this size, a fourth-rate ship of the line, might have three times that. Company policy is to run light on crew and heavy on cargo. Profit is king!'

Richard has already asked about the dimensions of the *Arniston*. She is 176 feet long and 43 feet at the beam, weighing 1,468 tons plus cargo. He tries to imagine the roles played by the crew on such long voyages.

He knows from the voyage to St Helena that there will need to be a surgeon, purser, boatswain, gunners, carpenter, sailmaker, armourer, cooper, caulker, butcher, baker, poulterer and cooks with mates to each of those trades. In addition, stewards, quartermasters, a master-at-arms, servants to the officers, midshipmen, and ordinary seamen.

'Nevertheless, you command a floating village,' Richard observes in genuine appreciation.

The captain shouts an instruction to a passing sailor, who tugs his forelock and runs towards the poop deck. 'I suppose that makes me the lord of the manor?' jests Simpson. 'Tell me, Mister Davey, what is it, exactly, that you do?'

Richard freezes. The captain promised discretion. 'I am a trader, as I explained. You have my cargo on board.'

Simpson looks away to study the horizon. 'You pay well, sir and I will not pry but I have called at St Helena for some years and never heard your name.'

The captain does not sound suspicious and Richard wants to keep it that way. He needs a plausible reason for washing up on one of the British Empire's most remote outposts.

'I am a writer. I travelled to Belgium to watch the encounter between Wellington and Bonaparte. I planned to write of my experiences in *The Times*. I was in Paris when France surrendered and obtained an audience with the emperor. He was surprisingly talkative and I germinated the idea to write a book while his celebrity is still fresh. I managed to get myself included in his party. Once on the island, I had to find a means of support while writing.'

Every word sounds hollow and implausible to Richard but Captain Simpson merely grunts and scowls as the fore-sail falls slack. A sailor flails in the air, attempting to regain his grip on a line.

Before Simpson can intervene, the boatswain is cursing and spouting orders in an argot so impenetrable Richard can only guess at the meaning.

'What's he like, Boney?' asks Simpson, relaxing onto the balls of his feet, riding the rise and fall of the deck nonchalantly.

Richard thinks for a moment. 'He is a man used to getting his own way. Clever, impatient, utterly convinced of the rightness of his opinions. He fervently believes the British responsible for the prolonged wars between our countries.'

Captain George Simpson scoffs, 'Surely you do not agree with that view? We fought the idea that men could overthrow the natural order, first their wretched revolution and then Boney's puffed up empire!'

There is an intractable conviction here. 'I am an observer. That is the writer's trade. You asked me what he was like. I did not say I agreed with him!' Richard is pleased with himself. He sounds sufficiently offended to deflect Simpson from labelling him a French sympathiser.

'Quite right. Forgive me. There is something delightfully ghoulish yet thrilling to think of the ogre locked up on St Helena.'

Richard wants to steer the conversation onto a different

topic. 'Captain, I wonder whether we might discuss a minor detour in your route? As you have no escort and are no longer in convoy, I should be grateful if you could land us on the eastern shore of the African continent?'

Simpson swings around to face Richard four-square. 'But that would place you beyond the reach of the Cape Colony. That is a land of lawless savages!' Simpson looks genuinely concerned. 'I should be sending you to your deaths,' he adds for emphasis.

'Captain, you are a shrewd man. I am willing to see you recompensed highly for such a service. Should you wish it, I will sign a document absolving you of any responsibility.'

The calculating glint is back in George Simpson's eyes. 'The owners expect me to keep to a tight schedule. We have already lost time on our outward journey.' Here the captain pauses.

Richard takes the hint. 'Nevertheless, with the right compensation, all parties might be satisfied, don't you think? I understand some trade passes through the Portuguese outpost at Delgoa Bay? Ivory perhaps? Enough to buy that chronometer you so desire!'

The captain looks down his straight nose at Richard. He is a good six feet tall, close to a giant for the time. 'I think we should continue this conversation in my quarters.'

Later, Richard walks on deck, mulling over his talk with Captain Simpson.

'Sail sighted off the starboard bow!' calls a young sailor trimming the rigging on the fore-mast sails.

All heads turn in that direction. The mate on watch, a

shaggy fellow with long black hair and a full beard, raises a telescope to scan the horizon.

'Looks to be a schooner. Heading our way. Red sails. Could mean trouble,' he barks each comment through his whiskers without lowering the telescope. His stance rises and falls with the deck, maintaining a steady image. 'Boy! Run to the captain's cabin. Ask him to be so good as to join me on deck. Now!'

There is something in the mate's tone that worries Richard. 'What sort of ships have red sails?' asks Richard nervously.

'Chinese junks, usually. It's a tradition with them. Colour comes from tannin. They use it to preserve the sails from rot.' Finally, the bearded mate lowers his eyepiece. He chews his lip. 'But this is definitely a schooner. She's sleek and fast and coming our way. Not a thing we can do to get away.'

Richard peers at the horizon but he cannot make out anything. 'Why would we want to get away from that schooner?' he enquires feeling foolish again.

'Because they're pirates, that's why!'

Captain Simpson crosses the deck and takes the spyglass. 'Pirates, you say, Jenkins? Let's have a look,' Simpson sounds utterly unperturbed. He is quiet for a full minute as he studies the oncoming ship. 'Odd looking vessel, that's for sure. Kindly inform the master-at-arms that his services are required. Crew to the gun decks, pass the word!'

Orders are shouted in relay and the men working on the main deck scurry below. 'If they think they're getting my cargo without a fight, they've got another thing coming!' The captain studies the canvas straining above their heads and then puts his face into the wind. 'We're making about six knots. The schooner can probably manage twice that. At this rate they will close with us within two hours.'

'Time enough to prepare ourselves, sir,' offers Jenkins, his eyes bright and his fingers twitching.

'Mister Davey, I suggest you go below and secure your party in your cabin.' There is no doubt Captain Simpson has dismissed him. Richard turns to go and the captain strides off to converse with the helmsman.

Richard opens the cabin door. The small space smells of unwashed bodies overlaid with a note of sickness. Emile is sitting up. He is still pale but able to chew on ship's biscuit and take a walk on deck each day. Bonaparte has almost finished Mungo Park's account of his adventures and sets it down reluctantly.

'You look like you've seen a ghost!' jests Emile.

'Pirates!' Richard blurts out. 'The captain has ordered us to remain in the cabin.'

Emile hauls himself out of his bunk and drops to all fours. He starts searching beneath his bed. 'Got it!' he exclaims, pulling his sheathed sword into view. 'I may be no sailor but I'm not going to sit idly by while we are attacked by brigands!'

Napoleon also stands. 'Find me some clothes! If it is my destiny to die at the hands of pirates, I shall do it dressed as a man not a maid!' His voice is stern and compelling. Emile lays his sword on the bunk and leaves the cabin.

'Sire, is this wise? Should the crew recognise you, our plans will be scuppered should we survive the pirates.' Richard knows he is wasting his time.

'And what do you think the pirates would do to me if I am

captured looking like this? I would be a particular disappointment, don't you think?'

Richard smiles wryly and gives up. He would feel the same in Bonaparte's place.

Emile returns with a bundle of clothes looking apologetic. 'This is what I could find, sire. I cannot attest to the fit.' Napoleon accepts the bundle, pulls out a red pair of breeches and unrolls a threadbare blue coat. 'They belong to one of the midshipmen. He made me pay a princely sum for them!' complains Emile as Bonaparte hauls the yellow dress over his head.

'Be content, Lieutenant. Anything is an improvement. If we are forced to fight, then so be it.'

Emile clips his scabbard to his white belt and checks the blade of his sword slides freely. He then pulls his saddlebags from beneath his bunk and extracts a pair of stubby cavalry pistols. Richard watches as he primes both and hands one to Napoleon. 'I have no sword for you, sire. Unless you wish to take mine?'

Richard hears the reluctance in the offer.

'Keep your weapon, Lieutenant. You are my bodyguard. I shall shoot the first pirate I see and take his blade!' Eagerness oozes from Napoleon. He pulls on a loose white shirt above red breeches and shrugs on the coat. The sleeves are too long so he folds them on themselves with difficulty, leaving his hands clear for action. His shoes are the same black slippers he has worn since departing St Helena.

Richard paces the small space between the bunks trying to decide what to do. He has no military skill. He was horrified by the sight of a man he killed and yet he has no wish to die.

'I need a weapon too. I can't just sit here waiting to be attacked.'

Emile looks hard at his friend before handing him the other pistol. He indicates the cocking mechanism and Richard tentatively takes the gun. It is heavier than he expects and his hand shakes. He turns away to hide the fact and forces himself to breathe deeply. It helps and his hands stop shaking. He sits down and looks at his companions. 'Surely we haven't come this far to be undone by a chance encounter with pirates?'

Napoleon is calm as he examines the small pistol. 'Chance is the constant companion of a commander. If she favours you then anything is possible, whatever the odds. But if she turns her back, well then, there is nothing to do but fight to the end.'

This is the Bonaparte of Austerlitz not Waterloo. Nevertheless, Richard finds scant comfort in such fatalism.

Time passes slowly. Richard checks his watch over and over as the minute hand drags sluggishly around the face.

All three of them jump at a knock on the cabin door. Emile is up, sword drawn before the body on the other side can speak.

'Captain's compliments, won't be long now. He asks you remain below. Gun crews are at the ready.'

With that they are left alone, listening to all manner of activity through the timber walls of the cabin. Running feet, shouted orders and the grate of metal against wood. There is a fearsome rumble as the gun carriages are run forward.

Their wooden box of a cabin is tucked close to the captain's quarters. Most of the accommodation has canvas sides that are stripped away as the ship readies for action. They are on the upper of the *Arniston*'s two gun-decks.

Sequestered as they are, Richard cannot tell what manoeuvres the ship is making. Waves slap hard against the hull and he hears the snap of sails coming up taut. Then, for a moment, all is stillness.

Richard tries to ignore the blood pounding in his ears. Emile is standing again, fingering the hilt of his sword.

Napoleon claps his hands together, eyes sparkling, 'Hold steady, my friends.'

A rolling explosion runs along the port side of the *Arniston*, as if the ship is being ripped apart. The deck thrums. Richard's ears ring painfully, as if he is trapped in a church tower as the bells peal.

Some seconds later they hear, dimly, as if through fog, another cacophony of cannon fire. There is no shattering of decks but they do hear one, two, three dull thuds against the ship's side below them, close to the waterline.

'The pirates are not yet in range. A few of their shot are skimming across the water. I wonder what elevation they are using?' Napoleon has shed twenty years. He is a young artillery officer again, puzzling at trajectories and distances.

Minutes drag by without any more firing. The *Arniston* heaves over hard leaving the three of them in no doubt the ship is turning. At last, she fires another salvo, this time from her starboard guns.

The onslaught on Richard's ears is not as uncomfortable because his hearing remains impaired, but the shudder through the ship attests to the force expended.

This time the return fire is immediate and finds its mark.

Timbers squeal and crack as they shatter. Beneath their feet the ship staggers. The shot is striking the lower gun deck from where screams summon images of carnage.

Richard imagines the injured dragged clear of the guns, bones broken and bodies pulped by the impact of iron balls. Others will be lacerated by the deadliest threat of all, myriad splinters of wood filling the air with shrapnel. Richard wonders how many guns are still in action on the lower gun deck?

It is not long before the *Arniston* manages another ragged broadside from starboard. It sounds close to a full complement from their hiding place.

Napoleon is pacing now, calculating what is happening from experience.

'Our attacker has fewer guns, perhaps half this ship's armament and their range is a little shorter too. This is an uneven fight.'

As if to emphasise his point, the schooner's return of fire sounds, a scattered burst followed by solo discharges, desultory and deflated.

The *Arniston*'s reply is rapid and imperious, barking in unison from her starboard guns, bellowing defiance and hurling destruction across the choppy sea separating the two ships. As soon as she has fired, the ship slews around, fighting her bow through the waves until she has exposed her opposite flank; she fires her two-tiered salvo once again, this time from the port guns that initiated the action.

'Why persevere in such an attack when you are so obviously overmatched?' questions Bonaparte. 'What desperation drives their captain to such folly?'

Richard and Emile can offer no explanation but Richard realizes he is no longer afraid. All the tension and torture of waiting was terrible. The shock of the initial barrage was debilitating but knowing the *Arniston* is more than a match for her attacker distances Richard from the fight.

He is an observer, just like that crowd gathered on the eve of Waterloo. Nothing but a freak accident will harm him now.

A new noise filters through his buzzing ears. It is rhythmical and mechanical. 'Bilge pumps,' Richard notes in a voice that sounds flat and unfamiliar. He imagines sailors at the pumps, moving handles up and down beneath calloused hands, driving the valves to create suction.

Then comes the sound of hammer and saw. The carpenter and his mate will have willing helpers as they patch the damage.

Emile is at the door to their cabin. 'Surely it is safe now? Let us inspect the scene, sire.'

Napoleon nods but a moment later the sound of incoming cannon fire begins again. There is little discipline to the barrage but Richard counts ten discharges.

All of them strike the *Arniston* and the whole ship shudders from stem to stern. Almost immediately, the ship begins to wallow, as if drifting beam on to the waves.

Emile groans and grabs the doorframe.

'I need to see what is happening,' insists Bonaparte, propelling the paling lieutenant ahead of him through the doorway.

The gun deck is strewn with sand and sawdust soaked in

blood. From the hatch, the smell hits them immediately. Richard recognises the acrid odour of the battlefield. His nose picks out discharged powder, a sulphurous stench, followed by the iron tang of blood and the sweat of labouring bodies. The scent of salt water offers some relief until the foulness of the bilges overwhelms everything.

Richard fights his gag reflex but Emile spatters the deck with the contents of his biscuit breakfast.

Huddled together they dash towards the ladder, across the open space so recently divided into canvas cabins, to clamber up towards the main deck.

The smell of hot metal and discharged gunpowder follows them as they blink at the man-made fog. Peering about, Richard tries to spot the pirate ship. There are small knots of struggling men scattered the length of the main deck.

The *Arniston*'s crew are distinguishable by their blue jackets as they hack and parry with swords and knives. Here and there a musket or pistol barks.

Richard leaps left to avoid a sprawling pair of fighters, locked together as they topple over, neither prepared to relinquish his grip for fear of the other taking advantage.

Curses meet curses, grunts echo back and forth along with shouts of defiance and pain. Emile's sword is clear of his scabbard as he fends off a desperate Arab with a groomed and oiled beard. The pirate wears voluminous trousers gathered at the ankle and a generous red sash. His wide chest is sheathed in a silk shirt topped by an embroidered waistcoat which hangs open. His eyes are as black as his hair and he grins maniacally, exposing improbably perfect teeth. The Arab's curved sword is broad and already dull with blood.

Richard freezes, a lost caricature in a *Boy's Own* adventure, until Bonaparte grasps his arm and points. A pair of pirates bear down on them. Richard lifts the small, heavy pistol, following Napoleon's example. Both men fire at the same time.

Their assailants are about ten feet away and both stagger at the impact from such close range. The weasely looking pirate charging on the right drops to the deck pole-axed but the giant Richard faces keeps coming. He is close enough for Richard to see the bloom of blood soaking his cream shirt at his left shoulder. His right hand is raised, brandishing a grappling iron on a short length of rope.

One stride, then two, brings him within a lunge of Richard and his rum-soaked breath buffets him. He staggers backwards, terrified, holding out the discharged pistol as if it is a talisman to ward off evil spirits.

Richard tumbles backwards as his retreat brings him up against a fallen spar. He hits the deck hard, bruising the base of his spine and knocking his breath from him.

He stares up at the leering figure as it swings the grappling hook in an arc towards his head.

Everything slows to a crawl as the vicious metal claw moves inexorably closer. Richard is mesmerised by the pirate's intricately tattooed face.

He has just identified the image of a whale on the man's cheek when it bursts apart in a spray of blood, sliced through by a scimitar's wicked blade. Richard is showered in blood.

Wiping his eyes, he can just make out, through a film of red, Emile and Napoleon standing back-to-back. Both men are grinning. Napoleon holds a curved sword at waist height, dripping blood.

The skeleton crew of the East Indiaman is proving a problem, even though they have crippled the schooner. The pirate boarding party know there is no escape but to seize the merchantman, so they fight to the last man, expecting no quarter.

Many of the *Arniston*'s crew are working frantically below decks to stop up the rents in her hull and keep her afloat. The majority of men were manning the guns until moments ago and many are incapacitated.

Richard is still sprawled on the deck.

'I count no more than twenty pirates left, sire,' observes Emile cheerily, having disposed of his Arab assailant.

'More than we have. I see eleven plus the captain.' Bonaparte points forward and Richard tries to spot the blue and gold uniform without success.

'Looks like he's got his hands full. He's cornered by three of them,' replies the lieutenant.

'I feel we are honour bound to rescue him from his predicament, Lieutenant. Wouldn't you agree?'

With that the pair move off, brandishing their swords and yelling something at the tops of their lungs. Richard thinks it is '*Vive La France!*'

He rolls onto his side and heaves himself onto all fours. The deck is slippery with blood and he struggles to get upright. He manages just in time to see his companions scaling the ladder to the forecastle.

Richard studies the pirate who so nearly ended his life. His features are slack, his eyes dull and his face something from a slaughterhouse. Richard prizes his thick hairy fingers open and frees the rope. He hauls the grappling hook from the planking, astonished that his attacker was able to keep it airborne with such ease. Although it is too heavy, he immediately feels better. It is an ideal weapon for a man with no training in firearms or swordsmanship.

Richard follows in Emile's wake, holding the rope wrapped around his left hand, grappling hook hanging menacingly.

To starboard, he sees a seaman overcome a pirate with a skilfully wielded boathook to the midriff and a downward blow to dislodge his cutlass.

Keeping to the centre line of the deck, Richard hurries past two more clumps of struggling limbs and clashing steel on the port side.

As he approaches the ladder to the foredeck, he is confronted by a leering pirate standing over the body of one of the ship's mates with a broad blade in his right hand. Blood pools around the fallen man's head.

Richard flings the grappling hook forward underarm. It is a clumsy motion but it takes the stubble-faced buccaneer by surprise, striking the underside of his jutting chin. One of the curved tines punches straight through flesh, bone and palate, to appear between the man's full lips in a spray of blood and shattered teeth.

Unable to dislodge his makeshift weapon, Richard pries a sword from the fallen man's hand and hurdles him onto the ladder.

Richard's head comes level with the raised deck in time to see Emile drive back one of three corsairs. Bonaparte wrestles a second and Captain Simpson duels with a third. Several bodies scatter the deck.

Climbing free of the ladder, Richard holds the sword in front of him and advances. He creeps towards the back of a long-haired, blonde privateer who is making his sword sing with measured flicks of his wrist. He dances forwards and backwards on delicate feet.

Simpson's blade is pressed back again and again until he is driven against the railing at the prow of the ship. As he skips out of the captain's range one more time, Richard drives the sword into the pirate's back with all his force. The hilt of the sword is designed for a single hand, so he has one hand inside its protection and his other behind the guard.

The sword has a slight curve and its final two inches dip to a point. This acute angle pierces the leather jerkin, shirt and skin of the swordsman.

Propelled by Richard's bodyweight, the blade slices through flesh and strikes the spine. Richard feels the blade slide along vertebrae before slipping sideways, tearing muscle as it goes. The shock of the impact on bone jars the hilt violently and Richard loses his grip.

Seizing the opportunity, Captain Simpson side-steps forward and thrusts the tip of his narrow sword into his assailant's throat. Despite the sounds of struggle all around, Richard hears a hiss of air. Throat bubbling blood, the skewered victim drops to his knees and topples sideways.

For a second, as the man falls, Captain Simpson and Richard lock gazes. Simpson nods his thanks before stooping to wipe his blade on the corpse of his fallen adversary.

There are four of them and only two pirates remain. One is a small, wiry fellow with lace at his wrists and striped breeches tucked into soft, brown boots. He fences with

Emile, cutlass against sabre, on a rolling deck; the pair are well matched.

The second marauder has Napoleon in a bear hug. He is a clear six inches taller and twice the weight but Bonaparte has a thumb in one eye socket, forcing a stream of invective from the red-bearded face inches from his own.

The captain turns to attack Emile's opponent from another angle, leaving Richard to help the former emperor. Once again, he finds himself without a weapon. Wringing his hands, he drops to one knee to pull the sword from the dead pirate's back but try as he might, he cannot free it.

Giving up, he spots a dirk in the man's waistband and tugs it free. He is light-headed and swallows hard to prevent his gorge from rising.

As he weighs the long dagger in his left hand, he sees the red bear loosen his grip on Napoleon just enough to reach for a similar weapon. It is housed in a black sheath attached to his belt by a loop of chain. Big fingers fumble to free the blade.

Richard knows what he has to do. He presses himself into the deck with his hands and one knee, a sprinter in the blocks. He has only ten feet to cover. Pushing off with determination, his rear foot slews awkwardly in a pool of congealing blood and he loses his balance. As he falls, he twists his head to keep Napoleon and his attacker in view.

He sees the glint of polished steel emerge from the sheath and shouts a desperate warning. 'Emperor, a knife in his right hand!' His voice fills a momentary lull in the ragged racket of the fighting.

Bonaparte turns his hip and stamps down hard on a

buckskin-shod foot. Emile finally pierces the defences of the cutlass-wielding pirate, thanks to a parry expertly deployed by Simpson, driving the sabre's point into his belly. He then closes rapidly and kicks the man's feet away before applying the *coup de grâce* with an arcing cut to the head.

Freed from the engagement, Captain Simpson appraises Napoleon with a thoughtful expression.

Regaining his feet, Richard closes the gap to the struggling pair and stabs at the burly giant's neck. Richard has to use an upward action that lacks power. The double roll of dense pink flesh is taut with effort and rebuffs all but the tip of the dagger.

Richard pulls it free and steadies himself for a harder thrust, only to be knocked from his feet by a flailing backhand. He is swatted away like an irritating fly. Sitting on the gore spattered deck, Richard can only watch as Emile, still resplendent in his uniform, drives his sabre between the exposed ribs of the huge pirate.

Slowly, the grip on Bonaparte weakens and he is able to pull free. Eyes bright with battle fever, Napoleon takes the cavalry sword from the lieutenant and runs the now kneeling pirate through, not just once, but over and over again. 'My name is Napoleon Bonaparte and I am still alive!' he yells into the breeze, his face and arms filmed with a spray of blood.

Captain Simpson helps Richard to his feet. The calculating look is back on his face.

Looking down from the forecastle, Richard sees all of the boarding party are dead. What of the pirates remaining on their ship?

He scans the port side without success so crosses to

starboard, keeping clear of a running deck hand. He sees little to starboard either, except a broken spar trailing torn rigging as it floats past.

Richard lurches against the rail, trying to adjust his gait to the awkward roll of the hull. Captain Simpson has moved away and is directing operations.

As Richard climbs down to the main deck, the prow strikes something solid. There is a ghastly grinding noise as the lame *Arniston* judders to a full stop.

Richard hears cries from the water as he falls from the ladder to the hard deck. His right ankle twists but holds his weight. He winces as he moves towards Simpson, worried what the captain might do with the information he has just discovered.

'That broke the schooner's back, sir. She's sinking fast. We took heavy damage from that last salvo. Carpenter and crew are doing their best to patch below the waterline. What are your orders?' Skelton asks the captain. He has a deep cut to one arm and is incubating a black eye.

Captain Simpson stands four-square on the slewing deck and looks over the side as the shattered remains of their attacker slips along the length of the *Arniston*'s hull. 'Scrambling nets over the side. If any of our small boats are intact, get them in the water. Pick up survivors!' The captain's voice is hard as steel but he is doing the humane thing. 'Mister Davey, I thought I gave instructions for you to remain below?' There is no criticism in his hoarse baritone. 'Never mind, I thank you, and your companions, for the assistance.'

Chapter Thirteen

The winds the sailors call Westerlies are growing angry. Captain Simpson reckons they are no more than a week from the Cape but the *Arniston* is badly damaged. The sky that had been blue, setting the sea to sparkling sapphire with its reflection, is now menacing.

Richard studies the dark grey line of a weather front as it approaches. The temperature drops and he shivers, wrapping his coat around his body and tucking his hands under his armpits. His hair is getting long and the increasing gusts tug at it in a way he rather enjoys.

Beneath his feet, he hears the urgent pumps, driven by exhausted sailors. Many are wounded and all bruised by their encounter with the pirates. Only three survivors were pulled from the wreckage. They work the pumps alongside the crew. Emile is down in the bilges lending a hand.

Richard has just emerged on deck after his latest shift. His hands are raw and he has blisters on both thumbs.

Bonaparte is confined to Captain Simpson's cabin under armed guard. Richard frets at the turn of events as he watches the weather change. The only thing giving him hope is that Simpson has not revealed Bonaparte's identity to the crew.

As the clouds swell and darken, pressing down on the horizon, the sea grows rougher. Whitecaps top the waves rolling irresistibly across the deep.

The rudder was damaged in the broadside duel. The carpenter's team have effected repairs and lashed it amidships.

They are now toiling to plug the breaches to the hull. Meanwhile, the *Arniston* is at the whim of the weather. She is holding course with wind and current, driven ever eastwards.

Richard is about to go below for an hour's sleep before taking another turn at the pumps when Captain Simpson appears from the poop deck. 'Mister Davey, might I have a word?' There is something oily in his manner that does nothing to still troubled waters. Richard inclines his head and waits. 'I have been giving things much thought,' Simpson continues, 'The *Arniston* is gravely damaged. We have no choice but to make for the nearest landfall. By good fortune that is Cape Town.'

George Simpson is another man who should never play cards; his calculating mind reflects in his sharp eyes and pensive frown. 'It will be a difficult journey,' the captain continues. 'We must restore the rudder's function if we are to beat north sufficiently. Otherwise, we will be swept past Africa into the wide desert of the Indian Ocean. I doubt this old ship's timbers will hold together for such a passage.'

Richard looks beyond Simpson to the tangle of severed rigging being unravelled by a pair of deck hands. Their calloused hands weave in and out confidently, coiling the salvageable lines at their feet.

'I understand,' offers Richard calmly, waiting for Simpson to reach his point.

'Should we reach safe harbour in British territory, I will face a quandary.'

Richard chews his lip and glances at the few intact sails arcing in the insistent wind.

'I am an employee of the Company and a loyal servant of

the Crown. I am also a man of modest means. I had to buy this command and my debtors are impatient. The future is dismal for a captain whose ship founders. I can save my reputation by reaching port but I will still be labelled a Jonah. Should the *Arniston* prove unable to continue to the Far East, then both the investments of the owners and my private undertakings will be frustrated.'

Captain Simpson pauses to study the weather and a flicker of fear tugs at his left cheek. 'However, we have on board a unique prize. Fortune has, for once, smiled on me and I am not fool enough to spurn it. Your travelling companion will prove a most popular visitor in Cape Town. News of his escape cannot be far behind us.'

Richard feels sick and grips the rail. The wind howls angrily, matching his mood. Invisible fingers coax eerie music from the taut strings of the remaining rigging.

Simpson lowers his voice and cups his mouth as he speaks close to Richard's ear, 'Imagine the celebrity that will attach to the man who recaptures the French tyrant!'

Richard waves his hands as if trying to chase such thoughts away. 'If you allow me to speak with your prisoner, I might arrange an offer that outweighs such considerations?' suggests Richard as confidently as he can manage.

The captain frowns, 'A knighthood, invitations to the best society parties, the chance to give up the sea and buy an estate of my own? These are the things I see in my future. Can your toppled dictator overmatch that?' He sounds resolved but leaves the door ajar.

Richard puts his foot in the gap. 'Let me try. What harm can it do?' Simpson nods.

The captain's cabin is at the stern, benefitting from large windows stretching the width of the ship. Despite this wall of glass, it is gloomy. The sky is bruised as the barometer falls.

Napoleon Bonaparte sits on the cushioned bench that runs beneath the windows, staring at the faint wake slipping astern. The guard shuts the door behind Richard. Bonaparte does not look round. 'What now, Captain?' he asks in an amused voice.

'Sire, it is I, Richard Davey. Come to see if we might not concoct an offer to deflect our grasping commander from his present intention.'

Napoleon springs up and gestures Richard to a seat at the captain's table. 'It appears I am Captain Simpson's roommate for the present. Tell me, how go the repairs? Will this ship make it to Cape Town?' Again, Bonaparte's mood is buoyant.

'The pumps keep pace with the ingress of sea water. The carpenter has patched the smaller holes and deployed canvas across the largest rent. In good weather we would likely reach the African coast but a storm is building fast.'

Napoleon nods. 'I see the skies darken.' He points to the stern. 'If this storm is savage, it will save us from the captain's ambition, no?'

Richard cannot understand Bonaparte's good humour. 'Sire, it is no joking matter. A choice between ignominious drowning and recapture seems short of attractive options.'

Dressed in the captain's cast offs, which are too long for him, Napoleon should look diminished but instead, sleeves turned up and breeches tucked into borrowed boots, he swaggers around the room.

As he paces, he slips his left hand between waistcoat

buttons. 'Very well, assume we successfully make landfall. What then? Should I offer the remains of my treasury to Captain Simpson in exchange for his discretion? He does seem inordinately driven by avarice.'

'As are many of modest means trying to make a place for themselves in this world,' replies Richard tersely. 'How much of your treasury were you able to transport, sire?'

The former emperor crosses to the bench seating and reaches into the storage locker below, pulling out his leather saddlebags. He hauls them onto the mahogany chart table and unfastens both pockets. He upends one after the other with obvious effort. Heavy gold coins cascade across the chart of the Southern Ocean.

Richard stares in amazement. 'How did you manage to carry all of that through Jamestown, it must be some fierce weight?'

Napoleon scoffs. 'I may be used to being waited on, my American friend, but it was you who cajoled me into a fitness regime. Besides, I needed sufficient funds to begin again. I hope to make contact with my supporters but they are thousands of miles away...' He shrugs in a way that eloquently completes the sentence.

Richard hears the guard outside shift position and glances nervously at the table strewn with imperial gold. 'Sire, tell me the captain has no knowledge of your cache?'

Bonaparte smiles and shakes his head. The coins slide across the chart as the ship rolls clumsily, the bulk gilding the outline of Africa.

'There is a wild looking storm brewing. I fear we are in for a rough ride,' Richard admits.

'Will Captain Simpson be amenable to an inducement?' demands Bonaparte, putting the conversation back on course.

'He is a calculating man, sire. He will weigh the certainty of your gold against the prospect of fame and fortune as your captor. I think he is prepared to take risks in order to advance himself. You cannot trust him, even if he agrees.'

Napoleon sweeps the coins from the table into the open saddlebags with his free forearm. His lips draw into a thin line and his blue eyes flare brightly. 'Very well, once he has us within sight of land, we will deal with the captain.'

Richard does not ask what Napoleon means. He simply nods.

For days the *Arniston* tosses from wave to trough. The crew struggle to keep a few stitches of canvas aloft to influence direction. Wind and current drive her south-eastwards. If they do not fight that trend, they will be driven past the Cape without any chance of reaching it.

Everyone is exhausted. Skin is raw from wind, dried salt, manning pumps and wrestling rigging. Sunken eyes stare out of frightened faces. Muscles spasm. Even Captain Simpson takes his turn in the bilges. Everybody has blisters except Bonaparte, sequestered in the captain's cabin.

Emile has stopped vomiting and drives himself into the knee-deep water below, working manically on double shifts, as if he can single-handedly save them all.

Food is rationed in case they have to face the vastness of the Indian Ocean.

Richard feels his arms strengthen although they ache. His

belly hardens and his legs are sure. He ceases registering the plunges and judders of the hull as it fights through seas hard as concrete that slam against its wooden membrane.

Taking a turn on deck, Richard ties himself to the rail with a length of rope, copying the commander, his mates and midshipmen as they stand duty watch.

Everything is grey. The sea broils menacingly, mirroring the angry billowing overhead. Clouds layer clouds, dark against grey, always churning. The wind tugs, buffets and blasts, agitating above and below the horizon. Air and water whip into a maelstrom mocking the little creatures struggling on the patched flotsam that is the *Arniston*.

Emile joins Richard and produces his own safety line.

'It is good to see you recovered,' Richard shouts into the teeth of the wind.

The lieutenant, wrapped in an oilskin, manages a grin. 'How many days has it been?'

'Since the storm started? Six, I think. We should sight land soon, if we have not been driven too far south.'

Emile frowns for a moment and then nods, as if he had to piece together meaning from the few words he snatched from the gale. 'What does Captain Simpson say?'

'By his reckoning we will be driven beyond the Cape. Our best hope is that the storm blows itself out. Then we can strike north-west.'

Emile looks unconvinced. Richard keeps talking, 'Although we have not sighted the sun for a week, by estimating speed and direction, the captain has a good sense of our latitude. The problem is longitude.'

311

Emile gives a shrug of incomprehension. 'Talk to me of horses, swords and women and I am a wise man. Babble about the oceans and I am all at sea!' The pair laugh at the lieutenant's quip.

'Longitude is the distance east or west from port. We know the distance from St Helena to the Cape. So, in our case, longitude measures how far we have travelled and how far to landfall.'

Emile looks at the waves and ducks as a huge plane of water plunges over the prow. For seconds they are beneath a silver canopy and then the spell is broken. They shiver, soaked to the bone.

Shaking himself, Emile pats Richard on the shoulder. 'Tell me more. It is best to understand an enemy.'

Richard is happy to oblige. Since quitting St Anne's, he finds teaching reassuring. 'Imagine a globe divided by lines running from pole to pole, spaced at intervals of fifteen degrees. That gives twenty-four lines,' Richard's teeth chatter.

Emile rubs his nose pensively. 'I have seen such globes. There are lines running horizontally too, is that not so?'

'Yes, exactly. They represent latitude, your location north or south, calculated by observing the sun at midday. But without longitude you cannot fix your station east or west and you need both to fix your position.'

The *Arniston* thrums from stem to stern and groans deeply. A cracking as sharp as the discharge of a cannon follows. Slowly, very slowly, improbably slowly, the main mast falls.

Richard and Emile are a little aft of the ship's centre line. The mast appears to be falling to starboard. Lashed to the port rail they are safe.

Then a huge wave shoulders their side of the ship as it loses momentum, drifting beam on. The teetering mast pauses as the ship rolls extravagantly and like a reluctant pendulum swings back. The mast is perpendicular again.

Richard and Emile are hypnotized. For a second, it appears the mast may remain upright but then, rapidly, it drops to port.

The two friends tear frantically at their knots, fingers wet and numb but urgent, nails clawing the rough fibres. Emile frees himself first and moves to help Richard.

'No time, get clear!'

A tail of rigging snakes down, striking the lieutenant across the face, knocking him from his feet onto the slick deck. The knot unravels and Richard yanks clear of the rail, throwing himself forward. He lands face down and aquaplanes for several yards before colliding with a broken spar.

A mighty crash announces the mast's impact with the ship's rail. It snaps it like a matchstick, crushing the main deck and bursting the hull's curved ribs.

With the mast acting as a second rudder, the *Arniston* ceases to be so jittery, settling into a rhythmic wallow.

Richard rubs the top of his head where he struck the cross-piece. It is tender but there is no blood. He twists around, desperate for a sight of Emile but all he can see is the massive main mast. Tip in the water, the mast's burst base weaves a lazy circle in the rain.

'Emile!' Richard shouts, 'Emile, are you alright?' The wind howls its fury and steals his words away.

'Axes!' bellows the first mate. 'Cut the mast free before it drags us under!'

Richard tries to stand but he is dizzy and his feet slip on the deck. Lying on the wet deck boards, he is frustrated by the interruption. The falling mast prevented him finishing his explanation.

He must tell Emile time is the key. Every fifteen degrees of longitude is an hour. Three hundred and sixty degrees gives twenty-four hours. Set an accurate timepiece to the time in your home port, then compare that with the time at your present location, using the sun or stars. The difference gives your longitude.

He tries to stand again and this time makes it, swaying quite at variance with the motion of the ship. He has to find Emile and tell him time is the key.

Crewmen armed with blades begin hacking at ropes, spars, anything that might hold the mast fast. When all encumbrances are shorn away, a party of sailors throw their shoulders against the mast. At first nothing happens and they are forced back by its grinding motion.

They try a second time but have to hurl themselves clear when the length of wood slides forward in staccato steps until half its length is over the side. The splintered base hangs at an angle close to seventy degrees.

The first mate gives another order Richard cannot make out and axes bite into the spire of wood, looking to sever it close to the crushed rim of the ship. Emile is on the other side of the mast.

Richard forces one foot in front of the other to starboard, shuffling urgently past the remains of mast before crossing back to port. He sees the lieutenant immediately, lying still and slack against the ship's side.

Richard kneels and runs his hands over his friend's head. There is no blood but he feels a large swelling.

The sailors swinging their axes establish a rhythm, attacking the stubborn mast from both sides until, with a final blow, they are through. The protruding length crashes onto the deck and the crew drag it away. They manoeuvre the felled mast stem to stern and lash it in place.

The sailors now try to pry the upper mast free from the ship's side but it has burst through the upper deck and wedged fast.

Richard drags Emile clear of the swarming activity threatening to trample him. 'Surgeon! I need the surgeon!' he cries in frustration, unwilling to leave Emile lying unconscious on the deck.

One of the axe crew glances over his shoulder. 'Busy below, sir,' he shouts. 'But his assistant's right here!'

Richard looks up to see one of the men put down his hatchet and cross to examine Emile. 'Knocked out cold. Nasty blow on his head. Best get him to his cabin. Nothing to do for him but wait. He'll wake up or he won't. Then you'll know.' His voice is kind but he is offering nothing.

'Know what?' whispers Richard hoarsely.

'Whether he's dead or not. If not dead, whether he's lost his faculties.'

Richard heaves up his last meal of ship's biscuit. When he has finished, he wipes his mouth with a trembling hand.

The trainee medic helps carry Emile to their cabin. As they negotiate the door, he wonders that it has survived both battle and storm untouched.

Hours drag by with Richard sitting braced beside Emile on his bunk as the ship endures the battering of the storm. Richard tries to bring him around by bathing his face with a damp cloth. There is no response. He tries willing Emile back to consciousness to no effect.

Finally, he tries talking him back from oblivion. 'I never finished explaining longitude,' he begins. 'It's quite simple really.'

Emile groans and moves his head. Richard carries on, his voice eager as he stumbles through degrees and hours. 'Our problem is that Captain Simpson does not possess a marine chronometer. The owners of the ship would not pay and he lacked the funds. So, he can tell us with reasonable confidence our latitude but he has no reliable way of establishing…'

'Longitude! Stop, for pity's sake!' mumbles Emile. 'I think your lesson is what gave me this terrible headache!'

Richard laughs and Emile manages a wan smile at his own joke. 'The ship still floats,' observes Emile as he struggles to sit up, back against the bulkhead.

'She is badly damaged and the storm is fierce. If we sight land soon and find a sheltered bay then all will be well.' Richard looks away.

'And if not?' Emile asks calmly.

'Then we will likely drown.' Richard winces as the words force their way out, bitter and resentful.

Emile is quiet after that. Richard thinks he has drifted off but then, just as Richard is closing his own eyes, he speaks again. 'I cannot think fate would be so cruel. If we were meant to fail, then we would have been caught trying to leave

St Helena. Yet here we are. Now it is up to us to ensure the emperor's survival.' Emile sounds stronger. 'You must discover the state of the ship. Best check the small boats too.'

Richard is glad of something to do after hours of inactivity in the stuffy cabin. He struggles to force the hatch at the top of the stairway and is wet as soon as he has it open. He licks his lips and registers the tang of salt. Wind howls all around.

There is no canvas left on either the fore or mizzen masts. Their surviving yardarms swing forlornly, festooned with shreds of rigging. Wood thumps against wood, metal grinds on wood, metal clanks against metal, rope flays wood and all around is wind and water. It is mid-afternoon but the sky is dark and storm lanterns burn defiantly.

Richard studies the damage. The deck is largely clear now. The wedged section of mast remains embedded in the ship's side but the sailors' axes have severed it above the waterline, releasing the *Arniston* from the confusion of two rudders.

Richard realizes the ship is riding more naturally beneath his feet. Looking aft, he sees two small boats hanging either side of the poop deck. They appear undamaged.

Spotting Captain Simpson talking to the quartermaster at the wheel, Richard edges along the intact starboard rail. 'Captain, forgive the intrusion. How goes it?'

Simpson turns red raw eyes to Richard. He looks as if he hasn't slept since the storm began. His eyebrows lower and creases furrow his forehead. 'From a company of near one hundred and forty, I now have less than ninety fit for service. We dare set no sail and this wheel is all but for show. We can move the rudder about five degrees to port or starboard thanks to an ingenious rig by Mister Bullington, our carpenter. We may keep her head running with the weather but I fear the first time we find land will be when the bottom is ripped out of her.' He sounds like a man resigned to having glory snatched from his fingers.

'Surely this storm cannot rage forever?' asks Richard hopefully.

'The pumps aren't keeping up with the leaks. The men are thigh deep down there and it's rising an inch an hour. Another day and we'll lose the lower deck, then the *Arniston* is just a floating coffin.'

A white flash slices through the gloom, like a tear in the fabric of the sky. Impossibly long wings harness the wind.

'Albatross!' spits the quartermaster crossing himself in a way that made the gesture pagan.

'I thought sailors revere the bird?' asks Richard puzzled.

'Most do,' agrees the quartermaster. 'But to my mind, they are storm bringers. Most birds mean land nearby but these giants soar day after day. They are the spirits of drowned sailors!'

Richard watches the massive bird wheel above them and spiral away into the darkness. He thinks about Emile's protestation. Does fate have other plans for them?

'So, we just wait for the ship to sink?' he demands brusquely.

'No sir, we fight north with everything we have. Africa is there somewhere. Better risk a wreck in shallow waters than out here in the deep.'

The next day a knock wakes Richard from a fitful sleep. He shuffles to the latch and lifts it.

'Captain's compliments, sir. Would you kindly join him in his cabin?'

Richard fumbles his watch from his waistcoat to find it is almost eight in the morning by St Helena time. They must be some two hours ahead of that. His stomach rumbles as he dresses and follows the orderly to the aft cabin.

He is shown in without ceremony to find Bonaparte and Simpson sitting at table, the remains of their breakfast before them. The cabin is suffused with a pale light. He stares out of the rear wall of glass and squints. Through a haze, sunlight shimmers on choppy water. He realizes the deck is only pitching gently.

'I trust you slept well?' the captain asks.

Richard nods to Simpson. 'It seems that albatross was a harbinger of good fortune after all.' He accepts the chair proffered by the steward who sets a plate and cup for him.

Bonaparte's grin and the sight of tea convinces Richard he is safe. As he sips the hot, fragrant liquid, he hears hammering down below. 'Repairs?' he enquires.

'Indeed. The pumps are holding their own again. Bullington has any spare men divided into teams, patching the biggest rent in the hull. He is cannibalising anything he can to get the rudder fully operational. When that's done, we'll try to jury-rig some canvas.'

Richard eats a bread roll, luxuriating in its fresh sweetness. The smell fills the cabin, banishing sweat, stale wine and tobacco.

'It seems fate is on our side after all,' muses Richard in a low voice to Napoleon. Captain Simpson has moved to his chart table and studies the sheet intently.

'Perhaps,' concedes Bonaparte, 'but we must not be complacent. In my experience, fate smiles on those who act. When land is sighted, we must place the captain in a position which compels him to cooperate.'

Napoleon is under guard and Richard survived the pirate boarding party more by luck than judgement. Surely this is asking too much?

'I will discuss the matter with Lieutenant Béraud.' The shrouds of mist part and the full glare of the sun reflected on the ocean scatters the cabin with dancing diamonds.

With the rudder serviceable, the *Arniston* tacks ever northwards, sails taut on her remaining masts. Two days pass and the sun shines from dawn to dusk.

'Land ho! Three points off the starboard bow.' It is the call everyone has been anxiously waiting for. Richard thrills to the news even as it makes his stomach queasy with relief. He turns to Emile who is quite recovered from the blow to his head.

'We must put your plan into action.' Richard follows Emile to their cabin. He waits as Emile searches beneath the bunk for his pistols. He is clearly having difficulty as his scrabbling becomes more insistent. His sword clatters on the deck boards as he thrusts his body further beneath his bed. He begins to curse under his breath.

Finally, he emerges and turns an anguished face towards Richard. 'They are taken!'

'Captain Simpson is a wily character. He has forestalled us,' Richard admits through clenched teeth. 'He means to secure his prize at all costs.'

Emile grips the hilt of his sword and loosens it in its polished steel sheath. 'It is of no matter. He could not steal this,' he pulls the blade free, turning its gleaming surface back and forth with satisfaction, 'because I always wear it now I am recovered from the *mal de mer*. To do otherwise is to insult the uniform.'

Richard admires his friend's spirit but does not relish a confrontation where one side has guns and the other a single sharp blade. 'Might we not secure a musket from another source? The master-at-arms is fond of his grog,' Richard suggests hopefully.

Emile looks sceptical. 'If we have time to get him drunk and purloin his keys. We might manage it tonight.'

'The crew have no idea who the captain detains in his cabin. I heard the cooks talking. They think he has run up gambling debts with Simpson who is holding him until his debt can be settled in Cape Town.'

Emile laughs. 'If the captain is foolish enough to play twenty-one with the emperor, I doubt he has two sous left to rub together.' The pair smile grimly.

'Let's seek out Simpson. Perhaps you can still get the drop on him?'

Emile agrees immediately and they head back on deck. Most of the crew crowd the port rail, craning their necks to study the thickening yellow watercolour smear separating unbroken sky blue from sparkling azure sea.

'Is it the Namib?' asks the cooper.

'Surely we're far south of Benguela?' insists the sailmaker.

'False Bay perhaps?' suggests an ordinary seaman.

'I do hope Cape Town's not far,' the butcher sighs wistfully, dreaming of fresh meat.

'Reckon we were driven further east. Maybe beyond any civilised settlement,' an old sea dog spits his gloomy words over the side.

'You mean there's no one there but savages?' a reedy midshipman's voice questions nervously.

'Not till you reach Delgoa Bay. If you count the Popish Portuguese as civilised!' Coarse laughter but scowls from the Catholics in the crew.

'Where is the captain?' enquires Richard.

'Trying to make sense of his charts!' scoffs the quartermaster, holding the ship's wheel casually on course with one hand.

Richard nudges Emile and they move away. 'If he's in his cabin, we may get the better of him. There'll be three of us.'

The guard on duty squats against the bulkhead, chin on chest, when they reach the captain's cabin. He jerks upright when Emile gently clasps his shoulder. Embarrassed, he makes no objection when they request entry.

Richard knocks and opens the door. Captain Simpson doesn't even look up from the chart table, assuming it is his steward or an orderly going about his business.

Bonaparte stands beside the engrossed commander but glances up to see who is entering. He nods to Emile and that is enough.

The lieutenant draws his sword in a fluid motion as he crosses the room, swinging the blade up to rest beneath Simpson's downturned head. He carefully runs the blade down the captain's chin like a skilled barber completing his party trick, until the point presses against Simpson's larynx.

A tick jerks across the captain's cheek.

'Now, Captain, you are my prisoner!' declares Bonaparte with glee, dexterously detaching the captain's sword which he has taken to wearing at all times since their run in with the pirates.

Simpson remains perfectly still for several moments and then, very calmly, extends his left forefinger to point at the chart.

All four men are shoulder to shoulder around the table. Richard pats the captain down and relieves him of a knife and one of Emile's lost muskets. The lieutenant reclaims it gratefully before offering it to Napoleon.

'See this section of coast. What does it say there?' Simpson's finger hovers while the three men look closely. '*Terra Incognita*. No one has even completed a hydrographical survey of the coast between Cape Town and Delgoa Bay. The features that are marked are few and unreliable.' Simpson lets his hand rest palm down across the area. 'We are somewhere along this coast, far beyond the reach of British authority. I fail to see how you intend to proceed.' He is almost dismissive despite the threat at his throat.

'You will furnish us with a boat and supplies and we will take any men who wish to accompany us,' Bonaparte commands. 'You will bring this ship close enough to the coast for us to make landfall safely. In exchange, I will leave you alive and you may do whatever you feel necessary once we are ashore.'

Captain Simpson tenses imperceptibly but Napoleon the card player spots it. 'No doubt, you contemplate shooting us out of the water with your guns. It will be difficult to issue that order from the small boat with us!'

Simpson's shoulders slump and he reaches for a chair, pulling it across the floor and collapsing into it quite deflated.

'I should like to borrow your key to the armoury, Captain,' requests Emile with a grin.

'Call in the guard,' Napoleon instructs, 'And order him to have a jolly boat made ready. If he questions your orders, tell him you need to scout the shoreline. I shall have this pistol on you the whole time.' Bonaparte grins.

Simpson complies. As the guard enters, Emile slips out with the key to augment their supply of weapons, while Bonaparte covers the room with the musket hidden inside his coat. Once the guard is gone, he starts listing the other supplies they need. By the time he has finished, Emile is back with an armful of armaments and blades.

Napoleon sends the lieutenant back out to find the captain's chief steward.

The slightly stooped but precise figure stands in front of his commander without the slightest suspicion. He does not write down any of the orders, used, as he is, to memorising everything. He leaves with a rejoinder to report back on the *Arniston*'s progress towards shore.

Minutes pass. Emile checks each of the weapons he has purloined and sorts through the ammunition stuffed inside a canvas holdall. He has three muskets, one of which is rifled, plenty of powder and shot, two naval swords and a cutlass which he adds to his pair of pistols and a third taken from the captain's desk.

He is wearing his sabre and offers one of the naval swords to his emperor. Napoleon makes to attach the sword to his belt then pauses. 'Lieutenant, I would crave a favour.'

'Anything, sire.'

'Will you exchange clothes with me?'

Emile freezes then looks down at his green and red uniform topping fawn breeches and polished boots. He remains immaculate. He hesitates and then unbuttons his tunic.

When the steward reports back, the pair have completed their swap. He is too discreet to notice. The *Arniston* is as close inshore as the quartermaster on duty dares bring her, he reports. Soundings are shallow but irregular.

Captain Simpson nods, 'Very well, Baines, ask the quartermaster to drop anchor. Have the intact jolly boat loaded with the provisions I requested and lower it. I shall be accompanied by these gentlemen. We will need strong oarsmen.'

Richard baulks at the jury-rigged ladder that is more rope than wood. Bonaparte pushes him aside and scrambles down into the gently rocking boat.

Emile is close at Simpson's side, his small pistol primed beneath the very coat Bonaparte had used just an hour ago. Richard watches the captain descend. He does nothing to signal there is anything wrong. Emile follows.

Richard takes a breath and swings himself out and around until he can clutch the heavy knots at the top of the ropes. He flails a foot in the air until it snags the first narrow step. Gingerly, he applies his weight and feels with his foot for the next narrow plank. He is sweating and his fists ache as he grips the rough hemp.

A swell causes the *Arniston* to roll and his right foot slips from the wood. He dangles, kicking his feet in panic until strong hands grasp his ankles. Looking down, he realizes he is no more than three feet from the bottom of the ship's boat.

Seated, he looks around. Their gear is in canvas bags tied at the necks with thick string and stacked neatly in the bow.

They are about to shove off when there is a commotion from above. The grizzled boatswain's face appears above the rail. 'Beggin' your pardon, Captain. But these three pirates wot we fished out are pleadin' to be put ashore. I've told 'em they're for the noose when we reach port. They say they'd rather take their chances in the wilderness.'

Shouts of agreement chorus behind him in an odd accent. Napoleon prods the captain and whispers in his ear.

'Send them down. They can replace three of our fellows.'

The swap of personnel is completed without incident and one of the sailors shoves them off. Clearing their oars, the crew pull for land with the surgeon's assistant at the tiller, having begged for the opportunity to set foot on undiscovered country.

The three pirates grasp their oars with particular enthusiasm, straining their backs for all they are worth and occasionally exchanging brief phrases in a patois that eludes Richard.

It takes some thirty minutes' unceasing effort to fight the slender craft into the shallows where offshore breakers mark an underwater reef. Captain Simpson indicates a break in the waves and the surgeon's assistant, squinting against the glare, turns the tiller to target the gap.

Richard feels the current snare the boat as they approach. The prow slides off course despite the rudder and frantic efforts of the port rowers. They are in danger of sweeping past the narrow neck that gives into the safety of a calm lagoon.

Forced to turn about, they approach again. Simpson swaps his crew port and starboard as half the men are blowing heavily. This time, anticipating the ferocity of the onshore current, the surgeon's assistant brings the little boat in at a severe angle, allowing the current to drive them towards the breach.

With a superhuman effort, every oar is dug and feathered, over and over, propelling the prow towards the gap. One man catches a crab, threatening the boat's momentum, but he recovers quickly and with one more pull they shoot into the lagoon's still waters.

Surrounded by hunched forms sucking in breath, chests heaving, throats rasping, Richard stands and studies the shore. He sees a wide, sandy beach backed by dense greenery.

As they skim easily across the calm waters of the lagoon, he starts to pick out more detail. More bushes than trees, the land rolling gently in folds of hills as far as he can see.

Looking to his right, the sweep of beach ends in reddish cliffs rising defiantly in the face of the ocean's assault.

To his left, the sands disappear into a haze of shimmering light. The air is warm but not hot. The mild breeze is pleasant.

The keel of their boat grinds into the shelving sand and comes to rest. Napoleon is first over the side, clutching his saddlebags. Emile lifts the sack containing their weapons free from the pile of supplies and hands a musket to Napoleon as he joins him, almost waist deep, holding the sack above the water's surface. Richard steps over the side into the shallow lagoon. The water is pleasantly warm. He too takes a musket.

'Captain, please instruct your men to carry our supplies ashore,' demands Bonaparte from behind his weapon. He speaks with such command Richard is not surprised to see the sailors begin the task before their captain relays the instruction.

In a matter of a few minutes, their little stock of supplies is ashore. The three pirates are studying the hinterland, heads together, chattering in their patois. Emile is standing beside them with his gun trained on the boat. Napoleon and Richard are with Captain Simpson. The rest of the crew stand nervously in a huddle, knee deep in water at the prow of the row boat.

'Well Captain, this is where we part. I wish you good fortune although I doubt you shall make it betting on my capture!' Napoleon's face is animated, his gestures incisive, his eyes afire.

Captain Simpson grimaces, 'Do not be so sure. You have made an enemy of me today and I do not die easily. It is my fervent hope we meet again. Perhaps I will get the jump on you? I doubt I shall be commanding any more East India Company ships after this debacle. The surviving cargo will not cover the owner's investment. Once we reach the Cape and make a report, I think I shall remain and seek new opportunities.' Breathless with defiance, Simpson stares at Bonaparte.

Splendid in his lieutenant's uniform, Napoleon looks impressed. 'You are not a man to be trifled with, I think? So be it. Be on your way and do what you must.'

With that, he waves his long musket at the boat. Captain

Simpson orders his men to the boat and within seconds they have pushed her off the sand and are beginning to pull out across the lagoon.

Bonaparte watches them for a few moments and then raises his gun, sighting along the barrel towards the receding skiff, where Simpson has taken the tiller. 'That man could be dangerous. Better he does not reach the British at the Cape,' mutters Napoleon as he controls his breath and swings the barrel slowly.

Richard steps forward to grip the tip of the rifle and pulls it down. 'Sire, I cannot let you kill him.'

Bonaparte looks daggers at Richard and tries to step around him. Richard keeps hold of the gun, frustrating any attempt to get off a shot.

'Lieutenant Béraud, shoot Captain Simpson before he is out of range! That is an order!'

Emile raises his rifle towards the receding boat. He stands stock still second after second without pulling the trigger and then, with a sigh, lowers the barrel. 'Forgive me, sire. He was too far away. Even with the rifling in this barrel, I could not make the shot.'

Napoleon curses and mutters as he turns in disgust from the sight of the oarsmen slipping through the break in the reef.

Richard keeps out of his way by joining the three pirates. 'Tell me, where do you come from?' he asks in friendly fashion.

All three men look surprised but the youngest of them, a pimpled face beneath a mop of sun-bleached hair, informs him, 'Guernsey. We were captured some two years ago and pressed into service. We are fishermen not brigands. That is why we were not with the boarding party.' His tenor cracks with uncertainty.

'Once you've killed a man, everything changes,' adds the tallest of the three, a man of middle years, heavily bearded and tanned.

The third man, barrel-chested and bow-legged, nods and spits into the sand. 'I say we have a chance to start again.'

That evening, sitting around a fire of brushwood, Richard tries to take stock. Bonaparte has shrugged off his annoyance and is once again full of energy, deep in conversation with Emile about his plans. Surreptitiously, he kneads his belly when he thinks no one is looking. The Guernsey fishermen are lying head to toe well within the light of the fire, already snoring.

He is alive. He has whisked Napoleon Bonaparte away from his captors and across thousands of miles of ocean to the coast of Africa. His friend Emile is with him and at least for the moment they have three more able-bodied men in their party.

They have found a stream draining the nearby hills and its water is fresh and pure. They have enough food to last perhaps a week now there are six of them.

Do what he may, Captain Simpson is sailing away to the west. He can cause them no trouble, directly or indirectly, for months. They are armed sufficiently to defend themselves against wild animals or any unfriendly locals.

He is comforted by his list of positives and lies down to rest. The flickering light of the fire conjures dancing shapes as he watches. Even when the brush is burned down to a glow of embers, he remains awake, the words of the Guernsey men repeating themselves like a litany.

He has killed a man, more than one. It has certainly changed him. Yet here he is, likely part of the first European party to step foot on this beach. A party that contains the deposed Emperor of the French, Napoleon Bonaparte. A man he has admired all his life and now knows too well. The man he abandoned his life to meet is too familiar to remain the focus of his existence.

Has it all been a terrible mistake? Is he just like Madame Odillet's husband, a weak man, a lost man, stranded by self-indulgence, outside his own time?

What would Aunt Patricia have to say? She might echo that other Guernsey fisherman, the square-set fellow with bow-legs. He has a chance to start again.